WOBEGON BOY

AUTHOR OF

Happy to Be Here
Lake Wobegon Days
Leaving Home
We Are Still Married
WLT: A Radio Romance
The Book of Guys

COMING SOON

The Denham Girls in the Persian Gulf
Problems in Modern Life
Snow Gently Drifting in the Hemlock Bushes and on the LP Gas Tanks
Teach Yourself to Dance in Just Fifteen Minutes a Day
Alternative Geography
Passionate Tissues
I Spell Correctly—And You Can, Too!

WOBEGON BOY

Garrison Keillor

VIKING

VIKING

Published by the Penguin Group
Penguin Putnam Inc., 375 Hudson Street,
New York, New York 10014, U.S.A.
Penguin Books Ltd, 27 Wrights Lane,
London W8 5TZ, England
Penguin Books Australia Ltd, Ringwood,
Victoria, Australia
Penguin Books Canada Ltd, 10 Alcorn Avenue,
Toronto, Ontario, Canada M4V 3B2
Penguin Books (N.Z.) Ltd, 182–190 Wairau Road,
Auckland 10, New Zealand

Penguin Books Ltd, Registered Offices:
Harmondsworth, Middlesex, England

First published in 1997 by Viking Penguin,
a member of Penguin Putnam Inc.

1 3 5 7 9 10 8 6 4 2

PUBLISHER'S NOTE
This is a work of fiction. Names, characters, places, and incidents either are the
product of the author's imagination or are used fictitiously, and any resemblance
to actual persons, living or dead, events, or locales is entirely coincidental.

LIBRARY OF CONGRESS CATALOGING IN PUBLICATION DATA
Keillor, Garrison.
Wobegon boy / Garrison Keillor.
p.   cm.
ISBN 0–670–87807–3 (alk. paper)
1.   Lake Wobegon (Imaginary place)——Fiction.   I.   Title.
PS3561.E3755W6   1997
813'.54—dc21   97–27240

This book is printed on acid-free paper.   ∞

Printed in the United States of America
Set in Aldus
Designed by Jessica Shatan

To Ellen, Helen, and Marcia:
three dauntless heroines
of the present day

WOBEGON BOY

Lake Wobegon

I am a cheerful man, even in the dark, and it's all thanks to a good Lutheran mother. When I was a boy, if I came around looking glum and mopey, she said, "What's the matter? Did the dog pee on your cinnamon toast?" and the thought of our old black mutt raising his hind leg in the *pas de dog* and peeing on toast made me giggle. I was a beanpole boy, and my hair was the color of wet straw. I loved to read adventure books and ride my bike and shoot baskets in the driveway and tell jokes. My dad, Byron, was a little edgy, expecting the worst, saving glass jars and paper clips, turning off lights and cranking down the thermostat to keep our family out of the poorhouse, but Mother was well composed, a true Lutheran, and taught me to Cheer up, Make yourself useful, Mind your manners, and, above all, Don't feel sorry for yourself. In Minnesota, you learn to avoid self-pity as if it were poison ivy in the woods. Winter is not a personal experience; everyone else is as cold as you are; so don't complain about it too much. Even if your cinnamon toast gets peed on. It could be worse.

Being Lutheran, Mother believed that self-pity is a deadly sin and so is nostalgia, and she had no time for either. She had sat at the bedside of her beloved sister, Dotty, dying of scarlet fever in the summer of 1934; she held Dotty's hand as the sky turned dark from their father's fields blowing away in the drought, she cleaned Dotty, wiped her, told her stories, changed the sheets, and out of that nightmare summer she emerged stronger, confident that life would be wondrous, or at least bearable.

I was named for my great-grandfather John Tollefson, who landed in Lake Wobegon, in the center of Minnesota, from Voss, Norway, in 1880. Lake Wobegon was a rough town then, where, all on one block, for less than five dollars, you could get a tattoo, a glass of gin, and a social disease, and have enough left over to get in a poker game, but Lutherans civilized it. They were hard workers, indifferent to vice. John and his wife, Signe, came from Voss and begat Einar, and Einar and Birthe (Birdy) begat Byron, and Byron and Mary begat me, John, the third of five children, with Bill and Diana ahead of me and Ronnie (Byron, Jr.) and Judy after.

It was a good place to grow up in, Lake Wobegon. Kids migrated around town as free as birds and did their stuff, put on coronations and executions in the long, dim train shed and the deserted depot, fought the Indian wars, made ice forts and lobbed grenades at each other, dammed up the spring melt in the gutters, swam at the beach, raced bikes in the alley. You were free, but you knew how to behave. You didn't smart off to your elders, and if a lady you didn't know came by and told you to blow your nose, you blew it. Your parents sent you off to school with lunch money and told you to be polite and do what the teacher said, and if there was a problem at school, it was most likely your fault and not the school's. Your parents were large and slow afoot and they did not read books about parenting, and when they gathered with other adults, at Lutheran church suppers or family get-togethers, they didn't talk about schools or about prevailing theories of child development. They did not weave their lives around yours. They had their own lives, which were mysterious to you.

I remember the day I graduated from tricycle to shiny new two-wheeler, a big day. I wobbled down Green Street and made a U-turn and waved to Mother on the front porch, and she wasn't there. She had tired of watching me and gone in. I was shocked at her lack of interest. I went racing around the corner onto McKinley Street, riding *very* fast so I would have big tales to tell her, and I raced down the hill past the Catholic church and the old black mutt ran out to greet me and I swerved and skidded on loose gravel and tumbled off the bike onto the pavement and skinned myself and lay on the tar, weeping, hoping for someone to come pick me up, but nobody came. The dog barked at me to get up. I limped three blocks home with skin scraped off my forearm and knee, my eyes brimming with tears, and when I came into the kitchen, she looked down at me and said, "It's only a scrape. Go wash it off. You're okay."

And when I had washed, she sat me down with a toasted cheese sandwich and told me the story of Wotan and Frigga. "Wotan, or Odin, was the father of the gods, and his wife, Frigga, was the earth goddess who brought summer, and the god of war, Thor, was the winter god, and the god of peace was Frey. So from Odin we get Wednesday, from Thor, Thursday, from Frey, Friday—Sunday and Monday, of course, refer to the sun and moon—which leaves Saturday and Tuesday. Wotan and Frigga had a boy named Sidney, and Thor had a daughter named Toots, and they fell in love and one day Sidney went to find Toots and steal her away, but Thor sent a big wind and Sidney rode his bicycle too fast and fell and skinned his knee, and that's why Saturday is a day off, so we can think about it and remember not to ride our bikes so fast." She gave me a fresh soft peanut butter cookie. She wiped the last remaining tears from my cheek. She said, "Go outside and play. You're all right."

In Lake Wobegon, you learned about being All Right. Life is complicated, so think small. You can't live life in raging torrents, you have to take it one day at a time, and if you need drama, read Dickens. My dad said, "You can't plant corn and date women at the same time. It doesn't work." One thing at a time. The lust for world domination does not make for the good life. It's the life of the raccoon, a swashbuckling animal who goes screaming into battle one spring night, races around, wins a mate, carries on a heroic raccoon career, only to be driven from the creekbed the next spring by a young stud who leaves teethmarks in your butt and takes away your girlfriend, and you lie wounded and weeping in the ditch. Later that night, you crawl out of the sumac and hurl yourself into the path of oncoming head-lights. Your gruesome carcass lies on the hot asphalt to be picked at by crows. Nobody misses you much. Your babies grow up and do the same thing. Nothing is learned. This is a life for bank robbers. It is not a life for sensible people.

The urge to be top dog is a bad urge. Inevitable tragedy. A sensible person seeks to be at peace, to read books, know the neighbors, take walks, enjoy his portion, live to be eighty, and wind up fat and happy, although a little wistful when the first coronary walks up and slugs him in the chest. Nobody is meant to be a star. Charisma is pure fic-tion, and so is brilliance. It's the dummies who sit on the dais, and it's the smart people who sit in the dark near the exits. That is the Lake Wobegon view of life.

When I was ten, I got absorbed in the Flambeau Family novels in the Lake Wobegon library and devoured them all in one summer, one by one, sequestered in my bedroom (*The Flambeaus and the Case of the Floating Barolo*, and the *Flippant Bellhop*, and the *Flying Bon-bons*, and the *Floral Bouquet*, the *Flagrant Bagel*, the *Flamboyant Baritone*, the *Broadway Flop*, the *Flustered Beagle*, and, finally, *The Flambeaus' Final Bow*). They were all about Tony, a boy of Manhat-tan, and his socialite parents, Emile and Eileen. Tony is a junior at St. Trillin's on West Eighty-ninth, All-City in tennis, an honor student, adored by his girlfriend, Valerie. Tony and his mother, an actress still beautiful at forty-one, and his father, the famed microbiologist, live happily together in their art-filled duplex apartment on the twentieth floor of the San Remo, overlooking Central Park, and solve crimes as they go about their elegant lives, hanging out in swank restaurants among high-rolling dudes and chantoozies, knowing who is real and who is from New Jersey. The neighbors across the hall, Elena and Malcolm Strathspey, a Scottish laird and his ballerina wife, come over for gimlets and to talk about ballet, opera, the O'Connell sculptures at the Guggenheim. For a boy whose dad ran the grain elevator in a small town where nobody had ever seen a ballet or knew a gimlet from a grommet, the Flambeaus were an inspiration. They were my secret family. Nobody else took out the Flambeau books, especially after I reshelved them under Foreign Language.

Sometimes, descending the steps of school, I would raise my hand as I came to the curb and imagine a taxi screeching to a stop and a bald man with a cigar clenched between his teeth saying, "Where to, mac?" "The San Remo." "Yes, *sir.*"

I put the Flambeaus aside as I got older. The miseries of adolescence somehow did not jibe with the Flambeau life, but in the back of my mind, I reserved New York for later consideration, after the tumult died down. Mother said, "John, you are not the first person who ever had hormones, so don't picture this as a great tragedy. Get over it. You're okay." And I was okay. Mother and Dad were un-Flambeau-like; they were reserved and didn't praise me for fear of spoiling me, and they didn't hug me beyond the age of six except sideways once or twice, but I was okay. I grew up and minded my manners and learned to be useful and didn't feel sorry for myself, and in my heart, I imagined myself possessing an Eastern elegance. And when I was thirty, I finally made it.

It was a desperate move. I was escaping from a girl in Minneapolis who wanted me to marry her and fulfill her dreams and secure her happiness. Her name was Korlyss, she was small and dark and of a mournful disposition, we met at the University and clung to each other for ten years, afraid to give up on a bad investment, I guess. We lived in Prospect Park, a sort of intellectual pueblo east of campus, in a tiny walk-up apartment with scarred tables and gimpy chairs and pine plank bookcases crammed with paperbacks. I was a bartender at The Mixers on Seven Corners, a grad-student hangout, and I sold ads for Minnesota Orchestra programs and did an all-night classical music show on the University station, WLB, and spent a dreary year in graduate school, and Korlyss sold lingerie at Dayton's. She was waiting for me to get my feet on the ground so we could marry and be happy. I kept almost marrying her for ten years. She was an extremely nice person. And then, walking along the West River Road one October day when the Mississippi gorge was a carnival of red and orange, she announced she might be pregnant. It just happened, she didn't know how. "Don't you love me?" she said. Maybe I did, but I didn't want to marry her. I offered her all the money I had, about five hundred dollars. She said, "I don't want your money." And the next morning, she packed a suitcase and three shopping bags and went to leave and the doorknob came off in her hand. "Maybe it's a sign that we're supposed to stay together," she said. I fixed the doorknob and opened the door. I offered her a ride. "No," she said. "I prefer to walk." I looked out the kitchen window and there she was on the sidewalk below, looking up at me, her baggage at her feet, as if she were Mimi in *La Bohème*. If only I would stick my head out the window and yell, "Okay! I'll marry you!" then all the neighbors would stick *their* heads out of *their* windows and wave their arms and cheer, and the mailman would dance a jig, and the orange school bus would stop, and out would pop a children's chorus to sing "When You Wish Upon a Star." But I didn't.

I was racked with guilt over Korlyss, believe me, especially when her friends called to say, "She really loves you," and her mother called, weeping, to suggest counseling. It was the absolute rotten worst thing I had ever done to anybody. I felt sick. I knew I had to leave town. Through a Mixers patron, an Episcopal priest who was fond of Rusty Nails, I heard that St. James College in Red Cliff, New York, on Cayuga Lake, had gotten an FM radio license and needed a manager to build a station. I flew out with a glowing recommendation written by the priest and another by me myself on the WLB letterhead, using the name Myra Groetz, and on the basis of the letters and a confident manner and a breezy interview over lunch and a good bottle of Beaujolais, I was hired for the job by Paul Burton, dean of students, a sleepy man with no chin, who for some reason was delegated to oversee WSJO. "I don't know the first thing about radio except that I don't care for it," he said. "It's noise, and it's one big reason why most people in this country go around without an intelligent thought in their noggins."

St. James College is an Episcopalian outpost heavily endowed by Christian bandits of the nineteenth century, a liberal arts school that administers a light coating of education to students lured by fine architecture and low admission requirements. When I saw it that fall, it smelled of richness. The groomed lawns, the oak trees with stone benches close around them, the trimmed hedges, the masses of ivy, the Georgian pillars of the administration building, Gilman Hall, and the curving stairs to the grand entrance, the lobby, a showroom of thick green carpet and rose-patterned sofas, and the dean's office, a large sitting room carpeted in crimson, with a small Chippendale desk—it all spoke well for the college's fund-raisers. The college lay on the crest of a ridge like a royal park, a golf course hugging the campus on the south, the arboretum on the north, and, below it, the town of Red Cliff (population 2,271), on a gentle slant near the lovely blue eminence of Cayuga Lake.

Among financially gifted parents of academically challenged students along the Eastern Seaboard, the college is known as St. Jude's, after the patron saint of hopeless causes, a place where you can pack off your SPASM child (Simply Pray And Send Money) and feel that, barring a felony conviction, he or she will get to wear a black gown and attend graduation and receive a sheepskin with the St. James crest ("Omnibus Omnia") on it. Tuition at St. James is equivalent to that at Harvard or Yale, on the theory that charity should not come cheap.

Oil paintings of benefactors hung in the lobby of Gilman—"the idiot children of the rich," said the dean, as he gave me a quick tour—and in the Bush Library, a four-story circular structure, concrete and brick and of a sturdy Bauhaus demeanor, with high beamed ceilings, the stacks dotted with study carrels, the building eerily empty, devoid of students. "They're all watching reruns of *Gilligan's Island*," he said. I glanced through the stacks and saw six shelves of Dante's *Divine Comedy*, four of Plato's *Dialogues*, the Variorum Shakespeare, Goethe, Chekhov, Macaulay's complete works five times over, all beautifully bound, all apparently unread. An entire room was devoted to atlases, another to rare books, both rooms majestic, with long oak tables and green-shaded lamps, both rooms deserted. "This is the place to come if you were looking to have an assignation," he said. "You could romp naked in periodicals and copulate on the carpet, and the librarians would be grateful if, after climax, you took down a magazine and thumbed through it." He gave me a baleful look. "We don't need a radio station—we need a literacy program."

I walked down the hill toward the lake. The grass really *was* greener here, and the foliage was denser, the trees and shrubs more various, than in Minnesota. The yards were more lush, and the standards of yard-keeping more relaxed. No Prussian horticulture, no home owners kneeling and trimming the borders with fingernail clippers. The lawns were clumpy, vegetation was allowed to loll, to spread, to luxuriate. I liked that. The houses were big, with big porches, vines climbing up the sides, here and there an American flag fluttering. The lots were deep. There were some dirt driveways with mud puddles—another good sign—and some leaning fences, and weather-beaten garages, a relief from the Scandinavian fastidiousness of back home. Here, people seemed to be appreciative of old things and could let them age and molder and crack. The old brick storefronts along Main Street that housed the usual college-town pizza parlors and sandwich shops and beer halls looked *old*, and the stoplights were old, from the forties, and hung over the intersections. Amazing, I thought. In Minnesota, county highway engineers would have torn those down long ago, replaced them with four $30,000 semaphores at each intersection, widened the street, and torn down every tree for a hundred feet, all in the interest of highway safety. Engineers run Minnesota, they designed it, they teach its children, and engineers are merciless men bent on the nullification of art and the worship of functionalism.

The only new building in Red Cliff was a small brick box of a post office, which sat next to the grand old post office, which housed a bakery, a Native American crafts store, a shop called Kathy's Kitchen that sold very expensive jams and jellies, a candle store, and a massage therapist. The Red Cliff Inn occupied an old Greek Revival mansion on the lake side of Main Street, and the Red Cliff County Trust Company faced it, in a granite temple with four pink marble pillars. Next to it was the Embassy Bar and then Parker's Antiques and then Colonial Laundromat and then a shallow creek flowing through a narrow rocky gorge. I stood and looked down the street and tried to imagine living here. The public library sat on the hill side of Main Street, in a crotchety brick mansion, and opposite was the Catholic church, St. Patrick's, a cross atop its small, square belfry, and down the street was a prim white Methodist chapel and the gray stone castle of the Presbyterians. A Genesee Beer truck sat double-parked in front of the bar. A pretty young woman in a Doris Lessing T-shirt, with an enormous bosom, passed by and smiled, and a young man with a wisp of beard, wearing a top hat and a paisley shirt and red-striped trousers— obviously a drama student—looked at me with a practiced sneer. *Hey,* I thought. *Home at last.*

Two weeks later, I was back, in a rusted-out pink 1978 Oldsmobile, my clothes in the back seat, my books in the trunk. I rented an apartment ("Carriagehouse: Elegant 1BR w EIK, oodles of charm") in what had been a garage, and went to work in a converted storage room in the college chapel, a refectory table for a desk.

The college chapel was a long Gothic pile that seated a thousand, with stone stalactites and high ribbed vaults, flying buttresses adjoining the apse, dark timbers and stone carvings and pennants and banners, the goddesses of Art and Science and Literature peering down, and you felt as if footmen and courtiers might enter, followed by fawning gentry, plump lords and powdered ladies, sallow-faced princes, and the monarch himself, dour and vast in his purple silk, limping from the gout, come to kneel in prayer before attending the morning beheading.

The Episcopal congregation of St. James was tiny, a few old ladies and a few hairy bison and me—I began attending almost every Sunday, trying to make up for the dirty deed I had done to Korlyss. In this cathedral we Christians would be like BBs in a boxcar, so it was reserved for convocations and academic events and Christmas. We huddled every Sunday morning in a tiny basement chapel for Mass, celebrated by Mother Sally, a hearty, sixtyish woman, who marched down into the congregation during the Exchange of Peace and hugged everyone as if testing us for ripeness. She raced through the prayers to allow extra time for her homily. She seemed to believe that God spoke in an elaborate code intended to get Her message past St.

Paul and the patriarchy of the early Church: the gist of it was that the Word is Womb, and the Womb is the Word. She was big on empowerment too.

My first year in Red Cliff was nothing but good. First, there was the great relief of not marrying Korlyss, of leaving Minnesota, the divestment of accumulated regrets. I joined a coed volleyball league and acquired a pleasant girlfriend named Jean, a librarian, who was enthusiastic and came and went at convenient times and never mentioned marriage. Dean Burton was a great boss. If I could catch him in his drowsy time, after lunch, he would sign anything put in front of him: extradition papers, a check for a million dollars, a death warrant, anything. The radio antenna tower was built on a hill west of town, the studios were constructed on the fifth floor of Gridley Hall—deep gray carpets, six-inch-thick soundproofed doors, cantilevered windows to reduce echo—and staff was hired (a gloomy bunch, I thought, rather Eeyorish, but okay for public radio) and WSJO went on the air on Labor Day, 1985, with a Mozart Marathon. President Postlethwaite came to switch on the transmitter, there were deans and faculty in full regalia, Mother Sally flung water on the microphones, and afterward, I sat in my big office and raised a glass of champagne to our business manager, Marian MacKay. I liked her. She was from Houston, she had that hands-on-her-hips Texas Woman style, she was young and smart and black, and she could *do* black if she liked and play African queen—and she also could whip through ten pages of budget figures and explain them to me in one sentence. On her résumé, she listed the Sam Houston Institute of Technology. I like jokes like that from a woman.

"To radio," I said. "To Mozart."

"He's the Moz." We clinked glasses.

"So how long you going to last here, baby?" she said.

I said that I was going to become a beloved old fart and stay until my eyebrows were as big as laboratory rats.

She gave me a sad smile. "You remind me of that Sorry Mutha song, 'Why Do You Try So Hard to Get What You Don't Even Want?' "

I told her it was a better job than what I had before. She said, "Baby, you and me are just *passing through.* The difference is that I know it and you don't."

One Sunday morning that September, before Mass, a man slipped into the pew next to me, a beefy man with a big head of permed brown hair, wearing a blue double-breasted suit and a blue shirt with a white collar.

"Hi. How are ya doing?" he said in a loud voice, reached over to pump my hand. Heads turned.

I whispered: "Fine."

"Something wrong?" he whispered.

I shook my head. Just then the organist cut loose with the prelude, something harsh and loud and medieval.

The man jumped. "Jesus Christ," he said. He grinned at me and said, "Wow. Cool."

He seemed never to have attended an Anglican service before, didn't know a hymnal from a prayer book, stood when he should have knelt, and when I rose to go forward for communion, he leaned over and whispered, "Where are you going?"

"Communion."

"Should I go too?"

I thought about this for a moment. I didn't want to have to give him instruction on how to receive the wafer, how much wine to drink. "Not this time," I said. "Next time. Catch you later."

After Mass, we shook hands again. "Howard Freeman is the name," he said. "New to town. Just started a law practice. Thought I'd find a church." We walked out into the sunshine and stood on the steps, looking across the lawn.

"Interesting sermon. She seems to like the word 'context,' doesn't she," Howard said.

"She is very much a contextual person," I said. "She can contextualize with the best of them."

"I must admit, I'm here looking for more of a spiritual dimension in my life," said Howard. "I've always meditated, but I thought maybe I needed something more disciplined." He looked at me confidentially. "Dumb-question alert: okay? Christianity believes in an afterlife, right? Or am I getting it confused with something else? Like Catholicism?"

I tried to explain about heaven. The Last Judgment. It was interesting to catechize a man my own age. Like explaining baseball to a European. We walked to Howard's car, and I invited him to play racquetball sometime at the Faculty Club. In Minnesota, you can issue invitations knowing that people will politely decline them, but Howard said, "Sure, how about tomorrow?" and he turned out to be a bull on the court. He won three games by wide margins, and I couldn't very well turn down his offer of a rematch without looking like a wimp, and so we became Monday regulars.

One day, sitting in the steam room, he told me about a house on Green Street two blocks from campus that was for sale, cheap.

"The owner is a lady drama professor named Sanders, who got canned for seducing a student," said Howard, "who happens to be the daughter of the guy who donated the money for the math building. They're hoping he'll give them a science hall too."

"I never heard about her being fired," I said.

"She was given a nice severance package. I negotiated it for her. One year's salary and a year on leave at half salary. Better than a Guggenheim."

"How much is she asking for the house?"

"However much she can get, to be perfectly frank, which is a lot less than she thinks. It's October, and who is in the market for a fancy house? Nobody, that's who. If you're interested, I'll see what I can do for you."

So I went to inspect the seductive lady's house. A two-story white Greek Revival manse, with a front porch and a terrace in the back. Excellent condition, newly renovated, said the lady agent who showed me through the place. There was a kitchen with Finnish cabinetry, and a living room with a blue ceramic Swedish fireplace and cherry wainscoting, and an oak staircase, and three upstairs bedrooms replastered and papered, with new oak floors, and two upstairs baths all marble and glass, one with a whirlpool.

"It's a peach," she said. "Bring your wife to see it."

I said I wasn't married.

"Well," she said, "I'm sure you would be very happy here."

Howard handled the whole deal. "Let me do this," he said, and he did it. He made an offer somewhat less than half of the asking price, and he withstood the fury of the agent, and he reported back almost daily. To him, it was like war. "There are no other prospective buyers. I know it. They are desperate. The agent is lying through her teeth about the college wanting to buy it for faculty housing. No way. The elephant is down, the tigers are circling."

And the next day he called and said, "They have surrendered!" He whooped over the telephone. He'd actually gotten the house for *less* than the original low offer. Something about a zoning variance that the seller hadn't disclosed. The agent was livid, but she capitulated. And a month later, I unlocked the back door and walked into the kitchen. It was a truly extraordinary kitchen, part science lab, part lounge. A cooking island and a ceiling rack for pans and two ovens, a stainless-steel refrigerator big enough to hold a hog carcass. In protest, Miss Sanders had left the place filthy and littered with packing materials; there was an arc of dried coffee on one wall where she had flung it from her cup. But compared to the dismal apartments I'd lived in, this was a fine home indeed. It cast a kindly charm on you as you walked from room to room. The master bedroom was long, with a ten-foot ceiling. One could imagine delightful things happening there. And then I saw on the master-bathroom mirror, written in foot-high red lipstick letters: THIEF. And underneath, in small letters: "someday someone will do this to you."

Nobody had ever put a curse on me before. Motorists had sworn at me, ex-girlfriends had called me names, but this was a specific curse: "As you did to me, so it shall be done unto you." I had sicced my gladiator on a defenseless woman and plundered her house, and now what would be a just desert? Probably something like prostate cancer. What goes around comes around. One morning, I'd get up and take a leak and the bowl would be bright red with blood, and I'd go to some specialist in the city and sit in a beige waiting room, listening to soupy music, thinking about my crumbling innards, pleading with God for a miracle, perusing tattered issues of *People*, thinking, *I am spending some of my precious last hours on earth learning more about Tammy Wynette.* And then proceeding to the examining room. Disrobing. Waiting for the arrival of the prostate potentate himself, Dr. Oh, and his various benedictions and incantations, and then the presentation of the posterior for the digital exam.

Yes, it seemed utterly clear to me. Cancer would be a fitting reward for having snookered poor Professor Sanders. I would enjoy a few months of the good life, and then the hand of death would tap me on the shoulder.

The Gibbs Farm

Howard recommended an antiques barn in Trumansburg, and I drove there and bought an oak writing desk, glass cabinets for books, a plank table for the kitchen and a hurricane lamp to hang over it and six white maple chairs. White wicker chairs for the porch. A series of watercolors of Norway: boats on a beach, boys wading in the sea, fiddlers around a maypole. Rocking chairs. A bobsled to hold firewood. Ships' chests. A church bench. A bust of Grieg. I hired a formidable cleaning woman named Ingeborg, who came every Tuesday and made the place shine. I snagged a gorgeous red Afghani carpet, dirt cheap, at an auction on a cold rainy day, and an oil painting of Bergen: the sailing ships tied to the piers, the brick warehouses, the green and white and cream houses behind, the green trees marching up the mountainside, the sunlight pouring into the valley—the last sight my ancestors had glimpsed of Norway. I hung it over the sideboard in the dining room. It reminded me of the painting of the Norwegian coast that hung in the Sidetrack Tap in Lake Wobegon, on the wall above the booth the bachelor farmers sat in: blue-green waves crashed on the rocks, spray flew in the air, a village of white stave houses nestled in a valley between mountains, two boys stood on the rocks, shading their eyes, looking out to sea. A copper plate below said, WHERE IS FATHER?

Jean and I liked to give small dinner parties, and so did the Brickmans from church, and they invited the Browns, who brought in the Sullivans and the Speeds—somehow the Hopkinses got in, though they were sullen and argumentative drunks and she was liable to rip into her husband—and Howard and his wife, Anne, became part of the circle, though Howard could be a pain. He had a permanent golden tan and smelled of a powerful musk that lawyers spray on themselves to warn other lawyers away. He always brought an expensive gift bottle of olive oil and made a big show of uncorking it and savoring its virginity. He was an olive oil bully, and an interrupter of other people's stories, and a haranguer. His wife was terribly polite to make up for him. She kept trying to turn the conversation toward the topic of elementary education.

When I look back on my thirties, I am stunned by the shallowness— how easy life was! Marian ran the station, Ingeborg kept the house clean, Jean appeared and disappeared like a friendly elf, I flew back home to Minnesota every July and every December, and I waited for tragedy to strike and it didn't. The newspaper landed on the front step, I read it, none of it had the slightest reality to me. What was most real was something missing from my life that was intimated in great music. I would look up from my desk to hear Jussi Bjoerling sing "Nessun dorma" from *Turandot* and suddenly know that my life lacked nobility and purpose. I was sleepwalking. People sat around my dining room table and actually discussed the merits of different brands of blenders, coffee beans, cheeses. They flew off to foreign lands and nothing happened: they came back and described their hotel rooms and the dinners they ate and how crowded the Louvre was. My thirties were a foreign country where there was no crisis, no suffering, nothing wondrous or noble, just nice people and a wonderful vinaigrette dressing. The noblest thing I did was to give parties and make people have a good time. Roast a pig on a giant broiler in the driveway. Put out a few cases of a nice Brunello di Montalcino. Circulate among the guests, barefoot, in shorts and white shirt, like Counselor John at the opening campfire, encouraging the gloomy and the shy and the sensitive to poke their heads out of their shells and have a good time! Parties are hard work. A good host has to keep moving through the crowd, breaking up cliques of mourners—the sarcastic feminists, the aging bohemians, the gloomy neurotics, the sad sacks of public radio, Mother Sally and her disciples, the unappreciated artists—introducing like to unlike, prodding people toward the Three Steps to Festivity: telling jokes, singing songs, and dancing. It was hard to get my crowd to the third step. In ten years, I succeeded perhaps four or five times—music blasting, heads bobbing, arms waving—and each time, people talked about it for weeks afterward, what a great party it was, and the next time, nobody would dance at all.

Suddenly my fortieth birthday loomed up like an iceberg. Months before, sitting in the steam room after racquetball, talking about it, I told Howard, "I am a guy trapped in a good job. If I had any balls, I'd quit." Howard told me about a former client, a pencil-necked geek from the math department named Larry, who won a $30,000 settlement from Wal-Mart for a microwave oven that blew up when he baked a potato, although it was pretty clear Larry had wrapped the spud in tinfoil. With the windfall, Larry bankrolled a sabbatical in Greece, and there he juggled around some old math formulas to come up with a magical algorithm crucial to the development of reliable voice recognition by computers, out of which sprang Loxware Corporation, and two years later he was worth $300 million, according to an article in *Esquire* on the Fifty Most Fascinating Men in America. Larry was on the cover. A former drone of the math lab, now at the helm of a schooner in the Aegean—he owned an island there—and though practically bald in his St. James days, now he had a great head of tousled golden hair.

"I met Larry when we were in AA together," Howard told me. Larry had lived alone in a house that reeked of garbage; he was addicted to crème de banana and licorice schnapps. He stood up in AA and said he had turned to liqueur as an escape from gender confusion, and now here he was, a winsome tycoon squinting into the sun and sailing the blue sea in the company of a twenty-year-old singer named Chantal.

If Larry could do it, why couldn't we? We sat, naked athletes in the steam, like Greeks at the baths at Delphi purifying ourselves before consulting the oracles, and Howard talked about going into business. "We're at that age when guys should go out and make their money," he said. I thought, *Maybe this is how big corporations start, with two naked men talking,* and then I thought, *With a jerk like Howard for a partner, maybe we actually could succeed.*

"What about a vineyard?" said Howard. But we knew nothing about growing grapes. I thought about selling antiques. But the towns around Cayuga Lake were teeming with antique shops already. "Designer ice cream," said Howard. Too boring.

One day, I had a wonderful idea—it sprang up at me from a bag of frozen corn I was pouring into boiling water: a restaurant, a *farm restaurant,* serving fresh vegetables grown on the premises. Proud salads, tomatoes and sweet onions, fresh herbs, creamed peas and onions, and sweet corn, ten minutes from field to table. You'd sit at a table with a linen cloth and drink a glass of Chardonnay, you and your love, and gaze out the window toward a field laced with green rows and see a man wheeling a barrow heaped high with sweet corn and potatoes and cucumbers and a basket of tomatoes—your lunch on its way—and the sheer goodness of it would make other lunches seem like chewing on old saddle blankets.

"That is the first absolutely new idea in restaurants since the salad bar," said Howard. "You've got it."

"Too bad I don't have the money," I said.

"Leave that to me," said Howard.

He went looking for investors, and they were not hard to find in that boom time, with the stock market going up and up, equity rising on every hand; and two months later, Howard drew up the papers of incorporation, with twelve partners putting in $50,000 apiece, including himself, and made a down payment on a two-hundred-

forty-acre farm about twelve miles north of Ithaca, near Taughannock Falls, and named it The Gibbs Farm, after Isaiah Gibbs, who
built the house in 1875.

Jean thought everyone was out of their mind. "A restaurant!" she
cried, as if I had said they were investing in cut daffodils. Her scorn-
ful expression was all I needed: I remortgaged the house, put in my
fifty grand, and became Investor No. 13.

One night in April, I drove to the farm, the house hidden by trees
until you came abreast of it, a fine white house, two stories, with four
dormers, a big red barn on a stone foundation. The partners gathered
under kerosene lanterns in the barn and uncorked champagne, and
Howard gave a speech. "We are men who are bonded to each other by
a common dream," he said, "and next year at this time, we will sit
down in our restaurant and break bread together. Here's to our
vision. Next year in the restaurant."

"Next year," they said, glasses raised, all smiling at me. I was
stunned. Two months after the lightbulb clicked on, and here we were,
on the road to triumph. All thanks to Howard, a can-do guy despite
his big hair and frat-boy manners.

"John," said Howard. "Want you to meet Steve, our contractor."
And I shook hands with a lean man with a blond ponytail down to his
waist, in white painter's overalls and running shoes and a Grateful
Dead T-shirt. Steve put his hand up for the soul-brother grip, but I
came in low for the standard handshake.

"This is a carpenter's dream," Steve said. "Thanks for the vision.
This is going to be an absolutely *primo* facility."

The three of us strolled around the property, the other partners
trailing behind. The house had a turret and high-pitched gables that
poked up above the weeping beech trees and willows. A big screened
porch wrapped around the front and sides. There were two acres of
lawn, where you could envision ladies in white dresses playing croquet. Behind the house was a rock garden, and beyond it were sheds
and the big red barn with double hanging doors, a windmill, an old
stone silo, several outbuildings in weathered shades of deep red. The
house was big, two full stories with a two-story wing in back. It had
been vacant for six years; the floors were littered with broken glass,

girls' names and "Class of 90 Rules" spray-painted on the walls. But it was basically sound, Steve said. He pointed out the fir paneling in the dining room, the granite fireplace and mantel with two stags and the letter G carved into it, the living room, thirty feet long, looking out at eighty acres of cornfield in the darkness.

The view reminded me of October nights in Lake Wobegon and the distant engines of tractors buzzing at midnight, headlights wavering, of corn pickers and combines and my dad working late at the elevator, supervising the trucks unloading until three or four in the morning. The old frame elevator with its four concrete silos and six smaller metal silos, the pipes and chutes connecting them, the bare, bright bulbs shining high and low, the dust rising—it looked as if rockets were being prepared for launch to the moon. Dad's office was next to the door to the dock and the truck scale. Everyone came and talked to Byron. He sat behind the gray metal desk in a ten-by-twelve room with a green shag carpet and an old green sofa that smelled of corn and bean dust, where farmers crowded in and drank a cup of coffee and chewed the rag for a few minutes. There is nobody so sociable as a farmer who's been bouncing across a field alone in the dark for four hours. They told jokes, complained about the government and their wives, talked about anything other than corn-picking. There were no wonderful stories about corn-picking, only gruesome ones. They preferred to tell jokes. Dad wore his old brown shirt and his DeKalb seed corn cap and his green corduroy jacket. He was happy. A river of corn and beans flowed into the elevator, tomorrow's weather looked good for picking, he was surrounded by Rollie Hochstetter and Roger Hedlund and Daryl Tollerud and Larry Kreuger, men he had known since childhood, and somebody was telling the joke about Ole and Lena celebrating their twenty-fifth anniversary and she gives him a hammer for a present. "That's for twenty-five years of lousy sex," says Lena. Ole slugs her in the shoulder. "That's for knowing the difference," he says.

Howard and Steve and I walked through the house, and Howard explained the loan from the bank, which had come through a few days before, and we walked out the back door, and Steve gestured toward the field. "And there's your real asset, the land," he said. I remembered a tomato from my youth, a tomato fresh and hot from the vine: I bit into it and the juice ran down my chin, the sweetness and boldness of the tomato burst upon me, the secret of life revealed.

"Are you sure you want to call it Griggs Farm?" said Howard. "Griggs sounds like someone chewing on sand."

"It's Gibbs, not Griggs," I said.

"Same difference. Why not Captain Crunch Café? Sounds friendlier."

If your lawyer who drew up the papers can't remember the name of the restaurant, should you be concerned? I wondered.

Steve was bringing his crew to the site in three weeks, Howard said. They would camp here. The work would start immediately. Steve was 95 percent certain that the restaurant could open next spring, two dining rooms, one in the house, a larger one in the barn.

The other partners got in their cars and drove home, and Howard and Steve and I sat on the steps of the house, the bright stars shining, and Steve rolled a joint and lit it and passed it around. He sat, legs drawn up under his chin, and talked about sailing as a deckhand on a freighter named the *Eleanor James* and how he was thrown off the ship in Athens for protesting the beating of a cabin boy by the first mate and was rescued by a black woman named Aleisha, who taught him Delta blues guitar and voodoo charms. He bummed around Europe from Greece to Finland to Turkey, playing blues on the street for spare change, and one day in Istanbul a stocky guy in a beret and a tie-dye T-shirt came up to him on a street corner and said, "Hey, cool," and it was Jerry Garcia, and the two of them traveled to India and Australia and Tahiti, and Steve spent three years with the Dead as Jerry's pal and bodyguard and keeper of the car keys, and through Jerry Steve met Moon Blossom, a poet and Sufi therapist. She and Steve moved to Alaska and lived in a geodesic dome on a glacier and were going to start an alternative performance space and then she died skiing into a fissure while high on psilocybin and Steve made her coffin out of spruce and got tuned in to wood and he built a boat and sailed it to Ireland where he studied cooperage at a distillery and went to Finland and apprenticed himself to the great Aalto Maarimakki and spent six years learning the art of cabinetry and returned to the U.S. to study Shaker design in New Hampshire, which was where Howard found him.

I got up to head for home. It took me a moment to stand up. It was some powerful marijuana. I walked carefully to the car and sat in it for a few minutes, rehearsing in my mind how to start the engine, how to move the gearshift to Reverse, how to back out, stop, put it in Drive. I thought, *There is a drug war on. I could be stopped by the highway patrol and go to prison for about ninety years. The prison doctor would discover my prostate cancer.*

THREE

Alida

My fortieth birthday was May 14, and I put on a garden party in my backyard. A birthday and Norwegian Independence Day and a celebration of the end of WSJO Pledge Week all in one, and I roasted legs of lamb on the barbecue and the wine flowed and I got about as drunk as I dared in the presence of my staff—drunk enough to be irritated by the gloomy talk I heard on the patio, the clumps of dough-faced academics muttering about Clinton's betrayals and the decline of civility and the pitiful ineptness of their students, and I got so mad I waved my arms and shouted, "People! It's a party!" They turned and stared at me, a lunatic.

"People!" I said. "We have met our fund-raising goals! I am forty years old! The Norwegian people are free from their Swedish oppressors! We need more wine! More music!" I got them to raise their thin, trembly voices in "Hey Jude" and "Zip-a-Dee-Doo-Dah" and "Blue Eyes Crying in the Rain" and "Amazing Grace" and "Up in the Air, Junior Birdmen," and then they sang "We Shall

Overcome," and a sweet memory of my younger, finer self brought tears to my eyes and I looked around at my comfortable, aimless life and wondered where I had jumped the tracks. Then we sang "Happy Trails," with a whole chorus of vocal clip-clops, with bass mooing, and as I let go a particularly good whinny, I turned and saw a solemn face studying me, the thin lips and beetle brows of my new boss, Dean Baird, who had taken over from Dean Burton in March. "Things have been allowed to drift around here," he had told me then. "I am not a drifter." The dean was not doing the clip-clops, and he did not seem to be having a wonderful time.

Around midnight, the crowd thinned out. Jean went home. She said, "You're acting weird. Please don't drink anymore," and disappeared. And a moment later, I noticed, standing next to Howard, a tall woman with curly close-cropped black hair, wearing dangly silver earrings, a white silk blouse, denim trousers, and sandals, who looked back at me in a frank way, as if she had been waiting to be noticed. She walked over and shook my hand.

"I'm Alida. Howard's sister, up from the city," she said. "It's a nice party. I like lamb. Howard tells me you speak Norwegian."

She and I sat talking on the porch as the other guests drifted by, saying good night. She was thirty-six and taught nineteenth-century American history at Columbia and was working on a book about Bolle Balestrand, a Norwegian immigrant who was Susan B. Anthony's lover.

"Never heard of him," I said.

"He was quite a dashing fellow. He was Thoreau's doctor, and later Lincoln's, and Susan's lover. He took photographs of her playing the accordion, wearing trousers, her hair peroxided, and after they broke up, he went along with General Custer to the Little Big Horn and then back to Norway and wrote his autobiography. I found it in the Library of Congress, filed under 'Stand, Last; of Custer.' So do you read Norwegian?"

"Of course. Some. Enough to get by."

"Maybe you could translate some of it for me."

"I'll do my best," I said.

The next morning, I checked out a book from the library, *Norwegian Made Easy*. Jean was at the circulation desk. She apologized for getting mad at me at the party, and I told her I thought we needed some time apart. "Why?" she said.

"Because my life is too easy. I need to think." I took the book home and pored over it and listened to tapes, and got some basic vocabulary in my head and a smattering of grammar, and I called Alida in New York and said I'd be glad to come down and take a look at Balestrand's memoir.

"I was thinking of going back to Red Cliff in a week or so," she said. "I liked it up there."

To learn the restaurant trade, I was working Friday nights and Saturdays at the House of Hash, managed by my friend Eric from the volleyball team, who stuck me in the scullery, washing dishes. The next Saturday afternoon, I looked up from a rack of steaming-hot plates I was pulling from the machine, and there in a cloud of steam at the back door, grinning at me, stood Alida, wearing khaki shorts and a Knicks tank top.

We walked through the town at dusk, under the canopies of elms and oaks, and onto the campus green, past the dark windows of the library, toward the chapel, with its tiers of steps and its pillars and its inscription about Learning and the Ennoblement of Youth. Across the lawn, a crowd of high schoolers from summer choral camp gathered around a bonfire in a parking lot alongside Dermot Hall, a women's dorm, and sang "Yesterday" with tender melancholy, as if they might never hear it again.

I was floating. I felt great. That's the thing about dishwashing: when you're done with it, everything that happens afterward is wonderful. You come out of the steam and heat of the scullery, and just the smell of grass and trees is pure pleasure after you've had soap up your nose. We sat on the top step of the chapel, looking across the great sward of lawn toward the flickering bonfire, and I took her hand

and leaned against her, laid my head on her shoulder, and thought, *This is what I wanted*, to feel her fingers wrapped in mine and her breath on my hair as she talked.

"Until I came across Bolle Balestrand, I never knew how impulsive Norwegians could be," she said. "I always—you know—thought of them as . . . well, sort of *settled*."

"As potato heads," I said. "Big blond phlegmatic people. Slow talkers. Mouth breathers."

"Sort of," she said. "I mean, very *decent* people—"

"But boring."

"Yes," she said. "Not that there's anything *wrong* with boring. I mean, compared to vicious or fraudulent, boring isn't bad."

If someone suggests you are boring, what do you do? I drew her chin toward me and put my lips to hers and gave her a long, searching kiss and ran my finger along her cheek and jaw and throat and shoulder and collarbone. When our lips parted, she drew a deep breath and blinked.

"I see you've kissed women before," she said.

"I don't recall if I have or not. I think you may be the first."

We sat, embracing, listening to the singers around the campfire, who had moved on to "Over the Rainbow."

"So where do we go from here?" she said.

"Come over for dinner," I said. "I'll cook."

"How do I know you're not the sort of man who likes to tie women to a bed and drip hot candle wax on them?" she said.

I said that we Norwegians would never waste candles like that.

I walked her into the chapel and around the ambulatory behind the altar, and kissed her again, and recited, " 'Let me not to the marriage of true minds / Admit impediments,' " learned years ago for Mr. Tuomey's sophomore English class, right up through " 'It is the star to every wandering bark, / Whose worth's unknown, although his height be taken.' " And then she kissed me. She took my head in both her hands and rubbed her lips along mine and slipped her tongue into my mouth and touched the front of my trousers. Lightly. But it boomed, it set off depth charges.

"What can I get you for dinner?" I said.

"I'd like you," she said, "but I'm leaving for Chicago early tomorrow."

"My favorite city," I said. "I'll come and show you around."

The next day, I ordered a ticket for Chicago and reserved a room at the Palmer House and told Marian MacKay I was sick. "Right," she said. "Sure." I drove to the Syracuse airport and flew west. I met Alida for drinks at the Drake, where she was staying. The following morning, I met her at the Women's Club, where she was on a panel discussing "Gender Models of the Post-Patriarchal Era," at which Alida said, in an innocent voice, "You know, there are generational differences that are greater than any gender differences I am aware of. Women of my generation are not obsessively angry at men, we do not hold them responsible for our lives. Period." A storm of fury descended on her head! Dowagers in straw hats hissed at her, and one panelist said, "That is the cruelest remark," and talked about her mother and her struggles in the trade union movement and got weepy, and Alida smiled at me sweetly and crossed her eyes and stuck out her tongue.

I took her to lunch and then to an interview with Studs Terkel. The two of them yakked about Darrow and Altgeld and Sandburg and Dreiser and the Haymarket bomb and the whole bloody history of Chicago radicalism, and I sat in the corner of the studio, wishing Terkel would hurry up and turn on the damn tape recorder and get the show on the road. Terkel kept relighting his cigar and talking his odd patois, like a bookie who had grown up reading James Joyce, and afterward Alida and I took a cab back to the hotel. Her hotel. We stood on the curb, under the brown awning. I asked if she wanted to look at architecture or take in a Sox game or go to dinner. She said, "What's wrong with going to my room and having sex?"

So I checked out of the Palmer House and moved into her room. It was one perfect day after another, five of them, and she kept calling New York and canceling things. The glory of first love, when a mortal man is filled with grace, and even silence is symphonic. Then I took a week of vacation and flew to New York with her. I cooked, did laundry, cleaned her apartment, was relentlessly good-humored, did my best to be irresistible, and, at the end, thought she seemed a little grateful to see me go. But a few days later, I got a note saying there was nobody in the world she would rather be with than me, she was longing for me, starving for me, she hoped I felt the same way about her, if I didn't she would be too sad for words.

She was, simply, the love of my life. She had turned up at a party, and now I didn't care if I ever gave a party again. She was it. No question. The advantage of a restrictive Lutheran upbringing is that it heightens the pleasure of love when you eventually get around to it, and Alida was a love worth waiting for. She was the woman to keep. She was smart and sweet and passionate, and also something of a princess, I found out. She could not tolerate background music. She did not drink out of plastic or paper containers. She took two showers every day and put on fresh underwear. She smoked two cigarettes in the evening and had one glass of wine, never more. She took a Walkman to bed, in case of insomnia in the wee hours, and the earpiece had to be in her left ear and the radio under the pillow, tuned to the BBC Overnight Service. I had to take my shoes off by the door—she could not bear to feel grit under her feet—and I could not clip my nails in her presence (gross!) and she could not abide the thought of nose-picking.

"You don't do it, do you?" she said. "I mean, not even alone in the bathroom. You don't stand at the sink and fish around for boogers, do you? Tell me you don't."

I told her I hadn't put my finger in my nose since I was in Boy Scouts. That I blew my nose with a tissue, the same as anyone else. It was a lie, but it put her mind at rest.

She didn't mind belching, was a connoisseur of it, in fact, and could bring up belches of such force she could articulate whole sentences with them—once, after a dinner at a Greek restaurant that included flaming cheese curds, she belched out "Whan that Aprille with his shoures soote / The droghte of March hath perced to the roote" in the elevator—but farting was beyond the pale, not even to be contemplated. If she heard even a whisper of a fart, she turned away and said, "Take that someplace else, thank you." She emitted a few sweet ones during the night, which I savored in the morning when she threw aside the blankets. She wrinkled up her nose. "I hope you don't think *I* did that," she said.

She was intensely jealous and didn't pretend otherwise; she could not bear to hear any reference to my previous loves, and so those chapters of my life had to be locked up. I didn't mind hearing about Simon, her old professor at Bryn Mawr, with whom she had a romance for eight years, which ended when his wife died. But she could not tolerate the mention of my days in Minneapolis when I lived with Korlyss, or in Red Cliff with Jean, or my trip to Greece with Ellie the fall Jean and I weren't speaking, or my affair with the dancer who did a month's residency at St. James—all off-limits.

"But it was part of my life," I said.

"Start a new one," she said.

Frankly, it was not such a bad deal to herd all my old girlfriends into a closet and close the door. I had thought enough about them: the first infatuation, the compulsive phone calls, the joyful couplings, the last sour, jagged moments. Women who are your best pals suddenly turn into peasant gypsy girls, their trust broken, their bodies defiled, their lives ruined by you, you big booger-boo. Sweet Korlyss, the night before she left, hurled wineglasses, one by one, at the back door, and tore my high school graduation picture to shreds, and lay on the couch sobbing. I had stolen the best years of her life and her only chance for happiness. If Alida did not want to look in that closet, well, fine, I didn't need to either. The past receded to a pale shadow when I was with her. She corrected my grammatical errors, which irritated me, and she *knew* so much and didn't hesitate to explain things, and that could be trying, and she was, I thought, a *tiny* bit self-centered— but it didn't matter: none of her personality seemed to be for effect. She was genuinely, utterly herself. She bounced on the balls of her feet. She whistled beautifully. She threw a softball accurately. She was an appreciative lover—she liked it when I went out of my way. I looked into her eyes and thought, *If I could live within that gaze, I would be a happy man.*

In Chicago, the weekend we became lovers at the Drake Hotel, we walked along the lakeshore to the Field Museum, and there she saw a replica of a sailing ship and stopped. "My great-great-grandfather owned a fleet of four clipper ships just like that one," she said. "He sailed out of Nantucket and traded in tea and ginger. Ezekiel Freeman—he had a black beard, and the look in his eye was like the crack of a whip. He was the last one in the family to earn any real money or amount to much."

We sat on a bench in the sun, looking out over the beach and the placid lake. "All of his descendants turned out to be cranks and eccentrics," she said. "His son, who was supposed to take over the business, ran away from the sea and founded a group called the Friends of Universal Reform, which attracted every crackpot on the Eastern Seaboard. Part of their credo was intellectual equality—the idea that everyone's ideas were as interesting as anyone else's—so the meetings went on for days. His name was Jack, and he changed it to Orion; he believed in the therapeutic effects of magnetism and slept every night with his head pointing north. Then *his* son, my grandfather, dedicated his life to proving that certain mounds and ridges in western Massachusetts were relics of a pre-Columbian Mayan culture. He camped out in the Berkshires, drawing maps of Mayan sites as they existed in his imagination. Not Mayan *cities* but places where Mayans sent their children for summer camp. When he was forty, he married the family's Irish cook, which broke his parents' hearts. They were freethinkers, but Catholicism was unacceptable, pure superstition, people praying to statues, so he was cut off from the family fortune and had to teach for a living, and so did *his* son, my father, and so do I. And that's the story of the decline of the Freemans. Brute capitalism followed by helpless whimsy and intellectual drudgery."

In the fall, I celebrated our love affair by having my house painted a deep gold with dark-green trim, and the front door a rich, deep red. Mr. Hall, the painting contractor, asked, "Are you sure?" and I was very sure, though when it was done, the effect was as if a parrot had settled in a flock of doves. A neighbor stopped as I was raking leaves and asked if I had gotten permission for the paint job. I said I didn't know that permission was needed. The neighbor said he didn't know either, he was only asking. "In some towns you need permission," he said, wistfully.

I had the kitchen painted a lighter gold and the floor painted green. Then the living room, pale blue. And the bedroom, pale salmon.

She came up the next weekend and walked around the yard, her hands clasped behind her back, and said, "I've never seen a house like this. Gold . . . green . . . a red door."

"In Norway they loved bright color," I said. "Because of the long winter. They'd have blue floors and green walls, or lilac, or pink, or yellow—and they loved gold, like this, this mottled orangy-gold. It was only when they got to America that they painted all their houses white. They got that from your people, the Puritans. My people were only trying to fit in."

"The Freemans were not Puritans, we were spice merchants. We sold pepper and ginger to Puritans; it was one of their few pleasures."

It was a sweet October day. We ate lunch on the porch. A blue-checked cloth on the table, poached salmon and a cucumber salad. And a glass bowl of cherries. We sat down, and a minute later, the neighbor shut off his lawn mower, and we could hear the radio in the kitchen, a Haydn string quartet. "I hope you know I love you," she said.

We walked to the Dairy Queen, and she told me about Bolle Balestrand's memoir. A Norwegian professor at Columbia had translated two chapters for her. She said that Balestrand was a sort of neuropath, who treated nervous disorders with colonics, herbal teas, and hot and cold baths. He arrived in Boston in 1852, a deckhand on a British frigate, and jumped ship and snuck away to Concord, pretending to be a reformed slave trader, and was taken in by the Alcotts and Emersons, the whole Transcendentalist crowd. They were terribly intellectual people, capable of looking into their cereal bowls and seeing the spirit of the universe. Their shadows, their heartburn, the ringing in their ears—everything pointed to a deeper Truth. An ice-cold bath was to them a religious epiphany. Emerson was the first to take one, and after he raved about it, everyone followed suit. Balestrand administered a powerful enema, which flushed you out, then he steamed you for twenty minutes and plunged you into forty-degree water, after which you drank a quart of hot tea made from dried poppies, and you walked out feeling like an angel. Constipation was epidemic in the nineteenth century, because people were afraid to drink the water. That's why Thoreau raised beans at Walden; when he said, "The mass of men lead lives of quiet desperation," he was referring to a specific problem.

Balestrand got things moving again, and the opiate tea cured all aches and pains, and he became the darling of the New England intelligentsia. Emerson introduced him to Whitman, and he gave Whitman the treatment, and Whitman wrote a poem that began:

> Scented effluence of my being
> Rushing from me so candid and rich and redolent of the earth
> And O so much of it!
> How much I contain'd! I contain'd rivers and the swamps of rivers,
>   the muck and mire of deltas,
> A thousand acres of corn could be raised on what was in me!
> I could feed multitudes!

Whitman took him to Washington and introduced him to Abraham Lincoln, who came to see him every week for almost two years. Lincoln suffered from insomnia due to nightmares—bells tolling, the sky black with smoke, horses rearing and plunging off bridges, women shrieking at the sight of dead men left on their doorsteps, widows dancing with widows—and he was convinced that history would revile him as a bloodthirsty baboon who had drowned America's innocence in blood. Balestrand steamed Lincoln and poured cold water on him and dosed him with opiate tea, and the Great Emancipator sat, stunned, dripping, his hair pasted to his head, mournful as a wet dog. One day, Lincoln was agitated about going to Gettysburg to give a speech. He said, "The thought of the butcher returning to the scene of the crime to speak over the victims! What jokes God plays on me!" And Balestrand showed Lincoln a speech that he, a humble immigrant, had delivered to the Neuropathic Society, about the obligation of the living to dedicate themselves to the unfinished work of those who had gone before and about neuropathy being the medicine of the people, by the people, for the people. Lincoln was grateful. He brought Balestrand the first draft of the Gettysburg Address, and Balestrand persuaded him to drop a long passage about the need for education in meeting the challenge of rapid social change.

"Did Balestrand ever claim credit for it?" I asked.

"Only in his journal. Along with Lincoln's check for ten dollars and his note, saying, 'Do you not think the phrase *the world will little note nor long remember what we say here* is somewhat silly? Why put ideas in their heads?' "

Nineteenth-century American history was a field as crowded as the Boston Marathon, but Alida had risen fast at Columbia, was well-liked in her department. I met her at her office once, when she was talking to her chairman, a short, heavy man with a gray crew cut and a bow tie, who pumped my hand and said, "If you take her away, I will plunge a knife into your heart. Do you hear?" Colleagues sought her opinion of their manuscripts, students smiled at her in the hallway and said hi. At lunch, in a walk-up Italian restaurant on 112th Street, she told me that she was in line to become a full professor when her book was finished.

"I got an offer from Berkeley," she said, "and I showed it to my chairman and he made me a better offer."

She had leapfrogged the feminists with their herstories, the progressive revisionists, the neorevisionists, the deconstructionists with their silly papers about history as pure text, wordplay, history as hissing wrist, as wistful hitting, as hidden story, stir-fry, antihistamine, and she had advanced despite hewing to an old school of thinking, wildly out of fashion, known as narrativism, which held that interpretation was a dead hand, a form of cartooning, and that narrative was All, the best filter of nonsense and political fluff, and that this was perfectly clear anytime you opened a book of history more than fifteen years old: the hermeneutics, the scholarly exegesis, the passages about "the viability of Eurocentric anathematization of

postmodern nonpatriarchal normative injunctions," were as interesting as a rotted log, and the only lively material was who said what to
whom after they did what when with whoever the other people were.

"How can you have history without interpretation?" I asked.

"It's a question of which comes first," she said. "And after slogging
through grad school and listening to professors straining for brilliance, a person comes to have a great respect for simple *facts.*

"If you could reconstruct one day of Jefferson's life, in which he
figured up his accounts, wrote a letter to a daughter, played his violin,
inspected his plantation and talked to his field hands, took a bath and
read a book, and went to a dinner and danced and flirted with someone else's wife, you would know more about the eighteenth century
than from reading every book on the subject. Historians rush to
make judgments, when we should be digging down deeper into the
plain facts that the past has left for us. The past *longs* to be remembered! The past is constantly sending us letters, dropping notes in our
path, phoning us up, trying to make dates for lunch. The past has no
wish to die. All the people I try to write about—Lincoln, Susan B. Anthony, Custer—they were jealous of their reputations to the day they
died, but death released them from the fear of public opinion, and
now they want to be naked and visible, and undressing them is what
motivates me, nothing less."

Her voice rose as she said it. People glanced her way. I was pretty
sure I was hearing a passage from a lecture, but that was okay by me.
I was touched that she wanted to impress me. She must be in love, I
thought.

All That Is Essential

Somewhere in the fall, what was between her and me ceased to be an affair and turned into an enduring romance, and we became two birds who know the way back to each other. Briefly, in November, she pulled back. "Is this going too fast?" she said on the phone. "I think this is going too fast." When she said goodbye, I wasn't sure if I would see her again or not. I imagined not. I set the phone down and sat in the kitchen and contemplated the farewell letter she would write to me, and as the sun went down and the house got dark, I promised myself that if she called it quits, I would not file an appeal, or plead for leniency. And the next day she called and said that she missed me and would come on Saturday.

We settled into a routine of every other weekend, at her apartment on Riverside Drive and 100th, looking out over the trees to the Hudson River, or my house in Red Cliff: we made love and talked late into the night, she smoked her two cigarettes; we slept, I curled behind her, my arm across her belly, being careful not to disturb the cord of the Walkman; and I awoke, she curled behind me, her arm over me;

and we got up and brushed our teeth, showered, put on clean underwear, drank our coffee from china cups, spoke grammatically, avoided background music, she belched a line from a poem, we walked, we talked, we made love, she showered; and then I kissed her goodbye and her eyes filled with tears and we parted.

A person could live his whole life exactly this way and be content, I thought. You wouldn't need to see the world, or be a raging success; it would be enough to be well loved.

Alida and I celebrated our first anniversary (and my forty-first birthday) in May in New York, at the Rainbow Room, waltzing to Gershwin and Berlin as the dance floor revolved and Manhattan blazed far below. She asked if I was happy, and I said I was. Really happy? Yes, that too.

I asked about her book, and she said it was coming along slowly. "How is the restaurant?" she asked. I felt a rock in the pit of my stomach. It was supposed to have opened that spring, but Steve's designs for the dining room in the barn (the Threshers' Hall, Steve called it) were complicated, and then, one February night, a carpenter had gotten into the Jack Daniels and wandered out to talk to the trees and left a cigarette burning on the kitchen counter, and the fire had gutted the kitchen, and now the bank was sending emissaries to remind the partners that the clock was ticking.

"But your brother is looking after it," I said.

"My brother," she said, "is the unstable one in our family. Howard dropped out of Boston College back in the sixties and drove around the country in a VW van putting on shows with some people—it was called The People's Circus, and he was a mime."

"A mime? My lawyer?"

"Indeed," she said. Howard had floated around the country in a psychedelic van, his face painted white, wearing slippers and a beaver hat and parachute pants and a candy-striped jersey, playing a character called Mr. Piper, who chased butterflies and picked flowers and was gentle and good. There was a juggler and a dancer and Howard, who also played banjo and sang songs like "There Was an Old Lady Who Swallowed a Fly." They did this for eight years.

"How did they stand it for eight years?" I asked.

"Tremendous sincerity, and a certain innate stupidity that was common at the time, and massive doses of Mexican reefer. They smoked reefer the size of Bering cigars. They were stoned *all the time*. By the way, that's where Howard met your contractor, Steve."

"No."

"Yes. Steve was the juggler. He was the brains of the outfit, so to speak. Finally, the police department of Provo, Utah, did them the great favor of arresting them, and they went through detox, and Howard woke up to the fact that he had spent the best years of his life as a nincompoop. He hustled off to the University of Hawaii law school, and managed to pass the bar exam on his fourth try. I love him, but if I'm around him for more than about half a day, I want to heave him out a window."

In the fall, she went away to Berkeley for a semester, rented a white bungalow at the top of a steep street, with the bay and Mount Tamalpais in the distance, and seemed pleased when I flew cross-country three times to see her. We hiked San Francisco and Sausalito and Stinson Beach, and sat on the dunes, our faces tilted toward the sun, and there was no talk of the future, of matrimony. The present was good enough. I told my parents about her at Christmas. "Bring her for a visit," said Mother. "Maybe in the summer," I said.

For our second anniversary, in Red Cliff, I bought her a diamond ring. And the day before she arrived, I had a scary talk with Howard over breakfast. "I'm not worried but I am concerned," said Howard. "We are having some finance problems, and the kindly vice-president at the bank has turned me over to some scary guys in Special Assets. No cause for panic, but I am concerned."

"Howard," I said, "this restaurant is our early retirement fund. In five years, you and I are supposed to give our suits to the Salvation Army and move to Provence and become philosophers."

"I am not joking," Howard said. "We've got problems. Special Assets is another term for repo men. Guys with skin problems. Big smokers. Three-pack-a-day guys who eat cheeseburgers for breakfast. These are not Chardonnay people, these are bourbon drinkers. Purposeful drinkers, with pitted skin and bloodshot noses. John, we are the elephant who went lumbering down the trail and saw the bale of fresh hay and went for it and the ground opened up and we fell in the hole and now the Masai are standing around the rim and buzzards are parked in the trees and hoping to eat our eyeballs."

"So fend them off, Howard. You're the managing partner. Work it out."

"I think we need to get together, you and Steve and me, and try to scale back—open the dining room—leave the barn for later."

"He's your friend, Howard. You deal with him."

"He's gone off the deep end on this Threshers' Hall," said Howard. "I think he thinks it's a temple of something. The guy is not making real clear sense."

Alida disembarked from the bus holding a cardboard box that contained the works of an 1882 grandfather clock with sailors and mermaids on the face. The clock, wrapped in a blanket, lay in the bus's luggage compartment. We set it in the front hall of my house and wound it and it rang four times, a bell that sounded like a trolley. I fixed a dinner of broiled tuna, and we ate on the porch, on the blue-checked cloth.

"This is for you, celebrating two years since I crept into your tent," I said, and slipped the ring on her finger. It was slightly too big. "I'll gain weight," she said. It was a blissful weekend. Though I was a little disappointed that nothing was mentioned about marriage. I wondered: was I supposed to bring it up?

Then, in July, she was on a flight from Nashville to New York, returning from a symposium on "The Cult of Southern Womanhood," when the jet blew an engine; there was a loud *whump* and a burst of light on the right-hand wing and the flight attendants put away the beverage carts and the plane descended sharply and the pilot announced that they would land at Dulles, outside Washington, instead—and what flashed through Alida's mind was that if she went down in flames, her body would be shipped to her mother in Amherst, Massachusetts, and that her nearest and dearest, namely me, would not even be listed in the obituary.

Only a true historian would think of such a thing during an emergency landing. A very tenderhearted historian.

Her eyes brimmed with tears as she said, "My sisters and brother, whom I see once a year, if that, would be listed, and my parents, who drive me crazy, but you—it would be as if you never existed."

She had come up from New York. Mid-July, and the air was wild with sweetness. She got off the bus wearing wraparound dark glasses, teary-eyed over my absence from her obituary, and we got in the car and drove to a nursery and bought red gardenias. "Do you ever think about us getting married?" she said. "I'm asking that purely as a question. Does the possibility ever cross your mind? I suppose it would be a terrible mistake, but . . ."

"I don't know if I even believe in marriage," I said, taking a conservative tack. "My brother Bill married a homecoming queen, who turned into one of the sorriest women you ever saw. Every Wednesday night, they go to marriage counseling, so that Elizabeth can tell a caring professional what she has told everyone else for years, that he is cold and blank and a blight on her life. They sit in a room and weep into Kleenexes and go home and say nothing until the next Wednesday. Who in their right minds would get themselves into that situation . . . ?"

"You're right," she said. "We're happy. We're not a couple, we're binge lovers. We make great weekends. Besides, I irritate you. I'm too self-centered."

"You're not, actually."

She snorted. "Of course I am. And I'm so rigid about little things. And it bugs you."

"It doesn't at all," I said.

"Well, you irritate me. You hum the same tune, you overtip, you leave the radio turned on without knowing it, and you put cilantro and ground pepper on everything. How could I marry someone like that?"

"I do not put cilantro on everything. Not everything green is cilantro. I use basil, I use tarragon."

"Anyway, we would get on each other's nerves," she said. "I know I get on yours."

"You don't. I adore everything about you."

We filled up the back seat of the Fiat with flowers. I said, "Let's go home. I want to make love to you."

"Fine," she said. And then, on the way home, she said, "Another thing about you that irritates me is that you bend over backward to avoid arguments. Why are you so afraid of disagreement?"

"You're wrong," I said. "I welcome disagreement. I thrive on it. It thrills me."

"To me," she said, "disagreement is a sign of being taken seriously. To you, it's a moral flaw. It's the Lutheran in you. It's that meekness. You go around meeking people. You're so self-effacing."

I told her to shut up about meekness or I would start yelling.

"It's true. You Lutherans are always ducking your heads. You instinctively apologize when you enter a room or when you ask someone to pass the butter. I've seen this; I'm a scholar, I'm trained to observe. You're brought up to avoid drawing attention to yourselves—to be vague, colorless. It's some old maidservant gene. My people are wacko and a bunch of wastrels and dizzy dilettantes, but they say what they think. Your people are taught to bow, to bootlick when necessary."

I looked into her cool brown eyes and said I would disagree with her anytime I felt like it. Literature, politics, feminism, you name it.

She made a snoring sound. "Feminism. Get real," she said.

I turned up Green Street and into the alley and pulled up to the garage. We hauled out the plants and set them in the shade under the big oak and I watered them.

"Feminism," I said. "The dead hand of political correctness. The charade of multiculturalism. The overthrow of Shakespeare and Dickens in the classroom, in place of which students pore over the journals of seventeenth-century vicars' daughters."

"Go argue with my mother. She's the feminist," she said. "I'll tell you what. Let's argue about you. You are one of the gloomiest people I ever met, and you don't even know it."

I turned on my heel and walked toward the house and yelled over my shoulder, "I am the most cheerful man in this town!"

"Only because I'm here," she shouted. She ran after me. I slammed the screen door and stomped into the kitchen. She was right behind me.

"I am *renowned* for cheerfulness. I am a giant of cheerfulness. A monster, even." I flung out my arm rather grandly. "Is this the kitchen of a sad man? No, it is not. I'm sorry that my happiness went unappreciated, but so be it."

"You grind your teeth at night," she said. "You cry out in anguish. People are chasing you and you're running as fast as you can and you can't get away. And you know who they are."

I asked her to kindly spare me the psychology.

"They are the ghostly figures from your childhood, John, and they get bigger the farther away you get. These people have got you on the run, and, John, when people make you run, they have more power over you than if you stand and fight them and *lose*. It feels like freedom to run, and it's exactly the opposite. The only way to get loose of them is to go back and tell them what you think and quit being so damn polite, and when you do that, then you won't turn into a blushing fifteen-year-old every time you're around them."

I had had quite enough of this conversation. I turned and lifted her T-shirt up over her head. I poured a little wine on her shoulders, to see her wince, and I licked it off her, the rivulets of wine running down her breasts and her back.

I took off my shirt and unbuckled my belt and let my pants drop to the floor. I knelt on the floor and pulled her shorts and her underpants down to her ankles and she stepped out of them.

"John," she said, "if you love me, why have I never met your parents?"

That afternoon, we lay together after love, naked, hair damp, my arm across her belly, and she said, "Are you sure you're Lutheran? Could I check your—don't you people carry some sort of ID?"

"Absolutely Lutheran," I said. "I fell in with the Anglicans for convenience, but I'm as Lutheran as they come."

"Then maybe I was not entirely accurate about Lutherans."

"You weren't the first. We've been consistently misunderstood."

"I would like to meet your parents, though," she said. She nestled her head against mine. "I promise to behave myself," she said. "I won't smoke or belch or anything." She made me promise to call my mother and invite them to visit. "Will they disapprove of me?" she cried. "Will they think I'm a snooty easterner from an Ivy League school?" I told her that my mother would see her through my eyes and my dad would see her through my mother's. So she'd be okay. But just the same, she should wear some clothes.

Talk Radio

It was a rainy September morning, the morning I would drive to New York for a memorial service in the afternoon and spend the night with Alida. I awoke to the gushing of water from the broken downspout on the gutter and the clanging of the clock in the downstairs hall, and I rose from bed, took out the plastic mouthpiece I wore to keep from grinding my teeth, did my deep knee bends and touched my toes. My feet looked gnarly, with shoe marks on them. I did fifteen jumping jacks and twenty sit-ups. I did twenty push-ups next to the bed, looking down at the dark-red Afghani carpet. The red couch under the window and the coffee table were piled with books, most of them Alida's. The room was dotted with little things of hers: her nightshirt under a pillow, her blue robe hanging on the bathroom door, her beaded moccasins under the bed, her lipstick and face cream and earplugs on the bedside table. Next to the bathroom door hung a large photograph of my favorite section of Riverside Park in New York, the promenade and flower garden below Eighty-ninth Street, with the park benches, the old couples taking the sun, the mothers wheeling their babies, an old lady pushing a grocery cart full of plastic bags, and a black Lab leaping for a Frisbee.

I stepped out of my blue pajamas and looked at myself in the mirror on the door. A middle-aged guy should check himself out every day and assess the devastation. I believe that. The flab around the waist, the wobble under the chin, the descent of the chest. My square jaw had gotten softer, my forehead higher, I was puffy around the eyes, I was getting a gut. People think that if you're six feet four you can carry extra poundage, but fat looks as jiggly on a tall guy as on anybody else. One likes to imagine that he could reverse the terrible things happening to the body, by ferocious exercise and self-sacrifice, but clearly I was no winsome youth. And an older guy has to be cheerful, I think. Young guys can get away with being sullen; it even looks good on them. But on an older guy, gloominess looks like indigestion. People think you had too much knockwurst for lunch. An older guy has to remember to lighten up and keep himself looking fresh. Smile at people.

A philosophy of cheerfulness is maybe an odd way of looking at the world, but an older guy absolutely has to keep his sense of humor. Even if he is lonely as a barn owl. The world is interested, up to a point, in the sorrows of women, but it doesn't give a hoot about the problems of a middle-aged Norwegian bachelor general manager, and why should it? So don't bother being unhappy; it only makes you look like a creep.

The cause of my troubles that fall was Dean Baird, who, since Dean Burton had trundled off to retirement in Arizona, had been pushing for change at WSJO: more Third World music, more diversity, more women's music, more African-American composers, more Hispanics. Every week, he sent along more suggestions: how about devoting Holocaust Month to Jewish music? why not set aside Mondays for women composers? and was there a historical index to blind, deaf, and physically challenged composers? He had pushed me into creating the position of public affairs director and hiring a gaunt, sallow-faced woman named Susan Mack, who had, in a year and a half, produced two documentaries, one on premature menopause and the other on mercury poisoning from dental fillings. The menopause one was a lulu, a marathon gripefest, an orgy of self-pity, women moaning and grousing about their sad lives and the uncomprehending world around them, and then some of those women showed up on the mercury-poisoning one too—the symptoms of *that* (forgetfulness, fatigue, depression, achiness) being symptoms of menopause as well. Plus there was the usual pious droning and technical jabber from various experts. A thoroughly mind-numbing piece of radio, so of course it received a du Pont Award, and Susan went on a speaking tour, yakking about why she had had all of her own amalgam fillings replaced and how this had improved the quality of her personal relationships. She created a national clearinghouse and hot line for mercury-poisoning support groups across the country and wrote a book, *Amalgam: The Enemy in Your Mouth.* And now she was producing a third documentary, on agoraphobia. She worked out of her home in Seneca Falls, and I seldom laid eyes on her.

She was a pill, and anyway I hate talk radio. Especially public radio talk shows. I loathe them. Drowsy voices dithering and blithering, obsessive academics whittling their fine points, genteel bohemians with their Bambi worldview, the earnest schoolmarms, the murmury liberals, the ditzy New Agers, the plodding Luddites, the sad-eyed ladies of the lowlands, all of them good and decent and progressive and well-read and *deeply concerned.* Concerned about children, about justice and equality, about the clouds in the clear blue sky. Everything they say is to demonstrate their Concern, to show their innate goodness, nothing they say comes from firsthand observation, they have no experience whatsoever, only concern, and the sign of their Deep Concern is their use of dozens, if not hundreds, of modifying clauses in each sentence, many (if not most) of the modifiers in some sense contradictory and therefore self-cancelling, which is a great deal (or at least more than what one might ideally hope for) of modification, the result being audio oatmeal, two hours of which isn't worth one Chopin Prelude, in my book. When you listen to Arthur Rubinstein play Chopin, you are no longer a liberal or a conservative or even an American, but simply a breathing sensate human being with a soul. Music lends you the freedom of your own mind. You listen to the Mahler Fourth Symphony or the Tchaikovsky Serenade for Strings, and it evokes scenes and visions of your own life and elevates them into the realm of art. Talk radio leaves you with nothing except a feeling of superiority to the poor schlumps talking on the radio.

I hate talk radio because I never cared for piety. I grew up among pietists; I know how they kill the spirit. Whenever I go to a party, if I get into the room where people are discussing the future of the American theater or the need for greater public awareness of the plight of the homeless, I back right out and go in search of the room where men and women are dancing in the dark, or the room where men are holed up telling lies about the time they and their buddies filled a guy's car with a hundred gallons of pig manure.

My great-grandfather John Tollefson was not a pietist, he was one of the Happy Lutherans: he loved to dance the polka, which is a Norwegian martial art, and to drink beer and tell jokes. He was the middle son in a family of eight living in a timber house with a sod roof on a mountainside farm near the village of Voss in Norway. He herded sheep to the mountain pastures and in the winter he attended school. He was a big sandy-haired boy with sleepy eyes, who, according to family legend, would walk three hours to attend a dance, and after a pietist preacher came glowering and pounding on the pulpit and persuaded people all through that valley that the fiddle was the instrument of the devil, and the dancing stopped, John was happy to set out at noon on Saturday and walk for six or seven hours to get to where a band was playing and pretty girls were waiting for partners, and hours later walk home, a little drunk, and arrive in time to wash his face and go to church and hear about the flames of hell that God was stoking up for dancers and drunkards.

I like to think that I take after him in certain respects. My ancestor suffered adversity and did not pity himself; he was a cheerful man, not a fatuous jerk. He was a carpenter and a stonemason who built stone walls that withstood a century of winters and are still standing in Lake Wobegon. That September, I was thinking maybe I should get out of radio and do something similarly distinguished with my life.

I left my golden house on Green Street and crossed College Avenue and walked across the greensward and around the back of the chapel. The sun had come out. Behind the chapel was Gridley Hall, patterned after Huntly Castle in Scotland, donated by a Gridley who had stripped the forests of northern Wisconsin down to the underbrush. The offices and studios of WSJO were on the fifth floor, not far from the chapel bell tower, and every day at noon, the walls shook as the bells pounded out the Doxology, the St. James school hymn, and the Pachelbel Canon in D. I walked through the sandstone arch entrance and up four flights of stairs and through the glass door ("WSJO—Public Radio for the Finger Lakes") and into the shadowy outer office, where my secretary, Fawn Phillips, looked up and smiled her golden smile. Her boyfriend, Trent, sat beside her desk, slumped in a chair under the Larry Rivers poster of Madame Butterfly. "Good morning, Mr. Tollefson," she said.

"It's a beautiful day, Miss Phillips," I said. "It's a work of art. It's a day by Monet."

She, on the other hand, was like an angel by Botticelli. Wavy blond hair tumbling down her shoulders, she smiled a pure Renaissance smile. I first saw her in church one Sunday morning, and Mother Sally told me Fawn was looking for a job. She had graduated from St. James, an English major, a star of the field hockey team, and the president of a group called Wounded Daughters of Distant Fathers. I did not think about WDDF when she came in to interview for the job. I hired her because she was angelic and only later discovered she could not spell or write—though now that she had Spell-check and Microsoft SynTax downloaded in her computer, she could write letters and put out the WSJO newsletter.

I said a cheerful good morning to Trent.

"Hey," said Trent. He blinked his gecko eyes and slid a couple of inches up in the chair and pulled in his legs. He wore baggy pants and a striped jersey and giant air-sole basketball shoes, his cap turned backward on his clumpy hair; earphones clamped on his head emitted a sound like tiny chain saws. He was twenty-one, a pizza deliveryman, a graduate of this liberal arts college, a walking testimonial to its shame. Under the chair was his skateboard. For her sake, I wished he would do a *grand jeté* off a curb and be run over by a gravel truck.

I walked into my office, followed by Fawn, and closed the door. The office was long, with the desk at the far end and a carpeted sitting area with a blue-striped couch and two mauve wing chairs and a teak coffee table, and, square in the middle, a bay window with a view of the quad.

"The dean says he needs to see you before you leave for New York," she said. "And Miss LeWin asked if you could come at ten instead of nine. Her cat is sick and she's waiting for the vet."

"Did you talk to her?"

"I talked to her housekeeper."

"Which cat is it?"

"She didn't say."

"Probably Snowball. He's the oldest." Miss LeWin was a major donor. I had been to her house and had memorized the names of all eight of her cats. Snowball was the easy one.

I saw a folder on the desk with big red print on it: IMPORTANT: RESPOND PROMPTLY. It was the minutes of a meeting of the Faculty Advisory Committee on Broadcasting, a committee the dean had assembled last year as a sort of Greek chorus. The dean posed questions to the committee, such as "Could WSJO do a better job of representing the aims and aspirations of minorities and the disadvantaged?" and the committee replied, "Yes, it could." And I, as general manager, was supposed to hustle up a report on how WSJO would proceed to represent the A & A of the M & D—all a game, of course; it had nothing to do with minorities. It was simply two guys in the driveway and the dean had the ball and I was on defense. He wanted to change the station to all-talk, to show that he could do it. It was that simple.

"I heard from a highly reliable source that the dean nominated you for a Wally Award," Fawn said. "I told you he has a lot of respect for you." The Wally was a national award for creative management in public radio, given annually at the NPR conference in Washington.

"Fawn, they give awards to guys right before they take them out to be shot. It's a kind of relaxant for the doomed. They give you the plaque and then they tie your hands behind your back and lead you out to deaccession your head."

"Anyway, he wants to see you," Fawn said. "Could I ask you something?" She handed me a CD. "Is this anything you'd consider playing on the air?" *Meadows of the Mind.* A singer named Loti. It had a picture of a misty pasture on the front.

"Let me give it a listen," I said. I pulled out the insert and saw that the lyrics were printed, lines like:

I float with the wind
I am open, listening, to my life
The wind-music of my life
Every day its magic reveals itself to me.

New Age music. Relaxation music for yuppies to listen to and get even farther into themselves than they already were.

"Her music comes from a very powerful place," said Fawn.

Loti looked to be about thirty, a slender Brünnhilde in jeans and a flaxen blouse, and there were endless thank-yous and acknowledgments, the sure sign of a New Age album. "Thank you Allan and Shondra for your strength and encouragement. . . . Thank you Shakti for being there. . . . Thank you Mufti for your faith in me. . . ." The list went on for two pages.

"If you're able to open yourself up to it, it's like a spirit bath," she said.

Like a brain wash, I thought. I said, "Sounds good," and was about to put a hand on her shoulder and say something about music, and then I pulled back. You have to be careful about touching a Wounded Daughter. What you think is a pat on the shoulder might be taken as groping for her zipper. I pretended to have pointed toward the window. "Looks like rain," I said. I told her I couldn't see the dean now, that if he called and asked for me, to say I wasn't in the office. "I'd like to get all my ducks in a row before I talk to him. Okay?"

She nodded, her eyes big, as if a major conspiracy were under way.

The desk was oak, massive, yellow. It once belonged to the president of the New York Central Railroad. Dark deals had been struck over this desk, unions busted, congressmen bought, virgins sacrificed to the Wall Street gods. Now there was a photograph of Alida on it, and a small wooden loon, and a University of Minnesota coffee mug. A copy of a memo urging staff to attend a reception at the president's mansion, jacket and tie, please, no running shoes. A stack of payroll checks to sign, and a stack of mail. And a folder labeled "LeWin Endowment." I started signing the checks—Joyce Mott, Susan Mack, Thomas Neil Cameron (why would a guy use three names? it was like going around in a linen suit, with a walking stick), the chief engineer, Ralph Montez (the only one who knew how radio actually *works;* the others were all from the humanities), the music director, Peter Pollard (must speak to him about all these justly neglected composers he's been featuring lately), Emma Clark (too shrill to read news, but what can you do), Priscilla Lee Wheaton (director of development, the courtesan division of public radio), Marian MacKay, Fawn.

Miss LeWin, whose mother was a Rockefeller, was eighty years old, diabetic, suffering from emphysema—her chauffeur carried oxygen tanks in the Cadillac—and I had been courting her for several years, coaxing larger contributions. And now that God was preparing to gather her up as a flower for His Bouquet, I was looking for the propitious moment to propose a LeWin Endowment Fund. A million dollars, locked up, the earnings earmarked for "the production of opera and classical music programs on WSJO." This would be my brilliant counteroffensive against the dean.

The dean had the angle on me. He was mustering faculty support to change the format of WSJO from classical-music-and-news to all-talk. But I thought that if I could only get that million-dollar endowment, it would carry the day with the president. Miss LeWin was a faithful friend of St. James. She had donated the carillon. She listened to WSJO. She adored opera. Her father had taken her to see Rosa Ponselle in *Carmen* when Miss LeWin was seven years old, and this experience was still vivid to her. She had hinted to me that she was in the process of rethinking her "legacy," as she put it, and was considering WSJO. The main competitor seemed to be a gay guy named Alan Dale, who wanted to start an opera company in Syracuse. He was a major cat-lover and often accompanied Miss LeWin on trips to the Glimmerglass Opera and the Met. He advised her on fashion matters. He had wormed his way into her good graces. But I had been doing my homework. Alan Dale was no Boy Scout. I pulled up the drive to The Poplars at 9:58 and parked under the portico, behind a cream Mercedes. I climbed the stairs and clunked the big brass knocker, and Miss LeWin opened the door, looking tired and distraught, her eyes lined with red, and her white hair, usually styled and sprayed, poking out from a scarf. She motioned me into the front hall. A short black woman with sweet eyes took my briefcase. Miss LeWin wore a brown silk housecoat with a large fish painted on each pocket, brown slacks, and a pair of pink slippers, and she looked thinner than ever, her face emaciated, the skin tight over her jawbone. I took her bony hand.

"I'm terribly sorry about your cat," I said.

"It's bronchitis," she said. "He's running a fever. The doctor is with him in the library. Would you mind if we sit in the hall, so I can be nearby when he wakes up?" She sat on a love seat under a painting of roses that I soon realized was a Renoir and was not a reproduction. I pulled up a chair. It was sweltering in the house. The heat was on. "I'm glad to see you looking so well," I said. "I hope you received my letter." She nodded and dabbed at her eyes with a handkerchief.

"As I said in the letter, we put your last two gifts—which were extremely generous, and thank you again—we put those into a sort of trust fund, the LeWin Endowment, from which we plan to use the annual earnings to underwrite classical music, and opera in particular. And I guess that what remains to be discussed is your feelings at this point about building that endowment to where the interest would be enough to secure the future of our music broadcasts."

As I said this, a short man in a tan three-piece suit emerged from the library, a black satchel in his hand. He wore large, round horn-rimmed glasses and had a brush mustache, and his head was shiny and hairless except for some blond fringe in back and a few curlicues on top. Dr. Mercedes, apparently. What a practice the man must have, ministering to the pets of the rich, giving annual checkups, listening to a cat's heart, taking its pulse, prodding its liver, examining its cataracts. The doctor nodded gravely to me, took Miss LeWin's hand, and whispered, "Snowball is sleeping. I've sedated her. Her vital signs are good, and that's all we can hope for. I'll be back after lunch." And he slipped out the front door and closed it without a sound. Not a click. Maybe he worked nights as a cat burglar.

The door to the library was open a few inches, and I could see, in the dimness within, a pile of white fur on a leather sofa. It was not moving.

Miss LeWin dabbed at her eye. "I'm sorry," she said. "I get so emotional about my cats." She said she had been to see Mr. Alan Dale, who showed her the old Palace theater, which he proposed to put his opera company in. He would name it for her father, the Arthur LeWin Musical Theater. She had once seen Lillian Gish in person at the Palace. It was the grandest place—boarded up for thirty years, but she remembered its gilded proscenium, the chandelier, the ceiling fresco of angels welcoming Caruso and Jenny Lind into heaven. "It seats two thousand," she said, "and I don't know if there are that many opera lovers in the area, but Alan does not lack for confidence. He wants to start immediately and renovate the theater and do a season of four operas starting in the fall, and he's talking about a program to mentor young singers, and he wants to put on performances for schoolchildren—I admire his ambition. Do you know him?"

I chose my words carefully. "Yes, I do. Of course," I said. "Alan is a good man. Very smart. Very ambitious. And I'm familiar with the Palace." I clasped my hands under my chin. "I'd recommend that you consult a structural engineer before you put money into it. I've heard that if a hundred people in the balcony stamped their feet in rhythm, the whole building could come down. Not a good idea if you're going to have schoolkids in there."

Miss LeWin's eyes widened, as if she saw oncoming headlights.

"Alan is a good man, though. Brilliant, in fact. I have great respect for him. He did that production of *La Bohème* in Minneapolis four years ago that caused all the fuss at the National Endowment for the Arts—you remember that? No? It was set in the East Village and Mimi dies of AIDS and Rodolpho is actually in love with Schaunard, and at the end the singers fling paint into the audience. Not my cup of tea, but the guy has his convictions. I think that anytime you have simulated sex onstage, you're going to offend a lot of people, but Alan went ahead with it. The one scene where the tenor and baritone stripped naked and jumped under the sheets caused a major hoo-ha in Congress, and they whacked about six million off the NEA appropriation, but I guess Alan did what he had to do."

She took a deep breath. Apparently, Alan Dale had not filled her in on his entire oeuvre. He had left out that *Bohème*, and perhaps he had also left out his *Traviata*, in which Violetta and Alfredo go around in bikinis and she sings "Sempre libera" sitting on a toilet. I bore down hard: "I must say, I believe in the classical repertoire. I really do. *Bohème, Turandot, Carmen, Traviata*—call them war-horses if you like, but to me, those are the doorways that a person goes through in order to discover opera. A six-year-old child could see *Bohème* and understand it and love it, and that child would care about opera forever! But not if that child sees the Queen of Spades played by a black countertenor in a leopardskin tutu. Not if *Carmen* takes place at a stock-car race and Don José is called Joe and Carmen is in black leather and the 'Habanera' is about carburetors. Call me old-fashioned, but people writhing around naked onstage and singing political slogans *does not constitute opera*, Miss LeWin. *I* don't think so."

The white fur in the library slid down off the couch and walked toward the door and opened its mouth in a silent meow.

"Don't get me wrong," I said. "There's a place for experimentation, but here at WSJO, our interest is in *broadening* the opera audience, and you do that by broadcasting the classic opera performances—exposing kids to the classics while they're young. You don't do it by putting on a freak show. And that's who the LeWin Endowment would benefit. Generations of kids, listening to the radio. Hi there, Snowball."

The cat emerged, none too steady on its feet, and eyed Miss LeWin's lap, gauging the distance, and thought better of it and sat on its haunches and meowed, a paper-thin raspy meow. "Poor darling," she said, and lifted the cat up, which took some effort—he was a hefty animal—and laid him on his back across her skinny knees. The cat struggled to turn over, but she held him down and rubbed his stomach.

"I have so much to do in the next few months," she said. "I am going in for surgery in October, and I want to get my affairs in order."

"If there's any way I can help," I said, "please let me know."

SIX

Mortality

Driving east toward the interstate, I felt pretty confident I had successfully steered the old lady toward radio and away from that finagler Alan Dale. The million did not seem out of the question. If only Snowball did not succumb to pneumonia. In that case, the million might go to shelter stray kitties. I thought of writing Miss LeWin a follow-up letter, about the tax advantages of the LeWin Endowment Fund, but I didn't want to come across as a bloodsucker. On the other hand, you shouldn't play the fish too delicately at this point; you have to make sure the hook is set.

The car came over a rise, there was a sharp curve ahead, and the road descended through a tunnel of green boughs and out onto the valley floor, past a field of hay, and through a farmyard, the house on one side of the road, the barn on the other. Beyond was a meadow where a hundred badly rusted combines and planters sat parked in parallel rows. Beyond the farm, the road turned sharp right and rose again, up through an apple orchard, winnows of dead grass in the ditch, low stone walls on either side, weeping willows, the crest of the ridge ahead looking over another broad green valley. At the top, I switched on the radio and heard the unnaturally deep voice of the music director, Peter Pollard, announcing the next work on the *Morning Concert*, a concerto for organ by Soler, and then a long silence, and then a shrill chord, like the air horn of an oncoming semi.

It was a four-hour drive from Red Cliff to New York City.

I was driving down for a memorial service for Charlie Koenig, a guy I knew from Lake Wobegon. Charlie grew up on a dairy farm, he was two years older, we played on the same football team. Charlie got a scholarship to Princeton, made captain in the army, became a banker, a sailor, a collector of fine old books, and died of a brain tumor at the age of forty-four. His wife asked me to speak at the service. I told her I hadn't known Charlie well enough. "Neither did I," she said, "but what does it matter now?"

I took the Sawmill Parkway and the West Side Highway to Alida's apartment, parked the car, took a cab to the church, and after the service I planned to pick up salad makings at Broadway Farms and a fish at Jake's and get to Alida's and have dinner ready when she got home from teaching her graduate history seminar at Columbia. And that would be my compensation for enduring Dean Baird and begging from Miss LeWin—Alida coming through the door pushing her bicycle, taking off her red helmet, setting her backpack on the table, kissing me, wrapping her arms around me, saying she loved me.

The service, in a side chapel at St. Thomas on Fifth Avenue, was conducted by a tall, graying rector who spoke through his nose and was working from notes. Even I knew Charlie better than he did: Charlie had given money to WSJO, and I took him to dinner once at La Réserve. I remember that he mispronounced the name of the composer Erik Satie. He told me he had bought a house in East Hampton, near Ralph Lauren's. "Not bad for a guy from Lake Wobegon, huh?" We reminisced a little about high school, which Charlie seemed genuinely uninterested in—he couldn't even remember the name of the coach ("Magendanz," I told him; "Oh," he said)—and mostly he talked about his new house, the heated pool, the clay tennis court, the problem of beach erosion. And now he was gone, his brain eaten by a tumor, his trim body cremated, his ashes cooling in a mausoleum in Queens, and only thirty people missed the poor guy enough to show up for the service. His wife sat in the front pew, prim in a gray tweed suit, and their three sons, home from Exeter. Nobody in the chapel looked as if they had ever set foot on a dairy farm.

During that dinner, Charlie Koenig got a little tight and told me the happiest time in his life had been as a young army captain in Heidelberg. The hard work was done by other men; he had an apartment off-base and a German girlfriend and learned German well enough to get along, and in German he felt that he became a better person, more direct, more affectionate, and they would go drinking with friends at cafés and he would tell (in German) stories about Minnesota, how it was flat as a table and got so cold in winter that spit froze in midair and jingled when it hit the ground, how stiff and unforgiving the people were, and as he walked around Heidelberg, he imagined settling down there and marrying Marianne, shedding the dead skin of Lutheranism, learning the art of living well. "I never felt so happy as I did there. Nothing since then has been half as good," he said.

"What happened?" I asked.

"I came back to America when my tour was up. I said goodbye to her in a sidewalk café. It was September. She cried. It was a wonderful bottle of wine. But I did the Lutheran thing. I came back to what I knew."

He was going to retire in a few years, he said, and go back to Europe and travel for a year and look her up. And then, a few months later, he conked out.

I sat in the cold church, the chapel organ wheezing like mortality clearing its throat, and I could feel malignant spiny things spreading in my brain. It occurred to me that I did not care for my fancy gold house and my empty life and I wanted to get married, and spring would be a perfect time for a festive wedding, my mother and dad and brothers and sisters flying in—a Tollefson family reunion. I would ask Alida to marry me. Yes, I would. She had almost crashed in the hills of Virginia and I was potentially dying of a possible brain tumor, and life is too short and precious to waste time treating a great romance as if it were a chemistry experiment, watching to see if it might eventually turn sour.

I would feed her tuna steaks and then over dessert I would propose marriage. I would say, *My darling Alida, you are the love of my life, and now all I need is a life to go with you. What I have, my darling, is a lifestyle, the life of people in commercials. I have a nice house and nice things and every couple of weeks I have you, the goddess Aphrodite, but I have no coherent story to my life. I am part of no struggle, have nothing at stake. I'm a fussy man in a blue suit who consumes fine wines. I'm a viewer of shows. My only story is my childhood back in Lake Wobegon. I need passion, blood, magnificence. You are the only magnificence I know. Marry me.*

I let myself into the front hall of her apartment and put the groceries on the wicker bench. The shades were pulled in the living room, to keep direct sunlight off the Navajo blanket that hung on the wall, but the sun streamed into the kitchen, which looked out on the Hudson. A tugboat pushed a barge upstream. I opened the refrigerator. Empty, except for skim milk and a few cartons of yogurt and odds and ends of vegetables. Alida kept the larder spare so as not to throw away spoiled food. I found teriyaki sauce to marinate the tuna in, and poured it in a bowl, and then I called Howard.

I said, "Howard, there's no reason for a meeting with Steve. There's nothing to discuss anymore. What you have to do is go over there and fire him and hire someone who can get the job done for us."

"It's not that easy," said Howard. "We owe Steve a lot of money. In the next thirty days, he's going to submit a bill for a hundred and eighty grand. I have no idea where that's going to come from."

I felt stupefied, as if hit on the head with a hammer. I could hear my dad saying, *I knew this would happen. Never should've gotten into this deal, John. I could've told you that. Restaurants. Terrible risks. Terrible. Shouldn't have done it, John.*

"That's for his percentage on the house and barn—his eight percent contractor's fee—and it's for materials and all the rest of it," Howard said.

"Does it include that stupid cornucopia?" I asked.

"Yes. The cornucopia is in there too."

"I told you to trash that cornucopia a year ago," I said.

"We've already got fifty thousand *invested* in the cornucopia."

"Howard, I've been fighting that stupid cornucopia from day one. The cornucopia is a sinkhole, it's a drain, Howard. It was Steve's idea, and it's going to eat us alive. It's five times the estimate *already*. Maybe six."

The cornucopia was for the lobby, to carry through the concept of vegetables, to pull everything together visually, to create a symbol, a logo—a horn of plenty, six feet high, fruit and vegetables cascading from it—but Steve had not told us it would be not a molded, factory-made cornucopia but a work of art, carved by his old mentor, the cabinetmaker Aalto Maarimakki, whose work was in the permanent collection of the Museum of Modern Art in New York. Nor that the cornucopia would be carved from rare South American woods, found in remote areas, requiring complicated export licenses, bribes to local officials, agents' fees. In other words, the most expensive cornucopia in America. A vacuum that sucked money.

"You're a lawyer," I said. "Sue him. The guy is way over estimate. It's that simple."

"Can't be done. The estimate was not included in the contract that we signed."

"Howard, I'm pleading now. Don't let this ship go down. Save us."

"I'm not a magician, I'm more of a *civil rights* lawyer, John. Real estate is not my strong suit. I'm doing my best. But don't worry. Steve is okay. There's no point in fighting him. Let's make him a partner."

I was just about to make my speech to Alida about wanting a real life, when she got out of the shower before dinner and, looking at me sweetly, said, "I was thinking today: I finally got my life the way I want it. Don't you feel that way?"

She said this standing naked, all five feet twelve inches of her, toweling off her hair. I lay on the bed and looked up at her. I had been thinking about brain tumors.

I said, "Actually, I've been thinking I'd like to leave Red Cliff and come to New York and be your wife. I'd be a good one." I told her she could use someone to cook and clean and do laundry. And as she rode her bike home from Columbia, exhausted, wouldn't it be nice to know that I was waiting for her, primed with perky conversation, ready to run a hot bath, pour a glass of wine, with a salad chilling in the fridge, the yogurt-mustard dressing all whipped up, the sirloins marinating, the risotto steaming, Alfred Brendel playing a Mozart sonata, the lights low, me smiling, cheerful, so at ease with my manhood that I could keep house and cook a great meal and then, as the occasion demanded, whip off my clothes and perform tender acts that most New Yorkers would never expect of a Minnesotan? *Wouldn't this be nice? Wasn't this what any woman would want?*

"Of course," she said, warily. "Of course it would be nice, until suddenly it wasn't so nice, and then what?" She sat on the bed and dried between her toes. "We're happy together. We get to see each other about every other weekend, which is perfect and exactly what every other couple in the world wishes they had too. I don't ever want to look up as you come through the door, John, and think, *Oh. Him again.* I don't ever want to be cool about you, darling."

She looked down at me, lying on the bed, hands behind my head, my heart quietly breaking, and said, "I am besotted and smitten with you, and I want to always be crazy about you."

It hurt to have my proposal of marriage tabled—before I could even make it—by a naked woman. To look at her black hair and china skin and her delicious shoulders, everything about her edible and savory, and to hear her say that, in her opinion, a little of me went a long way.

She tossed the towel into the bathroom and bent and selected a pair of white underpants from the dresser drawer and stepped into them, right leg, left leg, so graceful and neat, the quick glimpse from behind of her womanful nakedness. *I could never get tired of seeing that,* I thought. *If I were ninety-two, I would still struggle to rise from the bed, would reach for my walker, would pull the tubes from my arms.*

She sat on the edge of the bed and put her hand against my face.

"There is nothing so mean as the doldrums of marriage. I saw my parents go through it. Those sour arguments about money and in-laws and the stuff about *If you loved me, you'd want to spend more time with me.* Why would we ever wish that on us?"

"I don't think we would *be* like that, of course," I pointed out.

She leaned down and kissed me, her wet hair against my forehead, and stood up and pulled on a Knicks T-shirt and rummaged through her closet for the right pair of jeans.

I said that if she wasn't sure about me, I wished she'd tell me.

She pulled on a pair of black jeans and took them off and looked for a smaller pair. "John," she said, "I feast on you, I adore you, but I can only do it twice a month because I love my work too and I am not about to apologize for that."

"You don't need to."

"I would if you were here all the time." She turned and looked pleadingly at me. "Darling, I *enjoy* coming home alone and not hav-ing to talk to anyone. I do. I love sitting and eating takeout noodles from a white paper carton with my papers spread out on the kitchen table and writing until all hours and never having to explain to some-one why I am doing it. I like lying alone in a bed full of books and pa-pers and reading until I fall asleep and not having to say excuse me. I *enjoy* that, John—and then after a couple of weeks I get ravenous for you, and I can't wait for us to get back together and take our clothes off and make love like a couple of cougars. I *love* our weekends. We fasten onto each other for two complete days, no distractions, no any-thing other than us. We each have lots to talk about, we're each starved for each other's company. It couldn't be better. You want to see what marriage is like, go visit my brother Howard. He and Anne never make direct eye contact anymore. Sometimes they speak of each other in the third person when the other one is right there in the room. It's bizarre."

She pulled on a pair of blue jeans. "I lived through my parents' marriage," she said. "There was a war of attrition for you.

"My poor father. I never knew what he did, exactly. He was a biologist of some kind—he worked with fish, I think—but it was hard to know. He'd come home and grab the *Boston Globe* and hang on to it like a life preserver. My mother would lob a few sardonic remarks his way and he'd grunt, and that was how they conversed.

"We lived in Amherst, in a white Cape Cod house, and were perfectly decent, respectable people. He taught, she wrote poems and played music in an early-music consort—I can't stand the sound of a sackbut to this day—and we lived a genteel life and had all the advantages, except that our parents loathed each other.

"When I was four, Mommy decided she and I should be friends, and she took me to a Quaker women's retreat in the Berkshires, and one morning she stood up and read her poems. I had to listen to them. Her poems were about the movement, the struggle, the wounds she had suffered, and about me, about my becoming a woman, and I was so offended I jumped up and snatched the poem out of her hands and ripped it to shreds and called her an evil bitch. And after that she suggested it might be nice if I went away to school."

Lying on her bed in New York, listening to her talk, I wanted more than ever to marry her. I didn't think I could bear it if we didn't marry. I wanted to have children, a boy and a girl. They would be New York kids, smart and sociable, sweet-natured kids, and when they were four, I'd take them to Lincoln Center for the ballet, and to the opera when they were six. I could imagine walking down Broadway with them, past the corner markets with the tables of oranges and green peppers and tomatoes jutting into the sidewalk, past Zabar's and the Seventy-second Street subway station on its skinny island in the middle of the street. Their little hands in my hands, they'd be watchful, unafraid, savoring the crowds, the colors, the clownishness, the honking, the costumery. I wouldn't get a job. I'd be a dad. A daddy and a wife. Alida could go on writing, teaching, rising in the world, and I would bring up the children and every summer take them back to Lake Wobegon, to meet the characters in my stories and to learn the code: *do your job, don't tell lies, don't imagine you're exceptional, be glad for what you have, don't feel sorry for yourself.*

The alternative to marriage seemed grim to me. We would drift apart, exhausted by indecision, and then she'd fall for someone, *bang*, and marry him within thirty-six hours, and I would never recover: I would become one of those pleasant, careful men who live alone and somehow make a life out of small social engagements and a health club membership and looking after their parents.

"I am going down to the drugstore," she said. "Can I get anything for you?"

"No, thanks," I said.

"I'm going for a walk too, so I may be gone for an hour."

I almost offered to walk with her. I wished she would ask me to come. I waited, hoping for her to call out and invite me along, until the front door closed and the elevator came and took her downstairs.

If we didn't marry, it would be because she could see who I am down deep. Of that I was certain. That was why I had never taken her to Lake Wobegon. I was afraid that after an hour in Lake Wobegon, she'd know me all the way to the soles of my feet. Under my thin veneer of gentility, I was one of the large phlegmatic people. *Sumus quod sumus.*

Wobegon people are not so much fun to be with necessarily, you know. Not the warmest people you'd ever hope to meet. An embrace is rather intimate for us. A handshake goes a long way. Sometimes we just nod. We aren't all that keen about scholarship; we believe that any display of learning is purely superficial, that nobody is smarter than anyone else. We can be surly and stubborn and downright ugly. We are people of fixed principles, who drive in the passing lane at exactly the speed limit and wonder why drivers are passing us on the right and shaking their fists at us. We have produced no great humorists, only a few romantic writers, all of whom were romantic about other places. In Lake Wobegon, there is precious little romance; mostly there is weather, and only three seasons of it: either winter is just over with or winter is on the way again. Or else it's winter. Winter is what we talk about. We thrive in winter. Pain is satisfying to us. On the football field, our teams were mowed down like dry corn as the merciless fans sang:

WOBEGON
We said it once, we'll say it again
WOBEGON
Wobegon, Wobegon, that's our town.
We'll beat you up and knock you down.
Leonards, Leonards, that's our team.
You are the curds and we are the cream.
So pick up your trash and get out of the way.
The Lake Wobegon Leonards will win today.
Go, Leonards.

Our marching band played with a lurching rhythm—the result of forty musicians waiting to hear the beat before they play it—and our homecoming queens were not nearly so beautiful as they would be in a few years, when they moved away someplace where they could style their hair and dress up and not feel that everybody was staring at them and wondering: Who does she think she is?

Wobegonians looked at the outside world with suspicion, as a place where you send your money and nothing comes back. Most of my classmates had great trepidations about their chances in the outside world, and after graduation, at a drunken party at my old buddy Swanson's uncle's cabin, Swanny and I stood out on the dock and Swanny said, "Somebody said you're going to the University. Man, that's insane." To him, the University of Minnesota was a place where a guy could only get whacked hard.

If I took Alida to Lake Wobegon, I'd naturally introduce her to Swanson, who sold insurance there. He used to be skinny, the ball-handling guard on the basketball team, and now he looked like he'd swallowed the basketball.

Lake Wobegon is the home of the Chatterbox Café, where you belly up to the tuna hotdish, the pot roast and mashed potatoes with globs of butter mixed in, and get up from the table an hour later feeling you have swallowed a brick; it's the home of the Sidetrack Tap, where you can spend an hour, or two, or four, in the company of gasbags and blowhards and men deeply attached to their pickups. Swanson hangs out there, and my old buddies Leland and Mel. You sit and drink boilermakers and listen to guys talk about transmissions and supercabs and power seats and power mirrors until you feel your head melting, your brains leaking out of your left eyeball.

I was afraid Alida would see that I am a living replica of those people. Different hairstyle, same head.

She would be right. Look at my pitiful timidity before the dean, my fear of Steve, my meekness in declaring my love to her. My hometown is a world headquarters of meekness. Meekness carried to extremes. Endless apologies. Monumental hesitation in going through a doorway ahead of other people, so it takes an eternity to clear a room. A painfully polite people, uneasy in their skins, who raise their children to avoid exuberance. A child shrieks, and the parent says, "What did you do that for? What if everyone did that? Who do you think you are?" And so we learn to be dull as milk. But underneath the dullness is the fiercest sort of pride. We find it hard to see the difference between righteousness and the ordinary common sense inherent in Norwegians. If we aren't the chosen people, then why did God make us so close to the standard?

Guilt? Yes, of course, we have that too. Back in the woods there used to be a sign: REPENT. GOD SEES. GOD KNOWS. It was deep in the woods, on the theory that that was where people went to do that sort of thing. We were not brought up to experience pleasure, so it doesn't register with us, like writing on glass with a pencil. Dullness is our stock-in-trade, dullness honed to its keenest edge. The sun shines and people sit in the dark, mumbling the litany of conversation—*So how's Myrtle and Florian? Oh, about the same, then. And Carl? Yeah, he's fine*—people talking so slow you can hear the grass grow between the sentences. Someone tells a story about a fishing trip with his brother and stops and goes back to fill in some irrelevant background and the storyteller's wife butts in to correct a date—this footnoting can go on a long time—and hearing it is like listening to a man read pork prices for half an hour; it's not something you'd do for amusement.

It's the town where you are either Lutheran or you are Catholic, and this was decided back when you were a bead of sweat on your father's forehead. The Lutherans drive Fords from Bunsen Motors, and the Catholics drive Chevies from Krebsbach Chevrolet, and if you came to town in a Toyota, you would be watched very closely for longer than you'd think possible. In this town, Lutherans marry Lutherans, and Catholics marry Catholics, and when a Krebsbach fell in love with a Hansen, their mothers wept and cried, "But what if you have children?" and their fathers begged them to wait a year. The boy's mother said, "Some of my best friends are Lutheran, but dear child, if she is Lutheran and you are Catholic, then your children will grow up to be nothing at all." The boy scoffed. He said they would bring up their children to respect both faiths and to make their own choice. But of course respecting a faith is not the same as clinging to one. The wedding was held in the town hall, and the people on one side of the room knew that if the world were to end right then and there, the people on their side would be whooshed up into heaven and the people on the other side would have some pretty difficult questions to answer. When the groom lifted the veil and kissed the bride, everyone in the room shuddered. The reception petered out in half an hour, and fifteen minutes later, the couple drove away in the groom's car, which nobody had the heart to attach cans or old shoes to—you marry out of your faith, and you've got tin cans tied to you for the rest of your life.

Every few years, the King and Queen of Norway pay a visit to Minnesota, and they are driven around to Lutheran colleges and churches and old-folks homes and museums, where they inspect the rose painting and the hardanger lace and they make about fifty personal appearances in four days and at each appearance they wave to crowds of blue-eyed geezers and listen to a choir of flaxen-haired children in eighteenth-century peasant costumes sing in unintelligible Norwegian a song about maidens gathering birch boughs that nobody in Norway has sung for a hundred years and the King and Queen are given big plates of pickled herring and killer Norwegian pastry and they sit through a speech or two or three about the heroism and industry and faith of the emigrants, and after four days of this pounding punishment they fly home to Oslo and are whisked back to the palace and change into their jeans and T-shirts and open a bottle of white

Bordeaux, put a Duke Ellington CD on the stereo, and fix themselves a green salad and a plate of chicken quesadillas, and they look at each other and say, "Who in the hell were those people? They couldn't have been Norwegians! They seemed so—so backward."

SEVEN

Old Lover

Alida came up to Red Cliff in May for my birthday and our third anniversary. She would be in Washington for two weeks, ransacking the Smithsonian for Bolle Balestrand's letters to Susan B. Anthony; and then she'd spend June and July in Copenhagen, at the Royal Library, going through the papers of a poet named Bjornstjern Bjornstjernsen, a pal of Balestrand's. She'd live with friends in Copenhagen—a Danish-American couple, Jens and Emily—in their house in Taarbeck, between the Royal Hunting Park and the beach, a mile from the Klampenborg station where she could take the train in to the center of town. She wanted to leave June 15 so she could spend Midsummer's Night with them on the island of Fyn. They had told her how lovely it was, an all-night party, the sky still aglow at midnight, that mystic northern light.

I told her, "If you fall in love with someone, I'll be desolate, I want you to know that. So be on your guard. I know those Scandinavians. They drink like fish, they think nothing of nudity, everybody's in an open marriage, people adulterating left and right. You fall for a Dane, Alida, and it's your own responsibility. Some Søren or Peter or Kai comes and waltzes you around the garden and you toss down a couple aquavits and think it's love: don't come crying to me two years from now when you find out how cold and depressed and weird Danes are. They're not like us, honey. A dark and brooding people hung up on equality. Don't let *Babette's Feast* fool you. Karen Blixen was never highly regarded in Denmark, you know. They're suspicious of individuality. Anybody who crosses the street against a red light is considered a crazed eccentric."

"I like a man who has the sense to be jealous," she said. "I'm a very desirable woman. I'm glad you're aware of that."

"You have a romantic fling, and I won't be able to forgive you," I said. "So don't confess it to me. But I'll taste the deceit on your lips, I'll see the contrition in your eye, I'll know it by your being terribly sweet to me when you return."

"Then I'll remember not to be sweet," she said. And then she put her hand over my mouth. *Enough.* We were lying together on the chaise longue in the backyard. She had spent the afternoon in Seneca Falls, at the Elizabeth Cady Stanton house, and come back with steaks for dinner, which I had grilled—strip sirloins, very rare, with a thin slice of raw white onion, in a kaiser roll, with a barbecue sauce, and beans on the side—and we had finished a bottle of Barolo and I was about to open another. It was Seniors Day at St. James, when members of the graduating class get to run wild. Cars were parked bumper to bumper on Green Street, knots of pedestrians hurried off to parties. In the gathering darkness, the first rockets zipped into the sky and burst in spidery effusions of green and orange, the college colors.

"I remember when I graduated from Lake Wobegon High School, it was a hot day in June, and the seniors gathered in the cafeteria, in the faded blue robes and the mortarboards with the golden tassels. I loved the melodrama of it, thinking, *This is it, this is the end.* We lined up two abreast and marched out of the cafeteria and down the hallway past the band room and out the door into the sunshine and down the sidewalk, and when we came around the corner of the school, people at the football field a block away started cheering. They could see us. They were moved. You could feel the emotion. We marched onto the field past all these parents snapping our pictures, cameras flashing, the band was playing Elgar's 'Pomp and Circumstance,' and then we all stood and sang the Alma Mater."

I raised my glass and sang:

Shining Mother, we salute you,
Perfect grace of golden years.
Loving Mother, see your children
Bid farewell with shining tears.
Through life's dangerous lonely voyages,
'Long the coasts of grief and fear,
In our hearts we'll e'er remember
How you taught and loved us here.

"I could see other kids get misty-eyed, but I didn't shed a tear. The commencement speaker talked for twenty minutes, and when he sat down you couldn't remember a word of it. One of those self-erasing speeches. And then all hundred and one of us trooped across the grass and onto the platform and got our diplomas from Mr. Halvorson, the superintendent of schools, and he said my name into the microphone—*Tollefson, John Olaf*—and there it was, the terrible secret of my middle name, revealed, and I slunk back to my seat and people whispered, 'Hey, Ole.' And afterward Swanson and Leland and Mel and I went to Swanson's uncle's cabin and we got drunk, which we figured we were obliged to do, and that was that. We built a bonfire on the beach and stood around feeling profound, and one of us—not me—said something like, 'No matter what happens, even if we don't see each other for years, nothing will change, we'll always be as good friends as we are now.'

"I knew we wouldn't be. I knew I wasn't one of them. It was just a fact."

She kissed me. She told me I was the nicest lover she could imagine, and she cherished every moment and looked forward to August, when she would return. Nothing could be better. No Søren could interest her, compared to me.

"But you don't want to marry me?" I asked.

"We'll talk about it in August."

After she left the next morning, I thought, *What now?* It was Saturday. A chasm of two months yawned at my feet. I called Howard. Anne said Howard was at the farm. *Good,* I thought. *Maybe he's attending to business at last.* I walked to the office. The ash and maples along the street, the grass in the yards, the lilacs and forsythia and dogwood: a voluptuous green lay on every hand, hung overhead, came to my nose—an affluence of green, plants drunk in the noon sun. I crossed the street and headed toward the quad and inhaled the smell of new-mown grass from a triple mower piloted by a girl in shorts and a red halter top who wheeled around on the far sidewalk and headed toward me. The campus was deserted, peaceful. At WSJO, the May membership drive was in full swing, and as I came through the door, I heard my own voice reminding listeners that WSJO was a wonderful addition to their lives, and then Priscilla Lee Wheaton came on the air to mention the WSJO coffee mug, tote bag, and umbrella, the premiums offered for contributions of $30, $50, $100. Priscilla said, "We need the help of every single one of you out there who listens to WSJO and who values our programming. *Morning Edition, All Things Considered, Car Talk, Thistle and Shamrock, As It Happens, Fresh Air, The Morning Concert with Thomas Neil Cameron*—where would you be without them? If you listen, and you like what you hear, then go to your phone right now and give us a call and say, 'Yes! This is important to me and my family. I want to support this.' "

I picked up the Saturday mail on Fawn's desk. Circulars and bills, letters addressed to General Manager—you could tell by the handwriting which were the gripes, which were the fan letters; letters with job applications were always neatly typed and had a return address. I went into my office and closed the door. Membership Week is pure irony on public radio: you try to raise money to pay for your wonderful programs by stopping your wonderful programs and making a horrible scraping and whining and wheedling noise—truly dreadful, awesomely boring, and yet I always was fond of it. It was the only time when we did real radio, and looked deep into the microphone and tried to talk to people. Week in, week out, WSJO drifted along on audio feeds from NPR and taped concerts and long selections of recorded music, and then Membership Week came chugging in like a John Deere tractor, and everybody had to come out from behind the golden arras and dig potatoes for a few days.

A knock at the door, and the door opened. It was Marian MacKay. "You got a minute?" she said, and walked in. She was dressed up in a blue linen suit and high heels—*She wants to talk salary,* I thought—and she pulled a chair over to the side of the desk and put her hand on top of it, on a manila folder, and drummed her fingers and smiled at me. I smiled back.

"Membership Week. It's our version of penitence," I said. "The ritual foot-washing of listeners, the bending of the knee, the supplication, the flagellation . . ."

She smiled a cartoon smile and tapped her fingers and looked up at the ceiling. She hummed. She batted her eyelashes.

"Am I missing something here?" I said.

She said, "A woman would have noticed first thing when I walked in the door." I looked at her stomach. She laughed. "You're getting warm," she said. Then I saw the diamond on her finger. I kissed her on the cheek.

"It's not for another six months, so don't get all alarmed," she said. She and her boyfriend, who was finishing up at Cornell in veterinary medicine, were going to have a massive wedding in Houston—"two ministers, a choir and brass quintet, elephants, and slave girls waving fans of ostrich feathers"—and move to Casper, Wyoming, where he would do research for a year on a disease among male bison that causes them to adopt aggressive behaviors toward other males, unrelated to mating, called the Limbaugh syndrome.

"And what about you?" I said.

She would find something to do in Casper, she said. "And what about *you*? Are you and Miss Columbia going to get a life, or just be an item?"

"I'm not good enough for her," I said. "I'm a small-town guy and she's an Upper West Sider. I'll hang on as long as I can, and one day she'll dump me for Harold Bloom or Roy Blount, somebody her speed, and I'll be stuck with trying to line up dates. I'll be in chat rooms on AOL, with a screen name like HotNHeavy, talking to mature women and trying to get one to meet me at Perkins' for a tuna melt."

"Ha!" she said. "You're in demand, and you know it. You're straight, you're single, you're sober, you bathe regularly, and you talk in complete sentences. There's a million women looking for you right now." She tossed her head back and laughed. "*HotNHeavy*. That's a good one." Then she tried to look serious. "Sorry. Didn't mean to imply that you're not *sexy* 'n' shit." And then she laughed again.

I drew myself up straight. "Just because I'm of a Scandinavian Lutheran background, Miss MacKay, doesn't mean that I can't be as—as—" and then I heard the voice on the radio.

"As what?" said Marian.

It was the voice of Jean, my old lover, and she was saying, "Call now, it takes only a minute, and one of our friendly volunteers will tell you about the wonderful premiums we're offering this week for new members."

"As sexy as anybody else," I said.

Jean had volunteered at WSJO in the past, but I had never heard her on the air before. She had a pleasant voice, a low voice, but sweet. Musical.

"Don't tell me about it, okay?" said Marian. She stood up. "I don't want to know." She laughed. "I want to imagine." She put the chair back against the wall. "Does it involve the use of dairy products?" she said.

Jean was reciting the list of wonderful programs you could hear on WSJO. She had been a librarian for twenty years and read stories aloud to preschoolers—I liked her voice. It was stylish but without mannerism.

"By the way," said Marian, "if you all want to have a going-away party and wedding shower, my calendar is completely open."

I had run into Jean dozens of times in the three years since the end of our relationship (what a lame term, and how apt in this case), and she was always pleasant. At Flint Foods or Quality Liquors, at the library, she'd come over and ask how I was and mean it, and we'd talk about the radio station and people we knew. She was easy to talk to. She didn't seem to hold a grudge against me. She seemed to know about Alida and not to mind. I liked seeing her. I hardly ever thought about her, or about our long, uneventful romance, but when I ran into her, I enjoyed remembering her and the fabulous disparity between her plain looks and plump Girl Scout lady demeanor, and her secret sensuality, the way she talked as we made love, kept saying, "Oh, that was delectable, do that again"—and whenever I stood near her it all came back: the delicacy of her lips, her mouth tasting of warm ripe plums, the arch of her back and the way she chewed her lips and the wild look in her eye—and then we turned away and picked up our groceries and went home.

Go home, I told myself, listening to her ask for a phone call of support. *Go home and listen to the Mozart Requiem and put a cold compress on your lap.* But I didn't. I checked the volunteer schedule posted next to Fawn's desk and saw that Jean would be on duty until four. I sat in my office, reading through the junk mail, keeping an eye on the door—hoping she'd glance in and catch my eye and come in and we'd talk. I thought, *Go home and put this out of your mind. You get enough trouble in life free of charge; you don't have to go purchase more. And God doesn't fool around, mister. God shows you what you're supposed to do, and you are supposed to do it, and if you go against Him, He'll stop talking to you. There isn't anything fancy about it. Either you do it or you don't. So do it.* I listened to Jean on the air, talking about membership, and, at four o'clock, the news from National Public Radio in Washington, and a minute later, it happened just as I'd hoped.

We sat and talked for a long time. She was going on a canoe

trip in the Adirondacks with some women friends. It was an annual thing. What they saved on hotel and airfare, they spent on wine. Last year, they took three cases of a 1968 Chianti. "Such decadence," she said. "Librarians sunbathing on the rocks and drinking hundred-dollar wine out of Dixie cups."

She asked if I'd like to go have a drink. "Sure," I said, and we met at Dean's Steakhouse, a plush place with flocked burgundy wallpaper and brass gewgaws, where nobody I knew ever set foot, and we split an order of crab cakes and a bottle of Côtes du Rhône, and she asked if I was happy. I said I was. "Good," she said. "So am I." She said she enjoyed being single, that personal freedom was something few people were able to enjoy but that she did. She was looking forward to her fifties. "You get bolder as you get older," she said. I said that was true; the dogmas baked into you as a kid, in time you get over them. A dumb thing to say, but I said it. "Like marriage, for example," she said. She used to think it would be pathetic to be single and middle-aged; you'd be a lonesome old desiccated thing in a denim jumper and brown oxfords sitting alone in a tearoom eating your chicken salad and reading Danielle Steel; but that wasn't how it was—these were good years. You just had to remember to take things as they come.

Well, here I am, I thought. This mild-mannered librarian had enjoyed having sex with me in interesting places: in the St. James chapel, in her boss's office during lunch hour, behind a folding wall in the back of a Best Western banquet room where a woman was speaking about investment strategies to a group of retired teachers, in the choir loft of a Baptist church during her cousin's wedding, in the library stacks, and at the beach on Nantucket while standing in waist-high water, me thinking, *This is the sort of thing that can get your name in the paper, and for the next ten years, if anybody does a computer search for your name, they'll come up with Exposing Himself in a Public Place.*

We left Dean's. It was late, and we stood leaning against her car, and she said, quietly, "Would you like to come to my place?" And the honest truth was, I did want to. She didn't ask me if I thought it was *right* and *proper* to come to her place, asked only if I wanted to, and yes, I did, gosh, yes, but I lied and said I didn't, thank you, I was tired.

In fact, I was awake as could be: my eyelids were flying. "Well, you can't blame a girl for trying," she said, and kissed me lightly on the lips and told me to take care of myself.

I drove my car into the garage and walked up the path past the chaise longue where Alida and I had sat the night before and into the kitchen, feeling harrowed and torn. There are things you do that you can't explain, you can't defend, things you're just as amazed by as anybody else, and I was about to do one of those amazing things: pick up the phone and call Jean and say, "That invitation still open?"

But I managed not to. I went to bed and slept in my clothes, and in the morning, I thought, *Get me out of here.* I took a long shower, the spray like hot needles. I sang, "Just as I am without one plea/But that Thy blood was shed for me." Then I turned off the hot water and stood under the cold. I was afraid to look at myself in the mirror. I scoured the towel into my hide drying myself off. I put on a pair of blue-striped pants and a green-and-red-striped shirt, the ugliest clothes I own, clown clothes, and burned two slices of toast and ate them and went to eight A.M. Mass in the basement of the college chapel. I got there early, knelt and prayed, and did not feel like a good person in any way. There were four in attendance, an old couple and a girl in shorts and me. The room smelled tomblike and wintry. Mother Sally was gone on retreat, and the priest was one I had never seen before, an old man with a crew cut and a too actorly voice. There are plenty of those in the Episcopal ranks, priests who seem to relish being on stage and having all the good lines. Perhaps the man had been shipped here to learn humility. In the homily, he said, "We do not know ourselves but God knows us and so we must pay attention to His word and stop trying to make it more convenient to ourselves." I put my face in my hands, which somehow smelled of Jean's perfume, though I had not touched her except to kiss her good night. "We are not sufficient unto ourselves," said the priest. "Every good thing, every morsel of food, comes directly from God, who expects us to conform to His Holy Will."

After Mass, I walked across the green to Gridley Hall and climbed the stairs to the WSJO studios. Back in the dim bowels of the control room, Thomas Neil Cameron sat poring over the Sunday *Times*, eating a sandwich, as the Beethoven "Emperor" Concerto poured from the studio monitors. He had a squatty face and heavy black-rimmed glasses, like a minor Beat figure of the fifties, someone who might have trailed around after poets, hoping to pick up spare girls.

I sat at Fawn's desk and wrote her a note saying I'd be gone for a week. I wrote a note to Dean Baird—"My father was taken ill and I've gone out to see to him"—and sealed it in an envelope and was about to call the airport, when the telephone rang.

I picked up, hoping for Alida, and Sandra somebody from the *Syracuse Reader* asked to speak to John Tollefson. She was doing a story about public radio. I told her I was on my way out the door. "It'll only take five minutes," she said.

I talked with her for forty-five minutes, about listener support, about the Corporation for Public Broadcasting, about criticisms of public radio as elitist and politically biased, about its role in a community such as Red Cliff, and I had a feeling that the woman was not operating from plain old curiosity. There was a prosecutorial air to her open-ended questions, a mock innocence in her voice, references to nameless accusers: "Some people say it's wrong to use tax dollars to maintain what they say is a white, male, Eurocentric institution," she said.

"Some people say the moon is made of green cheese," I said.

"Are you saying it's *not* Eurocentric?" she asked.

"It's *ec*centric, if you ask me."

She was unamused. "How much women's programming do you do per week?"

I suggested that she listen to the station for a week, keep a diary, add up the total lengths of the things that had interested her, and that would be the answer.

"Frankly," she said, "I would rather sleep next to a dead person than listen to your station for even an hour. But thanks for the interview." And she hung up.

EIGHT

Home Alive

I drove at top speed to Syracuse and got a seat on a noon flight to Minnesota, feeling queasy about the state of my soul. Lutherans don't put great emphasis on hell, but that doesn't mean we aren't aware of one, and I could feel a place being prepared for me, a bed in the ashes, where I would toss and turn in the company of small, dishonest folk, connivers, chiselers, purse snatchers, adulterers. I walked down the jetway and stood in line outside the airplane door, looking at its steel skin, thinking, *You'll never get home alive.* I sat near the back of the plane, crunched in a middle seat, between a Vietnamese woman who slept with her head on my shoulder and a beefy man in a Vikings sweatshirt who fought me for domination of the armrest. The plane landed at two-thirty. I rented a white Firebird, and once beyond the outer ring of suburban slum north of Minneapolis, I put my foot down and drove eighty all the way, past cornfields and meadows with gloomy Holsteins parked on the hillsides, the meadowlarks singing in the ditches, the air sweet with grass. A little sooner than I expected, I came over the last rise and saw the Farmers Union grain elevator, and the sign whizzed past:

WELCOME TO LAKE WOBEGON
A TOWN ON THE GROW!

I took my foot off the gas as the road curved past the county highway department sheds, big snowplow blades parked in the tall grass, and over the railroad siding where the train carrying Babe Ruth stopped—that was in 1935, and my dad had been there. I passed a front yard that contained every lawn ornament known to Western civilization: windmills, cast-iron deer, plaster elves and gnomes, plywood cutouts of fat couples bending over and weeding, the woman's skirt pulled up and her polka-dotted bloomers showing. On Main Street, the town's one stoplight blinked green, and fresh plastic pennants fluttered in the breeze at the Bunsen Motors used-car lot.

A man in white T-shirt and white pants and a white apron stood in the window of the Chatterbox Café, drinking coffee, giving me a glum and wooden look. Two old mannequins stood in the window of the Mercantile, wearing green Bermuda shorts and green-striped jerseys, striking a pose of dated elegance. I turned up McKinley Street, past Our Lady of Perpetual Responsibility. Everyone along McKinley Street was out doing yardwork. Old ladies as delicate as wrens bobbed up and down, weeding their flower beds, and old men raked the grass. Mother was out working in the yard in her blue housedress, spading up the flower beds under the picture window. She looked up as I walked across the grass, and she leaned the spade against the house and put her arms around me. She was so thin, I could feel the ribs on her back. Her high cheekbones and puckish smile gave her a girlish demeanor, despite her gray hair and bifocals.

"I came to check up on you. Maybe I should have called," I said.

"No need to call," she said. "It's always good to see you."

She was putting in cosmos and marigolds and black-eyed Susans. It had rained that morning, and the yard was lush and thick. In the long backyard was a row of tomatoes, one of onions and carrots, a bed of strawberries, a few hills of cucumbers and squash. Bean plants crept up the poles beside the garage. On the trellis at the corner of the garage, by the raspberry bushes, yellow honeysuckle blossoms hung in the vines, and red blossoms on the dogwood, where two indigo buntings perched on a limb. Violets bloomed around the birdbath.

"I shouldn't ask," she said, "but are you in any sort of trouble?"

"Probably," I said, "but that's not why I'm here."

We walked around to the back porch. I braced myself. Always a shock to confront Dad's clutter and see how it had metastasized since the last time. Dad was someone who went downtown for a box of nails and came back with a croquet set, three army ammo boxes, *La Traviata* on 78-rpm discs, and a coyote trap. And if he saw humidifiers on sale, he might buy two or three of those too. Now that he was retired, he had time to attend auctions.

The porch had cluttered up some since my last visit. A pile of lumber scraps and a stack of storm windows. Boxes of air filters for cars Dad didn't have anymore. Bottles of ammonia and herbicide and various yard tools, some usable. Some old bikes, dried-out baseball gloves, a box of vinyl tile. Three metal detectors leaned against the wall. One of Dad's hobbies and so typical of him: he went looking for Spanish doubloons and came home with a pocketful of antique halfpenny nails. I opened the kitchen door. The counter was clear— Mother had fought Dad off in that sector. More power to her. The dining room had surrendered long ago when Dad took in Grandma's and Grandpa's junk; the garage and basement and attic, all gone, lost; the three upstairs bedrooms were under serious siege; the living room was an active battleground.

Mother made a fresh pot of coffee and poured two cups and sat down at the table opposite me and said, "So tell me everything about you."

"Not much to tell. I'm okay. I may be getting an award in Washington in the fall," I said. "An award for managers, called the Wally. Sort of like an Emmy, but it's a Wally."

"Your father," she said, "came across a speech trophy you won in high school." I remembered the speech, a piece of patriotic fluff about Dunkirk and D-Day called "Those Who Gave All." Terrible. To dishonor the heroic dead with cheap oratory. "Throw it out," I said.

I headed toward the bathroom, to check on the state of things, to see how full the house was. With Dad, things mounted up: a set of car keys left on a bureau would be joined by a stack of old postcards on a Hamm's serving tray, and then a box of goblets would jump up next to it, and the next day you'd find a Praying Hands plaque and a poster of the Northern Pacific Vista Dome crossing the Rockies. Stuff gathered on the floor, then jumped up on tables; stuff stashed in the corners edged toward the center. Boxes of *Reader's Digest* Condensed Books migrated up from the basement, bags of socks bought at burnout sales. You had to make preemptive strikes and not let the enemy dig in.

The dining room was a jumble of old books, antique bottles, three shoe boxes full of perforated steel discs for an old painted music box Dad had found at an auction. A seamstress's dummy stood by the hutch; a cradle, a wooden sled, duck decoys. Books were piled next to it on the floor, on them a sign: *Do Not Move—ASK—Please.* The dining room table had disappeared under piles of magazines that, according to Mother, Dad was trying to sort out: copies of *Life* with black-and-white covers—Irving Berlin, General Omar Bradley, the Rockettes, the battleship *Iowa*, Henry Wallace. But Dad could not throw stuff out; if it was old, if he could imagine a use for it, if he could think of someone he might give it to someday, he hung on to it. He would talk about getting things in order and make a big project of it and beaver away for a day or two, examining his possessions— open up an antique doctor's bag and look at the vials of pills, go through his collection of army insignia, unfold the weather balloon, look at a mimeograph (still in good working order), and riffle through a box of unidentified portraits taken in various studios around Blue Earth and Winona in the 1880s—and he'd pare away a couple of grocery bagfuls of stuff and toss it in the trash barrel, but somehow editing only stimulated the collection, spread it out, created gaps to be filled later.

I wondered if I'd be able to sleep in my bedroom, or would I have to order a Dumpster first?

Mother said, "So how's your history professor? Why didn't you bring her along?" I told her that Alida was in Denmark.

Dad came in from the garage, unshaven, wearing his old work uniform, the brown shirt with *Farmers Union* stitched on the pocket, the green pants. He was thin as always. A life of worry kept his metabolism whirring like a hummingbird's. "How are you?" I asked.

He ignored me. "Those phoebes are gone," he said. "The nest is empty. Thank goodness. The male was having conniptions every time anyone went out the front door."

"Marilyn Tollerud said their barn swallows took off on Sunday," said Mother. "Those four birds they had in their basement. The kids found them abandoned in the nest, so they brought them in and fed them dog food, and last week they were tossing the birds up in the air to exercise their wings and trying to teach them to fly and Daryl came out to see what they were up to and the screen door slammed and the birds took off like a shot."

Dad jumped up and darted into the dining room and came back with a packet of snapshots. One of his uncle Harald on a visit from California, taken in Grandpa's backyard beside the hydrangeas, Harald holding a sign that said *Cheese.* And a trick photograph in which Harald seemed to be holding Aunt Ray in the palm of his hand, and another of Dad's brother Carl and his dog, the dog wearing a porkpie hat and polka-dot necktie. Carl died of blood poisoning when he was eight, after a nail that stuck up from a porch step went through his shoe.

They said that my cousin Marvin, Ray and Art's son, who taught modern history and driver education at the high school, had taken too much Librium one day and lost consciousness during the behind-the-wheel instruction, and when he came to, the girl at the wheel was crying and it was dusk and the car was parked in a field of alfalfa near Sioux Falls, South Dakota, eight hours away. She had simply kept driving until she ran out of gas. She said she didn't know he was unconscious—his eyes were open—though he had said things that didn't make sense, about people being angry at him, people in Paraguay. They were angry at him for snoring and for killing flamingos. So Marvin was suspended for a week and taken off Librium and became a nervous wreck and on his way to the doctor's ran off the road and into a telephone pole and broke his collarbone.

"Ray is just beside herself," said Mother. Aunt Ray was a connoisseur of misfortune from way back, and Marvin was her masterpiece.

"Speaking of driving," said Dad, "I should show you my videocassette of the North Shore. I taped about two hours of it last fall when we drove up to see the leaves. It came out pretty well, considering. Gives you a nice idea of the landscape. There's a funny scene with the guy at the gas station. He sees me videotaping him, he starts singing. He was a cutup."

The video camera was Dad's latest discovery. He had recorded highlights of most of a day's drive from Billings to Yellowstone, as well as the South Rim of the Grand Canyon. He panned the canyon from left to right, and right to left, and got back on the tour bus and rode to the next promontory and taped more of the canyon from there, and now he had two hours' worth of the Grand Canyon at his fingertips, to revisit whenever he wished.

"We had Travel Club this week, and Irene Bunsen did Hawaii," said Mother. "She and Clint were there last winter and stayed at that old hotel on Waikiki with the banyan tree in the courtyard—"

Dad jumped up. "I've got a Hawaiian tune on that music box," he said. He hauled it into the kitchen.

"Don't you leave that box on my kitchen table," she said.

He put a steel disc on the music box turntable and cranked it up and out came "Sweet Leilani."

"I've got about three hundred different melodies," he said. "Paid fifteen dollars for this."

Down deep in his Lutheran soul, Dad believed in bargains. He felt there was no essential difference between cheaper brands and pricier ones—"They all come from the same factory; one just has a fancier label, that's all," he said—so, being no sucker, he always bought the cheapest kind. He coveted bargains so much that they became self-justifying. It was all right to buy junk he didn't need if it cost less than he had expected it to. "How much do you think I paid for this?" he'd say, holding up a birdhouse shaped like a grain silo. "A dollar!" That was a triumph, even though the birdhouse wound up in the dining room and was used to store pennies.

It was lunacy. He'd say, "If only I could find the time to get these things sorted out," but he had all the time in the world, and he used it to acquire more things. To lend an appearance of order, he made labels and created signage. *Door to Bathroom Is Behind You—This Is Closet:* it gave him pleasure to post that on the closet door; and on the bathroom door was *Bathroom: Light Switch Is to Left,* to save you from groping behind the door for the switch; and once in the bathroom, you saw *If Your Name Is Not Byron, Don't Use This Towel* and, over the toilet, *Hold Handle Down While Flushing.* He labeled shelves in the refrigerator, the cupboards; even the power switch on the television had a bright-orange sticker with *ON* written on it in red letters. He tried to fend off Mother with warning signs, such as *Do Not Remove Boxes from Bureau: They Are There for a Reason.*

We sat in the kitchen, drinking coffee, as Dad fished around in a shoe box full of discs and asked which tune we wanted to hear. Aunt Ray came in, and I stood up and gave her a hug. "I was going to take a nap, I am all worn out, but I can't sleep, so I thought I might as well come over," she said. "Did you hear about Marvin?"

"Yes," I said, so of course she told me the whole story. Marvin was applying for a disability retirement. "He is not the person he was," she said. "This thing has torn him to pieces inside." She sat sipping coffee and was full of bad news, as always. Her and Dad's oldest brother, Bernie, was deaf as a woodbox, living alone in Uncle Svend's old house, which was almost totally full of debris. "You can't get in the upstairs at all. He's worse than you, Byron," she said. Bernie never married. "He lives like a badger. He sleeps in an aluminum lawn chair next to the kerosene stove, he keeps the place at ninety degrees, it reeks of pine disinfectant and cigar smoke, and he changes his clothes once a week, if that," she said. "His favorite food is bacon, and he eats a pound of it a day, it's his entire diet, that and baked beans and boiled coffee. I check up on him when I can, but I have no idea what's going to become of him."

I thought, *He is going to die, Aunt Ray, that's what's going to become of him. Check the statistics on eighty-five-year-old men.*

Aunt Ingrid was at Holy Redeemer Home, tiny, hobbling around, fussing at the nurses' aides, suffering from high blood pressure and diabetes and irregular heartbeat, and, despite a lifetime of frailty, going on ninety-three. Aunt Ray didn't know what would become of her either. Aunt Ingrid was lost without her son, Bunny; dolt that he was, he had been her main comfort.

Mother said, "That coffee is cold; let me make you some fresh." And Ray sighed and said, "No, this is fine," as if cold coffee were all a person could expect in this world.

She thought maybe allergies were causing her fatigue. Art had told her maybe it was depression, and she told him, "*Of course* I'm depressed; if you were tired all the time, you'd be depressed too." She'd like to go see an allergist in the Cities, but Medicare wouldn't cover it.

"Let me at least heat that coffee up for you," Mother said. "No," said Ray, "I don't like coffee anyway, so hot or cold makes no difference, I only drink it out of habit."

Mother took Ray's cup and dumped out the cold coffee and poured in hot. "That dress looks good on you," she said. "You look nice in blue. It's good for your color." Ray said she wished she had nice clothes to wear, but she hadn't gone shopping for so long because she wanted to lose some weight first. Ray had been skin and bones all her life, but she thought of herself as a cow. She patted her tiny belly. "Look at this," she said. "All I do is eat."

The subject of food reminded Dad that Carl Krebsbach had been to his niece's wedding in St. Paul on Saturday and the church was almost full of people, and the organ kept playing and playing, and finally the minister came out and said the wedding was off and that a lunch would be served downstairs. "I guess the bride was standing in the back, about to walk down the aisle, and she turned to her sister and said, 'Get me out of here,' " he said.

"That must've been rough on the bridegroom," said Ray.

"Not half as rough as marriage would've been, I'll bet," said Dad.

Motes of dust fell through the sunlight. They talked on and on. The clock ticked. On the old radio on the table was a sign: *To Clear Up Static, Tap Center of Tuning Dial Sharply.* A string hung over the kitchen table, marked *Pantry Light,* and indeed, when I reached up and pulled it, thanks to a system of tiny pulley wheels, it switched on the pantry light, twenty feet away.

"What do you need?" said Mother.

"Fresh air," I said.

NINE

A Tour of Town

I walked down the hill to Main Street, thinking about Alida in Denmark seven hours ahead of me, her day almost over, curling up in a Danish bed, people walking under her window speaking Danish. I knew I would never come so close to betraying her again. Maybe the dinner with Jean was an inoculation against adultery. Evil can lead to good, surely it can—you have to believe so, anyway. What does a fool have except hope? Far out on the lake, a bright-green boat lay at anchor with an orange blob in it under a blue umbrella—Clarence Bunsen's boat, *Lebensfrieden*, the seats removed and an orange couch bolted to the bottom. "He likes to relax after he's sold a car, when he's feeling flush," Dad said once, "and the fish don't bother him at all, except the occasional one who needs help getting off the hook." Around his boat, just under the gunwales, Clarence had painted, in black letters:

O blessed mood, in which the burden of the mystery, in which the heavy and the weary weight of all this unintelligible world, is lightened.

He found this saying on a men's clothing calendar. Clarence was one of the Happy Lutherans, like Mother, a distinct minority in Lake Wobegon.

Outside the Chatterbox Café stood Mr. Berge, in an old brown plaid jacket, his white hair puffed out under a Pioneer seed corn cap. He told me he had heard that people were pulling in sunfish using croutons soaked in bacon grease for bait. I opened the café door and stepped in. The room was steamy and loud, the booths along the wall packed with farmers, a few stools open at the counter, so I sat down and ordered the hot beef sandwich. "You're John Tollefson, right?" said the waitress. "Yes, and you're Darlene," I said.

She wiped the counter in front of me and put down silverware and a paper napkin. "You graduated with my older sister, Cheryl."

"Right." She brought me coffee, and I put milk into it.

"Corn went in so late, I doubt it'll amount to much," said a man at the table behind me.

Another man said, "I was thinking I should've put in beans instead. There was a guy west of here put in pinto beans the past two years and did real well."

"Corn is the wave of the past. We've got to get over it. Get over beef. Look at these specialty crops, like sprouts and beans. There's more vegetarians out there than you might think."

"Irene Bunsen, you know—she became a vegetarian after her uncle choked on a piece of beef at a family reunion."

"Did he die?"

"No, but it sure took people's appetites away. They had to pry the meat out of his throat with a Swiss Army knife. It wasn't pretty."

"She makes this baked eggplant, and it isn't bad. I had it once at church."

"I saw Clint at the Veterans of Foreign Wars clubhouse in St. Cloud one time, having a steak tartare. Irene wasn't with him."

The hot beef sandwich came: two slices of white bread, two glops of mashed potatoes, four slices of overcooked beef, a lake of brown gravy. I glanced to my left: the man next to me, reading the newspaper, was my old football coach, Mr. Magendanz. I was a second-string end, back before the era of complicated plays, before the spreads and screens and draws, back when the Leonard offense consisted of a brief lunge forward by eleven men, most of whom then fell down. I'd line up opposite some enormous demented animal and lunge forward and get crunched and go back to the huddle and sneak a look at the girls huddled in the bleachers, shivering, exhaling clouds of steam. They had gone out of their way not to dress for the cold weather, a way of gaining independence from their mothers: to expose yourself to death and not die. The girls never looked at me; they were indifferent to my disgrace. Mr. Magendanz was indifferent to me now. He had folded the paper so that only the stock market listings showed, and he held it three inches from his face. He had to be seventy-five, at least. The guy who used to grab me by the scruff of my neck and yell in my face, "How come you go to sleep on me out there, huh?" Retired now, forgotten, drifting along like a dry leaf on an empty street, checking his investments. I wanted to lean over and whisper in his ear, "Your star tackle Charlie Koenig got rich in New York and he forgot your name, Mr. Morgandunce."

I ate my lunch in peace. Nobody shouted my name and clapped me on the shoulder and asked me how I was, nobody made a fuss about my being there. It was no big deal. Maybe they hadn't noticed that I left twenty-five years ago. Maybe they thought I was still around but didn't get out of the house so often.

I paid up, left Darlene a dollar tip on a two-dollar sandwich, and hiked north along Main Street, past Skoglund's Five and Dime, past Ralph's Pretty Good Grocery, the front windows half covered with hand-lettered signs announcing Scott toilet tissue, frozen pizza, peaches, root beer, Hi-lex, ground round, fryers, instant potatoes, Joy detergent. The bachelor farmers' bench in front of Ralph's was packed. Six old men watched me come toward them and then looked away as I got close, so as not to have to say hello. Uncle Bernie wasn't among them. One leaned forward as I approached and, putting a finger alongside his nose, blew a big clot of snot onto the sidewalk. That is one thing that keeps them bachelors, the nose-blowing, and the other is body odor. These men do not bathe regularly, so great is their self-confidence.

I cut through the alley to the swimming beach, where many people lay on the sand who should not appear scantily clad in public. Mounds of aging mottled skin, mapped with varicose veins, the flesh like hunks of clay gobbed on. Myrtle Krebsbach paraded down to the water in a two-piece silver lamé bathing suit. I was brought up not to stare, but it looked as if her suit could fall off her at any minute, and it wasn't anything you'd hope for. She pranced into the water up to her cellulite saddlebags and dove in and paddled toward the diving dock.

I walked up past the plain white frame Lutheran church to the parsonage next door. David Ingqvist's blue station wagon wasn't in the driveway, so I rang the bell, and my sister Judy answered, in old jeans and a white shirt, her reddish-blond hair tied back. "Hi, stranger," she said. She gave me a dry peck on the cheek and patted my shoulder. "This is a rare occasion," she said. "I had no idea you were coming." I followed her through the house, which looked as if too many basketball games and wrestling matches had taken place in it. The sofa and chairs sagged, defeated, and the carpet was worn down in places to the gridwork. She said, "Excuse me. I have to go fax something that was supposed to be in Chicago an hour ago—back in a jiffy," and peeled off toward David's study.

I sat at her kitchen dinette, strewn with papers. Churchy stuff. Bulletins. Study guides. She used to be my favorite sister, the smartest one in the whole family, the one who could've gone on to grad school—what a painful memory that is: Michigan offered her an assistantship, she was all set to go, and then she didn't; instead she married that lump of a Lutheran and clerked at Super Valu to put him through seminary and typed his term papers and kept house and cooked him hamburger hotdish—that was David's favorite, cabbage and ground beef and canned tomatoes. After Judy turned down Michigan, I never felt close to her again. We were pals for one year at the U, I a senior, she a junior, we cooked meals at her apartment over Vescio's in Dinkytown, we went to foreign movies, we biked along the Mississippi once from Minneapolis to Red Wing and camped out and told each other secrets, but she never told me she had decided to cast her lot with Mr. Vanilla. I don't know why she didn't tell me. I never asked.

A calm man, Pastor Ingqvist. I played tennis with him a few years ago, and he was quite calm losing 6–0, 6–0. He has no backhand. Not even a sense of backhand. There is no irony in him whatsoever. Probably that is a good thing if you are a pastor in Lake Wobegon, but wouldn't you need to go away somewhere for a few days where you could be sarcastic? Maybe there is a motel in South Dakota catering to the ministerial trade, a Holiday Inn with a big atrium that had a pool and potted trees, where flabby men in bikinis lie on chaise longues sipping Mai Tais and make withering remarks about their parishioners. I doubt that David would be capable of it.

She came back carrying a stack of pamphlets and plopped them down on a chair. A thin tome, "Why I Am a Lutheran." "It's not the work, it's the paperwork," she said. She shuffled the papers on the table into one stack. "We're in between church secretaries—the old one wore out and the new ones want real money—so I'm filling in, and ever since the church headquarters got computerized, they use *twice* as much paper. One thing I've learned about computers is that they make it possible for so many more people to get involved in every decision. Instant gridlock."

"You folks taking a vacation this year?"

She snorted. "Our church board feels that ministers shouldn't need vacations, they ought to just read the Psalms. If we're lucky, we'll go visit David's mother in Minneapolis and see a couple of movies."

A cat wound itself around my ankle. I picked it up and put my ear to its side, to hear the motor purring. The cat struggled and leaped onto the table and hunkered down on the papers like a hairy meat loaf. Judy poked it, and it leaped to the floor.

"It's enough vacation for me just to get away from the kids," she said. "A person gets tired of being a parent. I told David this morning, I have no further interest in running their lives whatsoever. If one of them came in and said, 'I'm running away,' I'd say, 'Go ahead, but first write out a description of yourself that we can put on the sides of milk cartons.' "

"Speaking of parents," I said.

"Yes?"

"Dad's collecting has gotten completely out of control. The man needs help. The dining room has disappeared, and he's eating away at the living room."

"I don't see that, but then I'm around all the time."

"Check it out. The garage is full, and he's starting to store things under a tarp in the yard. He's got an old two-bottom plow that he bought for fifty dollars at an estate sale, and he greased it, he put good tires on it, tightened up the nuts, had a broken trip lever welded, and it's all ready to go, except that he has no use for it, of course, and no intention of giving it to someone who does. Is this normal? I don't think so."

"He's not harming anybody," she said.

"I'm thinking of Mother getting crushed in a junk slide. It's incredible what the guy is squirreling away; it's like a spook house."

She let three beats go by, and said, coolly, "So what brings you back, John?"

"I committed a sin, and I came back to repent for it."

"Are you joking now?"

"No," I said. I stood up and opened the refrigerator, which was stuffed tight—an incredible array of inedibles—and got out a can of Coke and popped it open. The refrigerator door was covered with papers held on by magnets: Bible school schedules, Kate's soccer practices, swimming lessons, drawings by Will and Charlie, pictures of the kids, pictures of other kids—and I noticed a postcard that said:

The Parents' Prayer

You have accepted all our gifts and seldom said thank you. You have looked at us with contempt, loathed our company, ignored every shred of good advice we offered. We offered you art and music and literature, and you chose garbage and noise. We forgive you for each and every one of your offenses and we heartily pray that in the fullness of time God will give you children and that they will do the same unto you. They are our allies. They fight for us and for justice. God grant us the simple justice of grandchildren. Amen.

"I should take that down," Judy said. "David doesn't like it."

The phone rang and she picked it up and whoever it was had a lot to say to her. Judy sat hunched over, listening hard, murmuring, "I see . . . uh huh . . . okay . . . you bet . . . No, of course, I understand . . . ," and I paced the floor, drinking the Coke, and then waved and slipped out the back door.

The Ingqvist garage was made from boards from my ancestor John Tollefson's first house in Lake Wobegon, according to Dad. When I go home, I like to look at it and think about him. The story is that when he was eighteen, one fall day, over a supper of boiled onions and rice porridge, John Tollefson told his father, "I go to America next summer when the second crop of hay is in." His father stood and whacked him up the side of the head with his fist and said, "You've been sleeping with the butcher's daughter Signe. So you can marry her and go to work for him, and that's that. Let America take care of itself." Signe and John had enjoyed the old custom of night courting, spending some nights together with a ribbon between them the length of the bed. Among rural people in Norway, it was understood that couples might cross the ribbon—which was placed there for the parents' sake and had nothing to do with the couple—and it was considered no shame if the bride was pregnant on her wedding day. You should not have a child out of wedlock, but it wasn't important how far into wedlock it was born. So he married Signe, with no dancing at the wedding, only the usual reception with doughy people in Sunday clothes sitting in a circle and grumping about the weather and the goats, and they moved in with her parents, and John took up butchering. They gave him the job of extracting brains and kidneys and livers and collecting the intestines and cleaning them to use for sausage casing. His parents-in-law were pietists and allowed no lighthearted singing or foolish talk in their house, so John kept his mouth shut. Once, he traveled to Bergen for the wedding of a cousin, and he danced half the night, and the sun came out, and then he returned to Voss and the sky was cloudy. They had two daughters. Every night, he lay with Signe in their box bed in a little windowless room under the eaves, the babies asleep in a trundle bed, and he told her what a fine place America was. You could learn English in two weeks—it was not so different from Norwegian—but in any case, they would live among Norwegians there, good decent folk, and not among those lying, drunken Swedes. The land was free and it was rich black loam deposited by ancient glaciers; you could raise two crops, one in June and one in September. If you worked hard, you could make your fortune in five or six years, and then of course you could come back to Voss and buy a handsome house. And a shop—perhaps he would be a clothier or tobacconist.

He persuaded her that they should go, and then he earned money for their passage one freezing January night in 1880, on a wager. He got into conversation with a ship's captain in a tavern and bought him a whiskey. The captain's pocket watch was on the fritz, and John said, "I can fix watches," so he went to work on it. The captain was quite drunk. John helped him get drunker. John said he had always wanted to go to sea, that it was a good life for a man. The captain said it was a dangerous life and no good for a married man at all. John said he didn't know about that; he was strong, he was up for adventure. To toughen himself, he said, he went swimming in winter and he could swim for ten minutes in the river before he got cold. The captain said that a man would be dead within three minutes in such cold water. "Not so," said John. "It would depend on the man." He believed in individualism, he said. "Science is science," said the captain. He paid John for fixing the watch, and John said, "How much are you willing to wager to see me swim?"

They walked down to the shore and John took off his boots and coat and plunged into the black water and stayed for ten minutes, treading water, willing away the cold, and made it to shore, barely able to walk up the stony beach, and collapsed into the arms of the waiting men and was carried back to the tavern and given hot whiskeys, and he collected the hundred crowns he had wagered and went home and told Signe, and he brought home two beers and drank them in front of his father-in-law, the first beers ever seen in that house, and he told the old man that he was a prude and a stuffed shirt and no more Christian than a china figurine, and three days later, John and Signe and the girls left for America.

Mother told me that story when I was little, and I asked her, "How did he stay warm in the water for so long?"

"By fixing the captain's watch so that it kept time more quickly."

"But wasn't that dishonest?"

"Yes, it was," she said. "But what sort of man would care to stand and watch another man die?"

When I got home, Dad was napping on the couch and Mother was making chicken soup. She had bought three boiling chickens from Mrs. Luger, three old leghorn sisters who after years of egg-laying and chicken conversation were snatched up by Mr. Luger and decapitated, and now would be translated into the glorious afterlife of soup, the apotheosis of chickenhood, their bones boiled along with chopped onions and carrots and celery and parsnips, the concoction strained through a cloth, the excess fat ladled off, the meat cooked in it along with egg noodles and some tarragon and oregano and a pinch of dill and—crazy idea—some fennel, and all simmered to a peak of dizzying goodness. Some was for Uncle Bernie, she said, and some for Judy, and some for Marvin, to take the place of his Librium.

I got out a pair of gloves and a fork and a pail and spent an hour prying dandelions out of the front yard. Cars went by, people honked and waved—Mr. Berge rolled down his window and yelled, "I see they put you to work!" as if this were quite a witty remark.

It struck me, pulling up dandelions, how handsome they are, almost like marigolds, and how hard people work to coax along pansies and impatiens and here is a hardy perennial that keeps coming back no matter what. Maybe people have chosen the wrong side, and the tide of history is with the dandelion. Then there was a long rolling clap of thunder, like a pile of lumber falling. Black thunderheads had moved in from the west, and I could see a sheet of rain sweeping over the hill and across town. Bolts of electricity exploded in the sky. I ran up onto the porch as the first drops hit.

Mother was in the kitchen, looking at an old book of poems Dad had found in the highboy. Pressed between the leaves was a piece of yellowed handstitching that read:

Elizabeth Crandall is my name
And America is my nation.
Providence is my home
And Christ is my salvation.
When I am dead and in my grave
And all my bones are rotten,
If this you see
Remember me
When I am quite forgotten.
1845

A sweet little piece of stitching. A little girl had held this piece of cloth in her hands in 1845 and thought about her own death, preposterous as it must have seemed to her at the time.

"This is my aunt Eleanor's book of poetry," said Mother. "The Crandalls were on Grandpa's side of the family. When I was little, my aunt Eleanor worked in her garden, and I was so devoted to her, I followed her wherever she went and tried to do everything she did, and I guess a little of her love of gardening rubbed off on me."

Aunt Eleanor had a beautiful garden. Bees landed on her and did not sting, birds came when she whistled, and she always had the earliest tomatoes. "She was my ideal. She lived her life as best she could and never complained," said Mother. "On her best days, there was no one more generous and fun to be with, and on her worst days, she kept quiet about it. She loved to have people over for coffee. She laid out a nice white cloth on the table and set out her best cups and saucers and the creamer and sugar bowl, the good napkins, a plate of fresh cookies, and berries in season, and she sat at the head of the table and poured the coffee and it went on for hours. She was never in a rush. She was a country person. Hospitality was everything to her."

Two knocks on the door, and it opened, and there was my old classmate Leland, rain dripping from his face, grinning. We were on the football team, and now he has a fifty-six-inch waist and wears billowy shirts so you can't see his fat wiggle. His sandy hair is pretty thin on top. "I heard that you were on the run from the law," he said, pumping my hand. "Let's go have a beer."

Leland winked at Mother. "One beer. I'm a married guy, you know."

I looked down along the bar of the Sidetrack Tap, the dark oak scratched and gouged, the sky-blue Hamm's globe revolving over the backbar, and the Pabst lantern and a miniature Schmidt's beer wagon pulled by six white horses and a Wendy's lighthouse with a circling beam that reflected in the brass trim. Men leaned on their elbows, their faces seamed and shadowy. Clint Bunsen and Carl Krebsbach sat together, leaning against the bar, their heels hooked on the barstool rungs. Wally stood behind the bar, playing cribbage with Mr. Berge and LeRoy. "Fifteen-two, fifteen-four, fifteen-six," said Wally, and he moved his peg. LeRoy looked away in disgust. According to Leland, some teenagers had caught LeRoy dozing in the town cop car the weekend before and let the air out of his tires and then raced by, dropping cherry bombs. It was like Pearl Harbor. He gave chase and ran the tires right off the rims. The kids weren't from here, they were from Millet, up the road. West of Hansens'.

"Did you hear that Hansen's dog died? The ugly one?" said Clint.

"That was the dog that bit Carl the time he slid his car in the ditch, wasn't it?" said Leland.

"I remember that dog," said Carl. "The cinnamon-colored dog."

"How did that dog bite you?" said Mr. Berge.

"He bit me hard," said Carl. "Right in the back of the leg. Audrey was right there. I'd gone to borrow a snow shovel and the dog bit me and she says, 'What happened?' and I said, 'Your dog bit me!' and she says, 'That dog don't bite.' I said, 'Well, *some* dog bit me, and he's the only dog here.' And the dog was being very cool about it, wagging his tail, smiling up at me, so I didn't say any more, I went and shoveled out the car. He was a terrible dog. He bit a lot of people. I think he bit Berge once in the butt, didn't he? Show us the scar, Berge."

"He never bit me," said Mr. Berge. "Dogs don't bite Norwegians; we're too salty and we've got too many bones."

"He bit your butt, but never mind," said Carl. "That reminds me of the time my cousin's wife's sister got fired from the root beer stand and came to stay with him and his wife for a few weeks until she could find a job and get back on her feet." Carl pushed his empty bottle across the bar and Wally opened a fresh one and pushed it back. Carl took a boiled egg out of the jar by the cash register and began to peel it. "So this sister was there, and weeks passed, and my cousin finally asked about the sister's plans, and the wife said, 'Laura's still pretty shaky. Unemployment is rough on a person's self-image, you know.' And a few more weeks went by. The sister camped in the living room, where she watched TV, consumed quantities of food, and talked on the phone at length to people in far-flung places like Japan and Greece and New Delhi, and finally my cousin mentioned to the wife that in his opinion anyone with friends all over the world must have a good enough self-image to be able to work for a living, and the wife cried and said, 'Well, she's my little sister, I can't kick her out in this cold weather.' So my cousin went to a novelty store and he purchased a talking toilet seat."

"A what?" said Wally.

"A talking toilet seat. He brought it home and installed it in the bathroom. It had a little tape recorder under it, and when someone sat down on the seat, this growly voice said, 'Hey, get off of there! Can't you see I'm working down here?' So the sister-in-law goes into the bathroom and closes the door, and my cousin puts his ear up to the keyhole, and he can hear as she squeezes out of her jeans and sits down, and when she hears the voice say, 'Hey, get off of there!' she shrieks and bolts out the door and rams the doorknob into my cousin's ear and goes flying out the front door with her trousers at half-mast and falls on the ice and breaks her leg. In three places. Very complicated break. He was flat on his back, holding his head—his head rang for a week. This happened two years ago. The sister-in-law is still there, but now he is half deaf and it doesn't bother him as much."

"I never heard of a talking toilet seat," said Mr. Berge. "I wonder if that isn't a made-up story."

"Ask my cousin," said Carl. "Give him a call. He's in the phone book. Just be sure to talk loud."

"I stopped telling lies because it's too complicated," said Mr. Berge, winking at me. "You lie, and you have to remember what you said the first time. But I only gave it up recently. I could go back to it if I had to."

LeRoy said, "That oldest Hansen boy tried to sell me his Plymouth Fury, a car that was spewing out this brown oily foam—I couldn't believe it! I told him, Don't sell it to a *friend*, for crying out loud. What a turkey!"

"That was the car with the dumb sticker on it, the one that said, 'I love America,' " said Leland.

"What's wrong with that?" I said.

"I don't know, but if you had a bumper sticker that said, 'I love my wife and kids,' I would honestly wonder about you."

"I don't have a wife and kids," I said.

"Well, we've all been wondering about you for *years*, Leland, so welcome to the club." LeRoy turned to Carl. "That wasn't the time you pulled that trick with the oysters, was it?" he said.

"With the dog? Yes. I gave him oyster therapy." Carl had peeled the egg, and he salted it and bit off the end.

"I decided to teach that dog not to bite, so a few weeks later I went up to Hansens' to borrow a posthole digger or something, I forget what, and Audrey sent me around to the toolshed, and in my pocket I had a couple chunks of sirloin and a plastic cup with two raw oysters in it. The dog was trotting along beside me and I flipped him a chunk of sirloin and the dog caught it and swallowed it, *glug*, and then another chunk, and he swallowed that on the fly, and then I flipped him the raw oyster. He caught it in his mouth, and as the oyster was going down, the dog was trying to spit it out—you ever see a dog do that? He was gagging, down on his knees, trying to stick his paw down his throat. I took the other oyster and rubbed it on his food dish so that he would be thinking about oysters in the future. Then I told Audrey I changed my mind about the posthole digger, and I went home."

Mr. Berge did not seem interested in the story at all. He seemed anxious for the spotlight to come back on him. He turned to Clint and said, "I dug about forty-six thousand postholes for the U.S. Army in the Philippines. Nineteen forty-five. General Doug MacArthur. He'd lost the Philippines once, and by God he wasn't going to lose it a second time, so we strung up more barbed wire in two months than there is in the state of Texas. Dug ditches and strung fences. We used to march in formation from the barracks to the work site and little kids would line the streets and wave American flags and shout all the obscene words they had learned from American soldiers who were digging postholes. They'd yell terrible things. I don't even want to repeat it. It was the only English they knew."

"So did the dog learn his lesson?" I asked.

"I didn't go back to find out," said Carl. "Didn't see the Hansens for five or six years, though I recall that whenever I drove past there, that dog would chase me for almost a mile. He came running flat-out, his chin about an inch above the ground. A couple of times I clocked him at fifty miles an hour. I didn't go to Hansens' until the summer I went there for my nephew's wedding. He married their daughter Marie, and she wanted to have a garden wedding at home. So I got dressed up to go and put a tear-gas pen in my pocket, and when I got to Hansens' their dog saw me and laid his ears back and growled, and I just pulled out the pen and gave him a whiff of it.

"All through the wedding I could feel his eyes on me, and I kept my hand in my pocket. He was circling. Whenever I looked around, I could see him behind a tree or skulking around the house. I went through the reception line afterward and felt something brush my leg and I whipped out the pen and I almost gassed a two-year-old child.

"I told myself, Relax. And then, of course, the dog made his move. It was after the lunch and I was helping them carry dirty dishes into the house. I had a tray of pretty expensive cut-glass goblets, and I was going up the back stairs and I saw him out of the corner of my eye lunging toward me and I turned and dropped the tray and whipped out the pen and fired and the wind blew the tear gas right up into my face and I fell down, I couldn't see a thing, I rolled around, and the dog bit me on the lower lip."

"What did the Hansens do?" said Leland.

"They thought I was drunk. She told me to go home and break my own dishes. The dog was sitting there laughing so hard he was about to wet his pants."

"Anyway, that dog died last week," said Clint. "Died of old age. He forgot he wasn't as young as he used to be and got in a fight with a bigger dog. He died of embarrassment."

"The Hansens haven't spoken to me since," said Carl. "Six years. I see them sometimes at Ralph's, and if they see me coming up one aisle they'll scoot over and come down the other one. Sensitive people. One tray of busted goblets and you become a pariah. But that's Lutherans for you."

TEN

Bankruptcy

When I came back to Red Cliff, a week later, it was late afternoon. I had seen all of my relatives, eaten a yard of bratwurst, fished for crappies, heard dozens of stories of shame and degradation, and was cured of my fevered thoughts about Jean. I felt reconfigured for fidelity. On my way home from the Syracuse airport I tuned in WSJO. A Third World woman novelist on *All Things Considered* was chiding Americans for their lack of interest in the Third World, and I switched over to W100, the Folks Next Door station, and the announcer was talking to a man on the phone who had seen a little girl in a white communion dress walking along the highway toward Seneca Falls last night and when he turned around and drove back, she wasn't there anymore—he wondered if this had happened to anyone else. "We'll find out," said the announcer, and went to a commercial for E-Z Twist, a special wrench that opens even the tightest lids.

I got home and opened all the windows and sat at the kitchen table and longed for Alida.

There was a letter from Copenhagen saying that she was having a wonderful summer, though she missed me. She listed the delights of Denmark: the civility of the people, the sunshine in the parks, the lunches at open-air cafés, the elaborate generosity of librarians. Meanwhile, my summer wasn't wonderful at all: it dragged on through July without her. I mowed the lawn and watered the flowers. I listened to Mets games booming out from my neighbor's yard. I kept calling Miss LeWin and getting an answering service. Marian MacKay was gone on vacation, and twice I was badly humiliated by my inability to explain simple budgetary items to the dean. "I would expect you to have a better grasp of the numbers," he said, as if I were thirteen years old. He had told Susan Mack to report directly to him on her agoraphobia documentary; he wanted to make sure it was syndicated nationally. Howard was elusive, out of touch for days at a time. When I finally reached him, Howard said he had been under terrible stress, that the bank was after him, running searches through computer files, tracking his financial life. "Banks are destroying America, pal, they're all merging into gigantic holding companies, ripping the hearts out of small towns and eating them. Everything is malls now. It's like the Middle Ages. In fifty years, you'll have airports and freeways and a series of walled compounds like in Roman times. Don't get me started."

"Howard," I said, "you're the managing partner here. You're at the helm. We need you to focus right now."

I described to him the original beautiful vision of The Gibbs Farm. Its perfect location, near Taughannock Falls, the highest waterfall in the eastern U.S. (215 feet). Tens of thousands of tourists every season. But you come to see falling water and, hey, it's not interesting for that long; the water cascades, it roars, it splashes, it crashes, and you take a video of it, and read the educational billboard ("Ten thousand years ago, this area was covered by a glacier"), and five minutes later you're ready for something new. Water is water. Looking at a waterfall is no more, and no less, thrilling than running your bathwater. "How about The Gibbs Farm?" you say to your weary wife and kiddoes. "Let's go there. I've heard it's good." And you go. And it's better than good. Fresh sweet corn and beautiful salads served in a cool Victorian farmhouse with a screened porch, the windmill slowly creaking on a sultry August afternoon, free parking in the pasture, a shop selling Amish crafts and jellies and blankets and those simple wooden toys that cost about twenty-one dollars apiece. Rides on the hay wagon for the kids, old Dobbin chugging around and, at the reins, Zeke, a kindly coot in a red plaid shirt chomping on a hay straw, and a petting zoo with baby lambs and pigs, and meanwhile the parents are ensconced on the porch, sipping Pinot Noir at six dollars a glass and grateful for it.

"This is our dream, Howard. Don't let it die. It's the fourth quarter, we're behind by a few points, we've got to be smart now. If we can't fire Steve, let's look for new partners, get an infusion of cash, make the thing go."

"How about we raise some cash among ourselves?" said Howard. "I'm good for another fifty. How about you? Excuse me." I could hear Howard, his hand over the phone, talking to somebody who had come into the room. Then he was back.

"Basically, we've got five options," Howard said. "Aside from the chance we might win the New York State lottery, there are five different ways this can go. One, we wait until the bank sends in its goons, and we hand over the keys and say, Have a nice day, and we take a business loss on our tax returns and we all become better people. Number two, we file for bankruptcy and pray to God we get a judge who's a liberal Democrat and isn't fond of banks. Three, we find that the water supply is hopelessly contaminated by PCBs and operating a restaurant is out of the question and the bank throws up its hands, abandons its collateral, and we sell the property to someone who wants to turn it into a nursing home. Four, we go out there late at night and are careless with matches and the place burns to the ground and we pass the lie detector thanks to the use of beta-blockers and the insurance pays up, the bank loan is paid off, and we now own two hundred forty acres and some trees. Five, we raise more capital. Which way do you want to go, pal?"

"Howard, I am not on top of this the way that I thought you were. But what about refinancing? No?"

Howard went off on a tirade about interest rates and banks and what flesh-eaters they were, and finally I got tired of it and said good-bye and hung up.

The restaurant idea had started out as an innocent vision of happy people eating sweet corn, not as a finance project. It was about corn, like the corn we Tollefsons got from Mother's uncle Ernie, who planted a half acre every spring, enough for him and whichever relatives he was on speaking terms with, and our family made sure to be nice to him, fool that he was. We would drive out, Dad and Judy and Bill and I, and pick a few dozen ears, and we kids would husk them in the back seat as Dad drove home, where Mother had the water simmering on the stove. Dad slid the ears into the pot to cook for five minutes, and we all sat down and feasted on hot buttered corn, with a slice of pot roast on the side.

"There are four main pleasures of life," Dad used to say. "Sweet corn, and the love of knowledge, and the love of God, and the one that you boys thought of first." He winked at us. "The hitch is that nobody can have all four. No, sir. You have to sacrifice one. Most people I know gave up the love of knowledge. I gave up the fourth one. I have no idea where you children came from."

"Byron, we've heard that joke before," Mother would say.

We rolled each ear on a stick of butter, salted it, and chewed lengthwise, butter dribbling down our chins. It was sweet corn as God intended it, not the inert cornlike cobs in the plastic coffins in the supermarket. That was what our restaurant was all about. Forget about decor. You offer fresh sweet corn to people and they will come. But The Gibbs Farm was nowhere near that point. It was hung up on a wooden cornucopia.

I trudged off to Sunday morning Mass. Mother Sally had returned from retreat and was full of thoughts about living life contextually and the patriarchy and the trajectory of faith. She came down during the Peace and hugged everyone, even those who, like me, weren't in a hugging mode, and her homily was about the divine energy of the womb, and she invited anyone who cared to dialogue about the sermon to join her in the Russell Room at the conclusion of the service. I snuck out a side door. I'd rather drop a rock on my foot than dialogue with anybody, especially about energetic uteruses. I went home, feeling depressed, and slept for two hours, and woke up feeling as if my head had come unscrewed.

Alida returned from Denmark in August, tanned, handsome, happy, her Balestrand book almost done, and the moment she laid eyes on me, she smelled treachery. I threw my arms around her and kissed her ten or fifteen times, and she gave me a weather eye and said, "So how was your summer?" Something had happened, she could tell. She came into the house sniffing for the scent of Woman, looking for the spoor—an alien sock, a pot of eye shadow belonging to the Other. "Did you see a lot of people this summer?" she asked.

"Would you like a list?"

"Were you keeping one?"

Thank goodness she had the book to finish. She spent three weeks in Red Cliff, holed up in the small guest bedroom with my old word processor, a CPT, an antique, but she liked it because the screen was longer. "I do not want to speak to anyone on the phone, I don't want you to knock on the door and ask if I need anything, and I do not want to see my brother," she said. "I'm sorry to be rude. It's called PMS. Pre-Manuscript Syndrome." She wandered downstairs for lunch in her jeans and sweatshirt, flushed, a little dazed, distant, and I fixed soup and a sandwich for her. Every day at five o'clock, I walked her across the quad and through the arboretum and along a gravel road that wound up through a narrow valley to an abandoned white church and graveyard, where we turned around and walked back. "Maybe I should come and live with you and write books for a living," she said. "New York is a lousy place to write. Too many other writers. I walk down Broadway and see one of those crazy women lurching around screaming and I think, How many stories is *she* going to wind up in tonight?"

I cooked for her every evening—risotto, pasta, casseroles: writer food. She ate very little, she slept like an old horse. She didn't want to talk about anything in the future. "You plan Thanksgiving and Christmas," she said. "I'll go anywhere, do anything, except not with my family, okay? And especially not Howard.

"My brother is a big idealist, and that means he goes out and fights make-believe battles, battles that were over a long time ago. And then he orates about it. I can't bear to listen to him right now, or he'll drive me nuts."

And then, shifting gears smoothly, instantly, she said, "Did you have a nice summer without me?"

"It was a lonely, forlorn summer. I went home for a week, and otherwise I sat around brooding."

"Oh?"

"I don't think I got out my tennis racket four times."

"Who did you play with?"

I had played with Howard, as a matter of fact. Howard was porking up, what with the bad news about the restaurant, and was easy to beat. You simply volleyed deep and then hit a little drop shot near the net, and he charged forward like an enraged buffalo, and if he managed to return the ball, you lobbed it deep. It was fun. Like torture but without the guilt.

Howard was writing an article for *The Nation*, attacking big banks as a violation of the spirit of Jeffersonian grassroots entrepreneurship and a form of corporate Stalinism. Lying on the grass between sets, he told me he had formed a liaison with a group called Animals R Us against a bank that dealt in "the finance of murder"—it loaned money to feedlot operators—and ARU would, at the proper time, gather at the bank's doors and fling roadkill at employees on their way to lunch. Even now they were collecting squashed squirrels and skunks to show their contempt for the moneylenders.

"What does all this have to do with our restaurant?" I inquired.

"The bank is the driver at this point, we are the passengers," Howard said. "But there's still a First Amendment, thank God."

Howard came over one evening when Alida was upstairs working, walked in without knocking, opened the kitchen cupboard and got out a couple of glasses and poured a big wallop of Scotch into each one. He wore a T-shirt under his blue pinstripe suit. It said *I have seen the truth and it makes no sense.*

He said, "I'm forty-five years old, pal. I'm searching around for the second half of my life, you know what I mean? This restaurant was going to be it."

"Not to be a scold," I said, "but should you be drinking that much Scotch, Howard? You've got about half a pint there."

Howard waved the question away. He had met with Harry Chambers, the bank vice-president who had approved the loan three years before, and Harry had been very, very testy. The partnership was into the bank for $600,000—a twenty-year amortization with a three-year balloon, monthly payments of $3,500, secured by a first mortgage on the property, and the bank was now feeling that the restaurant was a shaky proposition. They were talking to a developer from Philadelphia about dividing the property into five-acre ranchettes with prefabricated ramblers on them. Big, boxy houses, the kind that are stapled together and sell for a half million. The bank could do as they liked because the partnership was nine months behind on the payments. I couldn't believe what I was hearing. *"Nine months?"*

"We got behind." Howard took a big swallow of Scotch. "Anyway, if this campaign of mine works, maybe we can bring the machine to a stop."

"Howard, your campaign is purely recreational. I hope you know that. Forget about economic justice and just visualize trying to use your common sense."

I felt queasy. I sat down, tried to collect myself, and said, "Howard, are you at all keeping track of things at the farm? I thought you were. Was I wrong?"

Howard looked deep into his whiskey. "Everything is in place," he said. "Julie at my office is signing checks. She's looking after the day-to-day stuff. We're behind at the bank, but I told you that a long time ago. Didn't I? I thought I did. If I didn't, I'm sorry. Okay?"

He reached down and picked up a plastic bag and rummaged through it and found a paper, which he thrust at me. "This is where we stand now."

I asked him when he had started carrying his papers around in a plastic bag. "What happened to your briefcase?"

"I'm not that kind of lawyer anymore," he said.

When he finally left, I thought about Charlie Koenig, the dead banker. Charlie would have been a big help at this point. I could hear Charlie say, "No problem. We'll buy out the loan. Let me talk to some people." And that would be it.

Upstairs, Alida's chair scraped, and I could hear the clicking of computer keys. I got out a sheet of paper and a pen and began composing a letter to my aunt Mildred Tollefson in Buenos Aires.

Back in my childhood, she was the head cashier at the Lake Wobegon bank and lived in a brown stucco bungalow on Van Buren Street, with a reflective chrome ball called a gazing globe and banks of hydrangeas in the front yard. She wore knit dresses and orthopedic shoes and pinned her hair in a bun. She was my favorite aunt. She loved to play Scrabble and Monopoly and double solitaire and any other game you could imagine. She thought like a child. Everything was impulse. She'd jump up and say, "Let's have ice cream," and scoop it into the bowls. The bank was like a game to her. She loved to tell me how dumb the others were at the bank, especially Prune Face, Hjalmar Ingqvist, the president. "The man is not firing on all his pistons," she would say. Mildred had been married for a few months to a tall, slack-jawed man named Norman, who was no great prize and suffered from nervous spells, and then he left town because they weren't right for each other. Norman was a bad chapter, and when he was out of the way, she never mentioned him again. She told me I was her favorite nephew. I shared my Flambeau Family novels with her and she loved them too, and one fall she told Mother she was planning a train trip to New York City.

"I need a break," said Mildred. "I'm worn out. I'm the one who runs that bank, not Hjalmar Ingqvist. Anybody with a brain in their head knows that. Hjalmar has no more idea how a bank runs than the Greyhound dog understands internal combustion. I'm there from dawn to dusk, working away until I can hardly see straight. It's time for the old gal to kick up her heels."

Mildred asked Mother if I could go along with her and see the city, and Mother said I couldn't, I was too young, so Mildred went alone. She came home and told me everything. She saw the Great Nina Nilssky play her Stradivarius at Radio City Music Hall. The Great Nina was driven onstage in a silver Rolls-Royce, from which she emerged in a silver fur cape and silver boots, and bowed so her forehead touched the floor, and played some wild gypsy thing on the violin, and then Rollo and His Flying Collies entertained with their madcap antics, and then the Great Nina came out in a red Rolls-Royce, wearing a maroonish fur cape, and played "Malagueña," then the stage revolved and ten women in white dresses played the "Warsaw Concerto" at ten white grand pianos, and then out came the Great Nina in a silver-pink Rolls-Royce, wearing a silver-pink fur cape, and did the "Minute Waltz" and "Flight of the Bumblebee," then "By the Falls of Minnehaha," as the curtains opened and actual water cascaded over a rocky ledge—and an Indian came out from the wings and picked up the virtuoso and carried her across the edge of the waterfall, where she paused to perform "Indian Love Call" and then bowed, climbed back in the Rolls, and was swept away, and that was the show.

"I wish you had been there," said Mildred. "Maybe next year." She bought a dress in New York that was not her usual navy blue; it was iridescent green and was slit up one side and low-cut. No one had ever seen her show cleavage before. She modeled it for us, her hair pulled back with two bright-yellow combs, and instead of her steel-rim spectacles wore a red pair with rhinestones in the bows, and glittery earrings. People always said that Mildred was as normal as the day is long, but days get short in the winter. "You've got to live while you can," Mildred said. "The clock is ticking."

She put the dress away and resumed her job at the bank, but she sometimes talked to Mother about wanting to cut loose and start getting some fun out of life. She had gone to cocktail lounges in New York, had danced with men, a man took her to Coney Island, and this experience had changed her. She had not had a philosophy of life, and now she did, and it was: "Live today, while there's life." She had married Norman to please her mother and father, and now she intended to please herself.

"The old horse threw off the traces," she said. "The cow is out of the stanchion. The pigs are in the corncrib. It's hard to keep 'em down on the farm once they've seen Paree!"

I looked forward to going to New York with her the following fall, but in the spring, the bank examiners deciphered an odd piece of accounting and discovered that a great deal of money had passed through Mildred's hands in the past few years. They were young; they could not believe that a Sunday school teacher who wore steel-rim spectacles would betray her trust. They pointed out the discrepancies. "No, no, no, you're getting three different things confused here," she said, and she studied the journal. "Let me take it home and figure it out for you."

So she took the journal home and burned it in her fireplace, and packed her bags, and drove to Minneapolis and flew to Miami and on to Buenos Aires. On her way out of town, she stopped to see us. The Tollefsons were eating supper. I was eleven years old. I looked up, and Mildred sprang into the kitchen and cried, "Ta-dahhhhhh!" and struck a Theda Bara pose, one hand to her bosom, one extended as if fending off suitors. She was wearing the iridescent green dress again. "It's time for the old girl to sing her number," she cried. She kissed me on the cheek and whispered, "When you grow up, come and find me, buddy," and went out the door, leaving behind a mist of rum in the air.

The story hit the Minneapolis paper a week later—SUNDAY SCHOOL TEACHER ROBS BANK; TOWN IN "STATE OF SHOCK." And I became the nephew of the famous Light-Fingered Mildred the subject of heavy-breathing newspaper stories. Kids at school whispered about her behind my back. I had played Monopoly with her—had we used real money? my buddy Swanson asked me. I slugged Swanson in the mouth and we rolled in the dust.

Mother never mentioned Mildred, except to say once, "Mildred's problem was that she felt sorry for herself. She sat in that little house and thought about all her problems and of course she felt trapped, but it was her own trap." Dad and Aunt Ray wrote to Mildred every year at Christmas, and she wrote to them. There was a neighborhood in Buenos Aires where fugitives from the Midwest had always settled: defrocked ministers, disgraced scoutmasters, adulterers, husband-poisoners, arsonists, and middle-aged unmarried small-town lady bank tellers. I had had the address for years and never written. I don't know why. Perhaps because I had nothing to say that seemed to me to be of interest to someone in Argentina.

I wrote now: "Dear Aunt Mildred, Many years have passed since you last heard from me, but that doesn't mean that you have been absent from my thoughts—far from it. I have fond memories of our times together in the old days, our long talks, our hard-fought Scrabble games, and on the strength of those, and of our old family ties, I am writing to ask if you could consider helping me with a peculiar financial problem"—and I described the beautiful sweet-corn restaurant and the fiscal morass into which it had sunk.

ELEVEN

The Wally Award

I got official word of the Wally Award two weeks before the public-radio conference in Washington, and I stayed home two days and wrote a speech. Three speeches, actually—one on funding, one on the commitment to excellence, one on communication and community. The letter from National Public Radio notifying me of the Wally said that a few remarks would be appropriate, five or six minutes, as I saw fit. It wasn't my idea of a good time, giving a speech, but maybe somebody would be in the audience from New York City, a foundation exec, someone with a job to offer. You have to put yourself forward to get those cushy jobs at prestigious nonprofits, you have to network and press the flesh and be willing to stand at a podium and hurl thunderbolts of boilerplate about multiculturalism, and afterward a guy in a houndstooth jacket offers you $90,000 a year to sit in a cool office in the East Fifties and bestow grants and attend the occasional conference on arts education.

I blended the three speeches into one, and Fawn typed it up, and it came out twenty-five pages. Way too long.

"That is so cool that you're going to get an award in front of all those people," Fawn said. "I wish I were there to see it."

"I am going to feel like a naked idiot in front of all those people. I am not a public speaker."

"Tell a joke," she said. "People like that."

"Like what? The only good jokes I know are dirty ones."

So she tried to think of one. She sat, fingers pressed to her eyes, concentrating. I wondered if the Wounded Daughters of Distant Fathers ever tell jokes at their meetings. Probably not, but then probably Wounded Fathers of Sardonic Daughters don't tell jokes either. "How about the one about the grasshopper who goes into the bar?" she said.

"You mean the one where the bartender says, 'Hey, we've got a drink named after you,' and the grasshopper says, 'Why would anyone name a drink Chuck?' You mean that one?"

"Except the grasshopper's name isn't Chuck, it's Bob," she said.

I drove Alida back to New York on the way to Washington. She had edited her second draft of the Balestrand book and was feeling fresh and eager to see the city. "You're awfully quiet," she said, as we cruised down the thruway. "What's going on with you?"

"I'm hopelessly in love with you."

"What's hopeless about that?" she said.

I was about to tell her, when she said, "You know what would be the nicest thing? If your parents could come for Thanksgiving." I said I'd get on the phone and invite them. "No, really," she said. "And if they can't come out here, maybe we should go there."

"I'm not sure that's a good idea," I said. "My father collects stuff like you wouldn't believe. Ever since he retired, he's been going to auctions full-time, and the house is a warehouse. It's depressing."

"We could stay with your sister Judy and her husband."

"He's the Lutheran pastor. Not the most stimulating company you'd hope to find. And you couldn't swear or say mean things about people. And if there was wine, I could only have one glass."

"I'd like to meet your family," she said. "One way or another."

"We could go up to Amherst and spend Thanksgiving with *your* parents. Wouldn't that be more fun?"

She let that hang in the air for a few miles. "Spending Thanksgiving with my parents would be like being in a bad play and not knowing your lines. They are divorced people living in a college town who have a lot of friends in common and are both active in saving the world and everything is quite civil between them except that they truly despise each other. My mother is an accomplished sufferer. She got the idea as a child that misery was a sign of intelligence. She had some kind of nervous breakdown when she was seventeen, and she has maintained it for forty years. My father is your classic passive-aggressive. They're two spiders weaving a gummy web around each other, constantly hunting each other, always escaping, and no, thank you very much."

My speech in Washington was a total wipeout, a lead balloon. I had imagined the worst but I wasn't prepared for it. I arrived at the hotel the night before, edited the speech, lay awake until three A.M., watching the Letterman show—in which a woman in a low-cut dress appeared with her tropical fish, who did cartwheels when they heard the "Washington Post March"—and then an old detective movie, low-budget; you could see the gangsters look up for the cue cards. Nothing is so somber and oppressive as a single room in a big convention hotel, the decor bland and yet hostile, as if designed by civil engineers or accountants, the immense TV, the hard bed that nobody ever had sweet dreams in. I awoke exhausted, hollow, at ten-thirty in the morning, showered, dressed, and went down to the ballroom, where important people stood and scanned the room for other important people. None of them looked at me for more than a second. I took my seat at the head table, along with some famous people I had never heard of, whose names I forgot immediately. They screeched and hugged, men slapped each other on the back, I pulled out my speech and looked at it. I picked at the lunch of veal medallions with potatoes au gratin and crème brûlée, and then the woman next to me—who produced segments of *All Things We Wish You Were Interested In*, as I think of it—started yakking about storytelling as the glue of community. She had come from a seminar that very morning at which Jonah Hadley had spoken on the subject. He was brilliant, she said.

"Jonah Hadley's Journal" runs every week on *All Things Considered*, an audio essay, a liberal sermon with sound effects. Hadley is a good writer in the worst sense of the word: humorless, tone-deaf, smug, predictable, all gesture, no smarts. He'll talk about sugar mapling in Vermont, and you hear the crunch-crunch-crunch of footsteps in the snow and the drip of the sap in the bucket and some extremely laconic Vermonters muttering something about syrup— they talk at a rate of twelve words per minute, which gives their mutterance an air of vast profundity—and then Jonah Hadley ties it all up with a whispery voice-over, something solemn and flabby about tradition as a force for sanity in our lives, a few sentences that manage to bring in de Tocqueville, Bob Dylan, the quest for the Holy Grail, the African-American heritage, a quote from an obscure Sufi poet, the crisis of male identity in the nineties, the myth of Sisyphus, and the Easter bunny.

The awards program began twenty minutes late, of course, and people at the head table were introduced, and some of them spoke, and the woman next to me stood up and said a few words for a long time, and then a man in a plaid jacket talked about the Wally Award for creative management. It was named for a station manager who died in 1986 and whose colleagues wanted to honor him because they felt bad about not having liked him much. I remember him. He had an ugly nose that looked like a yam stuck to his face and a laugh like a dying goose, and everyone avoided him like crazy, and now his name lives on in the form of a Lucite trophy. The speaker referred to the original Wally as "an innovator who was deeply committed to radio," a description that covers many sins indeed, and then everyone looked at me and clapped and I rose and was handed the Wally by a woman from NPR who smiled all the way up to her gums, and I took the speech out of my breast pocket and set it on the podium.

I looked up and smiled a sickly grin. I read the first paragraph: "There was a famous American naval captain of the War of 1812 who, when his ship went into battle, always wore a red shirt so that, if he was terribly wounded, his men would not see the blood and become demoralized. And now you know why I am wearing brown pants." There were titters in the audience, and a woman in a red suit sitting at a front table put her hand to the side of her face and rolled her eyes. Thus I launched into the speech I hoped would win me a job at the Ford Foundation, with a poop joke. Oh boy.

The speech was about how public radio, in the midst of the Balkanization of broadcasting, is creating an intelligent centrist voice, blah blah woof woof—I did a page of that and the crowd was quiet, and I wished I had told the joke about the engineer going to the guillotine. I plowed through another page, skipping over a long passage about a remote South American aboriginal tribe that knew nothing of toothbrushes or mirrors or cameras and was given a dozen cellular phones, which it incorporated into its religion as sacred totems and instruments of prayer—I skipped that and talked about the building of WSJO, and then I saw that the rest of the speech was laced with references to that South American tribe, so I had to backtrack and sort of summarize about the cellular phone thing, which took a while, and I fumbled around and the crowd got restless; they could sense what a flop it was, their blood lust was aroused, they exchanged knowing glances *(This is pretty awful, isn't it. Oh yes, this is a stink, all right)*—and suddenly I was in a gloopy passage about public radio as a telephone in a dark forest whereby the brave exchange their messages *(Where did this dreck come from?* I thought), and I felt thoroughly ashamed to be giving a speech this dumb and wasting everyone's time, I felt bitter shame rise in my throat, I was choking on it. I wanted to stop, if only I could find a stopping place.

And then the woman with the gums passed a note over to me: "Wind it up, thank you." That was pretty disconcerting. I flipped two pages and looked for the paragraph about the funding crisis in public broadcasting—it was somewhere in there. I searched, I skipped another page, and I looked up at the audience and grinned and said, "Almost to the end," and then there was a crash, as if someone had dropped a bowling ball.

It was Bob Edwards's head. He was sitting at the main table, two seats away from the podium, and apparently he had rested his chin on his hand and closed his eyes and fallen asleep, and then his elbow slipped and his head whacked the table: cups and saucers bounced, and people thought *coronary*, the voice of NPR's popular *Morning Edition* dead!—and then Bob Edwards raised his head and grinned, and people clapped! They practically gave him an ovation! I said, "And thank you very much for this fine award," and stuffed the speech in my pocket and turned and got out of there as fast as I could. Bob Edwards reached out to shake my hand, and so did the woman from *All Things Considered*, but I couldn't bear to talk to anyone. I had talked enough.

I fled through a door that said FIRE EXIT, which opened into a concrete-block stairwell, and ran three flights down the stairs, two steps at a time, thinking, *Dumb, dumb, dumb, dumb, dumb!*

One mark of a good general manager must be the ability to give a horse-hockey speech and shrug it off, but this hit me hard. I felt nauseated and dizzy. I sat down on the stairs in that silent stairwell and leaned my head against the steel rail and felt my heart pound and prepared to vomit. I thought, *You're forty-three years old and you're wasting your life. You're an old fart and you're losing your shirt on a restaurant and she is never going to marry you if she has any sense at all.*

And then the door opened above, and two men stepped into the stairwell and the door closed. One of them said, "What's wrong?" and the other said, "I saw McCullough coming and I don't want to talk to him, the big dummy. He's been a stone in my shoe for years, and now he's bad-mouthing my book, the big shithead."

I knew that voice. It was Jonah Hadley.

The first voice said, "You going up to the suite?"

Hadley said, "No, I had enough. I'm going home. Who was that gasbag they gave the Wally to? Geez."

"I dunno. Some jerk from New York. Pretty boring."

"New York City?"

"God, no. Upstate. He's from Minnesota originally."

They both snickered at the thought of Minnesota. Pretty hilarious to them. "Minnesota," said Hadley. "I should've guessed," and they chuckled. They talked about what a snoozefest the conference was, compared to other years, and my face burned. To be called a gasbag by Jonah Hadley! It was like being called ugly by a tree toad. If Hadley came down the stairs, I thought I might like to shove a finger in his chest and tell him his show is a blight on radio, but then the two of them slipped out the same door they came in.

I sat and felt blue and confused, and a moment later the door opened again and a woman called down, "John? John?" It was Susan Mack. I stood up quietly and tiptoed down the stairs and then my foot scraped and she cried, "John? Is something wrong?" and she came after me. I ran down five more flights of stairs, trying the door at each landing—each one locked—until I finally escaped into the parking garage. I dashed along the rows of cars toward a far wall that said ELEVATOR and followed the arrow around the corner and punched an Up button and waited, panting, perspiring, feeling like a jewel thief. I took the elevator up to the lobby, jammed with bodies, and made a sharp right turn toward the hotel elevators, where four security men stood, dazed from tedium. "You with the convention?" one of them asked. I nodded. A light flashed, a bell dinged, the doors opened, and I got on the elevator. I squeezed into the corner, behind a tall blonde in cool sunglasses, wearing articles of clothing not sold to members of the general public. Her bosom, visible on three sides, brushed against my arm; it felt like molded plastic. An immense shoulder bag hung under one arm, the sort that women in public relations carry, and she was talking on a cellular phone. "Everything's running late," she said. "Some creep stood up and talked about nothing for half an hour."

I went straight to my room, to clear out and head for home, and flopped down on the rumpled bed. I had sat here last night polishing the speech and added that painful phrase about the brave exchanging their messages. What a dumbbell! I threw my toothbrush and razor into the carry-on, stuffed in a dirty shirt and socks and underwear, and was almost to the door when the phone rang.

I picked it up, hoping for Alida, and it was Dean Baird at the college. "I'm on the speakerphone," he said grandly, "and President Postlethwaite is here with me." Then a loud crackling sound as the phone was moved. "John?" said the president in his richest, fruitiest voice. "Yes," I said. "John, I simply wanted to congratulate

you on behalf of everyone here—all of your friends—on this wonderful recognition of your achievements. It's richly deserved, and we
couldn't be prouder. Congratulations. I hope you're enjoying this
moment."

*Oh, Mr. President, if only you knew. What humiliations await us
all,* I thought. *I went to receive a prize, and I was struck stupid.* But I
said, "It's turned out to be a very good conference, and of course the
award is a nice compliment to the staff of WSJO and the faculty and
administration and everyone." A minute of aimless pomposity, and
we said goodbye.

Driving home that evening along the Hudson, the sun setting in
flames, I thought about my dumb life pushing a desk. What a wimpy,
wasted life it was, compared to my ancestors'. They worked in the
fields all day, and at night they built a blazing fire and drank and challenged each other to fight for the fun of it. A straightforward deal
compared to office politics. You didn't go to meetings and sit wooden-
faced in the downpour of bullshit; you drained your whiskey bottle
and stripped off your shirt and whooped, "*Whooooooo-haw!* What
fool among you dares to engage in a test of manhood with me, the
unbeatable Sigurd? *Whooooooo—yeow!* Look upon me, gentlemen,
and see what the standard shall be! A farmer and a Christian gentleman, and one who can beat the living crap out of any one of you.
Who would prove me wrong?" And then a younger man steps into
the circle and whips off his shirt and eyes you up and down and says,
"Sigurd, a wounded skunk on a country road has a greater understanding of trucks than you have of manhood," and with a ferocious
roar, the two of you fall into a clinch and roll in the dirt and sandburs
and pound each other, and finally, when it is enough, the others sepa-
rate you and stand you up and the bottle is passed and you grasp each
other's hands and grunt, "*Huh.*" Which means that you are true
brothers and your fight meant nothing at all except that you love to
fight.

Those men were giants compared to me. A privileged little pissant
who stands up and blathers in public—why hadn't I just said "Thank

you" and sat down?—and bankruptcy awaited me in Red Cliff, and my girlfriend had coolly declined to marry me. What disgrace awaited me in the future? Would I go on to host my own radio show like Jonah Hadley and be a privileged pissant with a vast pissant audience hanging on my every pissant utterance?

I imagined how it would be to pull over to the side of the road, write Alida a farewell note ("My darling, You had the misfortune to love a weak and spineless man, and I am sorry. I tried hard to resist this conclusion, but it is unavoidable. Please forgive me"), leave it on the dashboard, steal a boat from a marina, paddle out to the middle of the river, tie the anchor to my ankle, and pitch myself into the water and let my life be quietly obliterated. There would be a surge of adrenaline at first, and I would struggle like a dervish, but down I'd go, under the waves, and oblivion would come quickly: it was interesting to think of this, knowing that I wouldn't do it.

I switched on the radio. WSJO was in the midst of a major scream-fest, Wagner or the Berlioz Requiem or something, Amazons with their heads thrown back and their mouths open wide as grapefruit, their harpy hair stuck out, their spears in hand. I dialed around for something soothing, a girl with a guitar singing about the permanence of love—the Supremes, the Chiffons—and found W100, the Folks Next Door: two guys discussing field markings discovered in nearby Troy Township, the corn flattened and the earth dug up in concentric circles, no footprints to be seen; was it a visit from outer space, or kids doing wheelies? They were taking calls from listeners. Interesting to consider, the possibility of aliens reconnoitering in up-state New York. You never hear this sort of news on public radio, just people with advanced degrees talking about the need for retraining in the Information Age.

I cruised into Red Cliff, past the pizza joints, Al's used-car lot, Red Cliff County Trust, the Inn, the old brick storefronts, and onto Green Street, and into my garage, where I stuffed the speech in the garbage can. I stuck it down deep to discourage the garbageman from pulling it out and reading it. A gang of soccer girls, in sweatshirts and jeans, swaggered up the alley like sailors on shore leave. I walked to the house, sitting big and golden, a picture-book house with a pretty green lawn shaded by stately oaks, the neighbor's hedge, the screened porch with the wicker couch where I liked to lie and read the Sunday *Times*, and, off the porch, the flagstone terrace with the glass-topped table and chairs. *Why am I fruiting away my life?* I thought. *You'd think, looking at this place, that I had a few brains. What happened? Why did I go be a dork in front of five hundred people?*

I opened a beer, put Chopin on the CD player, Chopin the poet of lost dreams and failed ambitions. The pianist plonked a long melancholy chord and drifted into a meditation on defeat. Youth squandered on foolish arrogance, love accepted and carelessly discarded, the heart denied again and again, and then, *too late*, wisdom. I sat, elbows on the kitchen table, watching the sweep hand of the clock on the counter, and considered calling Alida, pressing my case, but I was too sad. I'd call up to unburden my heart, and she'd be standing by the door with her coat on, adjusting her earrings, blotting her lipstick on a tissue, gesturing to her waiting friends: *I'll be with you in a moment, as soon as I lose this guy.* No, I wouldn't call her now. I was afraid I might cry if I did.

I looked on the front porch for the mail, and there was the *Syracuse Reader*, a picture of me on the front, smirking, holding a wineglass. My house in the background. I felt light-headed. THE BEATINGS CONTINUE AT WSJO, it said.

The reporter was Sandra Welles, who had called me the day after my dinner with Jean. The story was a real torpedo. It referred to me in the first paragraph as a "cultural czar" and a "portly Lutheran Lothario" and to WSJO as "Uncle John's Cabin," and said I was a "self-appointed arbiter of taste" who was dictating a format of Classical Lite dinner music for fat cats rather than anything controversial or intellectually stimulating. It said that I had a "problem" with assertive women, being from the Midwest, and that I tried to "psychologically seduce" women in meetings and charm my way around them. I had paternalized the decision structure and made women feel afraid to speak up. It said that I had gotten drunk and groped women staff members at parties, and quoted a joke I told at a party. (A man goes into a bar and says to the bartender, "A beer for me. And let me buy one for that douche bag over there," and the bartender asks the douche bag what it will have and it says, "A vinegar and water.") It said that I censored a dramatization of *The Adventures of Huckleberry Finn* and that when it came to management skills, I took credit for the work of others, namely Marian MacKay.

My heart sank. These slanders had come from people who knew me. They worked at WSJO and had come to my house and drunk my wine and eaten my Chinese spareribs. There was a description of me sashaying around the backyard in a blue suit and a red T-shirt, leading the singing of songs, and it quoted someone as saying, "Seeing John Tollefson sing 'We Shall Overcome' is like seeing G. Gordon Liddy sing 'The Union Makes Us Strong'—the irony slaps you in the face."

I read it, every word, and then reread it, the blood pounding in my head. People I knew had rewarded my hospitality by sticking a fork in my back. "WSJO is a museum of European Music because to John, radio is decor, it's there to set a tone, not to communicate; it's like his golden house, his expensive grandfather clock, his $45 wine, his Finnish cabinetry. It's a soundtrack for the Gracious Life." And the photograph was taken by someone who came to my house as a guest. What treachery.

I walked to the sink and drank a glass of cold water and thought, *Let it pass. You have a good life, you're in love with Alida, be grateful. This is mouse droppings. Don't obsess about it. Sweep it up and put it out of your mind.* But the article loomed up, big as a barn.

Why would people be so angry and bitter toward me? I had built this station from the ground up and had managed it reasonably well, and what was their beef?

I went up to the bedroom and sat down at the computer. ("To the Editor: Your story about me is a parcel of lies and distortions, not worth a response, except to say what our almost 2,000 listener-members already know: that public radio is a public good. On a radio dial full of headbanger music and honkytonk and religious schmaltz and the steady whanging of commercials, public radio brings you worthwhile and even beautiful things. And it is a better thing to broadcast beautiful things than to publish lies about people. A royal flush beats a pair of threes. Sincerely, John Tollefson, General Manager.") And then I pressed Delete.

And then I wrote Alida a letter. ("My darling—I have decided I cannot give any more speeches about the mission of public radio or raise money for documentaries on menopause. I have become like those tomatoes you see in stores in February that are bred for long shelf life and taste like old tennis balls in your salad. They are not tomatoes, they are ideas of tomatoes. I am an idea of a person, a man in a blue suit. I need to have a life story. I want to do something noble, like get married and have babies. You're the one I want to have them with.") And I pressed Delete again.

The phone rang. It was Leland, back in Lake Wobegon.

"Tried calling you last night," said Leland. "Wanted to make sure you got home okay." He sounded as if he had been drinking for a while.

"I was down in Washington, giving a horseshit speech."

"Well, you chose the right city for it."

It was good to hear his voice. We talked about his youngest son, a senior at Lake Wobegon High and a center on the basketball team, and about my dad, and Leland said, "Did I ever tell you about a woman named Candy Legato? No? Well, this was after I came home from the army."

After high school, Leland enlisted in the army to avoid having to marry his girlfriend, Anne Marie Meister. He was stationed in Okinawa and wrote to her faithfully for two years, meanwhile discovering that he didn't really love her. He kept saying in his letters that he did, thinking repetition would make it true, but it didn't feel like love to him. It troubled him that he wasn't dying to get back to see her, because how could you not love someone so kind and good as Anne Marie?

"I came home and went to a bachelor party at the VFW in Millet. They said there was going to be a dancer, and we each dropped twenty bucks in the bucket. Everybody's hanging around, waiting, saying, 'This had better be good,' and around ten P.M. she drives up in a baby-blue Thunderbird, and she waltzes in and says hi and takes the money out and counts it and then she goes in the bathroom. She was in there thirty seconds and took off all her clothes and came out and danced. She had a tape machine. I forget what kind of music. Latin. Lot of percussion. She was pretty. She had big brown eyes. She was sort of tan all over, no bathing suit marks. Otherwise she was just real normal. Like girls we knew in high school except they weren't naked. She danced in a circle around the room and she sort of made conversation as she went—she'd say, 'So how's the corn crop? You think you'll get it in pretty soon? It's been kinda wet, though, hasn't it.' And guys said, 'Yeah, it's been real wet.'

"She danced up to me and she says, 'So how's your car running these days?' and I say, 'Oh, pretty good. Misses a little.' And she says, 'Oh, what do you think the problem might be?' and I'm looking at her and I'm thinking, *This is the girl of my dreams.* I asked her if she was dancing someplace else that night and she said yes, at the Boom Boom Room at the Romeo Motel on Highway Ten.

"So I went over there. You remember the Romeo Motel, right?"

"I saw it from the highway," I said. "I never actually went in there."

"You're kidding me."

"I didn't."

Leland cleared his throat. "Anyway, the Boom Boom Room was in this cinder-block building behind the motel. There were blue lights along the walls and a bar in the back and a stage and a sign that said 'No Dancing by Patrons' and about twenty dorky guys standing around drinking Singapore slings, nobody I knew, and then out came Candy Legato and danced. She was gorgeous. I felt really bad about her parading around naked in front of these clowns, and I hung round afterward and met her and twenty minutes later I was in bed with her in the motel. It cost me a hundred dollars and it took about ten minutes. I went out the door as fast as I could. So much for romance, I thought, give me marriage. I felt sick, I had tears streaming down my face, and the next day I asked Anne Marie to marry me."

"So what's the problem?" I said.

Leland sighed. "She found out about this little escapade from somebody. She said it's disgusting that I never told her. She said I could've given her a disease. She said she felt betrayed. Cheapened."

"She'll get over it," I said.

"I married her not knowing if I loved her or not," said Leland. "Which I guess was the best thing to do. I mean, where were the great women who were begging to be my wife, huh? In my dreams, that's where."

"I hope you're happy," I said.

"I've always been happy. I know how to be happy," Leland said. "Women can't do that for you, you know. A woman can make you happy for about ten minutes a week, and that's it. The rest of the time, you're on your own. So you still seeing that girl in New York?"

"Yes," I said.

"Lucky you," said Leland. "How come you don't bring her around to meet your old friends? Isn't she good enough for us?"

I said goodbye to Leland and trotted down to the kitchen and opened another beer and thought of the men in the Sidetrack Tap, that dark, warm cave of beer smell and smoke, the Norwegian bachelor farmers at their end of the bar, the gentry at the other, and the contempt that all of them shared for men like me, fools in suits doing rat's-ass work in offices, work that doesn't make a dime's worth of difference to anybody, the work of con artists, snake-oil salesmen; managers. My dad, back when he ran the grain elevator, came home from a visit to an agriconglomerate in Minneapolis and said, "Dullest people you ever saw—daylight is wasted on them." Some vice-president had invited him into his big carpeted office with plate-glass windows and a panoramic view of the Mississippi River gorge, and Dad was deeply unimpressed. "Young guy with a mustache, suit and a tie, shoes with tassels, poofy hair, dumb laugh, you know the type. Sits down and right away it's first names, like you're pals. Talks your head off, and— boy oh boy—there's nothing going on upstairs. The guy is all foam and no beer. All wax and no wick. A rocket without a payload."

That's me, I thought. *One more self-important lummox hurtling through space, trying to make an impact somewhere.* I didn't want to be a general manager anymore; I wanted to be something good. My

ancestors knew how to walk away from a bad deal. They looked
around them in Norway and saw it would be fifteen years before they
inherited a piece of the farm and it'd be a woeful and backbreaking
fifteen years and the piece would be too small. They did not agonize
over it, did not go into therapy, keep a journal, or call up talk shows;
they headed for America. When some of them got to the Midwest
and saw they had exchanged one bad deal for another, and then they
heard about gold in Alaska, chunks of gold that lay in streambeds for
a man to scoop up with his bare hands, they set down their tools in
the yard and walked away without hesitation, seeing their chance to
break out of the traces.

I sat in my decorator kitchen with its white Finnish cabinetry and
gray marble counters and thought of the fine meals Alida and I had
fixed and taken upstairs to bed and then were too busy to eat. I
bought the house four years before I met her, and I knew plenty of
loneliness here, when its elegance and warmth seemed to mock me,
and I would have plenty more loneliness when she bade me farewell.
The day was not far off now. I could imagine her calling on the
phone, and the coolness and resolution of her Hello would tell me
everything. She would be kind about it and tell me she loved me, but
she would not be so cruel as to leave things hanging: the door would
close, *click*, and that would be the end of it.

I had had three beers now, and felt dopey and morose. I toddled up
to bed and switched on the old Philco, a radio Dad gave me for Christmas years ago, and there was a woman calling in, whose daughter
created original silk-screen T-shirts, saying what a hard time talented
people have in our society and they never get the recognition they
deserve. A man called in to say he suffered from chronic leg cramps.
"I don't think people realize what a rough time people have who
don't quite qualify as handicapped. I mean, I have to park way at the
other end of the lot even though my leg hurts like heck sometimes,
so I can't attend as many athletic or cultural events as I'd like because
I never know if those leg cramps might kick in suddenly, and I'm just
saying I wish there were a little more public understanding."

The host thanked him for his comments, and then a guy with a
quiet whiny voice talked about how alone he felt in the world. *Hey*, I

thought, *the reason you're alone is that people who know you don't like you that much.* I thought of calling in and saying, "I wish there were more public understanding of guys like me. I like to walk around town in pink pants and lead my wolverine, Walt, on a leash and sing 'Whistle While You Work' in falsetto, and I am hurting no one by this, but people look at me as if I were a monster. I have a responsible job and pay my taxes and keep my lawn mowed, but because I dare to be an individual, people whisper about me behind my back. Why is life like this?" But before I could reach for the phone, I fell asleep.

TWELVE

Dark Lutherans

With the hundred crowns that he won from swimming in freezing water, my great-grandfather John Tollefson sailed from Norway with Signe and their little girls, Nissa and Anna, in January 1880. Two days out of Bergen, the ship ran into rough weather and the passengers lay belowdecks in the dark, pitching side to side, vomiting, moaning, terrified that God was about to drown them in the North Atlantic as punishment for having abandoned Norway. Steerage was two long halls with six rows of rough wooden bunks, four bunks to a tier, thin straw mattresses, three tin washtubs for chamber pots, the odor of excrement and urine and vomit and grease and terror. They arrived half dead in New York and rode a train three days to Minnesota, in a filthy coach with strange men leering at them, and spent February and March in a twelve-by-fifteen cabin ten miles from Lake Wobegon, with no amusement except checkers, an accordion, and a Bible. John purchased eighty acres north of town, rocky, covered with scrub pine, and worked all summer and fall clearing a few acres, and after Christmas, he rode the train north and worked as a cook in a

logging camp along the upper St. Croix River. Winter was the busy
season, when the lumberjacks could slide the logs over the ground
and onto the ice of the river to wait for the spring float to Stillwater.
Signe stayed home, locked in the cabin, praying, reading her Bible,
teaching her little girls that they must never speak to strangers lest
they be kidnapped and tortured.

He slept in the haymow of a log barn, where snow drifted in
through the cracks and the only heat came up from the horses in the
stalls below. He worked six days a week, and on Sunday he built a fire
under an iron kettle in the cook shack and heated water for his bath
and sat in it reading his Bible and jumped out and dressed quickly
and washed out the kettle and filled it with potatoes and boiled them
for dinner.

He returned home in April. Taking his lumberjack money to the
bank, he stopped along the way for a toot at the tavern, and a man
asked him if he knew the polka and he said yes, but it wasn't a dance,
it was a card game, and he was too proud to say he was unclear about
the rules, and he lost a hundred fifty dollars in ten minutes. So he lost
the land north of town. Signe was furious. She wept all night. She
said he had betrayed her trust in him, that they could never be happy
in America. He went to work sweeping floors in the tavern, saved his
wages, and learned a little English of the barroom variety. The place
was owned by a big red-faced man named Annenson, who bought the
bar because he'd been thrown out of every bar in town and he needed
a place to drink, but business was poor because he drank so much and
got belligerent and insulted the customers. In 1885, he sold out to
John for a low price.

John swore off drinking when he took over the tavern, which he
named the Harbor Bar. He was friendly to all kinds of people and
made them feel welcome. He was curious and loved to hear a story,
and if you told him a story, he never repeated it, nor did he sit in
judgment on it. He was in the tavern from noon to late at night,
drinking cold sassafras tea in a glass, a pleasant and hospitable man.
Other saloons were dark as tombs and stank of beer and urine, and
the Harbor had lace curtains at the windows and cloths on the tables
and rugs on the floors. It was a kindly institution, more forgiving

than the Lutheran Church, and if you came in the door sad and confused, you were treated as an equal, which you probably were already
and would soon be even more. If you cursed, you were required to
put a nickel in the kitty, which went to the orphans at Christmas, and
nobody minded donating to the orphans. Sometimes a man would
curse the damn orphans themselves with their damn running noses
and their damn fleas and their damn stink and to hell with all of
them, and put down a quarter, and feel better for it.

They were giants, his friends and customers, old Norsemen who
worked hard in the fields all day, came home at sunset, and ate boiled
potatoes and fried fish for supper, and on Friday nights they built a
bonfire in the meadow north of the church and drank whiskey, the
Lutherans on one side, the freethinkers on the other. As they got to
feeling good, they began to insult each other lavishly, showing off
their English with high-flown scatological allusions, and when they
used up their vocabulary, they started a game of baseball in the dark.
The bonfire was the infield and the pitcher threw the ball through the
flames and the batter stood over a flat rock for home plate and swung
at the pitch, and it was bare-handed baseball, no holds barred, and if
you hit the ball, you dashed for first base, taking the bat along with
you; there was no umpire to look out for you. And if you bunted and
the ball dribbled into the fire, an infielder dashed in and grabbed it.
You didn't bellyache about the rules, you just played. And if the
pitcher reared back and threw at your head as a spark flew in your
eye and you recovered consciousness on Sunday morning and your
head hurt, you didn't cry about it. That was *ball*, gentlemen, that's
how it was played. And after the game, they all came down to the
Harbor Bar, with the twenty-foot mural of naked goddesses on the
wall above the upright piano where a gin-crazed Bohemian rocked
back and forth and walloped out the polkas, and they drank and told
stories and made each other cry in the beer, and at five A.M. they
stood up and washed their faces and went out to work in the fields.

He owned the Harbor Bar for six years and sold it because the
pietists were after him, mainly his wife, Signe. She was one of the
Dark Lutherans, of the Haugean persuasion, who were in the majority in town. All of the Norwegians were Lutherans, of course, even

the atheists—it was a Lutheran God they did not believe in—but a chasm separated the Hauge Synod, or Dark Lutherans, who believed in the utter depravity of man and separation from worldly things and strict adherence to the literal truth of Scripture, and the Old Synod, or Happy Lutherans, who believed in splashing some water on babies and confirming the little kids and then not worrying about it, just come every Sunday and bring a hot dish. The Dark Lutherans said, You fool yourself, O Man, if you say God is in you, for behold you are a Whited Sepulchre and a Heap of Chaff and your end is near and it will not be a happy one. The Happy Lutherans said, in essence, God loves you and be glad that He does and can you please coach basketball this year?

The two factions were divided over the role of women and the color of the sky and how to make coleslaw, and they divided over the issue of "Will we recognize each other in heaven, or will our spiritual forms not have our earthly features?" A Dark Lutheran would say, My sainted grandmother is waiting for me beyond the pearly gates, free from suffering and care, and if you're saying I won't know her, you are ignorant of Scripture, you infidel, and to hell with you; and a Happy Lutheran might reply, It's not important to me one way or another, but if you think your face is something God would allow in a place of perfect bliss, maybe you ought to take another look. The pastor said that they should leave this matter with the Lord; but the Facial faction (or, as they called themselves, the Recognized) looked down on the Cloud faction (or, as they called themselves, the Enlightened) as secret Unitarians, and the Enlightened looked on the Facials as illiterate peasants who saw God as a Divine Grandpa serving up herring on rye bread and singing lullabies in Norwegian.

John Tollefson walked away from the church when the congregation split over facial recognition—he had no taste for religious bickering—but Signe believed in recognition. She also held with the Dark Lutherans in their denunciation of alcohol, and when he came home with the smell of beer in his hair, she refused to sleep with him. Tobacco, fiction, dancing, bright clothing, fancy hairdos, worldly attainments, pride in any form: the Dark Lutherans were down on all of it, but above all they were opposed to moderation and compromise in any form. The Brainerd Declaration of 1888 said: "We will not speak in moderation. We are in earnest; we will not equivocate, we will not retreat, we will be heard. Wrong is wrong. Untrue is untrue. The man who would write untruth, the woman who adorns herself with baubles, the dandy in his gaudy vest and scarf, the couple who indulge in lascivious displays of carnal dance—the love of God is not in such persons. And when they come to the gates of heaven, God will look them in the face and say, 'I do not recognize you, O unfaithful servant.' "

The Dark Lutherans held the Truth, and thus were rejected by the world, and their isolation was proof of their righteousness. They sang:

The gift to be righteous is the gift to say no,
And depart from the place you should not go,
Renouncing the company of unclean souls,
And thus we are added to the saintly rolls.
Deny, deny, shall be our delight,
And by separation to come out right,
And wait for the day when we all shall die
And find true fellowship by and by.

The Dark Lutherans were strict about dress, which should be modest—no trousers for girls, not even infant girls—and about the Sabbath: after church, you remained in a devotional mode for the rest of the day, sitting in a room with shades pulled, perusing a commentary on Habakkuk and Obadiah. The Happy Lutherans said, "Oh, what harm would it do to read *David Copperfield* on Sunday, or play baseball, or hear a Mozart sonata?" and the Dark Lutherans cried, "Do you care so little for Him who shed His life's blood for you that you cannot spare one day out of seven to think of Him and of Him only? Is this too much to ask?"

It was a miserable argument, and the Happy Lutherans lost, of course—how militant could you be, arguing for kindness and mercy? Could you screech and yell at the legalists, demand that they be tolerant, pound the table, threaten them with damnation if they didn't get themselves a sense of humor? One by one, most of the Happy Lutherans migrated south or westward to California, where they prospered. They were polite, able to get along with others (they had not gotten along with people back home, but that was because they knew them too well), they were steady workers and cheerful, and they accepted the California climate as God's gentle blessing on them.

The Dark Lutherans throve in a cold climate, believing that adversity and suffering were given as moral instruction, and so was sickness—the Darks were never much for medicine beyond the use of cold compresses and purgatives. Their religion was part Christianity and part ancient Nordic precept that the gods are waiting to smack you one if you have too good a time. Better to anticipate disaster. So they believed in the inevitability of suffering. If life was not miserable now, it would be eventually, so you might as well get an early start on the weeping and gnashing of teeth.

As often happens when great victories are won, however, all that the victors fought for quickly faded away. Absolute adherence to the truth is easier for people in remote rural areas, and as the roads improved, extending the opportunities for sin, nobody gave a fig about the recognition issue. It was dead as a mackerel in the moonlight. Soon alcohol snuck in by the back door, and half the Lutherans were snitching a beer here and there, and in the twenties, dancing came back, and after World War II, all of the strict rules for observance of the Sabbath were forgotten, and then television arrived, and then it was all over.

It was hard on the Dark Lutherans. They didn't really believe in forgiveness, so if one of their number fell into worldliness, there was no way back. A young man snuck away to a dance and embraced a buxom young woman as the saxophones played "Vaya con Dios," and specific carnal thoughts sprang to his mind—her green taffeta gown seemed to say to him, "It's so tight in here. Do you know what a clasp is? Do you know what a zipper is?"—and he escorted her to his car and they dashed toward the Peaks of Passion and leaped over the Cliff of Ecstasy onto the Hard Rocks of Remorse: that young man could never return to the fold and be one of the Chosen again. He had to go to

Minneapolis, or to California and the Garden of Eden Synod, where the sign in front of the church didn't say *Repent, O Wretched Man;* it said *Mistakes make better artists of us all as we weave new patterns in the fabric of our lives.* All that Dark Lutheran orthodoxy accomplished, in the end, was a dramatic loss of population.

One freezing February day, Great-Grandfather John was summoned home: his wife and daughters were sick with influenza. For weeks, he nursed them, and his wife looked up from her bed accusingly and said, "This is because of your infidel tavern. When will you listen to God? Must we all die before you change your ways?" She recovered, but they lost the two girls, who died on the same day and were buried in the Lutheran cemetery under a tombstone inscribed: "Below this humble monument there lies / Muzzled with dust, their souls in Paradise / Our cherished daughters quickly fled / To the immortal living from the dead."

In the spring, John sold the tavern—he thought Prohibition was imminent—and he took up bricklaying and stonemasonry, and the following December, Einar was born, who became the father of Byron, who was the father of John the Younger. John and Signe, after the deaths of Nissa and Anna, had six children in all: Einar, Hilda, Otto, Maren, and twin boys, Haakon and Harald. Einar grew up to be his siblings' taskmaster and treated them cruelly, being a very dark Lutheran indeed, and when they came of age, they all made their escape, the girls by marriage, the boys by migration.

Haakon went to Minneapolis and found the city exciting, full of theaters and ballrooms and restaurants, Swedish vaudeville houses on Cedar Avenue, the bars hopping every night, pretty girls strolling the streets in their stylish coats, and he found work as a printer's apprentice at a Norwegian-language publisher, Norske Bog, and learned the book business. Before he was twenty-five, he started his own company, Solskin, which published dime novels in Norwegian and Swedish for the servant-girl market. Norske Bog published inspirational books, but Solskin published novels in which blond men with bulging biceps held girls closely and breathed on them, and Haakon became wealthy quite young, and married an Episcopalian, built himself a mansion on Lake Minnetonka, learned to sail a boat, and got himself a St. Paul mistress. He wrote to Harald that he had wanted to escape Lake Wobegon and its "drunken hayseeds and angry old biddies and yahoos who try to cure goiters with mustard plasters and dumb clucks who sit and cry about seeing their mothers someday in heaven" and that in Minneapolis he found "go-getters and live wires" and "fellows who know how to have a good time."

Harald followed Haakon to Minneapolis and got work with a big fruit wholesaler and was sent to California to manage an orange grove north of Los Angeles. He did well in the West. He ran the orange grove and also, being youthful and well-built, got lucrative jobs in motion pictures. He played a Canadian Mountie in a Mae Swenson picture, *Tanya of the Tundra*, and looked fierce and swung a whip as soap flakes swirled around him and stagehands rocked the sled, but he found movie stars unpleasant, a bunch of shallow neurotics with the personalities of water buffalo—and then a director insisted that he color his hair, and Harald walked off the job. He felt that hair coloring was unmanly. He married the woman who was Pearl White's stunt double on *The Perils of Pauline* and was tied to the railroad track, and he changed his name to Harold Thompson. They had four children, Alma, Frieda, Dahlia, and Murray, and became disciples of Anna May Mowray, the founder of Radiantism, who received visions from friendly beings on the planet Jupiter, which she published in *Vast Essence Known Minutely*, the bible of Radiantism, whose cornerstone was nudity. Dropping your clothes was her answer to just about everything. And when they became too old for that, they became Universalists.

Harald's children prospered, of course, and built bungalows with red tile roofs and joined country clubs, and *their* children, of course, were completely de-Lutheranized and 100 percent free of any Wobegonian elements whatsoever and wouldn't have known a herring from a lefse, and if they ever looked back at Minnesota, they thought of it as a barren frozen plain populated by cranks and fanatics and people of no imagination whatsoever.

THIRTEEN

Thanksgiving

It was out of the question that Alida could get a job at St. James and move to Red Cliff and marry me. I knew about the St. James history department. In the midst of the Age of Information are certain small resistant pockets of feudalism, where old dukes rule with an iron fist, their reptilian eyes and great hairy nostrils searching out heresy and insubordination, and the department was run by such a tyrant. Why should Alida leave Columbia, where people loved her, to join a chain gang at St. James?

So one week, I looked for a job in New York, and the only offer I got was from Harry's Shoes on Broadway. "We have a lot of liberal arts graduates selling shoes," the manager said, and he quoted me a salary figure somewhat higher than what I made as manager of WSJO.

But my ego is much too delicate to let me take the foot of a stranger in hand and slip a saddle shoe on it. It would wear me down. Even for the love of a woman as adorable and dazzling as Alida. You would think that a man could make a small career sacrifice—give up his oak desk and his Botticellian secretary and kneel on the floor and sell shoes—but no, I knew I couldn't do it.

And it was true, our arrangement was the envy of our friends, especially friends who were couples, like Ginger and Neil. She was a model, skinny, with a pouty mouth and big brown eyes and breasts the size of Christmas cookies, and he was a writer at *Sports Illustrated*, and they married and two years later the light had gone out of their eyes. She had no idea how much he loved to watch football and baseball, he had no idea what it took to keep up that fabulous face and figure, and Neil said to me once, "You two certainly have it figured out, don't you?" and Ginger said to Alida, "I don't know why we didn't do what you guys did."

Two nights after my Wally debacle in Washington, I called home and invited my parents for Thanksgiving. "We'd love to come, of course we would," said Mother. "We'd love to meet her. I'm sure she's lovely. Does this mean you're going to marry her?"

I explained that we loved each other but weren't sure we'd be successful at marriage.

"Oh, there's no such thing as a successful marriage," she said. "There are marriages that give up and marriages that keep on trying; that's the only difference."

Mother said she would discuss Thanksgiving with Byron. "You know how he is," she said. Indeed, I did. Dad believed that Lake Wobegon is the center of sanity in the world and travel only reminds you of it, and once you have it firmly in mind, who needs reminders? And who would take care of the house? What if the furnace shut off and the pipes burst?

Dad was a Dark Lutheran. In my youth, he served for two years as scoutmaster of Lake Wobegon Troop No. 12, and when his term was up, the Scouts breathed a sigh of relief. He was a nervous wreck on camping trips, always counting and recounting our heads, startled at any sound in the underbrush. None of the Scouts believed in bears, but Dad did, and rabid skunks, bad water, escaped lunatics, falling tree limbs, tetanus, a whole shopping list of disaster. For him, the Boy Scout motto, "Be Prepared," was an invitation to paranoia. Sleepiness alarmed him, and when our troop camped out in winter, snuggled into our sleeping bags, crowded together like a pack of dogs, boys would wake up, terrified, in the dark—someone was shaking them. It was Dad, our scoutmaster, making sure we had not perished of exposure.

Mother called two days later and said they could come, but only for a few days. Dad was on the town council and there was a property tax increase coming to a vote sometime in November, and the Christmas party at the grain elevator, and of course he had to supervise the flooding of the skating rink.

A short visit would be fine, I said. Just fine. Frankly, I found it painful to be in the same room with Dad: we always had been skittish around each other, and any conversation was like ice cubes on a hot griddle, a series of non sequiturs. Dad was always walking out of the room in the middle of someone's sentence, yelling, "I can still hear you!" as he went and took a leak or got a book off the shelf with some paragraph in it that he had to read you in rebuttal. He could never come into your home without finding fault somewhere: a light fixture—how much had you paid for it? why had you gotten this kind? how long had your toilet been leaking like that? why did you buy those expensive towels? what was wrong with ordinary towels? He got on my nerves something fierce. "You stay as short as you like," I told Mother.

"How is your restaurant coming, by the way?" Mother said.

"It's still in the unfounded-hope stage," I said.

The next day, I got in my car and drove north, past the entrance to Taughannock Falls State Park, past rows of dry corn wrapped around the hills, to the farm, the white frame Victorian mansion in the grove of oak and maple and ash, surrounded by rolling fields, and the sign THE GIBBS FARM—DINING ROOM AND THRESHERS' HALL—OPENING FOR MEMORIAL DAY. It was October, time to paint a new sign.

I pulled into the drive, gravel crunching under the tires, and my heart soared, as it always did on coming here, and the closer I got to the house, the handsomer it looked. The turret and gables shone fresh and white above the trees, and the screened porch looked brand-new. The lawn was mowed to perfection, the hydrangea bloomed in the rock garden. Two old sheds had been torn down, and the big red barn was under reconstruction; the double hanging doors had been removed, and I could see the scaffolding inside and smell sawdust. The windmill had been restored and the old stone silo. I walked up to the house and pressed the brass button and heard the bell clanging deep within and stepped into a maple-paneled room with a pressed-tin ceiling salvaged from a storefront in nearby Aurora. Only the back entry, but the floor was tiled in black marble. Steve did good work and used the best materials; that was the problem. I walked into the kitchen, refitted with commercial ranges and ovens, a walk-in cooler where the maid's room had been, a circular steel staircase down to the wine cellar.

Steve came into the room without my hearing him and stood a few feet behind me. "What do you think?" he said.

I jumped. Blood rushed to my head. I turned and said hello and stuck out my hand. "Hoping to open up this place," I said. "Have we ordered the tables and chairs?"

Steve said he was waiting for Howard's approval on a design.

"Can't you buy them from a catalogue?"

"We don't want to fill up the place with junk."

"It's a restaurant. It's not a crafts exhibit."

Steve tossed his head back and chuckled. "In ten years, we'll look back on this fall as the darkness before the dawn," he said. He put a hand on my shoulder. "I'll never forget, crossing the Atlantic once from Gibraltar to Rio, one day of terrible weather after another, and you could sense land a couple days before you got there. The sailors called those days the shark days, because that was the dangerous time, when you could be distracted by the longing for land and a cable could snap and the next thing, your head was lying on the deck, cut clean from your body. That happened on our ship. A guy from Kenya. Anyway, we're in the shark days here, man. Gotta keep our cool. How do you like the porch?"

We walked through the house and onto the porch, which was beautiful, of course, and headed across the yard toward the barn. Steve's crew lived on the site, in a settlement of camper vans and tents and Airstream trailers drawn up in a circle in the barnyard, around a fire pit with log benches, and a sweat lodge made of canvas and birch logs, and a thirty-foot pole of stripped pine sunk into the ground, with two loudspeakers hanging from it. The settlement was deserted. "They took the day off and went to the movies," Steve said. "You want to take a sweat bath?" I declined.

The renovation of the house seemed to be finished, but according to Howard, the barn had unforeseen problems—the beams were infested with carpenter ants, the foundation was bowed out in back. We stepped into the barn. The scaffolding rose to the roof. A curved wall made of ash and birch strips, steamed and bent, hand-sanded and refinished and rubbed, stood alone in the middle, as if it were a sculpture.

"That's the divider between the entry and the dining room?" I asked.

Steve nodded. "What do you think?"

I ran my hands over it. "If I knew more about carpentry, I'm sure I'd be dizzy with admiration. But my concern is: when do we open?"

Steve said, "That's interesting you ask that. I remember the winter I was living in Aalto's workshop in Haukipudas, on the coast north of Oulu, and Aalto, who was a man of great simplicity, who himself slept on a mat and bathed in ice-cold water every morning and ate no meat and whose one indulgence was his pipe—he smoked this aromatic black tobacco; a cloud of his smoke drifted behind him wherever he went; it was like a sort of a blessing—he said once to me, 'Wood is memory, Steve.' I liked that: Wood is memory."

Steve did not speak English in sentences, he spoke in puffs of smoke, and at first I had thought it might be due to brain damage from some long-ago drug experience, some white powder in a Baggie, and after you snort it, you no longer think in terms of subjects and predicates; you think in terms of auras, nimbuses, coronas, sparks, bright-green dots. If you asked Steve when a project would be finished, he told you a story about rice farmers in India. He had stories about Jerry and Alaska and Ireland and the blues and the culture of Lapplanders and the mysteries of working wood, and getting a straight answer out of him was like pushing spaghetti uphill.

"Can we talk about that cornucopia for a minute?" I said. "This is where it goes, in front of this wall, right? Right. Listen. We've got to keep the costs reasonable on that. It's in the budget at five grand. That means we can't spend thirty or fifty or a hundred on a cornucopia. You get me?"

"Hey." Steve put his hand on my shoulder. I stepped back, and the hand fell off. "I want to show you something," he said. On a sheet of plywood sitting on two sawhorses was the blueprint for the Threshers' Hall, and Steve took a carpenter's pencil and showed how the barn would be configured into a boat-shaped structure, with broad screened decks along the sides rising to a handsome prow in front. "The boat motif is interrelated to the cornucopia motif—it has to do with the relationship of travel and sustenance, the shipping vessel and the serving vessel, which of course are Time and Space, and this whole vision of America as a sea, a sea of grass that was turned into a land of wheat. Thus, the Threshers' Hall That's the heart and soul of the thing. The land." Steve walked to a window, covered with plastic, and looked out. He turned. "I've got a lot invested in this place," he said, quietly. "My heart, for one thing. My soul, for another. I fell in love with this farm. This farm is what the Indians call a spirit-place. I'm not about to cheapen it. I want it to have the power to move people and be a life-changing environment."

He stood about two feet from me, his hands on his hips.

"I'd like to get the place open," I said. "As far as I can see, you're the one who's standing in the way of that. Why?"

"I can't discuss this in an adversarial way, John. I'm not a lawyer, I'm not interested in picking a fight with you. I'm an artist." Steve looked at the floor.

"You weren't hired as an artist," I said. "You were hired as a carpenter."

Steve looked up and grinned at me. "So you got a bonus."

The WSJO budget was due in November, and I had to find an ad salesman for the program guide, and hire a new announcer, and get bids on rewiring the tower—gophers had eaten the cables three times in the past two years—and now, at the dean's urging, Marian MacKay had spent six weeks getting WSJO on the World Wide Web. It was crazy, having a Web site. One more meaningless gesture in the world. Everyone I knew was reeling from the pressure of faxes, answering machines, computers—the data pouring in, paper mounting up, messages to be returned, E-mail to answer, Web sites and news groups to check: the rec.complaints group, alt.depression, alt.vague longings. Somehow, instead of simplifying people's lives, technology had managed only to speed up the rate of harassment.

I sat down at his big desk one morning and flipped through the stack of mail, and there was a form letter from Steve, printed in block letters on handmade paper, a letter addressed to "Friend" about cabinetry as a religious exercise, with a haiku ("The pine board is split, / The part I nailed to the wall, / The part I could not") and something about how one must relinquish control in the act of building and build "that which is already there but cannot be seen," and finally the announcement that Steve would lead a two-week seminar at Bard College on spirituality in modern design, called "The Cloud in the Tree," tuition $1,200 for the general public. And at the bottom, at the end of Steve's biography, after mentioning his work with Aalto Maarimakki, whose work was in the Museum of Modern Art, it said: "Currently working to complete the Lake Cayuga Meditation Center near Ithaca, New York."

I picked up the phone and called Howard. I got the answering machine. "Howard, this is John," I said. "Is there something I should know about the farm?"

Mother and Dad arrived the day before Thanksgiving, having driven for two days, thirteen hours a day, in order to save on a motel. Dad had driven the entire distance himself, Lake Wobegon to Red Cliff (he could not endure being a passenger with Mother driving, it terrified him), so he was pale with exhaustion, as well as highly nervous about meeting Alida. He came stiff-legged up the walk, carrying two ancient suitcases, shook hands with her at the front door, said,

"Howdy," and walked past her and looked at the ceiling, as if checking for water stains, then turned to me and said, "How much did you pay for this place?"

"I got it cheap, thanks to moral turpitude," I said. "Alida, this is my father."

"We met," said Dad. Alida and Mother exchanged a ladylike embrace and a kiss on the cheek, and Alida asked her how the trip had been.

"No problems," said Dad. "Smooth sailing all the way." He noticed the Wally Award sitting on the hall table. "What's that for? Bowling?" He examined the back of it, checking its durability.

"That is a coveted prize in public-radio management," I said.

"Never heard of it," he said. He inspected the living room and the dining room and poked his head into the kitchen. "Come in and sit down," I said.

"Been sitting for two days," said Dad.

They paraded upstairs, to be shown the guest room, and Dad glanced at the bookshelf in the upstairs hall. "You read all these books?" he asked. He said to Mother, "Some people accuse *me* of keeping junk around."

In the bedroom, he tested the mattress, and pulled the blind to make sure it worked, and flicked the light switch on and off. Then he was up and off to the bathroom, where he inspected the sink and the shower. "You tile this yourself?"

I asked, "Is the tile crooked?" No response.

Dad peered into the master bedroom, noticed the wall-to-wall carpeting, and asked if there was something wrong with the floor.

"No," I said. "Why?"

"Just asking," said Dad.

"Byron," said Mother, taking him by the arm. "Come and sit in the kitchen with me." She said to Alida, "The house is so lovely. I've been imagining how it might look, and it's even lovelier." She steered Dad downstairs toward the kitchen, and then he decided to look at the basement, seeing as the door was right there, and he descended the stairs. We could hear him roaming below, moving things, stopping to inspect, clucking to himself.

"He gets restless, cooped up in the car," Mother said to Alida.

A glass bowl of inky-black marinade sat on the white counter, six tuna steaks swimming in it, and a pot of small red potatoes simmered on the stove. The round kitchen table was set for four, the big white china plates with blue salad bowls on a white cloth with a border of blue and green flowers. A bottle of Beaujolais was open, four glasses next to it, and two baguettes baked in the oven. A bouquet of pink roses sprouted from a narrow blue vase on the cooking island, next to an open cookbook. Alida sat on the counter, in a red sweater and blue jeans, her long legs dangling down, barefoot, and Mother, in her beige pants and jacket, sat at the table, sideways on a chair, facing the stove, and I, in jeans and white shirt, stood next to Alida and poured the wine.

"John says you teach American history," said Mother. "I can't imagine a more fertile field."

"Nor can I," said Alida. "The nineteenth century. It's so much more interesting than the twentieth."

"I always thought that too," said Mother, "but I never dared say it."

"You wouldn't happen to have any beer?" said Dad, in the doorway. He had scouted the entire house, upstairs and down, made a couple dozen aimless remarks about things, gotten on my nerves, and now seemed as if he might climb in the car and drive back to Lake Wobegon. The man was relentless.

"Of course," I said, and opened the refrigerator.

"You wouldn't happen to have a Wendy's," said Dad.

"That's a local beer; they don't sell that out here."

"Oh," said Dad. "Well, that's okay."

I asked if a Seneca beer would do. "No, that's all right," said Dad. "I'll just have wine." He glanced at Alida. "I don't want to be a problem," he said.

I reached up into the liquor cabinet and pulled down a bottle of bourbon. "You care for this?" I said. Dad said, "Sure," and I poured him a slug with a couple of ice cubes and passed the glass to him and we all clinked glasses.

"Happy Thanksgiving," I said. "Happy Thanksgiving," said Alida and Mother. "Happy landings," said Dad. He tossed down his bourbon and set the glass on the counter. "I saw that picture in the dining room of you and Hillary Clinton shaking hands," he said. "I didn't know you were a Democrat."

"Been a Democrat ever since I knew better," I said. "I thought most grown-up people were."

"That's just what a Democrat would think," Dad said. "They are not people who keep in close touch with reality, if you ask me."

He squinted at Alida, his hairy brows wrapped around his eyeballs. "Democrats are people who trust in the goodness of bureaucracy," he said.

"Well, that's who I am, a good bureaucrat," I said.

My father believed in turning off lights that were not in use, and I heard him later, after dinner, descending the stairs to switch off the hall light and the light on the stove in the kitchen. While downstairs, Dad also turned the thermostat down. I thought it was cheerful to leave lights on and to keep the house warm. But I remembered my father's litany from years ago—I can repeat it in my sleep: "It's seventy-two degrees in here! What's the matter with you people that you can't put on a sweater? If people would just remember to close the door behind them, but no, every time I turn around, there's lights blazing away and a door wide open. How many times do I have to tell you to close the door? It's winter, for crying out loud. How much intelligence does it take to close a door? We're trying to heat the whole outdoors around here. Do you have any idea what the price of fuel oil is? It's staggering, that's what it is. I don't know where you kids think we get the money to pay for it. Is anybody listening to me?"

Dad was restless all Thanksgiving Day. He drank a cup of coffee from fresh-ground beans and complained that it was too strong. He riffled through the *Times,* but there was nothing interesting in it. He tuned in to a football game on TV and couldn't keep his mind on it. He and Mother went for a walk and got lost. Alida was locked up with her Balestrand book, and I spent the day cooking. I love Thanksgiving dinner. If you limit yourself to one turkey a year, the smell of it roasting in the oven is so rich, so familiar and overwhelming, you want to baste it every few minutes so you can drink in the aroma of crisping skin and crackling butter and the white meat simmering. Dad spent half the morning in the basement, repairing a bookcase that I was intending to throw away. Mother made the stuffing, a wild rice and walnut and sausage concoction, and lay down for a nap. Alida came downstairs, furious about the computer, which had lost a block of writing she was trying to move; she was almost in tears. "It was good," she said.

"Write it again, and it'll be even better," I said. "Trust me."

"I do like your parents," she said. "In case you thought I didn't. I do."

Thanksgiving evening, after dinner, after the table was cleared and the dishes were done, the four of us played gin rummy in the kitchen. Two candles flickered on the cooking island; their reflections shone in the glass cupboard doors. The Bach Brandenburg No. 3 played quietly, the cards slapped on the table. Looking at his hand, arranging his cards, Dad asked Alida if she knew what a privy was.

"An outhouse," she said.

"Exactly. You ever hear of privy-tipping?"

She hadn't.

"It's history," he said. "Nobody does it anymore. But we did it when I was a kid."

Dad had undergone a great mellowing. He had enjoyed a glass of champagne before dinner and a glass of red wine during dinner and now was on his second glass of champagne and was somewhat drunk, a remarkable sight—I had never witnessed this before. It seemed new to Dad too. He became vivacious all of a sudden. He discovered a Cary Grant quality within himself that hadn't been there an hour earlier. He shuffled the cards and dealt them with a practiced air, he caressed Mother's hand and hummed an old tune. He said, "John, my boy, this is an excellent wine," and he swished it in his mouth and swallowed it and chuckled in a suave way. Alida and I held hands under the table, and when the old man said, in a stagy voice, "Aye, that was many and many a year ago, in a kingdom by the sea," she squeezed my hand to remind me to be nice and not laugh.

Dad pulled a pencil and a crumpled sheet of paper from his jacket pocket and drew a circle with a sort of ulcer protruding into it and squiggly lines above it and said, "This is the lake, and this is Trapper's Point, on the east side of the lake, the side away from town." He made an X. "That's town.

"There was an old logging road that ran into the woods above Trapper's Point, and back in the twenties about six guys built fishing shacks on the point. Torben Saetre was the instigator of it. He was a Republican and married to Ruby, a yellow-dog Democrat, and over the years they pretty much came to despise each other. She said she didn't have anything against marrying a Republican, but she'd never be friends with one. When Franklin D. Roosevelt came into office, they pretty much gave up speaking to each other. Anyway, Torben got the idea of building himself a refuge on Trapper's Point, and he was joined by five other men, in similar situations, and they built these shacks. On weekends, they'd drive out to the end of that logging road and then hike down the hill to where the shacks were.

"The shacks weren't at all like cabins are now. They were one-room affairs, with a table and chairs and a bunk bed, and a woodstove and a pump and a sink with a slop bucket under it, and out back was a privy, a one-holer. And that was all. Pretty primitive. Their wives took one look at the shacks and that was it. No, thanks. Goodbye. Which of course was exactly what these men wanted.

"It was stricter in town back then than it is now. The Lutherans and Catholics didn't mix in town, but on Trapper's Point, they could and did. Men would go out there and drink a good deal, and of course in town they were pretty much dry. They would go out for a weekend, and play poker, drink whiskey, smoke their cigars, and have a good time. The one thing they never did was fish.

"Torben had a shack and Mr. Hoffman and Mr. Starr, the editor of the paper, and Mr. Diener, who was superintendent of roads, and Ralph's dad, and my uncle Svend had a shack too, though he didn't spend much time out there. I remember as a kid I could hear jazz music from that side of the lake late at night, and I asked my mother what it was and she said somebody was giving a party.

"Well, there wasn't much that went on in town that I didn't consider my personal business, and when I was twelve or thirteen and I had figured out how to sneak away at night and not get caught, I got a bunch of kids together to go over there and investigate. We had formed a club, called the Detective Club, and we slathered mosquito repellent on ourselves and got on our bikes and rode around the lake and up that logging road to where they had parked their cars and we lay up there in the bushes and looked down the hill and were quite amazed at what we saw.

"There was a bonfire on the beach and about fifteen or twenty men, about half of them naked as jaybirds, passing the bottle around. There was a Victrola on a kitchen chair playing a ragtime tune, and they were all laughing and carrying on. Some of the naked ones were running in and out of the water, chasing each other and throwing mud and whatnot.

"There were four of us boys up there crouched in the bushes, and none of us said a word; we were all shocked at how dumb they looked. They were drunk and acting like fools, and to us, it was just utterly disgusting.

"One of them had deer antlers on his head, and a couple of them were having a sword fight with two sticks with melted marshmallows on the ends. One of them was trying to throw a pair of shoes up into a tree. It was not the way we expected our elders to behave. And when we saw Mr. Starr come down the path toward the privy, carrying a lantern, we decided to take matters into our own hands, and we crept forward down the hill, as quiet as could be.

"Mr. Starr went into the privy, and he checked around for spiders and shut the door and settled himself, and we closed in and put our shoulders to the back of the privy, and we listened. He sat in there straining and fizzing, and just when he started to cut loose, we gave a heave, and the old guy felt the world turn, and the privy went tumbling forward onto the door, and there was a poof of flame when his lantern broke, and he came squirting out the hole as fast as he could.

"He came out headfirst, and he fell in the pit, and when we turned around to look—we were all the way back up the hill by then—he was kneeling on the ground, covered with slime, bawling like a calf.

"We were about to get on our bikes and head home, but I said, Wait. About ten of them came running up from the beach, and somebody took him down to the lake to wash off, and the others lifted the privy up and set it back over the hole.

"And then Torben looked up the hill, and he said in a loud voice, 'You boys go home now, or I'll make you wish you had.' Well, I had a lot of respect for Torben. He ran the grain elevator—he had the job that later I got—and he was one of the shakers and movers in town. He was a county Republican chairman, he'd been to St. Paul and met the governor, and he was just about the most important man in town, but on the other hand, he was drunk and he had these antlers on his head. He had grabbed a shotgun. Next to him was a fat man with a tablecloth wrapped around him. He yelled, 'We mean it, you little bastards.'

"I didn't think he had a right to call us bastards. I didn't think he had a right to say anything to anybody. We were ducked down in a thicket of sumac and ready to run on a moment's notice, but none of those men made a move to come up the hill, and then it dawned on me that they were afraid to. They were afraid of the dark. You could tell by the looks on their faces.

"They shook their fists at us and turned and went into Torben's shack, which was right there, and a moment later they opened the back window and we saw a match flare up and then the sparks of a fuse, and up came a rocket with a whoosh, way up high over the trees, and a big bang and a flash of light, and then they fired another. We heard them all chortling down there, and to us that was a declaration of war. We might've gone home until they set off those rockets and laughed, and then we decided to stick around. First of all, we went over to their cars and took off the distributor caps and heaved them deep into the woods. And then we slipped down to the last shack, Mr. Hoffman's shack, and we picked up *his* privy and moved it back a few feet so the pit lay in front of the door. And we snuck back up the hill to our hiding spot, and then the back door of Torben's shack opened and Mr. Diener came out, and Torben behind him.

"Torben was carrying the lantern and the shotgun. Mr. Diener went into Torben's privy, and Torben stood guard, and several minutes passed, and Torben kicked on the door and told Mr. Diener to hurry it up. But he couldn't. Torben told him to relax, and Mr. Diener said he couldn't, he was all clenched up, and Torben said, 'How about I heat you up a beer? It works for me every time.' He passed the shotgun in to Mr. Diener and went in the shack to warm up the beer. We waited a moment, and one of us lobbed a rock and hit the back wall of the privy, and Mr. Diener flew out of there like a pigeon out of a coop, his pants around his ankles.

"A couple of the older boys had worked for Mr. Diener on road maintenance crews that summer, and one of them said he'd like to get a coat hanger and run it through a knothole and see if he couldn't snakebite Mr. Diener from below. And then he had a better idea. We released the emergency brake on Mr. Diener's Model A Ford and got it rolling toward the edge of the hill. Meanwhile, Mr. Diener had gone back in the outhouse. We tried to stop the car, but it got away from us and headed down the slope through the brush and trees toward that privy.

"Mr. Diener must've been peeking through a knothole, because he yelled and came out of the privy, the gun to his shoulder, and he let fly with both barrels at that car rolling through the sumac, and he busted the windshield, but that didn't affect the force of gravity. The car bore down on him and crashed into the privy and sent it flying, and the right front wheel of the Model A went down in the pit and the car stopped, *whump*, and that pit saved that man's life.

"As soon as we saw he wasn't killed, we jumped on our bikes and raced for dear life down the logging road, and there was a lot of shouting back there, and some more gunshots, but we went straight home and got into our beds, and the next day there was nothing said about it. Those men had to walk home, and they all showed up in church in the morning except for Mr. Hoffman, who had broken his arm. He said he had fallen into a hole."

I had never heard this story before in my life. I wondered how many other stories Dad might have in his repertoire that I had never heard. But there were no more to be told that night.

"You people have gotten me drunk and taken my money at gin rummy," said Dad. "Shame on you for taking advantage of an old man." He gave Alida one last, suave glance. "Nice to have some good looks in the family," he said. And he and Mother said good night and went up to bed.

FOURTEEN

Rome

I drove out to the farm with Howard the week after Thanksgiving, Howard talking about opening a bed-and-breakfast in the farmhouse and getting some cash flow going. Something was better than nothing, he said. He wondered if maybe I would like to move into the house, bringing my own furniture, and be the innkeeper. The Gibbs Farm checking account was gone, he said, flat broke, and of the other partners, seven wanted to sell out their interest, even at a loss.

"Who could they sell it to?" I asked.

"Well, that's just it—they can't. What they don't realize is that Steve now has a de facto majority interest in the place. We owe him so much money that he's negotiating directly with the bank. Steve, I think, would be open to the idea of us leasing the house from him for a B-and-B, and eventually a restaurant, and he could have the barn for his meditation center. He's holding a men's retreat in the spring. You're invited, by the way."

The fields of corn stubble flew by, a meadow where two horses raised their heads to watch the car pass, a farm with a bright-blue silo.

"Steve meditates by sitting very quietly and watching his prey," I said. "And we've been retreating from him for three years."

"Let's not be unpleasant," said Howard. "We may need this guy."

The restaurant sign out front was gone. The house sat empty, majestic, in the yard. A truck was backed up to the barn, and Steve and his crew were unloading big round maple tables and antique church pews. The interior of the lobby had taken a great leap forward: the curved wall was finished, and the cornucopia stood on its pedestal, and the crew was busy setting up furniture in the dining room, which was mostly finished.

We sat on a window ledge, cooling our heels, and eventually Steve tore himself away from the unloading and walked over and said he was glad we had come, he had good news. He had spoken to the bank, and they were willing to refinance if the partnership was reorganized. The bank had suggested that he, Steve, become managing partner and that the other partners divide up a quarter interest in the property. Steve said he had argued with the bank, but they said take it or leave it, so he took it. The deal would be signed the next week if the partners didn't come up with two hundred thousand dollars. So that was where it stood. The good news was that we could continue as partners, howbeit silent ones.

Steve recalled a time he had traveled to India, to a little village called Rajapathaparamagudi, where pilgrims in their white robes streamed up the dusty road to Dharamudram, and how he had faith then that though he was penniless he would find food and shelter, and so he had, and now he had the same faith that the place would open in the spring. He did not care to have us operate a B-and-B in the house. That would only confuse things. His macrobiotic restaurant, called A Place of Sustenance, would open in the barn, and the Lake Cayuga Meditation Center would occupy the house. Steve hoped we both would come visit. "It's been a stressful time. I look forward to the day the three of us can let go and try to grab hold of some serenity together."

I looked him in the eye. "The time I'd like to let go is if you were hanging off a cliff and I were holding you by the wrist," I said.

"I totally understand your feeling that way," said Steve.

"You don't understand a damn thing."

"You've been wanting to say that for a long time, haven't you?"

"You're the biggest jerk I ever met," I said.

He stood there, smug, impervious, a vague all-purpose smile playing on his flat face. "I accept your anger," he said.

"You're a filthy thief and someday someone is going to do the same thing to you," I said, and stepped toward him.

And then Howard was steering me away, toward the car, and then the barn and Steve were in the rearview mirror, getting smaller and smaller.

Howard and I rode back to Red Cliff in silence. We pulled up in front of Howard's house, and he sat for a moment and looked over at me and said, "I hope you're not blaming me."

"Of course I'm blaming you. You were in charge."

"I don't think that anger is going to help matters," said Howard.

A week later, Alida and I flew to Rome for Christmas. It was her gift to me. We walked along the Via Condotti, through an army of Japanese tourists foraging at Armani and Ferragamo and Valentino. It was raining, a cold, drizzling rain. She clung to my arm, and when we stopped at the curb for a red light, she pulled me close and gave me a long, slow movie kiss. We strolled into a twisting narrow street, just wide enough for a taxi and a fat man and his dog, and came out at the Pantheon, the Roman temple, here since 118, when men were still alive who had watched St. Peter's crucifixion. When Martin Luther came to Rome, this great dome was already 1400 years old. We sat at a table in an outdoor café in the Piazza del Rotondo, holding an umbrella over ourselves, and drank creamy coffee and looked up at the temple, the dome, the granite columns scarred and pockmarked from so much violent history. Around the fountain in the piazza, where the men in business suits hustled by, armies had contended, bombs bursting, and men had put the blade to their enemies.

Martin Luther lived in a monastery off the Piazza del Popolo for two years and witnessed the corruption and excesses of the religious hierarchy, and here began the Reformation: here in this city, the

Church cracked and the northern part broke away and Lutherans were born, and though they were right to break away, their principles being sound, you wish that Luther had learned more from Rome than that the Church was corrupt.

In Catholic Italy, the custom survives, unimaginable to Lutheran Minnesota, of noontime siesta: close the shop for a few hours, let the customer go away—it's not so important; more important is to enjoy a leisurely lunch, nap, talk with your family. You could never convince Lutherans to enjoy ease and comfort and leisure. It goes straight against their natures.

We found a little restaurant we liked called Il Convivio and had dinner there every evening, eating whatever was brought us— delicate artichokes, mushrooms, chicken, savory clam sauces—and one night, a little flush with wine, she put her hand on mine and said, "I hope you know that I adore you. I could not bear to lose you, darling John."

I looked into my wine, teary eyed, and thought, *If you ask her now, she'll say yes, so ask her,* but I couldn't find the words. There simply weren't any. I put my hand in hers and intertwined our fingers and smiled at her and looked away, feeling lost. *Maybe we should get married.* That's a pretty poor way of saying it. (Maybe we shouldn't.) *Will you marry me?* The contractual approach. *I want to marry you.* But she knew that already.

"You're not losing me," I said. "I am securely attached to you."

And that was as close as I came to proposing marriage.

When I got back from Rome, Dean Baird was lying in wait for me. I walked into WSJO, scanned the mail for a letter from Buenos Aires, didn't find one, took down *The Decline and Fall of the Roman Empire* from the shelf and stood at the window and looked out on the great snowy expanse of the quad, and I heard a throat being cleared and turned, and it was Dean Baird. He closed the door behind him. He had his solemn face on. "We need to talk, John," he said.

He eased into a wing chair and gestured toward the couch, and I sat.

"John," he said, "there have been allegations made about you vis-à-vis possible sexual harassment, and I hope you understand it's my duty to check these things out, ugly though they are."

The dean said this looking past me, toward the window. He smoothed his silvery hair; his chipmunk nose twitched.

I said, "I hope you don't mean that piece of garbage in that idiot newspaper in Syracuse."

"I've been talking with a few of our staff members, and they corroborated some of the details in the story, John. Such as the joke about the douche bag, for example. Which I didn't think was funny." He pursed his prim lips. "Douche bag is a term derogatory to women, John. I'm sure you know that."

"A douche bag is a bag used to administer a vaginal douche," I said. "Vinegar and water used to be a common solution used in a douche. That's what the joke is about. It's not about insulting women. It's a joke about an actual douche bag sitting on a barstool. A guy wants to buy a drink for it, and the douche bag says, 'Give me a vinegar and water.' "

"Douche bags don't talk," said the dean.

"In jokes they do."

"I don't see the humor in it."

"Obviously not."

"So why did you say it?"

"It was funny at the time."

The dean sighed. He said he would rather not see the matter go before a meeting of the college's committee on human rights, but it might—though an apology from me might head off such a meeting.

"How about this joke?" I said. "A woman walks into my office and bares her breasts and says, 'Make me feel like a woman!' and I stand up and give her my pants and say, 'Iron these!' "

The dean did not smile.

"Is that sexist?" I asked.

"Yes, of course," said the dean. "You know it is."

So I said that I would apologize, and whom should I apologize to?

"She prefers to remain anonymous," said the dean. "Simply write a note to To Whom It May Concern and say you're sorry and—you know—explain about how you grew up with that sort of humor and you didn't realize how women felt about it, and now you do, and you're sorry, and sign it, and give it to me, and I'll see that she gets it."

I took out a piece of paper and wrote: "To Whom It May Concern—I understand that you were offended by my joke about the man buying a drink (vinegar and water) for a douche bag in a bar. I'm sorry. It's rude to tell jokes to people with no sense of humor. Next time, I'll just give you the vinegar and water. Sincerely, John Tollefson."

I put it in an envelope and sealed it and gave it to the dean, who said, "Thanks for making this easier," and shook my hand and left.

Now is the time to get out of Red Cliff, I thought, as the dean's footsteps disappeared down the hall. Don't wait too long.

FIFTEEN

Byron

Dad died early on a Tuesday morning in mid-January. He collapsed on the basement stairs at the age of seventy-three with a bag of frozen peas in his hand. I got the news over the phone from Bill, and my first thought was that it was a sensible death: cleanly, Dad had sat down and died while still in good health, at home, and he would never have to be conned into a nursing home and sink into the sloughs of infirmity, senility, degeneration. He simply sat down and gave up the ghost.

My second thought was that I must be a monster to have thought what I did.

Bill had spoken to Ronnie in Dallas and Diana in Tucson, and everybody was flying to Minnesota that evening. "It's snowing like crazy," said Bill. The funeral would be on Saturday, at the Lutheran church.

"I'm on my way," I said. I called Alida. "My dad died," I said.

She, unlike me, seemed genuinely grieved. She said with a quaver in her voice, "That dear man—oh, your poor mother. Oh, I'm sorry. I am so sorry. Should I come with you? I shouldn't, should I."

I hadn't even considered that she might. "No, you shouldn't. They'd be glad to see you and everything, but you wouldn't know anybody—"

"I'll cancel everything and come if you want me to," she said. "But you have to tell me."

"It's too much," I said. "Don't."

"Nothing would be too much, if you want me to come."

"It's okay," I said. "But thanks."

I packed my dark-brown pinstripe suit and a white shirt and drove to the Syracuse airport. On W100's *Party Line*, though it was only nine in the morning, people were arguing about the high school girls' basketball coach, Miss Waters, who believed that every player should get an equal amount of court time, regardless of ability. Snow was forecast, the announcer said, two inches. He said it in a mournful voice, as if the snowfall were punishment for his sins. Plywood paneling was being sold at a 40 percent discount, however, and that made the announcer cheerful again. Then a caller came on to ask if anyone knew how to get bloodstains out of a damask curtain.

At the airline ticket counter, the woman gave me a look of stark pity, as if I wore a name tag that said: Dead Man's Son. The plane was packed. I curled up in a window seat, stuffed two pillows between the seat and the window, pulled the thin blanket over me, and awoke as the plane taxied in gusts of blowing snow to the lighted windows of the Minneapolis–St. Paul terminal. A little line of drool trickled from the corner of my mouth. The woman in the seat ahead turned and gave me a look of disgust, and I guessed that I had been snoring.

I rented a black Pontiac and headed north on the interstate, traffic creeping along at twenty-five miles an hour. The road felt frictionless, as if I were at the wheel of a destroyer on the North Atlantic, and the shapes in the mist off to starboard weren't farmhouses but cargo ships in the convoy, and the windshield wiper was a sonar antenna tracking German U-boats. At any moment the whole thing could blow up, but a man's got to do his duty, and either you go forward or you go hide somewhere, and yes, sir, I believe we're going to win this war.

When I was a kid and the family drove home at night from visiting Mother's relatives in the Cities, Ronnie sat between Dad and Mother, Bill and Diana and Judy and I crammed into the back, I standing behind the front seat, my chin next to Dad's head, watching the parade of approaching headlights, their beams filling the car with a big whoosh of light; I'd smell Dad's hair oil, his aftershave, trying to get the feel of what it was like to be a man driving a car. Dad loved to drive. He would have been happy to go all night. He steered with his left hand low on the wheel, thumb and finger on the spoke, and he never sped or tried to ace out other cars. He drove with his right arm across the seatback, touching Mother's shoulder, as the radio played a sexy singer like Julie London or Eartha Kitt. Diana liked to bonk Ronnie on the head because it sounded like a watermelon. Ronnie whined, and Mother told me to stop it. I didn't say anything. I was imagining driving, how the wheel felt, how it would be to be alone in your own car. Just you.

It was two in the afternoon when I reached home, snow drifting in the streets, the house a dim shape in the storm, all the lights on, Mother in a gray housedress, waiting at the back door. "How were the roads?" she asked. "Not that bad," I said. I kissed her on the cheek and she put her arms around me and we clung tightly to each other for a moment. "It's good to have you all safe under one roof," she said. The junk on the porch had thinned out. "Where are the metal detectors?" I asked. Mother said that Dad had given them away. He had been cleaning house over the holidays.

Everybody was there in the kitchen: Ronnie and Bill and Judy; Diana stood up to give me a hug. She has put on some weight since she became a vegetarian. She struggled to her feet and brushed back a shock of blond hair. Tears ran down her puffy cheeks. She wore a lacy white dress and big turquoise jewelry, earrings the size of juice glasses, enough beads to fill a bread box.

"Daddy's gone," she said. "We'll never see him again in this whole world." She motioned toward a tall, tan woman with a crew cut and said, "This is my partner, April." The tall woman gave me a stiff hug. She was dressed in khaki pants and khaki shirt, no jewelry.

Ronnie was perched on the counter, in green pants and a short-sleeved shirt with *I Am the Way* embroidered on the pocket. His blond hair was cut short, scalped almost, and it glistened with oil, and his face was badly nicked from shaving. "Nice to see you," Ronnie said, in his squawky voice. "Been a while." His legs dangled down, new white shoes with tassels, white socks.

Bill sat at the table, looking gray and haggard, his face slack, and I shook hands with him, and hugged Judy. "Hi, stranger," she said.

"Would you care for spaghetti?" said Mother, already filling a bowl with a long skein of pasta. She dumped a cup of red sauce over it and added another, and set it on the table, with a paper towel for a napkin. "Well," she said, looking around at our silent faces, "here we all are."

Dad died on the next-to-top basement step on his way upstairs from having taken to the basement a box of rubber binders that Mother had told him to get rid of, binders saved from his years of running the grain elevator, thousands of binders, a lifetime supply. While in the basement, he fetched a bag of peas from the freezer in the laundry room, which he kept full of hamburger patties, fish sticks, vegetables, hash browns, as his hedge against disaster. He also kept silver dollars in a flour sack stashed behind the paint cans under the basement stairs. And then disaster struck as he climbed the stairs. Dad suffered from arrhythmia, and as he approached the top, he must have lost his breath. He sat down. Mother heard him gasp. She called to him, "What's the matter?" and he said, "Nothing. I'm all right." She was making spaghetti sauce. She put a little more seasoning in it, and then opened the door to the stairs a moment later, and he was gone, slumped against the wall, the bag of frozen peas in his right hand. His eyes were open, and he was dead. She sat on the stair beside him and put her arm around his shoulders and smoothed his hair and kissed his cheek. She told him she loved him and always would love him. And then she took the frozen peas from his hand and put them in the refrigerator and called the rescue squad. They came five minutes later and tried to revive him, and Dr. DeHaven came over and pronounced him dead and had him taken to the funeral home run by Dad's old buddy Mr. Lindberg.

Diana said, "He was unconscious, and you took the peas from him before you called the rescue squad?"

"He didn't need an ambulance; he was dead," said Mother.

"But how did you know that?"

"I could see it to look at him. And I checked his pulse."

"You didn't think you should call a doctor?" said Diana. She looked around at the rest of us. I ate my spaghetti. Bill and Judy drank coffee. They ate cookies from a box that neighbors had sent over. April did not take her eyes off Diana. Over the table hung Dad's three-by-five index card, *Pantry Light: Do Not Yank.*

"Dr. DeHaven? No, it never occurred to me," said Mother. He had done a cardiogram on Dad in December and said everything looked fine, said Mother. Dr. DeHaven was a big hulk of a man and a chain smoker, obviously a firm believer in mortality, and when he said you were okay, it made you uneasy.

"He sat there unconscious, and your first thought was to make sure the peas didn't thaw?" said Diana.

"It was silly, wasn't it," said Mother. "I don't know why I even thought of it."

And then Diana clapped her hand to her mouth. "Those weren't the same peas . . ."

"Yes," said Mother. "Actually, they were. Of course they were."

She had put the peas in the spaghetti, with the tomato sauce. The death peas.

"We ate the peas Daddy held in his hand as he died?" Diana whispered.

"Dad touched everything in this house," I said. "You're sitting in his chair. What's the problem?"

I took a forkful and held it to my mouth, smelled the sweet, uncomplicated sauce: it reminded me of when I was in sixth grade and Mother had me sent home every day for lunch because Mr. Benson, the teacher, liked to humiliate kids and Mother thought she needed to boost my morale. She fed me her spaghetti and we had grown-up conversations. She told how much she had loved her one year at the University of Minnesota. One year was all that Grandpa Petersen could afford. "I knew I must make the most of it," she said, "and get all I could in one year," so she attended every free lecture and concert, haunted the library, soaked up her classes, wasted no time making friends, because she had only the one shining year.

I noticed that the dining room and living room had been cleared away somewhat. The stacks of *Life* were gone, the row of four school desks. *Door to Bathroom Is Behind You—This Is Closet* was still posted on the downstairs closet, and other signage remained, but there were patches of bare floor where I wasn't used to seeing floor. "The week before he died, he took three carloads of books to the Good Shepherd Home in Little Falls," said Mother.

Bill and I cleared stuff off the beds in our old bedroom so we could sleep on them. A doll buggy with two cracked and balding china dolls, two red wooden runners from a bobsled. An oil portrait of a tiny dog in a noble pose, entitled *Toby*. A brittle canvas sign from a carnival freak show: *See Carlo the Human Smokestack*100 Boxes of Cigarettes a Day*A Puzzler to All Medical & Scientific Men*. An immense vase painted with a scene of a millpond with ruined mill, drooping willows, full moon, and a canoe paddled by a man in a white shirt, a maiden reclining in the bow. Our old maple desk by the door was stuffed with book reports and class projects. "It isn't a home, it's an interpretive center," I said.

Bill sat on the bed. He did not look well, and he had been silent all afternoon. He was fifty-one, and a few months before, he had gone to see a doctor about rectal bleeding and they stuck a probe and a camera up him, after having him drink six gallons of an oily liquid to flush his intestines out: he'd told me this in a letter but not what the doctor found out. It grieved me to think of my big brother, a man with a poor self-image to start with, having to be reamed up the colon.

"How's your colon coming, by the way?" I asked.

"Fine," Bill said. "How's yours?"

"Are you okay?"

"Tell me what okay is, and I'll tell you."

I was about to say, and Mother knocked on the door, which was open, and walked in. "I want you to do something for me," she said.

She held up a brown grocery bag. "Take this over to John Lindberg at the funeral parlor. These are the clothes I want Dad to be buried in."

I looked at the bag. A plain old brown bag.

"It's his work clothes," she said. "I want him buried in the clothes that we always saw him in."

Bill and I walked up the street to Lindberg's. The snow had stopped falling, and a few dutiful souls were already out shoveling walks in the dark. It was a light, dry snow, and it glittered where the porch lights shone on it, and in the dark it glowed.

I said, "I wonder what it's like to embalm people you've known all your life. To cut their arteries and drain out the blood and clean them up—"

"Let's not talk about it."

"But when you take over your dad's undertaking business in the small town where you grew up, you figure you're going to know the clientele."

"Lindberg never married, did he," said Bill. It sounded so mournful. Unmarried. To be known by what didn't happen to you.

Lindberg's was in the same old big white house with the curved veranda on Cleveland Street, a driveway alongside the house running under the little portico with the double door, through which generations of Wobegonians have been carried for their funerals. The old black Cadillac hearse sat, nose out, ready to take Dad to church on Saturday and then to his grave.

I knocked at the back door, and Mr. Lindberg opened it. He was tall and plump, with a wild shock of white hair and watery blue eyes. He wore an old brown wool suit and a brown plaid shirt, a tuft of white hair poking up at the neck. He led us into his tiny kitchen. Beyond was the funeral parlor. The kitchen was his office, his larder, his den, and upstairs was his bedroom. He plopped down on a white kitchen chair, and Bill took the other. I stood and leaned against the counter. Mr. Lindberg gave us a sorrowful look.

"This is a hard one for me," he said. "I knew your dad all my life." He took a deep asthmatic breath. "We used to raise hell when we were kids, you know. I've been putting off going down there and working on him." He nodded toward the door to the basement.

Mr. Lindberg offered us coffee. I said yes, and the old man poured a mugful and said, "How about some flavoring in it?" He pointed to a bottle of Old Crow. "It's just to keep the flies off you." I nodded, and he poured a wallop of whiskey in and handed it to me. I took a sip. It was powerful. The smell made my nose hairs tingle.

"Oh yes," said Mr. Lindberg, "your dad was a rambunctious young man before your mother settled him down. I remember when he took the pastor's Model A apart on Halloween and reassembled it in the church basement. I imagine you boys didn't hear about that."

"He told me about tipping over privies," I said.

Mr. Lindberg chuckled. "Torben Saetre. He used to get very apprehensive whenever Byron was nearby. Your dad used to drive around in a car that when you flicked a switch under the dashboard and revved up the engine, a flame six feet long came out the tailpipe. We'd cruise up and down Main Street and just amaze people.

"I remember your dad playing a joke on a guy on the football team named Finsen, who was quite taken with himself and drove a red roadster, which he always parked in front of school where it could be appreciated. Everybody was duly impressed, and one day your dad snuck out and threaded a wire loop into the upholstery in the front seat on the driver's side and ran the wire out the back. A couple nights later, Finsen was parked by the train depot with his girlfriend, and your dad and I crept up from behind with a car battery and waited until it got very quiet in the car, and then the girl said something like No, or Don't do that, and your dad touched that wire to the battery and it sent a thousand volts through the seat and poor old Finsen flew out the door like a bat out of hell, and when he stopped, he discovered he had soiled his pants. Your dad and I took off running, and we spent the summer working on threshing crews in North Dakota. It was a great summer. I heard that Finsen died young. Apoplexy, I believe."

Bill handed him the paper bag and said, "Well, we won't keep you, Mr. Lindberg. We came over with Dad's clothes."

Mr. Lindberg set the bag on the table. He leaned back and smiled and shook his head. "I remember when we moved a boxcar onto the grade crossing and blocked the road. We were twelve or thirteen years old. It took thirty boys to get that boxcar moving, and we got it where we wanted it and ran away, and the freight agent—an old guy named Jacobson—he refused to move the car off the crossing. It sat there for a whole week. People south of town had to drive five miles out of their way to get in. Jacobson said, 'Those boys put it there, let them move it.' There wasn't much freight business here then, so the siding wasn't in use that much. Finally, one Sunday, everybody from church went down and moved it back."

"Mr. Lindberg," I said, "I'd like to go down and see my father." My heart was pounding as I said it. I half hoped the old man would say no, but Mr. Lindberg pointed me to the door to the basement. "Right down there," he said. "I haven't started on him yet; he's just the way he arrived."

I descended the stairs, into a cold cellar with a sour chemical smell. A refrigerator hummed in the corner. Two large tubs stood against one wall and a row of cabinets against the other, and in the middle was a table, and there, covered by an old rubber sheet, lay the body. I stood at its side for a moment and then pulled the sheet back.

My father lay curled on his side in a fetal position, his eyes closed, his mouth slightly open as if sucking wind, the hands clenched. I touched a hand, and it was cool. I put my hand on top of Dad's head and smoothed his hair. I could not remember ever touching his hair before. Showing affection did not come easily to members of our family. The body seemed restless, straining. I stroked the head, and I put my other hand on my father's cool, dry hand. Affection was hard for Dad, and it is hard for me. Norwegians are not a people given to kissing and hugging. Even direct eye contact can be uncomfortable. I had seen Dad and his brother Henry stand back-to-back and converse. Dad was always turning away.

The only time I heard Dad talk about love, as such, was in describing a horse that Uncle Svend gave him when he was seventeen. Dad went to live with Svend on the farm, because Dad and Grandpa didn't get along. The horse was named Beauty; he rode her bareback every day after chores. He hated school, he was shy, he wasn't in the clique of town kids who ran things, but he had that horse. "I loved that horse. She made you feel like the Prince of Paris," Dad said.

One morning, he went in the barn and Beauty was moaning and sweating, rearing up, and Dad saw that the old icebox that held the oats was open. She had worked the latch open and eaten half the oats and she was foundering on it. "A horse can't vomit," Dad explained, "so the oats were fermenting in her gut and she was bloating, which cut off her circulation, and there's a place in the middle of the hoof, if it doesn't get blood, it gets so painful the horse can't walk, but you have to keep the horse walking, you can't let her lie down, because that makes it worse."

He walked her up and down all day, but then he fell asleep for a few hours, and when he woke up she was lying on the ground and he couldn't get her up. She was trembling in agony. He called the vet and the vet was out on a call, so Dad had to get the gun and put her away himself. Dad wouldn't say more, but I could imagine him crying, putting his arms around her neck, then putting the muzzle of the gun to her beautiful forehead and thinking about how much he loved her and the gun going off and the boy, numb, in shock, reaching for the shovel, digging the pit beside her, using a board for a lever, rolling her in.

I bent down and kissed my father's hand. I whispered, "Goodbye, Dad," and right away my eyes filled with tears. I pulled the sheet back over him and climbed the stairs, turning the light off behind me.

Bill and Mr. Lindberg sat in silence at the table.

"I'm going to take my brother down to the Sidetrack Tap and buy him a beer," I said. "Mr. Lindberg? How about you?"

The old man shook his head. "I've got work to do," he said. "I put it off long enough."

Bill and I walked around the side of the house, past the hearse, and he said, "Why'd you do that?"

"I wanted to see him before he gets all made up, that's all."

"What did he look like?"

"He looked like our father."

We walked down Cleveland to McKinley and turned toward downtown. The Christmas lights still hung over Main Street. Dad was
gone, and maybe Bill didn't have long to live: he seemed so preoccu-
pied, as if some dark secret was flying around in his head. Maybe Bill
wouldn't tell anybody if he did have cancer. That would be par for the
course for this family. I could imagine Bill going off without a word
to die in a hospice, doped on morphine, too weak to even switch off
the TV, nobody of his family present to comfort him, only infomer-
cial hosts trying to sell him a weight-loss skin cream as he descended
into eternity, a true Tollefson, a stoic to the end.

The Sidetrack was dim and smoky. A twangy song played on the
jukebox, the deep, mournful voice of a man sorry for his misdeeds
while still committing them. A few patrons sat staring up at the TV
like a row of rock bass on the dock, the reflection playing on their
faces. Wally stood, one foot up on a beer case to ease the pain in his
back. Three Norwegian bachelor farmers sat in the bachelor booth,
beside the door to the men's can, their grizzled old faces and ropy
necks lit by a match flaring up. They had a bottle of Four Roses and a
bucket of ice and three glasses and were looking up at Mr. Berge, who
stood, one hand on the door to the men's can, serenading them. His
face was flushed, his eyes shone, as he sang:

Oh, the shepherd, he lay in the tall green grass,
His faithful dog lay by his ass,
His faithful sheep licked at his balls
Through a well-worn hole in his overalls.
A magpie perched on a limb nearby
And watched this scene with an evil eye.
Then the dog, he barked, and the sheep, she bit,
And the man, he yelled, and the magpie shit.

We sat down at the end of the bar near the door. Wally said, "That's
why Evelyn refuses to tend bar—she got tired of the smutty jokes."
He pulled two glasses of beer and filled two shot glasses with rye
whiskey and reached across the bar and shook our hands. "Your dad
was one of the finest individuals I ever met," he said. "I knew him

since we were in the fifth grade together. It's hard to believe he's gone. I don't know what this town is going to do without him." Bill put down a five-dollar bill, and Wally waved it away. I saw a sign above the bar: *I want to die peacefully in my sleep—like my grandfather— not screaming in terror like the passengers in his car.*

"I wish the funeral were tomorrow," said Bill. "It's depressing hanging around here."

"I noticed."

"Look out," said Bill. "Speak of depressing, Harley's coming over this way."

I felt the big hand on my shoulder and turned, and Harley sat down next to me, unshaven, long gray hair under his orange cap, and he pulled out a hankie and honked. He and Dad used to duck hunt together.

"How's everything?" I said. Harley rubbed the back of his head gingerly.

"Slipped on the ice getting into my pickup the other night and hit my head. Don't know if it's a concussion or what. Slid under the truck and lay there and my sheepskin coat froze to the ice and if it hadn't been for the fact that I was able to wiggle out of the coat, I'd be a dead man right now. Me and your dad together. Two funerals on the same day."

Having survived this close call, Harley had felt Lady Luck calling to him, and he drove to the Mille Lacs Indian casino and won several hundred dollars at blackjack, when an elderly lady in an orange pantsuit and a brown wig dropped her purse and like a true gentleman he bent down to fetch it and collect the stuff that dropped out of it, and when he came up, all his chips were gone and so was the lady. The dealer said, "I thought she was your wife." Harley tore out to the parking lot and saw a white Caddie pull out, a lady at the wheel, and he chased her and made her pull over, and then it turned out to be another lady. She had called the sheriff on her car phone meanwhile. It took Harley three hours to clear things up, sitting in the sheriff's office, being lectured at like a teenager.

"Let me buy you a drink," I said.

Harley ordered a double bourbon on the rocks.

"Yeah," he said, "I thought it'd be my lucky day at cards, because it was on that very day in 1957 the St. Paul Saints invited me to come to their camp in Florida and try out. They had scouted me when I pitched for the Whippets in the State Men's Tournament. The scout was a little guy with a big cigar named Ricky. I was working for the rendering plant, picking up downed cattle, so baseball looked good to me, but Hazel about went nuts. She was my first wife. Scary woman. She told me that anybody could see I didn't have the stuff for pro ball; even she could see it. I rode the dog down to Florida and hitch-hiked twenty-five miles to the ballpark and got suited up and went out and warmed up and a coach waved me over to the mound to throw. There was a batter at the plate, and the coach said, 'Don't mind him—he's only there to give you the strike zone.' Well, they forgot to tell the batter that, and he swung and hit a line drive that bounced off my forehead, and when I came to, I was in a hospital bed. They said I owed a hundred fifteen dollars for the X-rays and whatnot. I had to shinny out of there, not a dime on me, and hitchhike back to Minnesota, and it was raining to beat the band, and who wants to pick up a wet hitchhiker? Worst time of my life. I slept under bridges. I stole tomatoes out of people's gardens."

I put down a fiver and signaled for Wally to refill Harley's glass.

"You wouldn't mind if I had a beer too, would you?" Harley said. He took a swig of whiskey and chased it with a long swallow of beer.

"Anyway, I got home and Hazel was fit to be tied. She called me a sapsucker, said she rued the day she met me. There I was with these ferocious headaches, and only whiskey seemed to relieve the pain, beer didn't do the trick. I drank and she called me names and one night she came at me with a pistol and said, 'I'll bet you think I wouldn't dare,' and I said, 'I'm not thinking anything,' and she said, 'That's your problem,' and she shot me. I came to three days later in General Hospital. They decided to leave the bullet in. I pretty much recovered, except I can't remember songs. Nothing. You could play me 'Happy Birthday to You' and I wouldn't remember ever having heard it. I was a big Buddy Holly fan, and now I hear 'Peggy Sue' and I can tell it's music but it doesn't mean anything to me. Otherwise I was normal, except for the headaches, and sometimes I'd have a seizure and they would have to hold my tongue down. Otherwise I was okay."

I signaled to Wally, and Wally poured Harley another shot of bourbon and a glass of beer.

"Yeah, they put me on muscle relaxants for a while, until I turned out to have this overwhelming urge to drive toward bright lights. Some kind of obsession. I'd see headlights approaching and have to pull over to the shoulder so as not to drive head-on into someone. Once, I picked up a hitchhiker and asked him to drive and he did and I dozed off, and when I woke up, the car was in a parking ramp in St. Paul and my billfold was missing. But that's another story." And he turned to me and said, "Johnny, can I borrow ten dollars from you until Wednesday?"

It was so sudden, I couldn't think of how to say no. I pulled out my billfold and gave Harley a twenty. "Thanks," Harley said. He turned to Bill and said, "It was a pleasure meeting you. I was a good friend of your dad's." He tossed down his drink and stood up, thanked me again, and when we left, a few minutes later, he had changed the twenty for two rolls of dimes and was engaged in cribbage with Mr. Berge at the end of the bar and seemed to be winning.

Everyone was in bed when we got home; the house was dark. Bill tiptoed up the stairs, and I picked up the kitchen phone and called Alida. I sat on the counter and looked out the window at the backyard, lit by a streetlamp in the alley, a cone of light on the snow, the garbage cans crowned with snow.

Alida was excited. Her book had been accepted by Vandal-Pigeon in New York, and the editor said it would come out in the fall. Based on the three chapters she sent them, they thought it might actually sell. They were hoping she might entitle it *Lincoln's Cold Shower*, and she was holding out for *Bolle in America*. But it was good news, wasn't it?

"An author," I said. "You'll need to buy a new suit."

"What's on your mind?" she said.

"You. You and me."

"You sound sad."

I didn't think I was nearly sad enough. My father was gone, leaving a bleeding scar, and what it revealed was the deadness of my own life.

"I wish I had shown my father a little more affection, that's all. I mean, if you don't show the people you love that you love them, then what's the point? I wish it weren't so hard for me to be a loving person. I don't want to go through life being this cold, smug, wisecracking, oblivious jerk. On the other hand, if I had ever put my arm around Dad, he would've jumped three feet and had a heart attack right there. I'd've put my arm around him and caught him as he fell."

I told her about Diana's bruised feelings over the death peas, the strangeness of April, the work clothes, Mr. Berge's song about the shepherd, Harley's string of mishaps. I left out my visitation with Dad. I was afraid she might think it was creepy.

I hung my pants on the chair, over Bill's, and crawled between the cold sheets and listened to the deep silence of Lake Wobegon on a snowy January night. My ancestor John Tollefson had heard the same silence, the majestic dreamlike breadth and depth of soundlessness that some people hike into the North Woods wilderness in search of and other people turn on radio talk shows to avoid.

I was wide awake. I reached down to the bottom shelf on the side of the desk, and there, in the exact spot where it sat in my boyhood, was the Flambeau Family novel that Mildred gave me for my tenth birthday. I pulled it out, and opened it, and read, in the light from the streetlamp in the alley: " 'Darling, it's Carlos, calling from Barcelona. Can you speak to him?' Emile took the phone. 'Carlos,' he said, and winked at Tony, who sat, knees drawn up under his chin, still in his dressing gown at six o'clock in the evening. He had trailed Gonzaga for two days and slept for eleven hours, and now they were going to see *L'Elisir d'Amore* at the Met."

SIXTEEN

Family Matters

On Thursday morning, the wind had died down, the sky had cleared except for streaks of high cirrus clouds. The low sun made long shadows of trees across the shining snow.

"A beautiful day! Let's all go to the Chatterbox Café for breakfast," Mother said, but Diana said no, she wasn't ready to face people yet, and Ronnie said it was too cold for him. So we fixed eggs and sausage. In the basement freezer, Dad had thirty-seven tubes of Jimmy Dean sausage. I counted them.

Ronnie drank a cup of hot water. He gave me a clipping from the Dallas paper about Texas painters and composers. It said that the climate of the Midwest is not conducive to a modern lifestyle and so the area would see greater economic decline, losing population to the Southwest, which was where the important cultural activity of the twenty-first century would take place, something along the lines of the Italian Renaissance. Business produces art, the article said. Economic vitality is the key to culture. You don't get great art where there's economic decline.

"I thought you'd be interested in that, seeing as you're the artistic one in the family," Ronnie said.

"One advantage of the Minnesota climate is that you always know if your fly is unzipped," I said. Ronnie reached down and zipped up his barn doors.

Ronnie was doing okay in Texas, and that was a relief, sort of. He was so quiet as a kid, you figured he might grow up to become an ax murderer. His grades were okay in junior high because his ear for multiple-choice tests was good—in Lake Wobegon, the correct answer is usually c—but in eleventh and twelfth grades, there were essay tests, and he did not shine. He once wrote in a test, "Well, this is a very good question, what is laissez-faire economics, and it goes straight to the deeper question of what economics is about. Laissez-faire economics was practiced extensively by the French, sometimes with greater success than at other times, but always the principle was that of fairness. Fairness in economics was a totally new concept. The French pioneered this, and it has also been tried in other countries." He showed me the test. He got a D on it. "How was I supposed to know all that stuff?" he said.

He was a spooky kid. Once, he and I helped a farmer burn off weeds in a field outside town, and the fire was moving along, and Ronnie said, "What if it was God's will that this fire should burn all those houses because people in those houses had done terrible things? Then if we tried to stop the fire, we'd be going against God's will." This was not normal talk for a Lutheran boy. That was Baptist talk.

When Ronnie graduated, he didn't have a career planned, so he went to Dallas with his best (and only) friend, Merle. Mother cried after he walked out the back door, carrying an old cardboard suitcase, wearing a yellowish linen suit Uncle Art gave him. She was right to worry. He and Merle stayed drunk for about four years. When Bill went to visit him and they drove around Dallas, Ronnie pointed at a park and said, "That's where everybody goes to throw up."

And then he was nuts for about a year, mad as a hatter, talking about money-making schemes, about talcum powder, how poisonous it was, about ions, how he was going to get an ionizer. And then the Rev. Packwood spoke to him over the radio.

Ronnie was drunk in the back seat of a car one night, and in the front seat were two men whom he couldn't remember having met, and the Rev. Jeeter Packwood of the Church of the Revealed Lord came on the radio and said that the world was nearing an end, the Tribulation was about to begin, and, according to prophecy, a great earthquake would divide North America into five continents—one of which, the Deep South and Texas, would be under Christian rule, a sort of New Confederacy with cities of gold and jasper and ivory palaces and millennial joy, and Ronnie said, "Thank you, Jesus!"

The men dropped him off at his apartment, and he never saw them again. They were angels sent by God, he told Mother. He packed his things and went in search of the Church of the Revealed Lord, found it, was born again, quit drinking, forgot about money and ions and talcum powder. He met Serena, who was plump and wore a plain white dress and bonnet and was submissive and never spoke unless spoken to first, which suited Ronnie to a T.

"She shall be your helpmeet," said Rev. Packwood, "but first the Lord has a work for you to do. My brother Jasper Packwood and his wife, Sister Fern, are serving in the mission fields of Ecuador, among the M'a H'ano people, and they need a little help, as Fern is suffering from her nerves. You go lend them a hand, and I'll be happy to marry you and Serena in the spring."

So off to Ecuador he went, and was met by a M'a H'ano man at the airport in Quito. A man in cut-offs and sandals and a T-shirt from Sea World, holding up a sign with Ronnie's name on it. "Truck," he said. The man drove for six hours over roads as rough as a plowed field. The heat was merciless, steam rose from the forests. Ronnie was stupefied when the truck pulled into a compound and stopped. Thirty huts with corrugated-tin roofs sat higgledy-piggledy around a cinderblock chapel. Right away Ronnie noticed that here at the M'a H'ano Revealed Lord Mission Church, the women went around naked to the waist.

And after supper, everyone gathered for a communal bath in the river. They all stripped and took a bar of soap and walked into the water and lathered up. Including Sister Fern and Brother Jasper. Ronnie took off running. He tore up to the chapel and waited there, and he went to Brother Jasper Packwood that night and said, "How come you people go around naked? Where does it say that in Scripture?" And Jasper explained that the M'a H'ano could only comprehend the gospel if it was adapted into their culture. They were gentle folk who loved singing and dancing and did lovely beadwork and weaving and wore their finest clothes every day, and there was no word for "late" in the M'a H'ano language, so it was impossible to translate "Now is the time of salvation" or the parable of the foolish virgins into M'a H'ano. He said, "As well as the M'a H'ano learning from us, we must also learn from the M'a H'ano and adapt the gospel to their culture instead of trying to change them to become like us."

"I thought that changing people is what the gospel is all about," Ronnie said.

Ronnie worked with a gang of M'a H'ano men digging a ditch and was frustrated with how slowly the work advanced. The M'a H'ano took long breaks, squatting in the dirt, rocking back and forth on their bare feet, jabbering away in their high-pitched birdlike voices, and Jasper took frequent coffee breaks himself. There was a different rhythm to life here in the rain forest, he explained. "Yeah," said Ronnie, "there's slow and there's slower." It was a rhythm that suited Jasper. He sat drinking coffee on the veranda, brushing bugs off his hair, and staring up at the mountains, humming, reading a book.

Ronnie wrote to Pastor Jeeter Packwood: "Dear Pastor, I regret to report that the Lord's work in Ecuador has strayed from the path and gotten into deep water. People go naked, men and women together, including missionaries, and I believe they are on drugs. Please advise."

Rev. Packwood arrived a week later and found that the M'a H'ano had indeed been medicating the missionaries with a white powder from the M'a H'anowah'a plant, a powerful narcotic, which they put in the coffee. Jasper and Fern, big coffee drinkers both of them, had been flying high. Jasper insisted it was a form of sugar, and Rev. Packwood said, "Sugar, my foot. That is an illegal substance. I am taking a sample back to the U.S.A. for testing."

He and Ronnie flew home by way of Miami, and there in the Miami airport, Rev. Packwood told Ronnie to collect the bags from the baggage carousel while he, Jeeter, used the men's washroom. Ronnie did as he was told, and as he put the bags onto a cart, a German shepherd employed by Immigration & Naturalization got a whiff of Jeeter's suitcase and lunged forward, and Ronnie, who had been scared of dogs since boyhood, made a run for it and was tackled in the concourse by six agents, who then found the envelope of M'a H'anowah'a in Jeeter's shaving kit.

Ronnie refused to finger Jeeter. He said the powder was his own, gotten from a friend in Ecuador, and he refused to name the friend. He was charged with possession and pleaded guilty and went to prison in Rochester, Minnesota, for four years. Mother visited him every other week. She said he seemed quite content in prison. He read his Bible and listened to tapes of Jeeter preaching and did his calisthenics. And when he was released, he flew to Dallas, and Rev. Packwood married him and Serena, and there was the perfect ending for Ronnie: he was saved, he had the millennium to look forward to, and meanwhile he had a hovering kindly presence to fix him breakfast and do his laundry.

After breakfast, I went downtown to see my old buddy Swanson, who was mad at his wife and his old man. "People take me for granted," he grumped. We went to the Chatterbox for coffee. Swanson said he had not recovered yet from New Year's Eve. He and Mel and Leland had gone to Mel's house and drunk beer and Jim Beam and then, to make their hangovers more interesting, had tossed down some champagne and peppermint schnapps. He awakened at noon on New Year's Day, feeling like the victim of a cruel experiment, and was still, three weeks later, not quite over it.

"It was too bad about your old man," said Swanson. "A great loss." On the other hand, he said, when your number was up, it was time to go. Look at our classmate Richard Hansen, the carefulest man who ever was, who never smoked, never drank, didn't eat red meat, jogged religiously, and died on a mountain road north of San Francisco when the tailgate of a semi ahead of him sprang open and suddenly the road was yellow with bananas and his car skidded out of control and smashed into a eucalyptus tree. There was no postponing fate. When it wanted you, it would find you.

I came home and cooked lunch for the six of us, a pork roast and caramelized potatoes, with the spaghetti and death peas as a side dish. April peeled the potatoes. We watched one of Dad's many mini-TVs, a man spraying cold medicine up his nostrils and looking joyful, as if it had lightened his burden in life considerably. April told me Mother had gone to St. Cloud with Ronnie to buy a down comforter for Uncle Henry, who was flying in from California and who chilled easily. April said that Diana was lying down, exhausted from everything. "Has your family always been this quiet with each other?" April said. I felt an urge to slap her.

"We communicate intuitively," I told her. "Not everything needs to be stated, you know."

"You're kidding, aren't you," she said.

I told her that people who know who they are don't have to go around describing themselves. They don't have to take constant inventory of their feelings.

"Yes, you're kidding," she said.

She and Diana had met at a seminar called "Changing Your Life Story Through Positive Projection," conducted by a man named Mel Loman, who had been a heroin addict sleeping in doorways in San Francisco and now was a multimillionaire, thanks to the way he had opened doors for thousands of people. "You would probably think it's cuckoo, John, but it certainly worked for us."

"Great," I said. I noticed that she was peeling wrong—peeling away from herself, not toward—and she didn't dig out the eyes with the tip of the peeler but kept peeling until the eye was gone, a major waste of potato.

"The breakthrough for Diana was when she became a hostage in that bank holdup and sat blindfolded in a tourist cabin for two days and she discovered that she had been an emotional hostage herself all her life; that changed her," said April. "I wish she would write a book about that hostage experience."

"How did it change her?" I asked. I hoped Diana would not write a book.

"It showed her that the search for answers is in itself a valid answer, that life is a process of constant healing and becoming, that everyone is on the same trip. That's what."

Diana had graduated from Lake Wobegon High, class of '64, won a Shining Star scholarship and went to St. Cloud State and fell in among Unitarians, which she loved—no mournful hymns, no Nicene Creed, no draggy sermons about our sinful natures; just intelligent people sitting in a cheerful room on Sunday morning and talking about what we can do to make the world a better place. And then one sunny morning she woke up with a nervous breakdown and couldn't get out of bed and was taken to a psychiatric ward and put in with a dozen doughy-faced women in blue gowns, who lurched around talking to the furniture. Diana spent two months there and then decided she did not wish to be crazy. It was February. She went to Tucson, worked in the bank, was hostaged, discovered her previous emotional hostagement, and since then she had taught Listening Skills in a senior citizens' center, made clay picture frames, taught creative writing for people in abusive situations, given tours of "Psychic Tucson," been a day-care giver, a meter maid, a video rental clerk, and the custodian of a major apartment complex, and it was clear to everyone in the family that Diana's search for identity was the one stable fact in her life. Now, according to April, she wanted to be an aromatherapist.

When Mother and Ronnie returned with the comforter, the kitchen smelled of pork roast, and I was whipping the potatoes. Mother plopped down in a chair. "How is Alida?" she asked. I said that Alida was fine.

"I hope I don't have to wait too long before I see her again," said Mother, and then she began to weep. "I keep trying to remember what I said to your father that morning before he went downstairs. I wish I could remember that I kissed him or told him I loved him, but all I can remember is telling him to take the rubber binders down to the basement. I hope I didn't say it in a mean way. He was in a good mood that morning. He talked about you, Johnny. He had found a term paper you wrote, about the Battle of Gettysburg, and Dad thought it was quite impressive." She blew her nose. "He thought a lot of all you kids; it just wasn't in him to say so."

I checked the pork roast and took it out of the oven.

"I sat down on the step by him and put my arm around him, but I think he was gone then," Mother said. "But maybe he could hear me."

Ronnie stood behind her, his hands on her shoulders, and she patted his hand. "I do think he knew that I loved him," she said.

After lunch, we all trooped up to Lindberg's Funeral Home to see Dad, laid out in his coffin. We walked through the front door, into air heavy with the scent of old flowers, and I took a deep breath and stopped. Suddenly I could imagine my own coffin being wheeled along this hall to the hearse, my carcass wedged inside, Mother weeping, my brothers and sisters trudging along, a few dozen Tollefsons lumbering behind them, and up to the cemetery they'd go and someone would say, "Well, it's for the best. He wouldn't have wanted to linger the way he was." Not true! I want to linger a long time, until they find a cure! "He wanted a simple funeral, no eulogy or anything of that sort." Heck, no. I want major eulogies, a gigantic funeral, bushels of flowers, spare no expense. And they would sing "Called from above, a heavenly race by birth," and watch me descend into a hole in the ground, and an assistant dean of St. James, a small man with dandruff who could easily be spared for pointless occasions, would shake Mother's hand and extend the condolences of the president, the dean, the staff of WSJO.

Dad looked unlifelike, waxen, like a fallen mannequin, but the work shirt and pants were a nice touch. There was even a plastic pocket protector and three ballpoint pens in his pocket. Ronnie glanced down and turned away, stricken. Diana got weepy and leaned her face against April's bosom and whimpered about how hard it was to see him cold and dead. Mr. Lindberg came in. Bill inquired about the weather forecast, and Mr. Lindberg said he had buried people in all kinds of weather, rain and snow and once when a tornado was skipping along the horizon. "It was an old bachelor farmer, and there were only ten of us at the graveside when that tornado hooked around and headed our way, and everybody dashed for cover, and I didn't want him to blow away, so I cut the rope, and the coffin landed in the grave like a ton of bricks. We all hid under a tree, and the tornado skipped over the cemetery, and I went to close up the grave, and the coffin lid had sprung open and his eyelids too, and he lay there, hands folded, looking up at me as if he were hoping it was the resurrection and that somebody'd buy him a drink."

I stood behind Mother and Diana. The tip of Dad's nose poked up from the satin lining. I remembered the old song he liked to sing, about the father who walked through the blizzard to meet the train he thought was bringing his son home from a distant city:

Oh, the Prodigal Son missed the late train home
And went out to drink with his friends.
And the one who most loved him lay dead in the snow—
He'll never see Daddy again.

"The Jews bury their dead the same day," Mother said on the walk home. "They put the body in a box and put it in the ground and go home and grieve for seven days and then it's over. They've got the right idea. I don't know why we drag it out like this."

I called Alida in New York that evening from Dad's chair in the living room, his old maple table next to the chair with a loon lamp on it and an ashtray full of paper clips for marking interesting passages in books, a glass jar labeled "Nuts" half full of marbles. She was in the kitchen. Her friends Suzanne and Bucky were coming for dinner; she had bought a chicken in lemon tarragon butter from the deli and a quart of risotto and a pint of succotash—it was all in the oven, the bread would go in in a few minutes, the deli salad was resting in the fridge, the wine was open, a New York Chardonnay. There was thick fog on the river; you couldn't see New Jersey.

I asked what she was wearing.

"Jeans and a white shirt. Why?"

"I want to imagine exactly how it looks," I said. "What are you going to serve the chicken on?"

"The white platter with the Italian flag on it. And I'll put out the big white plates and the red salad bowls."

"Talking to you is like tuning in to my real life."

"How are you all holding up?"

I said that we were all doing as well as could be expected under the circumstances.

SEVENTEEN

Friday

The snow came down hard again Friday morning. The schools were closed because the snowplows couldn't get out because the doors of the Mist County garage were frozen, according to the radio. It was the *Top of the Morning Show,* with Ole and Toivo. Dad's brother Henry was sitting listening to it when I came downstairs at six. Henry had flown in from Los Angeles the night before and arrived in Lake Wobegon at five. It was like seeing Dad sitting there, except tanned and with a better haircut and wearing an expensive tweed jacket and a white shirt. "Took me three hours just to get through the Cities," he said. "Cars in the ditch everywhere. People here have forgotten how to drive." He was a Minnesotan gone to Santa Monica for almost forty years, but he still knew how to drive through a snowstorm, by God. Ole was saying, "Ja, it's a cold one, Toivo. You know what you get if you sit on the ice and freeze your hinder? You get polaroids." "Ja, Ole," said Toivo. "That reminds me of the one about Sven. He was goin' out on the lake ice fishing, but he was scared—what if a bear come after him? So he asked Hjalmar. 'Oh,' Hjalmar says, 'that's no problem. You just run fast as you can, and if the bear gets too close, you reach back and grab some and throw it at him.' 'Grab what?' says Sven. 'Oh, don't worry,' says Hjalmar, 'it'll be there. It'll be there.' "

This was the show Dad listened to every morning over his bran flakes. Two idiots peeling off moldy jokes, mostly about excrement or sex or avoiding work. Dad sat in this chair and ate breakfast and pe-rused the auction bulletins in the back pages of the *Herald Star* and listened to Ole and Toivo.

"How is your mother holding up?" Henry said.

I said she was fine. I gave Henry the down comforter and sent him off to bed and ventured out to salt the sidewalk. I looked for salt in the garage among half-empty paint cans and old storm windows, old tools with broken handles waiting for the tool resurrection. There was a thick rubber belt from an escalator that Dad had brought home when I was fourteen years old. Here it lay, right where we had un-loaded it three decades ago. Next to it was a bag of salt. I trod gingerly around the house to the front walk. A perilous task, salting. I could imagine slipping on the ice and waving my arms in some weird way and slipping a disk and spending a year or two on major painkillers. A teacher at Bill's school slipped while shoveling snow and fifteen years later he was in India, eating lentils soaked in yogurt and waiting for the Rama Lama to come and place the sacred banyan branch on his back and chant the disk mantra—ice could do that to a person.

At nine, Aunt Ray and Uncle Art came over to visit with Henry, who was asleep. Judy arrived, with a loaf of rye bread. Mother made a fresh pot of coffee, put out a plate of crackers and herring and cheese, radishes, ham salad, pickles. We sat around the kitchen, drinking cof-fee, picking at food, passing time, snow falling outside the window, the old Regulator wall clock clacking in the living room. Dad bought it at auction; it had hung in the school library when he was a boy. It reminded me of that old song:

Many years without slumbering (tick, tock, tick, tock),
His life seconds numbering (tick, tock, tick, tock),
But it stopped short, never to go again,
When the old man died.

The herring reminded Art of a man named Harry who disappeared in a cornfield in 1955. Art couldn't remember his last name. They cut down the corn, thinking his body might be there, and found only his coveralls. He had given no indication of anything being wrong. Just disappeared.

We sat digesting that information for a while, and then Diana asked Mother why she decided not to bury Dad in a suit.

"He hated suits," Mother said. "He was one of the first to quit dressing up for church on Sunday morning. He went in his everyday clothes and was proud of himself for doing it. He loved his work, and I'm going to have him buried in what he wore when he was happiest. Burying him in a suit would be like burying him in a white taffeta dress."

"Well, it's up to you," Diana said.

"You do what you think best, Mary," said Aunt Ray, and then she sniffled and blew her nose. She had been crying all night, Uncle Art said, and he was worried about her getting dehydrated. She said she felt bad that she didn't have anything nice to wear for Byron's funeral. She hadn't been shopping for clothes for months, because she needed to lose weight first. She didn't think Marvin could come—he was a mess, and had admitted himself to the Veterans Hospital chemical-dependency program. And Uncle Bernie—he was running a fever of 102° and jabbering about oats and cussing out a farmhand named Howard who died in 1986. It was one thing after another.

The funeral service would be on Saturday at ten A.M. in the Lutheran church, David presiding, and then we would take him up to the cemetery and bury him, and come back to church for lunch, Mother said.

"We're going to sing 'Children of the Heavenly Father, safely in his bosom gather,' and we'll read a psalm and the passage about the corruptible putting on the incorruptible, and David is going to preach on the verse 'I will never leave you, nor will I forsake you,' and I think it would be nice if somebody did a eulogy." Mother looked at me.

"I can't. I'm sorry. I would go to pieces," I said. "It wouldn't be a pretty sight."

"I'll do it," said Diana.

"Fine," said Mother.

Ray looked at Mother, pleadingly. "Don't you think it's a sign of respect to bury a man in a shirt and tie and a jacket?"

"No," said Mother. "Alvin was buried in a shirt and tie and a jacket." Alvin was the town drunk, an old ballplayer who started tucking into the whiskey when his playing days were done and spent thirty years as a living example of the vast squalor available to us if we care to search for it. He died in a doorway with a quart bottle of peppermint brandy. His children had him cleaned up and stuffed into a starched white shirt and a suit, and he made a far better corpse than human being.

"It's just that—" And now Ray's eyes filled with tears, and her lips got flubbery. She said, "I hate to think of people seeing my brother—in his coffin—in some old work shirt."

"If they were going to look down on him, they had a whole lifetime to do it in; I don't see why they'd wait until now," said Mother.

Henry came downstairs, looking chipper in a ski sweater and black pants, and Mother poured him a cup of coffee. "I hope we're not getting ourselves a blizzard like that one in '41," said Henry. "That was a doozy."

Judy said that Mr. Hoveth, the Grand Oya of the Sons of Knute, had spoken to her about the Knutes' participation in the service. Mother rolled her eyes. "He and the High Chamberlain and the Bard of the Lodge and the Old Scout would like to come in their lodge regalia and do the Touching of the Forehead," said Judy.

"Whose forehead?" said Mother.

"Dad's, of course. It's a ritual of theirs."

Mother sighed. "I'm not in the mood for a circus," she said. The Knutes go in for the King Arthur aspects of fraternaldom, the swords and capes and plumes; they don't just do good works like the Kiwanis; they like to swashbuckle.

"Our father was a Grand Oya," said Henry. "I thought of him when I saw the statue downtown. Remember his sayings, Ray? How they drove Mother crazy. 'If *ifs* and *ans* were pots and pans, there'd be no trade for tinkers.' She'd go right up the wall. 'Listen too hard and you'll always hear something bad about yourself,' he'd say. To a poor sailor, all wind is against him. Don't judge the dog by his hair. Do your best and leave the rest. It's a foolish goose who goes to the fox's church. In silk and scarlet walks many a harlot. Mother'd say, 'What is that supposed to mean?' "

"Anyway, Dad was fond of those old Knutes," said Bill. He explained the forehead ceremony, a ritual greeting between Knutes, whereby the older brother taps the younger on the forehead and the younger is supposed to say, "Ost vest hjemme bedst." East or west, home is best. And the older one should reply, "Gaa altid lige hjem." Always go straight home. And then they turn around once, humming, and say Oya! and hook the little fingers of their right hands, and pull, and say, "Paa dommedag er vi alle lige." On Judgment Day are we all alike. He added, "But that part they leave out of the funeral rite. Only the tapping of the forehead would be done. And they would leave out the part where they fart."

"Pardon me?" said Mother.

"When they hook their little fingers—oh, never mind."

Judy said, "What they want to do, Mother, is process to the front of the church, stand beside the coffin—"

"Which will be closed at that point," said Mother.

"Of course."

"I'm not going to have anyone tap him on the forehead."

"No, no. They'll tap on the coffin and say, 'Go straight home.' "

Mother smiled. That was Dad's customary good night to departing guests: "You go straight home now, don't stop on the way."

Mother got up to cut slices of Judy's rye bread. She sliced an onion and set it out with liverwurst and mustard and a long reddish herring that looked like a person's tongue. Art fixed himself a liverwurst-onion-herring sandwich that made Diana blanch. She put her hand alongside her head as a blinder, to block the view of it.

I didn't see how we could avoid having a Knute presence. Dad was a Knute, period, who tried to get his sons to join. He'd told us about ancient rune blocks proving that back in the twelfth century the Vikings possessed amazing scientific knowledge. For example, though they didn't know about internal combustion, they possessed the secret of cruise control. Dad said you could learn a lot about Norway and ancient history through the lodge, but we boys weren't interested. When you saw the Knute contingent on Norwegian Independence Day, in their horned helmets and deerskin capes and red sashes festooned with buttons and medals and cheap jewelry, it was obvious that scholarship was not the main deal. And who wants to be a lodge brother with his dad?

"One other little detail," said Judy. "They need to bring their ceremonial hoop and walleye."

"It's a wooden walleye," said Bill.

Judy nodded. "The Chamberlain lays the hoop on the floor and the Oya steps inside it and then he is given the staff with the golden walleye to hold, and then he says the part about going straight home."

"Over my dead body," said Mother. She stood up to make a fresh pot of coffee.

"Maybe they could do it before the service," said Bill, trying to be helpful.

"I'm not going to have people fooling around with hoops and a fish," said Mother. "Next question."

"Did you ever hear about their initiation ritual?" said Uncle Henry. "You have to pick up a quarter with your bare butt."

Diana groaned. "Do we have to hear about this now?" she said. "Could this wait?"

"They set a quarter down on a wooden bench, and the initiate has to drop his trousers and pick up the quarter between his cheeks without using his hands. It's not that easy. Try it sometime—you'll see."

Mother said she doubted that Byron ever did that. He was squeamish about nudity. "I didn't see him without his clothes on until we'd been married three years," she said. She got up to slice more herring. And then she turned, paring knife in hand, and told an old story about Dad.

"I remember the last time Byron went hunting. The time he came home naked," she said. "That was a great day. I always hated deerhunting. He'd sit at the table cleaning his rifle and he'd put the barrel up to his eye and I'd have to leave the room. And to hunt during mating season . . . I said to Byron, How would you feel if you had been courting me and getting excited and then you got a whiff of stale beer and saw an unshaven man with a bright-orange cap pointing a gun at you and there was a blast of flame and everything went black? Byron said it was every man's dream to die exactly that way.

"Anyway, I remember the last time he went hunting. It was with Bill."

Bill smiled. "That was the time with the duck decoy."

Uncle Art smacked his hand on the table. "By God, I love this story," he said.

"Never heard this one," said Henry.

Mother sat down and continued. "Byron was intrigued with those giant duck decoys that the Knutes bought back in the fifties. Those sixteen-foot floating fiberglass decoys that the hunter was supposed to lie inside and look up through a periscope in the duck's head and when he saw ducks flying in, he'd kick open a trapdoor under the tail and fire.

"They weren't particularly seaworthy, and what's more, they seemed to frighten away ducks. Maybe the size of them made the lake look too small, I don't know. Two of these decoys sat moldering in back of the Knute temple, and Byron took one and hauled it up to the woods for a deer blind. He called it the Trojan Duck. He set it next to a deer path and came out the next morning with Bill and a box lunch and a sleeping bag and a big Tupperware bowl full of raspberry Jell-O with sliced bananas, mandarin oranges, crushed walnuts, and miniature marshmallows, covered with Miracle Whip, which he told me deer are crazy about, and he set that out on a tree stump for bait. He told Bill to go up the trail a hundred yards and wait there, and if the deer got past Byron, to shoot it. And then Byron climbed into the decoy with his sleeping bag and lay down to wait for the deer. And then a deer came and started eating the Jell-O."

It was interesting to hear Mother tell this story without Dad interrupting her to correct her on every little thing.

Bill said, "I didn't want to be involved, so I went about two hundred yards up the path and found a tree to lean against and sat down. I was wearing a red-checked wool jacket and an orange cap with a wreath of branches on it. I sat very still until I felt myself go into a sort of trance."

We all laughed. Bill always had the ability to remain perfectly still. He would sit on his bed upstairs with a magazine open on his lap to a picture of African women balancing water jars on their heads, and listen to Mother call to him, and not move a muscle.

Bill said, "I sat with the rifle between my knees, locked in this trance. And then a chickadee landed on the barrel of the rifle. I sat and looked at it, and I didn't move. I couldn't move. The chickadee didn't move either.

"And then a deer came leaping up the trail with white foam on her lips. She saw me and she swerved into the brush and I heard a gun go off and it was my gun. And a moment later, all these chickadee feathers came fluttering down on me. And then I got up to go look for Dad."

Mother said, "That deer was the one that Byron saw through the periscope, feeding on the Jell-O. It was a doe, her front hooves were up on the stump, her face down in the Tupperware, and then she looked up with a white Miracle Whip mustache on her upper lip, and then she bolted.

"Byron kicked open the trapdoor and climbed out and caught his foot, and the decoy flipped over and he fell out on the ground and saw a skunk about six feet away. It was the skunk who had spooked the deer. The skunk was after the Jell-O, and when he saw a man come out of the rear end of a duck, it was too much for one day. He turned his back on Byron and cut loose. Byron said he must've been a teenage skunk, he was so full of bitterness. The smell hit Byron and it took his breath away. He dropped the gun and staggered up the trail and tore off his clothes as he walked. He could hardly see where he was going, his eyes were so teary, and he felt dizzy and about to fall over.

"And then here came Bill, who had just killed a chickadee."

Bill said, "Dad was naked except for his boots. He looked terrible. His face was red and he was crying, and I couldn't bear to come within twenty feet of him, so I said, 'I'll sing to you and you follow me,' and I sang 'Rock of Ages' and 'Leaning on the Everlasting Arms,' and we got to the pickup truck and he climbed in back and I drove him home."

Mother said, "He looked like death on toast when he got here. I sprayed water from the hose over him and tossed him a bar of soap, and he washed and rinsed himself a dozen times, and I got out the copper boiler and filled it with hot water and he soaked in that, and we poured tomato juice over him, and lemon, and baking soda, and after four hours of soaking and rinsing, we were able to take him inside. He said that all this time he was praying that the Lord wouldn't let him die, smelling as bad as he did, because nobody would come to his funeral; they'd have to cremate him.

"He never hunted after that. He told me he'd always wanted to quit and he was only looking for a reason. His guns are still in the basement, though."

"Of course," I said.

Henry said, "By gosh, I never heard that story before."

Mother stood up. "I'm tired," she said. "I need a nap. I'll make dinner tonight. How about we have a nice bottle of wine with it?" Fine, said Henry, so he and I drove to St. Cloud in his rental Lincoln in search of wine. Snow was still falling, and the tire tracks on Main Street were almost a foot deep. Cliff was shoveling in front of the Mercantile, Luanne Halvorson in front of her beauty parlor. Clarence Bunsen was sweeping off the row of used cars at Bunsen Motors—he paused to wave, and Henry saluted back.

"I hear you're thinking of getting married," said Henry. "That's great. Did I tell you that Alice and I almost got divorced a few years ago?"

"Nobody tells me anything," I said.

"We came within an inch of it," said Henry, "but then our kids all went into therapy about the same time—you know, the kind where the whole family sits in a little room and says terrible things about each other—and that brought us back together. We sort of united against the kids. The reason we almost split up was because after I took early retirement, we found out that we couldn't stand to be in the same room with each other. She drove me nuts. She was always finishing my sentences for me. I'd pause for the comma, and she thought it was a blank to fill in. And she was mad at me because I made fun of that stupid book she wrote about the spiritual aspects of gardening. She sent me an E-mail that said, 'There is no reason to go on living a mistake we made thirty-seven years ago. I have found out what love is and someday maybe you will too. I wish you all the best, whatever that may mean in your case.' It hurt me pretty bad. I asked Byron what to do, and he said to do nothing.

"Turned out she was having an affair with a guy named Brett or Brad, or Shad, who did research on her book. Fine, I said, God bless you, enjoy your sex life, long may your tendrils intertwine."

We found a liquor store in a shopping center, but it sold only wino wine, and we drove on in search of something good. We found a shop called Uptown Liquors near the Super 66 truck stop, and went in, and examined the wines. There was a Château Grand Marais, 1978, for only fifteen dollars—a legendary Burgundy. I had seen it in New York for eighty. I took four bottles, and I asked the clerk, a young man in a stocking cap, a cast on his left arm, if there were more in the storeroom, and he went back to look.

"So Alice was all packed up and ready to move out, but then Brent, or Chad, or whoever, said his ex-girlfriend was still emotionally dependent on him and needed time for closure. So Allie stayed home. And then our kids started coming unraveled. Alan was in Chicago— he was in theater, acting in those plays where the actors crawl around in their underwear on a pile of truck tires, waving flashlights and free-associating—and Kevin dropped out of architecture school and moved home to become a songwriter, and Emma got engaged to this sad sack anesthetist in Boston, and a week before the wedding, he ran off with the best man. We already had the plane tickets, so we flew to Boston and had dinner and ate bad mussels, and four hours later, sitting around in our hotel, we looked at each other and started throwing up."

The young man emerged from the back, lugging a case of Château Grand Marais. "Got three more," he said. "How many you want?"

"All you got," I said.

"Anyway, Kevin was writing songs and he asked for my honest reaction, and I said, 'You want honest?' and he said he did, and I said, 'Kev, the urge to perform is no indication of talent.' He walked out into the night weeping, and two days later he came back and told me he hated me. Then Emma moved in with an idiot who gave up the practice of law to raise purebred sheep, and they lived like serfs in a cabin without insulation or electricity, surrounded by miserable animals they couldn't deal with and losing money in the process. And Alan went to New York and got a job tending bar in the lobby of the theater where *Cats* played, and an ad director saw him and liked him, and Alan got hired to do that commercial for Chucky potato chips."

"Right," I said. "I remember that."

"The one where he ate the chip, grinned at the camera, and said, 'A-hum daddy, hum daddy, hum daddy hum,' in a frog voice. It was cute. He earned a hundred thousand dollars in one year from that and sent Allie and me on a trip to Thailand and we went—Thad's ex-girlfriend's therapist asked him not to have contact with Allie—and in Thailand, we discovered that sex was still good, and that was nice to know."

The young man came back with the cases on a dolly. I paid, and we carried the wine out to the car and put the cases in the trunk. The snow had let up for the time being, and a plow truck passed by, its blue lights flashing.

"We came home from Thailand, and two weeks later, Alan was arrested in Oregon for sexual abuse of an eleven-year-old boy. Alan was on a bike trip, and the kid came up to him at a rest stop and said, 'Hey, Chucky Chip—do the A-hum daddy, hum daddy, hum daddy hum,' and Alan said, 'Get out of here, you little prick,' and under Oregon law, that's sexual assault.

"There Alan was, a rich New York actor with an earring, accused of molesting a sixth grader, so he hired an expensive lawyer, who got the charges dropped and settled with the kid's parents out of court and Alan was free, but it cost him two hundred thousand dollars. I had to remortgage the house."

We got in the car, and Henry headed west for Lake Wobegon, behind the plow truck. The landscape was pillowed in white on either side of the black strip of asphalt, a feathery lightness.

"Alan came home emotionally drained. One night, he accused Allie and me of using him as a pawn in our personal struggles for dominance. He said that we had never accepted him as a complete person. He talked for two hours, and it was boring and whiny. I went up to bed at two A.M., and she was waiting for me in the bedroom. It was pitch black. My arm brushed against her, and I let out a shout that made the neighbor's lights go on. She said, 'You excite me too.' The police arrived when we were in the middle of it. Alan let them in. Our door was locked. It was the most wonderful sex, and they stood out there asking if we were okay. Alan got upset and had to call his therapist, and he came right over at three A.M.—he charged two hundred dollars an hour for house calls, and I was paying for the whole thing, of course—and I told the therapist to get out. He was a very deliberate man in a beige turtleneck, the sort who, just before he does anything, tells you he's going to do it. 'I'm going to ask you a question now.' 'I'm going to be quiet now and let Alan talk.' A real slow-motion guy. The cops were there, and the neighbor, and Kevin woke up and came down. The therapist called up Emma and she came over, with her shepherd, and all of us sat in the living room, and the three kids lit into us and said we had never known them as people, only as trophies, and the neighbor said he had always taken me for a passive-aggressive, and the cops put in their two cents' worth, and I listened to all that I cared to, and I said, 'I'm sure we made our mistakes, but compared to you rotten kids, I'd say we did pretty well with our lives.' I told everybody to get out of my house, and Allie and I ordered Thai takeout and sat up and talked until noon and made love like a couple of bunnies. We've been thick as thieves ever since. Last week, Emma said she'd like to get back in contact with us. Fine, I said, take us out to dinner. Alan quit acting and became a mailman and he's better now, and Kevin—I don't know. He's in Hawaii. How are you?"

"Fine," I said. "I've never been in therapy, and I never had to think about divorce."

A gothic saga, Henry's tale, a saga of exiled Wobegonians losing their moorings, but how normal was my family? One brother in Dallas waiting for the millennium, and a sister caught up in narcissistic dog snot about self-realization, and another locked in the proprieties of being a pastor's wife, and another brother sunk in a joyless marriage and a possible case of butt cancer, and then there was me, with a foundering restaurant and giving horseshit speeches and being flim-flammed by a hippie, and now I was in hot water for telling a joke about a douche bag.

Mother slept late into the afternoon, and I fixed a cassoulet for dinner, one of those dishes that take no time to make and taste better than they have any right to. I sautéed onions in butter and added wine and fresh basil and dumped in layers of white beans and chunks of chicken and sausage and baked it, and it was downright tasty, especially with a great fifteen-dollar Burgundy. I stashed the four cases of Grand Marais in the basement, next to the freezer. After the table was cleared and dishes were washed, we sat in the living room, near the spot where the Christmas tree always stood, with the mountain range of presents beneath it, the red stockings hanging, stuffed, the Christmas oranges in the toes. Dad used to set up the model-train tracks on this floor and turn out the lights, and he and I would watch the North Coast Limited go clattering around behind the couch and through the legs of the table.

"It was sad going into the Chatterbox Café today," Diana said. "I saw Margie Detwiler. God. You look at her rear end as she walks away, it's like two dogs fighting in a potato sack."

"It's the Blessing of the Snowmobiles Sunday at Our Lady of Perpetual Responsibility," I announced. "They're expecting five hundred of them."

Mother said those snowmobilers were crazy, racing around in the dark, blind drunk, killing each other. "It was seven years ago last November that Art's nephew DuWayne drowned in the lake," she said. "He was out snowmobiling, and he walked out on the ice to test it, and it tested well until, about a hundred yards from shore, DuWayne broke through. He floundered around and yelled and nobody could do anything and he died out there."

Diana snorted. "Snowmobiling and deer-hunting and beer-drinking—it's all a form of natural selection, isn't it. A way of eliminating poor breeding stock."

Ronnie stood up and announced he was going to bed. Everyone

said good night, and Mother said, "Don't let the bedbugs bite." We listened to Ronnie go up the stairs and into the upstairs bathroom and close the door. Sure enough, he turned on the water in the sink and let it run. Ever since he was a kid, he had done that when he peed, so nobody could hear what he was up to.

"Remember when Ronnie went forward in church?" said Diana.

"He did it three times," said Bill.

"At least three," said Diana.

"I never heard about this," said Henry. Mother said it wasn't that interesting a story.

Diana said, "This was when he was about nine or ten. He started to cry during a Pastor Tommerdahl sermon about stewardship. It was dry as dust and delivered in that foghorn monotone of his, and Ronnie started quivering and he said, 'Why—am—I—like—this?' And Dad leaned over and said, 'Shhhhhh. We're in church.' But Ronnie stood up and went lumbering up the aisle to the pulpit and knelt down, and Pastor Tommerdahl looked on in utter amazement. He was a guy who believed in sticking with the program no matter what. But he had to kneel beside Ronnie, and Ronnie was crying and nobody could understand a word of it, and meanwhile everyone was thinking about their pot roasts in the oven, and finally Mother went up and retrieved him."

Mother turned to April. "It's amazing the things your children remember from when they were young."

"So you don't have conversion experiences in the Lutheran Church?" said April.

"We have them privately," I said. "Basically, Lutherans don't believe you can get rid of guilt by bursting into tears. We believe that you work off guilt by serving on committees. That's what leads people to coach youth basketball and be on the church board, you know. A good sense of guilt."

Mother said, "I learn so much when you children come home."

"Your average peewee-hockey coach is a guy who is paying back for a weekend in a motel with an aerobics instructor named Trish," I said.

"I never thought of it that way," said April.

"Oh yes," I said. "The best high school teacher I ever had was carrying on an affair."

"Mr. Tuomey," said Bill.

I nodded. "When people run somebody out of town for messing around, they're losing the person who could've run Vacation Bible School for the next twenty years and never expect a word of thanks."

"Speaking of which, whatever happened to Bob Andersen?" asked Diana.

Mother said she had no idea. He had gone off to New York years ago. She hadn't heard a word about him since.

"He was the only boy I ever loved!" Diana said.

"He went to New York and became a dancer," said Mother.

"He was the sweetest person," said Diana, "and he and I hung out together. He knew every song in *The Music Man* by heart. The Krebsbach boys beat him up because he was effeminate. Nobody stood up for him."

Bill said he didn't remember the Krebsbachs beating up anybody.

"They beat him up after school under the bleachers down by the ballpark. He once put his arms around me and sang 'Till There Was You.' " She hummed a few bars of the tune.

"I'm going to cry at the funeral. I hope it doesn't embarrass you," she said. "I cried when we buried our dog Weenie. Remember?" She looked at April. "I cried all afternoon."

I told her she'd have to cry buckets to beat Aunt Ray.

"I am learning to let my emotions out. I am a recovering Lutheran," Diana said. "I am getting over the idea of emotional distance as a mark of normality."

"You were brought up with no such thing," said Mother, standing. "Your father and I cared deeply about all of you, and on that note, I am going to bed. Thank you all for an interesting evening." She kissed us each good night, and we listened to her footsteps in the hall. Then we heard breathing. It was Uncle Henry, asleep in Dad's chair, his mouth open.

"Speaking of beating people up," I said, "I found a loaded forty-five automatic in Dad's tool chest, and a bundle of fifties, brand new."

"You didn't," said Bill.

"I found a gun and a pack of cigarillos, a sundress, and a magazine full of pictures of blond women with breasts the size of cantaloupes."

"You're kidding, right?" said Diana.

"There was also a picture of Vincent Foster and a map of the Texas School Book Depository." I stood up. "There was much about your father you didn't know. Good night, everyone." I took Uncle Henry's hand. Henry opened his eyes and shuddered. "Come on, Uncle Henry, time to hit the hay," and I helped him up from the chair and towed him toward the stairs.

EIGHTEEN

Chatterbox

The bedroom was awash in light. There was a full moon. The trees in the Andersens' yard across the alley cast faint shadows. I undressed and crawled into my old bed and burrowed under the blankets. One of the blankets smelled of smoke from having gone on a camping trip once.

The last funeral I attended in Lake Wobegon was Jim Tuomey's, my old English teacher, shot by a hulking bullet-headed man named Myron Magendanz, a second cousin to my old football coach, when Mr. Tuomey was bringing the man's wife back to the Magendanz farm at four o'clock in the morning. It was a cold November night, raining, and Mr. Tuomey was dressed only in a blue paper hospital gown at the time. He collapsed in the mud of the Magendanz farm-yard with a bullet in his abdomen and died in the cold and the rain, curled on his side, alone, nobody to hold his hand.

He and the wife had been parked in his green van on the one-lane dirt road along the lake between the swimming beach and the boat launch. She had parked her brown Toyota behind him, and the two of them were in the van when the town cops, Gary and LeRoy, drove up in the patrol car, and Mr. Tuomey rolled down his window to talk to them. They could see the figure of a woman next to him, but they didn't try to see who it was. They didn't want to know. The rain was coming down in sheets. Gary told Mr. Tuomey to drive carefully, and that was that.

Perhaps the encounter with the cops threw the lovers off stride. They drove to the Romeo Motel on Highway 10 outside St. Cloud, near the state prison—a motel shielded by evergreens and famous for its round beds and Jacuzzis, its theme rooms (Jungle Love, Sheik of Araby, Gone With the Wind, Roman Orgy, Sunset Strip)—where Mr. Tuomey checked in around eight P.M. under the name "Mr. and Mrs. Lawrence H. David" and got the Casanova Suite, where they were in bed three hours later when the mirror fell off the ceiling and landed on their backs. The fire department arrived at eleven-fifteen P.M. in a hook-and-ladder, siren screaming, and six firemen in black-and-yellow slickers piled into the room and found them naked, bleeding, the bed littered with broken glass. They were wrapped in silver insulated sheets, and their blood pressures and temperatures were taken. Mr. Tuomey, though in shock, pointed out to the firemen that the mirror had not been properly installed: the screws did not penetrate the joists; the mirror had been fastened to the acoustic ceiling tile. He urged them to check the other rooms in the motel. The fire captain responded that he did not need to know any more about the Romeo Motel than he knew already.

The lovers were taken to the St. Cloud Hospital emergency room, where, minutes before, sixteen high school wrestlers had arrived, banged up from a bus rollover. At one A.M., the resident on duty and a nurse began plucking slivers of glass out of Mr. Tuomey and Mrs. Magendanz, which took an hour, and then there was paperwork to be completed. A taxi took them back to the Romeo to pick up the van. Their clothing had glass fragments in it, so they kept the blue paper hospital gowns on and drove back to the beach for her car. The road was now a river. She had parked half off the road, and her wheels were mired in mud. He laid old roofing shingles down for traction, but the car could not be moved. And then, gallant man that he was, he drove her home.

He pulled into the barnyard, and Myron Magendanz came out of the house with a shotgun. He told the jury he was going deer-hunting, but he was wearing green coveralls, not hunting clothes. He was quite distraught. Mr. Tuomey got out of his van and walked toward Myron, the blue paper gown half sliding off him, and he held out his hands and said something about having wronged him and wanting to make things right, and Myron shot him in the stomach. Mr. Tuomey turned and took two steps and toppled into the mud and lay dying with the rain pouring down on him, the paper gown pasted to his body. The wife ran screaming into the house and locked the door and Myron stood outside pleading with her and finally she let him in. When Gary and LeRoy and the sheriff arrived, a little before five, Mr. Tuomey was quite dead.

About sixty people attended Mr. Tuomey's funeral, including his wife and his two sons and their wives, some teachers, a few old students. I flew in from New York. I felt I had to be there. David Ingqvist preached on forgiveness. He said there is less need to punish people than one might think, that people are quite able to do this for themselves. Some weepy man read Shakespeare's "When in disgrace with fortune and men's eyes," which made little sense under the circumstances, and a woman teacher did a big purplish reading of "Intimations of Immortality," and there was no reference to what had happened; everybody just sang hymns and talked about hope. I walked out into that cold fall day, wondering how a man could be so foolish at the age of sixty-one. To have an affair with the wife of a hunter. And to go to the Romeo Motel. And she wasn't even good-looking. It must have been the excitement of the chase. That tail-twitching, head-upraised sniffing of the air, the urge to follow the scent and deal with the consequences later.

Moonlight flooded the room. A car crept up the alley over the packed snow and pulled into a garage, and the motor stopped. Bill's and Diana's voices floated up from the living room. I heard the mice in the attic having their supper. Heard a dry leaf as it landed on the roof and slid down into the gutter. Heard my father whispering in the attic. Heard Mr. Tuomey reciting "Come live with me and be my love" in front of our English class, his eyes shining when he came to "And we will sit upon the Rocks / . . . By shallow Rivers, to whose falls / Melodious byrds sing madrigalls."

People in town were tight-lipped about the murder. Dad, a man who was full of stories and information, would only shake his head and say, "A messy business." Myron was charged with first-degree murder, was tried and acquitted by a jury, and sold his farm, and he and his wife and their three children moved to Montana. Leland was on the jury. They deliberated for two hours. I once asked Leland about the trial, and Leland snapped, "We're not allowed to discuss it." Which I knew was untrue. "A jury is accountable to the community," I said. "A jury is accountable to its own conscience," said Leland, "and mine is resting easy, and end of subject."

I awoke at five-thirty, an hour before the alarm, and realized it was Saturday, the day of Dad's funeral. Bill was sleeping on his back, mouth open, and I picked up my clothes and tiptoed out and dressed in the dark hallway. The sign on the wall said *Mind the Top Step: Carpet Tends to Bunch.* I didn't want to clatter around in the kitchen making coffee and maybe wake up Mother, so I pulled on a parka— Dad's old green one and his scarf and gloves—and slipped out into the dark and walked down McKinley Street to the Chatterbox Café. It was bitterly cold, thirty below, easily. A day with that sense of crisis so satisfying to Midwesterners, when they feel their character being tested. Dad loved to go out on a cold day like this. He loved to go around and check on old people and make sure their heat was working, which it always was. I walked fast. Thirty below hurts. A temperature at which physical matter wants to stop and become permanent, such as water, which is 97 percent of what a person is, after all.

The windows of the café blazed at the foot of the long hill, and figures stirred within. All was still except for my footsteps in the snow. The front walks of the houses along McKinley were shoveled, the edges straight, beveled, which seemed odd considering that people hardly ever use front doors in Lake Wobegon: front doors are emergency exits. If someone knocks on your front door, it must be a Jehovah's Witness, and you open the door and say no, thank you, I have my own church. But if you don't shovel the front, people might think you were ill and would come shovel it for you. The brick tower of Our Lady of Perpetual Responsibility loomed up to the left, and a figure shrunk down into a parka stood by the door and his cigarette glowed. An altar boy waiting for six A.M. Mass.

It was chilly in the café, and everybody had his coat on. There were four empty stools in a row at the counter between Clint Bunsen and Mr. Berge, and I sat nearer Clint, who said, "I'm awfully sorry about your dad, John." Clint wore a heavy ski sweater, blue and white, and a baseball cap—to conceal hair loss, I guess.

"It's not the same without him in here," said Mr. Berge. Dorothy looked at me from the door to the kitchen. "You look as handsome as ever," she said. "How about me?" said Mr. Berge. She snorted. Mr. Berge asked me if I was going to move back home now. I said I didn't think so. "Anybody who moves here now should have his head examined," said Dorothy.

She explained that it was chilly because the furnace had gone out. When she arrived at four A.M., it was forty degrees inside, and she called Carl Krebsbach to come and replace a switch. A new furnace. She shook her head. It was all this new electronic digital-schmigital baloney.

"My brother's furnace went out, and he called a guy in St. Cloud to fix it, and he charged him two hundred eighty-two fifty for a pilot burner," said Clint. "A hundred fifty would be more like it."

Dorothy said that Carl was going to come back and install a banister on the basement stairs so somebody didn't fall and break their neck.

"I'm no carpenter," said Mr. Berge. "Mainly I turn raw materials into scraps." He said the good thing about a furnace going out is that the cold can kill off any fungus you may have. His neighbor had had fungus. Squirrels filled their gutters with acorns, and water leaked through the shingles and ran down the walls and spread a rare fungus through the entire house. The neighbor's wife swelled up to twice her size and had to be put under a plastic tent in the hospital and the family could only visit with her by way of video camera.

Darlene brought me a coffee cup and returned, two pots of coffee in her hands. "Got the weak stuff for the old folks, and we got the regular if you need a kick in the pants," she said. I ordered the kick in the pants.

"This may seem odd," I said, "but I'd sort of like to have what my dad used to have for breakfast."

"Why, of course," she said.

"They canceled school yesterday," said Mr. Berge. "I couldn't believe it. School canceled. They sure didn't do that when I was a kid! Not every time it went below freezing, they didn't! We went to school no matter what, and that's why we could read and write. But back then, kids dressed warm, they didn't go around in their summer clothes the way they do now. I saw Lyle's kid gallivanting down the street in a windbreaker and jeans and sneakers. So they have to cancel school if it gets cold, and that's why kids don't learn. I mentioned Switzerland the other day to my grandson, and he didn't know where it is. He's thirteen. Switzerland!"

"I'd rather know where Florida is than Switzerland," said Clint.

Darlene brought Clint a platter of scrambled eggs and hash browns and sausage and refilled his coffee. It was going to be a long winter, he told her, so maybe she should take another Caribbean cruise like she did two years ago, when she entered the Last Chance Talent Contest and worked up "Will You Still Love Me Tomorrow" and sang it on-stage in her blue sequined blouse and the ship hit a swell and the spotlight wavered and she stepped off the front of the stage and into the drinks of some people from Ohio and sprained her right ankle and came home on crutches. "I wouldn't mind hearing that song my-self sometime," he said. "Especially the choreography." She took a swipe at him with her dishcloth. "You meet nice people on those cruises," she said. "A lot nicer than you meet as a waitress."

Carl came in to check the thermostat. The sun came up, and the pink-and-yellow sunrise hit the ice and fog on the front window. So pretty. I turned to look at it. Winter is aesthetically superior to other seasons, but most people prefer comfort to aesthetics, a terrible truth about the American people, and you see it wherever you go. Myrtle and Florian Krebsbach came in, two old people with waxpaper skin and drippy noses, and after them came a man in a down parka, who said to Darlene, "Tell Dorothy that Mr. Olson from the high school is here for the pies." He pulled his hood back and patted his hair, rearranging it over his bald spot.

Florian announced that he had gotten up early to make sure his car would start, and it did, and as long as it was running, he figured, why not go have breakfast? Myrtle came along in case he had a coronary. Darlene brought them old people's coffee and two caramel rolls, big as softballs, full of nuts and gobs of candy.

Clint said it was twenty-three below zero this morning. "That's too cold," said Dorothy. "Time to think about Florida."

"Amen," said Myrtle. "I was fed up with winter before it even got here. I was sick of it by Thanksgiving."

"You ordered eight pies, right?" said Dorothy. She read off the list: three apple, two cherry, two lemon meringue, one pumpkin.

"Maybe I should get a couple more apple," said Mr. Olson. Clint asked what was the occasion, and he said it was the annual banquet for the football team.

"Florida is infested with flies. They don't mention it in the tourist brochures, but they've got big green ones, horseflies, deerflies," said Mr. Berge. "You slap those suckers, and it only irritates them."

"It only bugs them," said Clint.

"Bug lotion has no effect whatsoever on those Florida flies. A crucifix helps, but you have to hit them really hard with it," said Mr. Berge. "You can get cracks in your windshield from them; it's like hailstones. I saw a man in Orlando who had been swarmed by flies, he had pits in his skin as if he'd been pecked by roosters."

Dorothy packed the pies in a box, in two tiers, with cardboard between, and Mr. Olson carried it out the door, taking short, flat steps on the ice, set the box on the ground, opened the back of his green minivan, and placed the box inside. Then he proceeded to get the van stuck on a hump of ice. He had parked directly in front of the café, where everyone could see. The front wheels got hung up, and the back wheels spun.

Florian watched. He said, "There was a couple in Sauk Center who wrote a bad check for plane tickets to Florida, and when they got back home they put them both in jail and their children were put into foster homes."

"Not a bad deal," said Carl. "Free trip and then free child care." He had sat down next to me and ordered French toast and bacon. "Long time no see," he said.

"It's two hundred bucks for the cheapest ticket to Florida, but you have to buy it thirty days in advance, so I never bought one because I couldn't wait that long," said Myrtle. "But you could go standby, I guess."

Mother and Dad had wanted to fly to Florida in the winter back when Grandpa Einar was in a coma, but then he showed a flicker of recognition, so they stayed home, enduring the cold, the snow, and then the lingering after-winter, the gray season, March and April, the months God created to show people who don't drink what a hangover is like. They couldn't go because what if Grandpa regained consciousness just before he died and looked up and asked the nurse, "Where are Byron and Mary?" and the nurse said, "They are at the Del Ray Motel near Sarasota, sunning themselves by the pool, sipping mixed drinks"?

Dorothy looked outside and grimaced. "What is that poor man doing?" Mr. Olson had gotten a lug-nut wrench out of the back of the van and was chopping violently at the ice around the rear wheels. Mr. Berge glanced back over his shoulder. "The man needs salt," he said. "Darlene, take this salt shaker out to Mr. Olson and ask him if he'd like to hear you sing a song too."

Florian said, "I knew a guy who had a forty-foot cabin cruiser on Lake Mille Lacs and he was welding a handrail onto his boat and deerflies came after him and he tried to fight them off with the acetylene torch and one fly got up under his T-shirt and bit a hole in him so deep he dropped the torch and dove into the water. The torch landed in the cockpit of the boat, and that sucker caught on fire, and he was under the dock in six feet of water, and those flies dive-bombed his nose every time he came up for air. He could see the flames on the boat, and there wasn't a thing he could do about it. He swam underwater to the neighbor's dock, and those flies followed him, and then the fire reached the cabin cruiser's propane tank, and it blew up. The guy's wife came running out of the house, thinking he was in the boat, and the flies went for her, and they both wound up with bites so bad they required fourteen thousand dollars' worth of plastic surgery. The insurance company sent a man around to investigate, and he wouldn't believe the guy's story. He knew nothing about deerflies; he was from Chicago. Two years later, the guy settled with the company for ten thousand dollars, about one-fourth of the market value of the boat. He sold the house, and he and his wife moved to the Caribbean. They have hurricanes to contend with down there, but that's nothing compared to deerflies."

"The Caribbean is different from Florida," said Mr. Berge. "Entirely different."

"It's not the cold; it's being cooped up when the roads are bad that gets me," said Myrtle.

Mr. Berge said it wasn't so bad with four-wheel drive.

"The advantage of four-wheel drive is that you can get stuck in more remote places, and get yourself stuck deeper down," said Clint.

"Talking him into four-wheel drive," said Myrtle, nodding toward her husband. "That'll be the day."

Mr. Olson was now back in the van and spinning his wheels again. He pressed down on the gas and held it down, and the tires screamed at high pitch and black smoke rose from the rear wheels. After a while, he stopped. He got out and hacked some more at the ice under the tires. "I think you better go help that man before he ruins his transmission," Dorothy said to Clint. Clint glanced up from his scrambled eggs. Mr. Olson climbed behind the wheel again and again spun the tires, until the smell of burning rubber drifted into the café. "If he can wait two minutes, I'll be there," said Clint. He rounded up the loose eggs and potatoes with his fork, corraled them against a slice of toast, and ate them, just as Mr. Olson, on his third attempt to chop the ice, stabbed his right front tire in the sidewall, and the front of the van dropped four inches. "Oh boy," said Clint.

"Look out," said Dorothy. Mr. Olson stood looking at the flat tire in silent rage. Then he kicked it, hard. He was unaware of his audience. He hauled the spare tire out of the back—he had to remove the box of pies to open up the lid of the tire well and then he put the box back in—and jacked up the front end of the van and changed the tire.

Clint had put on his jacket to go out and help, but now he sat back down to finish his coffee. "No point interrupting a man when he's doing good work," he said.

Mr. Olson cranked the lug nuts back on, and then, when he opened up the back of the van, in his fury he flung the jack and the wrench in and he yanked the box out, forgetting that it contained pies, and he shouted a curse to the sky and threw the box on the ground. And then he remembered. He opened the flaps of the box. Pie filling was leaking out through the corner. He looked inside and then reached down and grabbed a cherry pie and flung it as hard as he could into the street. There was a burst of red, and the pie tin skidded across the street, and a driver hit the brakes and honked.

"Was there a warranty on those pies?" asked Carl. Dorothy was on her way to the door and stopped. She didn't want to embarrass Mr. Olson by speaking to him in his condition. He kicked the side of his van, making a dent just below the gas cap. He was about to kick the box of pies, and he called on God to send hellfire down on the entire situation, and right then the world slipped out from under him. He twisted and waved his arms and landed on the side of his butt. We ran outside, Clint and Carl and I, and Mr. Olson was lying slightly on his side, his left leg bent funny. Carl knelt down and told him not to try to get up.

Clint said, "Can you move your leg, Mr. Olson?"

Mr. Olson lay with his cheek against the ice. His anger was dissipated now. He did not tell God to damn this. He didn't seem to be in pain. He appeared to be deep in thought.

LeRoy pulled up in the town cop car and got out. "Somebody fall?" he said.

"No, he just got tired and lay down," said Carl.

LeRoy ignored that remark. He reached in for the radio mike and jabbered into it and came and looked down at Mr. Olson and put two fingers against the side of his neck and pulled up one of his eyelids. LeRoy is a tall man with a big beak, who, back when it was fashionable, let his hair grow long, and then most of it fell out. "It was the weight," people keep telling him. "Your scalp was not meant to hold on to hair that long."

Since he lost his hair, he has gotten more officious, and now he looked at Carl and said, "I'm going to have to make a report and put your name in it."

"Fine," Carl said. He was lifting Mr. Olson's head and putting a scarf under it.

The volunteer fire department paramedics came, and I recognized Bud from Bunsen Motors, a man I remember as rather strong and not mechanically gifted. Once, he checked Dad's oil and rammed the stick right out the bottom of the oil pan and then closed the hood so hard the ornament came off in his hand. I hoped that Bud would not be attending to Mr. Olson's leg. He might shove the splint up into his chest cavity.

I went inside and Darlene brought me Dad's breakfast: blueberry buttermilk pancakes with two strips of bacon on the side, and a prune juice, large. The paramedics covered Mr. Olson with a silver insulated blanket and put him on a gurney.

"What do you want done with those pies?" Carl asked. Dorothy said she would take them up to the high school herself. "Poor man," she said. Mr. Olson was gazing up at the sky. "He's okay," said Carl. "The rest will do him good."

The volunteers had some trouble getting the gurney's wheels to fold up, but at last they loaded Mr. Olson into their van and drove away. "I tell you, this is my last winter," Myrtle said. "Man was not meant to live in this place."

The platter of pancakes made me feel bloated, so I took a walk, past the Sidetrack Tap and the Sons of Knute hall. The sun was low, and my shadow stretched forty feet ahead of me, as if I'd been run over by a steam roller, rolled out like a cookie. I walked up the hill, up to the cemetery, drifted over with snow. Someone had plowed the road and shoveled a path to Dad's grave, which was covered by a green tarp. The snow obliterated the granite pedestal on which the dark angel stood, in the monument to the Grand Army of the Republic, so she appeared to be standing on the snow, as if she had just skied over from Millet, carrying her broadsword and shield. The Memorial Day ceremonies always take place in front of her, the VFW honor guard standing at parade rest, the grade school children in formation, and the ladies' sextet, with my second cousin Audrey Tollefson, the worst singer in town. She loves to sing, though she can't carry a tune in a laundry basket. She is the one who will jump up in any public gathering and ding on a glass and say, "How about we all sing 'Home on the Range'?" and people think, *How about you stuff a rag in your mouth?* and then she'll launch into it, and her voice is so horrible, everyone sings loud to drown her out. "That was wonderful!" she'll say, and it is. Lutherans can sing, no doubt about it. They go into four-part harmony like geese go into V-formation, with only a few stragglers.

I used to go up in the cemetery when I was a kid, especially if Bud was digging a grave—I wanted to look inside it—and one day, as I looked down into a fresh-dug grave, Bud told me about coffins that had to be moved to another part of the cemetery, coffins he'd opened and found the satin ripped to shreds from the buried person trying to tear their way out. "Yeah," he said, "it happens a lot more than you'd think. Only way they can really be sure is, just before they close the coffin, if they slap 'em real hard on the cheek, but you know, they don't want to offend the grieving family—even though it doesn't hurt 'em if they're dead, of course, and if they're alive, why, that's exactly what you want to know before it's too late. But they don't do it, for fear of giving offense, and so they wind up burying a few who are in very deep comas. I don't say there are all that many, but it's something you'd rather avoid if you could. I always come up a couple days after we bury one and put my ear to the ground, just in case they might be down there banging on the lid."

"Have you ever heard that?" I asked Bud.

"I thought so once."

"And did you dig it up?"

"No. I wasn't sure if it was a voice I heard, or what. So I didn't dig it up. But maybe I should have." He looked around to make sure nobody was near. Then he said, "Would you like to see where I heard the voice?"

Of course I did.

It was not far from the grave Bud was digging. He pointed to the spot, and I put my ear to the ground and thought I heard a sigh, but I couldn't be sure.

"Let me listen," Bud said, and he didn't hear anything.

I listened again, and there was no sound. Only my own heart pounding in my ears.

Now I lifted up the green tarp and looked down into the hole, the concrete vault where Dad would lie. Dad had dug graves when he was younger. Had helped Bud dig Grandpa's, in fact. I scraped away snow with my feet, looking for Dad's aunt Maren's grave. Grandpa's sister. She ran away at the age of nineteen and married a soldier the day before he was shipped off to World War I. She was already expecting his child. She died of influenza, her unborn child dying with her. Nothing was ever heard of the husband. He vanished in France.

Somewhere nearby was a stone that said "Let Him Who Is With Oxen Cast the First Stone," a mistake at the granite works; I couldn't find it. But here was Grandpa and Grandma's, Einar and Birthe. A hard man, Grandpa, who made up his mind about people early on and never changed his opinion. He was one of the Dark Lutherans, all right. He was a butcher, who arose at five A.M. six days a week and went to work in a brown porkpie hat and a tie and white apron. Grandpa wrote me a note on my graduation: "Each man to his work. Do your job, no matter how lowly, and do it the best you can, and nobody can look down on you." Every morning, Grandpa made a pot of Ole Bull coffee. He was a real Norwegian, so the smell of coffee was an emblem of the good life. His dog drank coffee out of a bowl. When Grandpa got old and the doctor made him cut out coffee, Grandpa almost died of heartbreak. Growing old made him ill-tempered in general, and when he had to quit working because he got forgetful, he was so mad he didn't want to see anybody again. Eventually, it was more convenient for him to go into a coma, where he remained for six years, stored in a crib in a dim room in a nursing home twenty miles north of Lake Wobegon, where Dad went to sit with him every

Sunday afternoon and watch football or baseball on the television set over Grandpa's bed. Dad always took a little flask of fresh coffee and put it to Grandpa's lips.

He died one summer, and in the fall we put Grandma on the train at the Milwaukee Depot in Minneapolis. She was going to Paradise Valley, outside Phoenix. She had never flown on a plane in her life and wasn't about to start now. She took crates of stuff with her. The train was backed into the shed, the porters shouting. The conductor stood by the last car; hot vapor rose from beneath the cylinders, hot water dripped from under the boilers. The hissing of valves, the throbbing of compressors; smoke rising from the stack; sighing sounds from inside. We followed Grandma along the train to her car, and her bags were hoisted up, and she kissed us all in turn. I smelled her powder and perfume and felt her cheek, and she said, "You be sure to come visit me, Johnny, because I'm not coming back up here except in a box."

Grandma was content at Paradise Valley; it almost made up for her hard life. She went every morning to her exercise group and enjoyed a long lunch and a bridge game and a gabfest with her cronies and then a nap. After her nap, she had her hair done by a Mexican woman named Charo and then went to dinner and to a movie. Grandma said, "The town girls always wore the nice clothes and went to the hairdresser, and we farm girls always had to wear hand-me-downs and those awful cardboard shoes." She put on a shimmery gown with big painted roses for dinner. Then, getting up from lunch one day, she fell and hit her head and suffered a concussion, which she didn't bother to tell anyone about, and when Ray went to visit a few weeks later, Grandma was lying on the couch, disheveled, unwashed, the TV blaring, surrounded by empty tuna fish cans she'd been eating from.

Dad flew to Arizona that night, and Grandma flatly refused to come north with him, so Dad went before a probate judge and stood there and said that she was mentally incompetent and asked the court for guardianship. The judge asked Grandma if she understood the proceedings, and Grandma said she did. She announced that she had no wish to continue living in a country where this sort of thing could happen. She wished to go to Mexico with Charo and live out her remaining years among the Mexicans, a decent people with respect for the elderly.

The judge said he thought she sounded pretty competent to him. So Grandma got to stay in Arizona. She said to Dad, "You can wait until I'm dead before you bury me." She told him she would never speak to him again for the rest of her life. She told him this many times in the eight months she had remaining. She was a tiny woman, with fierce dark eyes and hair like a white mist around her head and transparent skin, the blood vessels and bones visible underneath, and she died of a brain hemorrhage while shopping with Charo in a mall, in a china store, while making a difficult selection between butter dishes, a warrior fallen on the field of battle.

I cleaned the snow off Grandpa and Grandma's stone and turned away and looked out over the town. Steam rose from the chimneys. On the lake, a few boys skated around the hockey rink, and nearby was the old jalopy parked offshore for the Sons of Knute "Guess the Ice Melt Contest," one dollar to guess the day and the hour the car would fall through. Two men emerged from a car and walked into the café. One of them looked so much like Dad. Wiry. A bundle of nerves. He stopped and kicked the snow off his boots and went in the café. "Hey, I died and then I realized I forgot something, so I turned around and came back," he said. "And now I forget what it is. Isn't that something? Anyway, they gave me twenty-four hours before I have to go back. Anybody want to play gin rummy?"

NINETEEN

The Lady in Black

At nine-thirty, washed, combed, in a fresh white starched shirt and my brown suit and a tiny Norwegian flag pin in my lapel, I stood with my arm around Aunt Ray inside the front door of Lake Wobegon Lutheran Church, watching people arrive for the funeral. Aunt Ray wore navy blue, and a white cloth corsage was pinned to her dress. Art was parking the car. "It certainly is a tribute to him, isn't it," she cried. "He was so well loved in this town." My fellow pallbearers stood nearby, waiting for the hearse, Clarence and Wally and Carl and two men wearing Knute ties emblazoned with golden walleyes. Mother waited in the vestry with David Ingqvist. She wore her best blue knit dress, long-sleeved, with a black wool shawl over her shoulders, her silvery hair tied in a French knot.

I asked Ray if Aunt Mildred had called.

Aunt Ray squeezed my hand. "Yes. She said she couldn't come. Funerals depress her. And she can't take the cold." Mildred had lived in Argentina for thirty years. She missed Minnesota, according to Ray, missed birch trees, snow, hydrangeas. She subscribed to *Reader's*

Digest and ordered Jell-O and tapioca pudding and Kraft macaroni and cheese dinners from a wholesale grocer in Texas.

"I honestly never thought he was ever going to die, I never envisioned it," said Aunt Ray. She clung tightly to my arm. Tears ran down her pale, damp face, framed in its girlish ringlets, her bright-red lips crumpled, and she put her face against my jacket. I looked away, out the little window in the door, and I spotted a tall woman in a fur cap and a long black coat come striding along the street and cross it and ascend the steps. It couldn't be her, but it was. It surely was. I opened the door and stepped out into the blazing-white cold, and she ran up the steps and threw her arms around me. Her cheek was chill. Her eyes watered from the cold.

"I'm astonished," I said. "Stunned. Absolutely knocked over. As always."

"Good," she said. "I'm frozen solid." I kissed her and led her into the church.

"Aunt Ray," I said, "meet Alida Freeman."

My aunt looked up at Alida, who had taken off her cap and was rousting up her curly black hair. "Thank you for coming," said Aunt Ray, and her lower lip trembled. "It means so much at a sad time." Alida patted her hand, and then Mother tapped Alida on the shoulder and she turned and they embraced. "I can't tell you how pleased I am," said Mother. "I am just tickled pink to see you."

"I couldn't not come," said Alida. She shook hands with David, in his white surplice, and gave him her most winning smile, and tendered a hug to Judy and Diana. I took her coat, to hang it in the cloakroom. Alida had come in black, a long black skirt and a chemise top, with a simple silver necklace. Mother took Alida by the elbow. "You stick close to me, I'll protect you," Mother said, and smiled at me: "You tend to your business."

How lovely Alida looked! I felt a warm glow at being the man associated with her, seeing people notice her. How completely herself she was, so untrammeled, unabashed. So delicate, extravagant, and tender. She smiled at me and stood in graceful anonymity, observing the current of people in big coats shuffling past her and into church, burly men and women of neutral demeanor, women cowed and bent, who chose their clothing for its dull effect, as protective coloration. Alida stood, a queen in their midst, shining with purpose. I reckoned she had flown to Minneapolis late on Friday and spent the night in a hotel and arisen early and driven north, calculating the distance, maybe killing an hour in a café so as to be exactly on time. Perhaps she had stopped at the Chatterbox, to ask the whereabouts of the church, and Darlene and Dorothy had looked at her, a Woman of Mystery, and wondered, Where did Byron know her from? An illegitimate daughter perhaps? His lawyer? No, she was his son's lover, who moved heaven and earth to make this loving gesture. I was touched by the pure goodness of it. I decided that before the day was over, I'd ask her to marry me.

She and I stood next to Mother, backs to the wall, as people came streaming through the doors. Aunt Ingrid entered, ninety-three, in a maroon outfit, pushing her walker ahead of her, a white aura of hair around her head. A young couple came in with a baby so ugly it took your breath away. It had bulging eyes, a beetle brow, a knobby nose, and an immense mouth; it looked as if it had been born under a rock. "Not a relative," I whispered to Alida. Bill's wife, Elizabeth, came in, gaunt and thin-lipped, in a white silk tunic, and Uncle Senator K. Thorvaldson, who had flown up from Florida with his cousin Frank and Frank's wife, Eunice. They all lived in a mobile-home park called Miracle Corners, near Tampa. Dad's cousin Lena came in with her dog, Bruno, at her side and a strip of toilet paper stuck to her shoe. She was eighty and practically blind, and so was the dog, but she had the church memorized. As a pup, Bruno once snatched a sunfish out of shallow water in his jaws, and he still liked to wade in the water up to his armpits, hoping for another, a waste of time, but what's time to a dog? Aunt Ray removed the toilet paper from Lena's shoe, and then Art came and took Ray into the sanctuary.

And then the hearse pulled up in front. I took a deep breath. I kissed Alida again. "You don't need to look after me," she whispered. "I won't break." I stepped out into the sunshine, the blast of cold air, and lined up with the other pallbearers, and we marched two abreast down to the curb. Mr. Lindberg opened the back door and we lifted Dad's coffin out and brought it up the stairs and into the church. A light load. David and Mother and Diana and Judy and Alida waited in the vestibule. David stepped forward and held up his hand. Blessed be the God and Father of our Lord Jesus Christ, the source of all mercy and the God of all consolation.

The organ began to play "When peace, like a river, attendeth my way," and Mr. Lindberg said, "Press in close, boys; it's a tight aisle." We moved forward down the aisle, little kids turning and gawking, the bank of flowers straight ahead along the altar rail, and I heard Ray's melodious sobbing. We set the coffin on a table. I remembered sitting at that table with crayons, coloring Joseph and his coat, and now Dad's coffin lay on it. I hoped someone had checked to make sure the table legs were glued in.

Mother sat in the second pew, on the aisle, head erect. The air was sweet with flowers. I eased into the pew and sat between Alida and Bill. From back up in the choir loft, a soprano sang "It is well, it is well, with my soul." During the second verse, Diana started trembling and buried her face in April's neck and cried, and that got Ronnie going. He ducked his head and sobbed a couple times. I looked straight ahead at David Ingqvist, head bowed at the pulpit. O God of grace and glory, we remember before you today our brother Byron. We thank you for giving him to us to know and to love as a companion in our pilgrimage on earth. Diana cried beautifully, crooning, as women do, but men are awful; they don't get the practice, and when they do cry, it sounds like an animal caught on barbed wire. Ronnie sounded like a killer who has confessed after two days of interrogation. Ray was crying for good now, and some other people; a faint gurgling spread through the room, a definite liquidity, and I noticed Bill's head tilt forward and a hand dab at his eyes.

Ronnie had his head down and was going to town now. God, don't let him stand up and speak in tongues or do some other dumbass Texas thing, I thought. Wave his index finger in the air or start baying and whooping. This is not a Baptist church, after all, where evangelists with bad toupees roam the aisles like wolverines, crouched, eyes aglitter, playing your heartstrings like a ten-dollar guitar. From the corner of my eye, I saw Mother, in profile, beaming up at her son-in-law in the pulpit thanking God for Dad, for his years of service to the church and to the community, his friendship, his counsel. Counsel, hell; Dad was bossy. Diana sat weeping onto April. I imagined people in the pews behind us thinking, *My, those two gals are affectionate toward each other*. Ronnie reached into his jacket pockets, one and then the other, and dug into his pants pockets, and I got out a clean handkerchief and handed it to him. He took it and blew his nose. A big blow. Oh, thanks a lot, Ronnie. He offered the handkerchief back. I shook my head. The prayer continued. David was now asking God to make each of us mindful of our responsibility to carry on Dad's work. So that means we all have to fill up our houses with bad art and useless junk? I wished Aunt Ray would get a grip on herself. She was moaning now. People around her were weeping. Weeping is contagious behavior, like vomiting. Suddenly I could imagine leaning forward and spewing out my breakfast; wouldn't that be interesting? When I get home, I am going to draw up instructions for my own funeral, and number one, there won't be one, and number two, it won't be like this. And then, to my astonishment, I felt tears creep into my eyes. David was asking God to comfort the family in its grief, and suddenly I who had felt very little felt heat behind the eyeballs and saw the altar crinkle and the image above it of the Good Shepherd and the inscription over it: I AM THE BREAD OF LIFE. HE THAT COMETH UNTO ME SHALL NEVER HUNGER. The letters rippled. I couldn't read the words for the tears in my eyes.

My ancestor John Tollefson sat in this church when the inscription was in Norwegian. A tear ran down the side of my nose. Stop that, I thought. Fool. I pinched my wrist. I thought of the joke about Ole and Svend coming home and finding Lena in bed with the mailman and Ole and Svend get beers out of the refrigerator and sit down in the kitchen and drink them, and finally Svend says, "What about the mailman?" and Ole says, "Let him get his own beer." The room was blurry. I felt shaky and queasy. I tried to take a deep breath. Alida's hand found mine and squeezed it.

With my other hand, I pressed against my eyeballs. I used to do that as a kid, for the experience of seeing yellow and pink and purple flashes on my retinas, a profound experience to a kid, like mescaline was to other people. Dad told me, "You're going to hurt your eyes." A river of sparks crossed the blackness. Where was Dad now? Was he drifting through the cosmos, a little black cinder in a mist of electrons? Was he in the clean, illuminated paradise that I imagined as a child, Lutherans in white garments floating through ivory halls, singing in four-part harmony? Or was Dad in hell, which might be very much like his own home? Boxes of junk around, an eternity of small thoughts and stupefying routines, dumb jokes, endless polkas played by a band with two trumpets, both slightly sharp.

Uncle Henry walked up to the pulpit and read the chapter about the corruptible putting on the incorruptible. It sounded like a paragraph of a mortgage contract. Alida put her hand on my knee. My funeral would be nothing like this at all. Donate the body to medical science, and spend the funeral money on a salmon dinner and a fine wine and a good band. If they want to weep for me, let them do it with the taste of grilled mushrooms and a 1988 Barolo in their mouths and listening to Butch Thompson play "How Long Blues" and "Please Don't Talk About Me When I'm Gone." No grave for me, thank you very much. Donate the money to the scholarship fund. Spend it on swing sets for the park. Don't invest it in granite.

David stepped back into the pulpit and spoke about Jesus never forsaking us. The merciful goodness of Our Lord should be made visible in all our lives. The first principle of the Christian life should be kindness and gentleness, and also the second, and the third. Ray had settled down now, and so had Ronnie and Diana, though I could tell she was geared to start up again anytime. Not a peep out of Bill. Mother had not moved a muscle. It isn't such a bad family, or odd, I thought. One dysfunctional high school counselor, one forty-three-year-old bachelor, one millennialist, one lesbian, but Judy is normal, a mom, a wife, and one out of five isn't bad. And David is a good man, though listening to him preach is like waiting at the crossing for a freight train to pass, and after a hundred boxcars have gone by, the train stops, and sits, and begins backing up.

The caboose came along after only ten minutes, a short sermon, amazing, and then the mayor of Lake Wobegon, Eloise Krebsbach, walked up and spoke about Dad's service on the town council. Her glasses were too big for her. They made her look like an angry insect. She spoke without notes and said that Dad was a good judge of human nature and knew how easily animosity and suspicion can get the upper hand and poison a community, and so he had been a peacemaker, listening to people and nudging them toward a consensus, not the most thrilling or self-fulfilling job, but one that needs to be done. "Thank you, Byron, for all you did for this town," she said quietly, and sat down. That got Ray going again. She had rested during the sermon and was ready for a new round of weeping.

She sobbed away, and Clarence Bunsen stood up, a tall, bald man with a good-sized gut on him, one too big to hide, so he let it hang out like a mailbag. He told about Dad organizing the Fourth of July and how particular he was about getting the details right—the bratwurst had to be fresh, the beer cold, the speeches short, the parade should start precisely on time, the fireworks should be spectacular, there should be masses of flags, and everyone should form the Living Flag on Main Street, as they have done every Fourth for years and years. Dad was devoted to maintaining the tradition of the Living Flag, whereby four or five hundred people wearing red, white, or blue caps stood in tight formation, making the Stars and Stripes with the tops of their heads.

I clearly remembered the Living Flag as an hour of overpowering tedium, waiting under the blazing sun in a grumpy crowd pressed cheek to jowl as Dad yelled instructions through a bullhorn from his perch on the roof of the Central Building. Maybe Dad was up there now, invisible, bullhornless, looking at the situation down on earth, willing the confused masses to please line up and take form, amount to something. Be a flag. Interesting that the man who whipped the town into shape for the Living Flag had lived in such a rat's nest of mishmash and foofaraw and was helpless to put his own house in order. Mother said he was trying to, that he was throwing things out, but she was only making excuses for him. Dad was a pack rat. He accumulated things because he was afraid of nakedness and silence and flatness and darkness. Afraid of Death. As we all are. But how extravagant his fear was. He must have heard Death breathing in the next room, and somehow he took comfort by gathering around him a set of skewers, a stained-glass St. Francis, a silver medal with the head of Dwight D. Eisenhower, a chunk of wooden cornice, a gold cornet, an old black phone, boxes of sheet music, chauffeur badges, plumed caps, a squirrel trap, a gavel, shin pads, shoe trees, spurs, candle snuffers, a lithograph of Luther, a racing program from the 1940 Minnesota State Fair, a leather billfold made at Bible camp, a chafing dish with no cover, the finial from something, a jigsaw puzzle of the skyline of Bismarck, North Dakota.

The Knutes trooped up front, and the Grand Oya spoke of Dad's pride in his Norwegian heritage. The Old Scout held the wooden walleye on a pike, the Bard held the hoop. They all looked at the coffin and said, "Go straight home."

And then I saw the bouquet of white daffodils, in a green vase at the altar rail, next to the flowers from the Bunsens. From the daffodils trailed a white sash that said *John and Alida*. How good of you, my sweet lover, to arrange for flowers—and in a town without a florist! How sweet to see our names linked publicly in a church, almost like posting the banns. John and Alida. In figuring out name order, it is common to put the duller person first. Oh well. I leaned toward her and was about to thank her for the flowers, when I noticed a stirring at the end of the pew, and the green bulk of Diana arose and headed forward. I closed my eyes. Please don't be as stupid as you can be, Diana. Please don't talk about rebirth. Don't introduce April. Please don't take this moment to plead for tolerance of gay people or explain your complicated feelings about Dad and your take on things, your reactions, your insights. I speak for the others in this. Don't tell us about your life right now. But I had to hand it to her. She had guts. She walked up and stood in the pulpit and broke down and bawled and apologized for it, and as she wept, she said what a good dad Dad was and how he always did stuff with her, explaining things to her, telling her stories when he tucked her into bed, singing her songs. . . . Whose dad was this? Not mine, I thought. She kept right on talking, and even though her face caved in and her shoulders shook and she could say only a few words at a time, she kept going. It was astonishing to see how she had transcended her upbringing. This is not Our Weeping Redeemer church, this is the Lutheran church, after all, where people sit quietly and then go downstairs for coffee. People with so much self-control, it's a miracle if one of them can cry. And then Diana started to sing.

She sang, "Come and sit by my side if you love me,/Do not hasten to bid me adieu." She gestured for everyone to sing, as the organist tried to find the key and follow, and then she sailed right into "God be with you till we meet again." It was nice to see my own sister show no fear of what other people might think of her. Alida sang, Mother sang. As we all sang the chorus, "Till we me-e-et," the high note touched the heart of Bruno the fishing dog, and he raised his head up from the floor by Lena's feet and sang along, a little flat. People laughed. Mother turned and smiled.

And then David prayed a short prayer and everyone stood and sang, "Children of the Heavenly Father / Safely to His Bosom gather, / Nestling bird nor star in heaven / Such a refuge e'er was given." Mr. Lindberg walked up the aisle, and the pallbearers assembled, and I reached down and plucked a few white daffodils and put one in my lapel and the others in my pocket. I took hold of the handle, and we lifted Dad and carried him out of church and into the cold January day and down the six steps and across the walk he had shoveled hundreds of times, and Mr. Lindberg opened the rear door of the hearse and we rolled him in.

Send for your rubber-tired hearses, and send for your rubber-tired hacks, they're taking your father to the graveyard, and they ain't going to bring him back. He was your dad, and you have done him all kinds of wrong, you rascal you. Ronnie stood shivering on the curb in a tan topcoat. We climbed into cars, Mother with Aunt Ray and Uncle Art and me and Alida, and Diana and April and Ronnie and Henry in the Grand Oya's van with him and the Old Scout, and Bill and Elizabeth with Judy and David, and then came about twenty more cars, Dorothy and Ralph and Mayor Eloise Krebsbach and Clarence Bunsen and Roger Hedlund and a delegation from the grain elevator, and the others. The procession moved slowly through the deserted town, the wind blowing gusts of snow from the piles along

Main Street, and up the long hill and under the cast-iron arch into the cemetery, and up to the path that had been shoveled through the drifted snow to Dad's grave.

The mourners assembled around the hearse, bending against the wind. Alida and Mother had their arms around each other's backs, huddled together.

Mr. Lindberg lined up the pallbearers and said, "If anyone slips, the others stop and stand until he recovers, okay? It's not too heavy. We'll roll him onto the bier from the foot. Okay? Let's go." And we started along the icy path. Pastor Ingqvist walked ahead, and Mother and Alida followed the coffin, then Bill and Ronnie, who looked stunned from the cold, as if he might crack open, and Diana and April, and Ray and Art, and Uncle Henry.

The coffin was so light that for a moment I thought it might float away. We shuffled over the frozen ground and set the coffin on the bier and the crowd tucked in around it, huddled close, heads down, like cattle.

Pastor Ingqvist glanced up and ducked his head and did the committal service quickly. For I know that my Redeemer lives, and at last He will stand upon the earth; and I shall see God. None of us lives to himself, and none of us dies to himself. As we live, we live to the Lord, and when we die, we die to the Lord; so then, whether we live or whether we die, we are the Lord's. He said that Dad was not here, he had gone to be with God according to the promise of faith, and that he was in a place where there was no suffering, no weariness, only perfect and unceasing happiness. I thought of the topography of Alida's bare shoulders, her breasts, her rib cage, the swale of her belly. Since God Almighty has called our brother Byron from this life to Himself, we commit his body to the earth from which it was made. I looked down at my feet and saw that I was standing on top of Grandpa.

TWENTY

The Wake

We left Dad lying in the cold. Just up the road from the cemetery arch, a man sat in the cab of a truck with a backhoe, reading a newspaper, waiting to lower the coffin down and close the vault and fill the grave. We trooped away, women dabbing at their eyes, men stone-faced, and on the way to the gate, my arm around Alida, Diana slipped up next to me and whispered, "Did you ever think as the hearse goes by that you may be the next to die? They'll take you out to the family plot, and there you'll wither, decay, and rot."

I said, "They'll wrap you up in a big white sheet and drop you down about six feet. And all goes well for about a week, and then your coffin begins to leak." She hummed the last part: The worms crawl in, the worms crawl out, the ants play pinochle on your snout. "I want to see the coffin put in the ground," she said. "Why won't they let us?"

"It was a dummy in the coffin," I said. "Dad is in Buenos Aires. With Mildred and the Siamese twin cousins. Soon as we're out of sight, Lindberg'll whip up here and retrieve the merchandise."

"Oh God," she said. "The Siamese twin cousins. I forgot about them."

"It's just as well you and I *didn't* have children," I said.

We drove back to church for a lunch served by old ladies in white paper caps with *Peters Wieners* printed on the sides. "I hope they didn't put too much onion in the potato salad," said Mother. She took Alida's arm and led her to a long table in the corner covered with Jell-O molds, the winners of the annual Luther League contest. "They were going to move this for the funeral," Mother said, "and I made them leave it. Byron loved Jell-O." There was a grayish Jell-O in the shape of a human brain, and there was a South Seas lagoon, and Jell-O in the shape of sushi, and then there was the Last Supper, Our Lord and His apostles in lime-green outfits, with strawberry faces, sitting at a coffee-colored table, and of course that won first prize—even though the brain was a better piece of work. Second prize went to a green Jell-O mold in the shape of the state of Minnesota, with canned oranges and miniature marshmallows embedded in it. "Byron loved this contest," said Mother. "He had a creative Jell-O contest for Toast 'n' Jelly Days for years. He thought up so many things: the Toast Race and the Blanket Toss. And the Dunk the Pastor booth was his idea. That booth has raised so much money for the library."

The crowd was starting to come in from the cemetery, stamping the snow off their boots upstairs, clumping down the stairs, David and Judy and Art and Ray, pale and purplish, and some old people whom I didn't know.

I told mother I thought it was a good funeral, and then I could say no more. She nodded, tears in her eyes, and turned away.

Bill's son Scott arrived, along with a girl with six earrings in each ear. "This is Scott's friend Melanie," said Bill. "Her ears whistle when she shakes her head." Melanie scowled.

Scott said, "What is the word for a chain of churches?"

"A chain—you mean a synod?" said Bill.

"Right. Synod. What synod was it that our family came from in Norway?"

"The Hauge Synod," I said. Odd that a Tollefson had grown up not knowing the word "synod." It made me wonder if Scott was clear about the Trinity. Or monogamy. Scott said, "Say, Dad?" and whispered something, and Bill reached for his wallet.

I turned away toward the food line, and Senator K. Thorvaldson came over for a word. He was flying back to Florida on Monday, he said. "Frank and Eunice and I found a mobile home park in Tampa where you get a trailer, furnished and everything, for one twenty a week, but I may have to get my own place," he said.

"The park is well-kept, but we've got a Wax Museum of Crime on one side of us and a replica of Graceland on the other, and people crossing back and forth between the two, and it's amazing what they will do on your lawn. We write letters to the city council, but it does no good. Frank and Eunice have the bedroom, and I sleep on the living room couch, which folds out, but the crossbar catches you right across the kidneys. I've been getting up nine or ten times a night to pee. And their dog, Roof, he sleeps in the hall, and sometimes he doesn't recognize me in the dark. And Frank—he's a nice enough guy, but his politics get on my nerves." Frank believed that the Clinton administration was bringing America to the verge of communist dictatorship. He was a regular participant in radio talk shows, said Senator K. "I can hear him yelling in the next room," he said. "I'm trying to take a nap.

"Anyway," said Senator K., "I won't take up your time, but if you could write me a letter sometime, I'd appreciate it." Then Diana tapped him on the shoulder, and he turned away.

I told Alida how, when I went off to college, he and Aunt Margaret and Grandma and Mother and Dad all insisted on driving me. An early character-building experience. You arrive on campus at the age of seventeen with an entourage of elderly relatives who are in the habit of narrating their experiences aloud. They see a sign that says Residence Hall for Women, and one of them says, "Oh look, there's a residence hall." And one says, "Yes, it's for women." And another one says, "Oh, so it's not a men's residence hall, then?" And the other one says, "No, it's for women." It was like a Samuel Beckett play.

Judy came up with a ham salad sandwich on a plate and offered it to Alida. "Don't believe what this man tells you about Lake Wobegon," she said. "He hasn't been around here for years. He's living in the past."

Alida bit off a hunk of sandwich. "I'm starving," she said.

Judy introduced her daughter, Kate, who smiled at Alida. "Mother said you teach history," she murmured politely.

"At Columbia," said Alida.

"I'm thinking about going East to college," said Kate.

"A good idea," said Alida. "Going away to school is getting two educations for the price of one."

They talked about Eastern schools, and I turned toward the food table, and a heavyset woman with thin painted eyebrows and big black hair stepped into my path. "Remember me? I'm Jennifer," she said. Art and Ray's daughter. "I just moved back here from Denver. I'm thinking about going to real-estate school."

I tore myself away, pretending to look for someone, and got into the food line behind David Ingqvist, who was listening to Uncle Art talk trucks; David looked dazed and sleepy. "Back before they had power steering, I was driving this old Kenworth, and man, you had to horse that guy around a corner when it was loaded, had to stand up and haul on the wheel with all your might," said Art, who feels that trucks are of universal interest. He told about the time he drove his Kenworth into somebody's kitchen in Sioux Falls, and it turned out that the husband of the woman Art almost killed as she stood at the stove fixing supper was also married to a woman in Worthington, Minnesota, an hour east of there.

"Makes you wonder, doesn't it?" said Art. He has told this story hundreds of times, often to the same individuals on consecutive days, but frequent usage has not taken the shine off it for him. How he climbed out of his cab into the living room of a bigamist. He shook his head. "Everybody's got secrets, I guess. We'd probably be amazed if we knew what some people have got going on."

An old man grabbed Art's shoulder and shook his hand, and Art said, "Ted, you old cuss, what do you know for certain?"

"Not a whole heck of a lot," said Ted.

Someone behind me said, "What he paid for that boat and motor makes those two northerns the most expensive fish in the Western world. You'd pay less for fresh marlin."

The food line moved slowly. The lunch was only cold sandwiches and beans and potato salad and fudge bars, but people were weighing their options carefully. Art studied the sandwiches—ham salad, tuna salad, egg salad, cheese—for a whole minute before selecting cheese and tuna. The basement was packed now, a loud drone of voices, people eating standing up. "John!" A big hand clapped me on the back, and I turned and said hello to Clarence Bunsen and thanked him for his remarks at the funeral. "Your mother looks well," he said.

I told him I was worried about her having to deal with that house, that I wished there were senior citizen apartments in town.

"Your dad tried to get that started," said Clarence, "but in this town it takes years. I'll never forget when he and I were both on the council and I was speaking up for . . . I don't know what—tennis courts or something—and I said, 'Either this town moves forward or else it moves backward,' and he leaned over and whispered, 'I wouldn't offer these people a choice like that.' " Clarence put his head back and laughed. Just beyond the tip of Clarence's nose stood Alida, her back to me, talking to Kate.

Who is this wonderful man people keep telling me about? I wondered. What happened to the crabby old guy I thought was my dad, the one who collected junk and never was satisfied with anything I did?

I took ham salad and egg salad, a dollop of beans, a scoop of potato salad, two fudge bars, and a cup of coffee. The old ladies in the Peters caps smiled, as I remembered old ladies smiling whenever a man took a big helping of their food. As if to say, "Have plenty to eat, dear, because, you know, you aren't going to live that long, eating the way you do." I took my plate and stood by Alida, who was talking to Aunt Ingrid now. People wandered around, saying, "How are you?" *Fine, how's yourself?* "Not bad." *And your kids?* "Fine." *What you been up to lately?* "Oh, not much. Yourself?" *Oh, not much.* There was a picture on the wall of an old man praying; he seemed to be saying, Lord, get me out of here. I asked Alida if she wanted to leave. "No," she said. "I like this."

Aunt Ingrid stood, her waxen, bony hands gripping the walker. "Sitting aggravates this condition I have," she explained to Alida and me.

"How are you doing otherwise?" I asked.

"Not bad for someone who's falling apart."

Aunt Ingrid was telling Alida about how she left Lake Wobegon and went to work in Minneapolis when she was fifteen years old. July 1919. "I kept house for a retired Methodist minister, who was nice to me and gave me books, and when he asked me to marry him, I said I would but I wanted a dowry. I wanted him to give me four thousand dollars. It was just a figure that came to mind. I was sure he wouldn't do it. But I guess he loved me. I invested that money in stocks and bonds, and it has taken very good care of me. My husband and I had Lester, and two years later my husband died of a stroke. He was good to me. I never remarried. People didn't back then. My son went into television. He had a children's program that was very popular. He died two years ago." Lester was Uncle Bunny on Channel 5. He came on between the Little Rascals cartoons, in his rabbit suit, with his puppet pals, Ole Owl and Betty Badger, to do the Happy Birthday Club. Whenever Lester used to visit his relatives in Lake Wobegon, I thought it was thrilling to be related to that famous face from TV, who wore a linen suit and smelled good. Not until I was ten did it dawn on me that Uncle Bunny was a man without a clear thought in his head. But he was pleasant and as happy as if he had brains, maybe happier.

Thinking of Uncle Bunny now, I felt the old fear of heredity: I am related to these people, and I may share more of their traits than I am willing to admit. There might be an Uncle Bunny inside me, or a Senator K. Thorvaldson, who believes that the Lutheran Church is the rock on which civilization rests and that other churches are basically a bunch of heathens hunkered around a fire, trying to comfort each other by telling funny stories. Maybe the traits don't appear until you reach your fifties, and then you turn into the same lumbering dolt that Lester was after Channel 5 canned him. A man who lived in the dim recesses of his couch.

When it was over, Mother stood in the foyer of the church, saying goodbye to everybody, thanking people, offering them flowers to take home, assuring them that she would be just fine, thank you. She told Carl Krebsbach that he should come and help himself to any of Dad's tools. She told Grace the librarian to come and help herself to the books. She hugged Kate and told her how lovely she was, and she hugged Judy's two boys. Clarence and Arlene Bunsen hugged her and said she should come bird-watching in Arizona with them in February, and she said she might take them up on that. Clint Bunsen said to bring the car in for an oil change, it was overdue.

"Let us take you home," I said, when the crowd had thinned out.

"I'll go home with Alida and Ronnie and Diana," she said. "I want you and Bill to take Uncle Art and go down to the Sidetrack Tap. They're having a wake there for your father. It's men only. You go."

"I'd rather not stand around and get drunk, Mother, thank you."

"Please. For me."

"This is cruel and unusual punishment," I said.

She smiled and patted my shoulder. "You have to," she said. "They will be so hurt if you don't," and she crossed the room and rescued Alida from the grip of Aunt Ray and marched Alida away, Alida giving me a big wave on her way out the door.

A crowd of forty or so men stood waiting when Bill and Art and I came through the door of the Sidetrack Tap. Someone sang out, "All right, now we can start!" and there was applause, and somebody yelled, "He was a hell of a guy, your father!" and there was cheering. The place was hung with silver crepe paper and tinsel from New Year's Eve and a few red and white balloons. Wally had set out bottles of liquor on a white towel along the bar, and glasses and a bucket of ice and a bowl of cheese curds. The beer was in an ice chest. Most of the men had helped themselves to the whiskey, the most expensive brand, and Uncle Art nosed in and popped a couple cubes in a glass and poured in about six ounces of Johnnie Walker.

"That isn't iced tea, you know," I said.

Art ignored me. He looked around the room, nodding to each man in turn, and then raised his glass. "That's one less here and one more there, they laid him in the ground. Speak well of the dead, for we shall join them very soon." There was a grunt of affirmation, and everybody tossed down his drink. I opened a bottle of beer, and Wally took it away from me.

"That's for the feed salesmen," he said. "Let me get you the good stuff." He filled up a glass with whiskey, and handed it to me, and clinked it with his own glass, and I took a swallow. It tasted like battery acid. I blinked back a tear and smiled a sickly smile, and Uncle Art grabbed my elbow and put his mouth up to my ear and whispered, "I'm going to say something, and then Bill makes a toast, and then you do."

I told him that I didn't have much to say.

There was one thing I could say: "My dad was generous to strangers and hard on his own kids. He never lost his temper, except with people he was related to." Then Uncle Art dinged his glass and hopped up on a chair. The whiskey had made him boyish and pert and put a glow in his withered old cheeks. He looked like a victorious alderman on Election Night.

He thanked Wally for the fine hospitality, and he thanked all who had attended the service and burial and said it had meant a great deal to the family to see the fine turnout on that cold day. "It's a cold day for us all, but now it's time to close up the ranks and go on. He had a good death. He went suddenly, he was home with his dear wife, here in his old hometown, surrounded by love and respect, and he went downstairs and *pfffffft*, he was gone."

He turned toward Bill and me with a grand gesture and said, "Two of Byron's boys are with us. Billy is up from the Cities, and Johnny came all the way from New York."

When he mentioned New York, you could feel the crowd wince, but there was applause, and Art nodded to Bill, who stepped forward. He had a clear liquid in his glass. He made a little speech about Dad's kindness, proposing that everyone should do a good deed in memory of a generous man, and there was another round of grunts, and the glasses tipped up again.

Art nodded to me, and I stepped up alongside Bill. I raised my glass. "I propose that, in honor of my father, you all show a little mercy toward your sons," I said. Some men chuckled, and Art said, "Skol," and there was a soft murmur of *skols,* and the glasses went up.

Then Wally dinged on his glass. "I was seventeen years old when Byron's grandfather John Tollefson died, who came here from Norway—and I remember he spent his last afternoon in this bar. He was ninety-two years old and still feeling frisky. I read somewhere that the great Stradivari made a beautiful cello, and inside it he wrote: Made in my ninety-second year."

Mr. Berge said, "That's what I'll write on my wife's thigh. 'Berge was here in his ninety-second year.' "

"Berge was there with what?" said Swanson. "His ballpoint pen?"

"A guy drinks your liquor, he thinks he's entitled to tell you about his home life," said Wally.

"Byron was a good guy," Mr. Berge said to me. "He told me he wasn't interested in making new friends anymore because it would take too long to tell them all his stories, and he was right. You spend your life in one town, married to one person, and it's just more economical—you don't have to keep explaining things."

I saw Swanson and Leland and Mel sitting at a back table, feeling no pain. The old gang. Like walruses congregating on the rocks, bellowing, flopping around, discussing walrus matters. Swanson was pouring bourbon into a glass of ice. He looked well schnockered already, and Leland not far behind. Mel had a bottle of beer.

"So how's life in the big time?" said Swanson.

"Just like life in the small time," I said.

"How come you didn't bring your girlfriend?" said Leland. "I was hoping to meet her. You going to marry her?"

Swanson held up his glass. "Poor Tollefson, lying down on the same bed of nails his friends did. Learning nothing from their sad lives."

"She looks very nice," said Leland.

Swanson laughed. "They always do, at first. They give you a whiff of what's in the oven, and pass a few appetizers, and you marry them, and bang, they put on fifty pounds and they go around angry all the time."

"Remember that night in the motel?" said Mel. "The night we picked up those girls at the roller rink?"

When we were seventeen, the four of us borrowed Leland's dad's car and rented a motel room in St. Cloud and stocked it with beer on ice and a bottle of orange brandy and then went to the roller rink to pick up a few girls and have a party, the sort where people get very relaxed and turn out the lights and amazing things happen. We rented skates, and Swanson went up to a group of girls and asked if any of them wanted to play Shirt Poker. You shuffle the cards and deal, and when you take a trick, you put the cards into someone else's shirt, and whoever has the most cards in his shirt wins. They said, "Oh, get lost." Leland thought he had two girls talked into Shirt Poker, so we returned to the motel and waited for the girls and meanwhile started in on the beer. Swanson got a lug wrench to break up the ice so he could put ice in his orange brandy, and he broke a hole in the sink. The girls never arrived, of course. We watched *The Tonight Show* and fell asleep with the lights on and the TV blaring, except for Mel, who sacked out under a picnic table behind the cabin, and when it started pouring rain at two-thirty A.M., he kicked down the door to get back in the room. We drove off in a panic, headlights off, leaving the busted sink and door and the beer-soaked carpet, and the motel owner called the sheriff, who called Leland's dad, whose car we had driven, and the four of us were sent down to the sheriff's office to have the fear of God instilled in us. A pockmarked deputy named Chuck sat us down in a bare room and spoke about what prison is like. He said that the prison van was on its way. We would stay there until the trial. In prison you eat baloney sandwiches for all three meals and sleep in a room with bright lights, where perverts snuggle up next to you and guys will cut your ear off with their switchblade if you look at them cross-eyed. Chuck illustrated the way perverts snuggle. We were scared out of our wits and crying, except Mel, who insisted he hadn't done anything, and Chuck kept getting up and looking out the window for the prison van, and finally Mel started crying, and then he let us go.

"That deputy made a deep impression on Mel. He never got in hot water after that," said Swanson.

"Twenty years the man has lived in abject fear," said Leland.

"Between fear of prison and his wife, Mel has been kept in check his entire adult life," said Swanson.

"Awwww," said Mel. "Don't get started on me now."

Swanson said he was taking a diet supplement that was supposed to perk you right up and increase your self-confidence and also increase your sex drive. "Sex at our house has not improved with the years, and it wasn't that good to begin with," he said.

"So what does this supplement do for you?" said Leland.

"Well, I think it increases my sex drive, but unfortunately it doesn't increase my wife's. Anyway, it's supposed to make you live longer. Whatever that's worth."

Leland snorted. "You'll be deaf and wearing diapers and have a nasty case of Alzheimer's, and we'll lean down and say, 'Congratulations, Swanny, that hormone did its job, all right!' "

Swanson said, "Well, that's right. Longevity absolutely goes against nature. We're programmed to degenerate, you know." He had read about this in a book. How nature only wants you to find a female, mount her, impregnate her, and then get out of the way, go die, and let the young take over.

"Nature is totally uninterested in old age. Once you've had your kids and raised them, nature has no more use for you. Passing on wisdom to the young? Ha! Don't make me laugh. Nature knows that past the age of twelve, your kids have nothing to learn from you whatsoever. That's why those teenage hormones kick in; it's nature saying, Get away from those people, don't listen to them, go find a mate. No, old age is purely an artificial idea." He poured himself another glass of bourbon.

"Just like marriage. Completely wrong. A man wasn't made for that life. The bachelor farmers got this all figured out.

"I came home the other day, my wife was sitting watching this idiot on television who'd written a book about body rhythms. Basically he was coming out in favor of coffee breaks and naps. I said, What is this tripe? And she said, 'Oh, you'd never understand—it's about listening to your body rhythms.' Ha! If I'd been listening to my body, I never would've gotten married in the first place.

"A bachelor farmer is all body rhythms. He wakes up in the morning and gets dressed in his old clothes and does a few chores, lets out the cat, pitches the empties from last night onto the pile beside the garage, toasts him a couple frozen waffles and slathers them with butter and syrup and they're good, so he has two more, and all this time nobody has said to him, 'Why don't you ever talk to me anymore?' He has a right to remain silent. That's his body rhythm. He puts on his barn jacket and goes out and works for a couple hours on projects for which there is no logical explanation, he sorts out coffee cans full of stuff, he shores up things, he pours some concrete, and then maybe he crawls back in the sack for a couple hours or he reads a book, and suddenly it's three in the afternoon. There is nothing special about three P.M., it is only a point on the clock, no law says you can't have lunch then. He opens a can of beans and eats a few off the top and shakes some ketchup on and horseradish and turns on the radio and the weather forecast is for more snow, which is fine with him. He puts mustard on a wiener and eats it. He feeds the cat and drives to town and parks the truck and goes into the Sidetrack Tap and gets a beer and a bump and now he may speak his first words of the day. Or he may not. It is up to him. This guy never had a social security number or a bank account. Never paid income taxes. The government never knew he existed. He keeps a big dog around the place, who goes after strangers like a werewolf. He hasn't bathed today and maybe not yesterday. Why? Because he knows who he is. He may or may not support the President on any particular thing, he may be an atheist, or not, but one thing is sure: this man is not driven by the fear of his wife. You can see this in the way he walks into the bar. You can see that this guy is not operating on a strict schedule. Nobody is going to burn his butt if he doesn't get home by six o'clock. Nobody is going to rant and rave if he has beer and brandy on his breath. Moral disapproval is not a big factor in his life."

Swanson leaned forward, stabbing his index finger at me.

"When you care what a woman thinks about you, you start look-ing for a safe place to stand," he said. "You try not to make mistakes. You think, If I can just keep from making her mad at me, I'll be okay. So you don't eat beans out of a can. You buy Italian beans, and you cook them with garlic and sixteen spices and chop up pepper and onion, and toss in thin slices of imported sausage that costs ten bucks a pound and grated parmesan cheese, and serve it with a fine wine. And are you happier? No. And is she happy? No. Because no matter what, nothing you do can ever taste good to her."

"My goodness," said Leland. "I believe the man has had a bad week."

"I am speaking for every man in this room," said Swanson, "whether he dares say so or not." He refilled his glass. "Marriage is a rotten deal for men. I speak from experience. You don't know what misery is until you find yourself in bed with an angry woman."

"So divorce her," said Leland.

Swanson snorted. "And where am I going to go live? Fargo?"

I stood up. "I've got to go take a leak and think about this stuff," I said. Uncle Art was at the bar, telling Wally about the bigamist in Sioux Falls whose house he hit with a truck. Bill sat alone, brood-ing, no easy thing in such a crowded room. Nobody had gone home that I could see. It was a fine drunken party. Even Clint, a Luth-eran and former mayor, was drunk. He put an arm around my shoulder and patted my back. "Your dad was so proud of you," he yelled, over the tumult. "He was always talking you up." I yelled, "I wish he'd told me." "Yes," said Clint, "so does he." We squeezed into the men's room, which was full, men standing three deep at the urinal trough. Harley was telling Mr. Berge that today was the an-niversary of the day the Saints called him to come to training camp. Mr. Berge asked who the tall woman at the funeral was. Someone said in a falsetto voice, "You mean me?" Carl said that Byron sure would have loved this party. Clint started singing "For He's a Jolly Good Fellow," and we all sang, and more men crowded in, and we sang:

He's waiting for us in heaven
He's waiting for us in heaven
He's waiting for us in heaven
And he's got the beer on ice.

And the verse about "The fish have peed in the water, so drink your whiskey straight," and "I've got a girlfriend in Fargo, and two in East Grand Forks," and "The bear went over the mountain, to see the burlycue," and "We won't go home until morning, when all the beer is gone," and "What's the point of a party, if everyone don't get drunk?" Verse after verse. Men banged on the door and yelled, "Hey, let me in!" and someone sang a verse in Norwegian and there was one about a fart that blew up the belfry and others about the cow who sat on the parson and mineral oil and whiskey and the Lutherans who get drunk on rum cake, and on it went. A bottle was passed around, and Mr. Berge repeated his song about the shepherd, and we did "Roll Me Over in the Clover" and "Waltz Me Around Again, Willie," and it was all for Dad, to show we loved him and considered him no ordinary man but a man worth being loud and foolish for.

I went home blind drunk and wide awake. I fixed myself a glass of Bromo-Seltzer in the kitchen. Bill snored on the living room couch. Out the kitchen window, I could see the Adolphsons' kitchen lit up next door and the old man opening the fridge and taking out a bottle of milk. He wore a ratty purple bathrobe, his teeth were out, he looked like hell. What a dreadful thought, that you might get that old yourself someday. Go around looking like an old pooch, your neck all ropy.

I opened the basement door and looked at the step where Dad died. Maybe we should put a brass plate on the wall. I sat on the step. I imagined how you might sit down to catch your breath and you take a breath and it's not enough, your heart flutters, and someone calls to you and you say, out of habit, "I'm fine!" but you know you're not, you know that the unthinkable has got you by the ankles on a Tuesday morning in January, and in that moment, the utter foolishness of your life is clear to you—you sit holding a bag of frozen peas, in a house full of junk, the sum and substance of your time on earth, and then, mercifully, God yanks the plug.

I heard a rustle, and Alida sat down on the step beside me and put her bare arm around my neck and kissed my cheek. She wore a silver satin nightshirt I had never seen before.

"I missed you," she said. I kissed her, and she closed her eyes and purred.

"I'm drunk."

"Your mother has given us her bed, and she is upstairs in your bedroom."

"My head is spinning."

She took my head in her arm and cradled it against her cheek. "We'll go on together," she said. "You and I, John. I've thought about you the last couple days. When I decided to come out here, I thought, *Well, that's it. You made up your mind.*"

"I'm drunk and I want to marry you," I said.

"I accept you, as drunk as you are. How drunk are you, actually?" She swiveled my head slightly away from her.

Then she helped me to my feet and down the hall to my parents' bedroom. I lay on the bed, on Dad's side, and she pulled off my shoes and socks and my trousers and covered me with a blanket, and I lay in Dad's trench and slept.

TWENTY-ONE

Mildred's Reply

When I came home to Red Cliff a few days later, after a stopover in New York, my backyard was drifted over with fresh snow; the trees stood pale and bare in the cold twilight, the crown of branches like delicate pencilwork on a gray-blue wash of sky. The sight of it did not warm my heart. It did not feel like a homecoming, but like a return to an outpost. It was not my home. It was a station.

I walked in the door and found a bundle of mail on the kitchen counter and white tulips in a vase. And a pot of soup in the refrigerator. The clock in the hall was ticking away. It was four-thirty P.M. Ingeborg the cleaning lady had left a note beside the flowers. ("Welcome home—soup in the fridge—enjoy!") Chicken soup. I heated a bowl of soup in the microwave, and the smell of it reminded me of Mother, and I phoned her. She said it was snowing again and Swanson had come and shoveled her walk. It was sweet of him, but he looked so exhausted afterward, she was afraid he might collapse, and she had him in for coffee, and then he stayed for an hour and talked about his problems, which exhausted her. Though it was nice to break the silence in the house, which was overwhelming. She had bought a dog from a man near Holdingford. A terrier-Chihuahua mix. The man lived in a mobile home back in the woods, a plump man in a tight blue jumpsuit. His walls were covered with pictures of circus clowns. The dog was brown, with black markings.

"His name is Toby," she said. "He and I spent a restless night, and I now think we are going to hit it off, if I can just remember not to step on him and break his leg."

She had a dog, and she had a book she was engrossed in, about a vicar's daughter in a village in the Cotswolds, and she had spoken to Alida, and Alida had said she would come for a visit, with or without me, in the summer, after final exams.

"I like her very much," said Mother. "Her coming out here on her own last week was a mark of true character, I thought. We old ladies appreciate someone bothering to attend funerals, and when she flies halfway across the country and drives on strange treacherous roads on the coldest day of the year to get here, then I take my hat off to her."

On our last night in Lake Wobegon, Alida and I had gone out to Swanson's fishhouse with Uncle Henry. Swanson was in bed with a hangover. We drove out in the rental Lincoln, and Alida clutched at my leg as the car rolled onto the ice and headed for the village of fish-houses in the middle of the lake. "How thick is this ice?" she asked. "Two feet at least," I said. I didn't know, but two feet seemed like a good solid figure.

"I used to skate out here on my dad's speed skates," I told her. "Skate away from the rink and out here in the dark, and I'd look up at the Milky Way and wonder what would become of me, if I'd have a life of glory or a life of disgrace. I still wonder, but it's not the thrilling question it used to be."

Swanson's was an eight-by-fifteen plywood-and-particleboard crate with one window and one door, which creaked bitterly from the cold when I opened it. We stepped inside. Alida had never seen a fish-house before. It had a plywood floor, and a crude wooden bunk bed at one end; the upper bunk was full of fuel cans, cooking gear, blankets, an ice auger. Four old white kitchen chairs stood around a white wooden table pitted with cigarette burns. I lit a fire in the kerosene stove and put a fluorescent lure on a line and lowered it through a hole in the ice and handed the other end to Alida and told her how to work the lure: two gentle upward jerks, then let it down—two up, one down—and Henry set a line and tied it to a table leg. He had brought a flask of bourbon and a six-pack of beer and a sack of sandwiches. The stove burned the chill off quickly, and Alida caught a sunfish, a good half-pounder, and Henry said, "This is the life, isn't it?" We took off our down jackets as the room heated. I went outside to pee, and when I came back, my uncle was telling Alida that a liberal arts education is useless, a poor preparation for life. "It's four years of dancing school," he said.

Alida bent over her line, tugging it gently, letting it fall. "Some of us like to dance," she said.

"My kids went to college and it didn't make them one bit smart, but it gave them the idea that they were brilliant, and afterward they couldn't bear to be disagreed with by their inferiors. Sending them away to college isn't in our best interests. Education tends to make them less useful. And a pain in the wazoo, to boot."

"So what do you recommend instead of college?" asked Alida.

Henry pondered this for a moment, picking at his teeth, looking down into the hole. "I'd send them away, for one thing. Run them out. Like my uncle Otto. He was Dad's youngest brother, and Dad was rough on him. There were four boys, and Haakon went to Minneapolis and got into publishing, and Harald went to California and ran an orange grove, and Otto left home as soon as he finished high school. He headed west on foot. Dad had a photograph of the family taken the day Otto left, and he was the only cheerful one in the bunch; the others looked like they had been buried and dug up. He wore a black frock coat, a boiled white shirt, red suspenders, a French voyageur scarf around his waist, a gold embroidered vest, blue overalls, high-heeled boots, a stovepipe hat, and a goatee. They filled him up with buttermilk pancakes, and he headed west and got on a dirt road that was Highway 12 and crossed North Dakota. He was six feet four and he had a long stride, so he made good progress, and when he reached Montana, he was no longer a Lutheran. He was a medicine

man. He had run into a half-breed and bought from him a medicinal
formula combining sassafras, buffalo grass, oil of peppermint, and
grain alcohol, which he named O-ho-no-ma-wa-hee Aromatic Balm,
the Sacred Spirits of the Cheyenne. He got to Billings and learned
how to manufacture the stuff for six cents a bottle and sell it for
seventy-five, and within a month, he had a pocketful of money."

Uncle Henry reached for the bourbon and took a swallow. He gave
his line a tug, to see if a fish was parked on the end of it.

"Life was miserable in Billings. Winter was brutal, living condi-
tions were bad, the houses were dark, squalid places, the companionship was none too inspiring, and the only amusements were waiting
for trains to arrive and waiting for fights to start. It was a place where
hardworking God-fearing people, after a few months, started to wonder if maybe whiskey might not do them some good. They weren't
ready to belly up to a bar, but medicine was another matter, and O-
ho-no-ma-wa-hee fit into your purse or pocket.

"Otto had himself a whole little medicine show. He had a trom-
bonist, who also did sword swallowing, and two Sioux Indians who
demonstrated feats of motionlessness for hours. And Otto learned
the art of public speaking. He gave rip-roaring gaudy speeches, which
people liked back then. He looked good in a top hat and black frock
coat, and he became the finest pure orator in Montana. He could rise
up on his toes and bay and cry out with the best of them, and one day
when James J. Hill's train was late arriving in Billings for the dedica-
tion of the new freight depot and the crowd was getting restless, the
town fathers asked Otto to step in."

Uncle Henry stood up and grasped his jacket and puffed out his
chest. "Otto stood up there at the podium, and he said, 'As I cast my
eyes across this sea of upturned faces filled with the optimism and
joy that are the very hallmark of this great city of commerce and culture which so recently was uncharted wilderness and now is in con-
tention as one of the leading cities of the land'—and he went on in
that style for ten minutes before he even came to the predicate—'as I
cast my eyes to those magnificent snow-capped mountains that adorn
the horizon of this great city, even as it says in Scripture, "I cast my

eyes unto the hills from whence cometh my help" '—the crowd was awestruck at this great oratorical sentence—'and looking toward the horizon, thinking of the boundaries of man's knowledge and of the wonders of the future that you and I shall not see but our children shall—aye, our children shall see them—' The crowd leaned forward, and when finally the sentence ended, fifteen minutes later, they gave him a standing ovation. It was not the longest sentence ever spoken in Montana, but it was respectable for an amateur."

Uncle Henry sat down. "Otto could speak off the cuff as easily as you could spit prune pits. He could talk for a full hour with only one or two thoughts to keep him company, and when people suggested he run for Congress, he said he'd be delighted. He had done well for himself, selling flavored grain alcohol to nondrinkers, but the market was drying up now that Montanans could walk into any pharmacy and purchase all the cocaine they needed. Otto campaigned on the back of a manure spreader. He said, 'This is the first time I have spoken from a Republican platform.' He made speeches against Wall Street and the railroad barons and their terrible greed at the expense of the honest workingman and tradesman, and he was elected with sixty percent of the vote and went to Washington, where he discovered that his outspoken opposition to the railroads had raised the cash value of his vote on railroad bills considerably. A Republican in favor of free enterprise got chicken feed for his vote compared to the People's Champion from the High Plains. Otto once told my father that bribery was simply a case of the free market at work simplifying the decision-making process. He had a fine time in Congress and did not overexert himself. He met with the Northern Pacific and Great Northern lawyers, who were helpful in advising him on regulatory matters. He passed antitrust laws that had about as much effect as a fart in a cyclone, and every two years he put on his old clothes and came home to roam the state and thunder against the Special Interests and the Malefactors of Wealth, and the Republicans put up some squinty old guy with bad breath, and Otto was elected to four terms."

Uncle Henry cleared his throat and opened a beer and passed it to me and opened another for himself.

"I don't want to interrupt your story," said Alida, "but did your uncle Otto ever come across a fellow Norwegian named Bolle Balestrand?"

Uncle Henry pondered the name for a moment. "It sounds familiar. That wasn't by any chance the fellow who was with Custer at the Little Big Horn, was it?"

"The very same man," said Alida.

"Well, I'll be darned. Oh yes. That man was responsible for ending Otto's career in Washington. He also was a masseur, was he not?"

"He may have been. He was a neuropathic healer who gave enemas and hot and cold baths."

"Yes, indeed," said Henry. "Otto went to him once for shortness of breath, and he pumped so much water into him that Otto could feel it coming out his ears, and then all hell broke loose, and Otto said he rose six inches into the air and remained there for about half an hour."

"So you met Otto?" I asked.

Uncle Henry nodded. "I'd go out to New York City on the train to visit him and bring him fresh vegetables. My mother felt that you couldn't get the proper food in New York City. I'd take a bag of carrots and potatoes and corn, and chuck them out the window between Minneapolis and Chicago."

"Where did he live in New York?"

"Up near Grant's Tomb, on Riverside Drive."

"That's not far from Alida's!"

"He moved there after he got beat, running for a fifth term. There had been a bill that would allow the railroads to trade parts of their original land grant for parts of the Crow Reservation and thus open up forty square miles for copper mining, and Otto was going to vote for it, and then Balestrand started talking to him about the Indians and what a rough deal they got, how they were robbed, and the two of them shared a bottle of O-ho-no-ma-wa-hee, and Otto's conscience was aroused after years of lying dormant. He voted nay. The bill passed, of course, and in the fall, the Republicans put up a cowboy against him, a Rough Rider in the Spanish War, a husband and a father of six, with a level gaze and a square jaw and a cleft in his chin, and the Republican newspapers accused Otto of wanting to give Montana back to the savages, and he was thrashed in the election. He was given a patronage job in the New York post office and spent the last twenty-two years of his life in the city. He collected his stipend and walked up and down Broadway, admiring all the new apartment buildings. He was known as the Mayor of Grant's Tomb, because he liked to sit on a park bench there when the weather was nice. People would come up and ask him a question, and Uncle Otto would jump to his feet, grab his lapels, and make a speech, even if they had only asked for the time of day. He would say, 'Time is a timeless concept that has led mankind badly astray, especially as we record age, which we do from the time of birth, and yet it is not elapsed time that really concerns us, but time remaining, and that is something that we cannot know. A youth of fifteen who will die tomorrow is older by far than an elder of seventy-two who has ten years remaining to him. And so we should not concern ourselves with time, except as we must arrange meetings or journeys by public conveyance.' And then he would look at his watch and give them the time."

"Did he have descendants?" I asked.

"None that we know of. He never married. He was too busy having fun to get married. And he couldn't bear to be interrupted."

A moment later, Henry got a strike. He almost fell off his chair, but he wrapped the line around his hand and hauled it in, and up came an immense northern, his prehistoric jaw jutting out, three silver spinners hanging from his lip, the razor teeth poised to snap, pure primal hatred in his green eyes. "Easy," said Henry. He laid the fish on the floor and pulled the old spinners from his lip and splashed a little beer on him. "Have a good life, old-timer," he said, and held the pike in the water as he recovered his senses, and let him go, and he dove down into the depths.

"He had a good life, Uncle Otto. Most of them had good lives, except Einar. Your grandpa. He was the careful one, who watched his money and worked hard and avoided extravagance. He never indulged an impulse to have a good time, and finally he quit having impulses. He was miserable, and he was good at making everyone else miserable."

"Interesting," said Alida, "but what does this have to do with college?"

"College!" said Uncle Henry. "What college? Uncle Otto never went to college a day in his life. I told you, he left home right out of high school."

My first morning back in Red Cliff, I awoke late, feeling feverish and achy, with a headful of sludge. I wrapped myself in a white robe and made a pot of tea. On WSJO, on *Morning Edition*, they were talking about Jack Kerouac—it was the anniversary of something—and a woman talked about the sense of adventure Kerouac brought to literature and read a passage of highway-driving from *On the Road*. A dreary writer, Kerouac. How antique it seems, the cool hipster lingo of the forties, how empty, compared to which Emily Dickinson's poems sound as if they were written this morning.

I called the office and told Fawn that I wasn't feeling well, and she said that Dean Baird wanted to speak with me.

"I'll call him tomorrow," I said. "If anybody else needs to reach me, tell them I'm checking my E-mail." I phoned Howard's office and got a recorded message, a woman saying the number had been disconnected. I called Howard's house, and Anne said Howard was depressed. He had spent two weeks in bed, listening to old Grateful Dead albums, and would not speak to anyone. "We're in terrible shape. I am thinking of applying for food stamps," she said. I told her I thought it would not be a bad idea.

I went through the mail—the catalogues, the pleas for money from the Pancreas Foundation, the American Depression Association, the Fund for the Coyote, a drive to raise money to organize a grassroots demonstration in which everyone who supports environmental protection would honk his car horn at precisely one P. M. on the first Monday of every month. And there was a note from Steve the contractor, on an Ansel Adams notecard with a picture of ice on the branches of a tree in a canyon: "I am very sorry about your father. I lost my own ten years ago, and as the Irish say, when your father dies, you lose your light. In all this wrangling over money, it's easy to lose sight of what's

real. Peace, brother." What sort of creep would send condolences to
someone he had cheated?

I tell you, a Midwesterner pays a high price for good manners. As a
child, you're taught not to interrupt, but interruption is a necessary
skill in any negotiation. When someone tries to lead you down the
garden path, you have to say Whoa, or else he will steal the shoes off
your feet. Midwesterners don't interrupt, and they are brought up to
eschew craven self-interest and to sacrifice for the common good. So
they get rooked. Politeness is their undoing. There comes a point in
every negotiation when you have to set the pistol on the table and
say, "Stop lying to me and tell me what this will really cost."

I missed my old dad. Suddenly our long argument was over, and
now I could think of so much more to say. Why hadn't I been more
decent, written Dad letters, tried harder to get to know him? I took a
shower and put on a pair of jeans and a scratchy wool sweater. I
wished I could ask Dad about this restaurant deal. Dad would have an
idea how to proceed. Maybe his Dark Lutheranism was a first line of
defense against cheese merchants like Steve.

And then I saw a letter from Buenos Aires, from "M. Tallia-
ferro"—Aunt Mildred had changed her name. It was six pages, typed,
single-space, on onionskin paper.

Dear John, Your letter arrived as I was about to leave for the finca,
which I own in partnership with my cousin David, and I wanted to
respond to it in some fullness of detail. I have been out of contact
with your family for so many years, I thought that surely a few
more weeks would not be an imposition, if that is what it takes to
clarify matters.

Every family has its tale of lost fortune, I suppose—my friend
Raymond had an uncle who sold his patent on the steel reinforcing
rod for a pittance in order to finance a day at the dog races—and
you have every right to be curious about the lost Tollefson fortune,
which for years lay up in the woods on the eastern shore of Lake
Wobegon, about a half mile due east from the sandbar island where
the flocks of herons rested on their way south. I don't know how
much you know about these things, so forgive me if I go over famil-

iar ground. It was there in the woods that my uncle Haakon built a magnificent two-story summer house in the sunny years after the end of the First World War. It was off-limits to us as children because he went there with his mistress, but I remember it had a copper roof and a tower with a turret and a wrought-iron fence around it, and it was there that he was murdered in 1932. Of course you know about that.

She went on to say that, though Harald Tollefson prospered in California and Otto did well for himself in Congress, the richest of the brothers by far was Haakon. He went to Minneapolis with two pairs of corduroy trousers to his name and twenty years later lived in a rambling Spanish villa on Lake Minnetonka and golfed at the Minikahda Club. His Solskin Publishing Co. made buckets of money on Vanessa Van Swenson novels about bright girls from small towns who take the train to New York and find secretarial work and learn how to trade their youth and beauty for the security of marriage to wealthy, cynical businessmen who provide them with fashionable clothes and big houses with phenomenal bathrooms. There was very little sex in Vanessa Van Swenson; the best parts were the descriptions of bathtubs and whirlpools, mirrors, marble counters, thick towels as big as bathrobes, bathrobes as big as blankets, baskets of soaps and shampoos and creams and astringents. Coming into the bathroom, the heroine always lit a candle, as one would do in a chapel. And then she dropped her gown and studied herself with a practiced eye. Long pages were devoted to the inventory of skin and hair, the terrible insults of aging, the elaborate remedies for each insult.

Haakon was a strapping six-foot man, handsome, with long sandy hair swept back, who went around in riding boots and knickers and carried a blackthorn cane. He and his mistress, Carmel, rode in a black Packard driven by an ex-welterweight named Rex Tanner. She had long black hair and bright-red lips and was swathed in mink. Haakon's wife, Karen, occupied the Minnetonka house and attended the symphony and organized charity balls and did good works among slum children. She accepted that Haakon had Carmel and that the house in the woods was for them. She did not much resent the arrangement because she loved her circle of friends, who were far pleasanter company than her tempestuous husband, and anyway she had, so to speak, abandoned the marital bed after the heartbreak of bearing Siamese twin sons, Donald and David.

They were a source of pain and embarrassment and were kept at home and privately tutored and sent to summer camps in Canada. They grew up to become—even more embarrassing—professional ballplayers and touring carnival attractions along with the Crocodile Man, the Aztec Midgets, the Wild Borneo Boy, Monsieur Petou the musical flatulist, the fire-walking Swami Mahananda, and the Montezuma Mountain Man, the only living human being to attain a body weight of one thousand pounds.

Haakon despised baseball, a game for idiots, their way of lending structure to tedium. His sons played catcher for the Minneapolis Norsemen (1926–28). They were four feet tall and joined at the hip and used one big chest protector and two mitts, and were effective defensively though they were slow throwing to second base: Donald, the twin on the left, was right-handed and David, on the right, was left-handed. Nature had been doubly cruel to them: throwing was awkward, shaving was delicate, and mealtime was no picnic either. The elbowing got on their nerves, and in their younger days, the boys got into frequent fistfights—not a pretty sight, pummeling, scratching, shrieking—and people would rush in to break up the fight, and it took the boys a long time to cool off. Sometimes they wore a padded wall between them.

The fans loved them for their pluck and courage, however, and naturally they were great celebrities in Minneapolis. They went around in green plaid suits, white gloves and spats, diamond stickpins in their bright-red ties, and girls enjoyed dancing with them. Haakon, however, considered them a curse on him. He said, "Why must you make such a spectacle of yourselves?"

"We *are* a spectacle," Donald said. "There is no escaping it." He grabbed the large whitish rubbery cartilage that linked him and David at the hips. "What would you have us do with this? We didn't ask to be born this way."

Haakon offered them a large lump sum if they would go play their baseball in South America, where he wouldn't have to hear about it. So they did, for the Buenos Aires Campesinos, and in Cuba, in the summer of 1930, they hit an inside-the-park home run against the Havana Camerados that brought them international acclaim.

A newsreel photographer happened to catch the play perfectly: a towering fly ball to right center that caroms off the glove of the Camerado center fielder as he leaps and crashes into the fence . . . the Tollefson twins racing around second base, their inside arms around each other's backs, their little legs pumping . . . the ball rolls to the right-field corner, where the right fielder chases it down and snatches it up and rifles it homeward . . . the twins steam around third, both grinning . . . and the throw is a little high as they slide into home, Donald's left foot hooking the corner of the plate under the catcher's tag . . . and the Cuban fans pour onto the field and hoist them up in the air and parade them around and around the bases, as the organist plays rumbas and tangos. It was shown in movie theaters around the world—two freaks, their faces lit up with joy, a glorious three minutes of film—and Charlie Chaplin wired them to come immediately to Hollywood.

Of course, Haakon was disheartened by this turn of events. He had sent them south to become anonymous, not celebrated. He cut off their monthly allowance and wrote them out of his will. That was what drove them to join the carnival. "People are going to stare at us, no matter what, so why not charge them for the privilege?" Donald wrote to his grandfather John Tollefson. And off they went with the carnival, up and down South America, as far north as Galveston, Texas.

Though small, they were strikingly handsome, with blue eyes and wavy sandy hair, and wiry, and they worked hard to put on a good show. A trade paper, *Carny Cornucopia*, said, "The Tollefson Twins' cheerful demeanor and steady line of patter and surefire jokes is a welcome relief to carny-goers. So often one gets a guilty feeling from freak shows, as if one had paid cousin Walt a nickel to eat dogfood. But the T.T. are real crowd-pleasers." They were married to two Argentinian girls, Carmen and Roselita, in a double-ring ceremony, and they purchased adjoining homes in Buenos Aires, the husbands going

back and forth, spending a day and night in each, the visiting twin remaining silent, inert, during marital intimacies. They begat seven
children between them, all of them perfectly normal and bright, and
sometimes one of the children would button its overalls to another
child's and go around in tandem, for the companionship of it.

Haakon refused to acknowledge his grandchildren. He felt that his
sons were taunting him when they appeared in movie shorts, jumping on a trampoline, riding horses, swimming, tap-dancing to "Tiptoe
Through the Tulips." He felt that in Minneapolis he was looked down
upon as the father of freaks. Shameless ones. He canceled his club
memberships, and he put Solskin up for sale, and he spent an entire
summer at the lake with Carmel.

Haakon and his brother Einar never spoke, but Haakon came to
visit his father and mother, John and Signe, and one day he brought
the beautiful woman with black hair to meet them. He said, "I am
getting a divorce. I want you to meet my new wife." Signe wept, for
the shame, but John brought out the brandy and poured three tiny
glasses full and toasted their happiness.

Haakon never invited anyone to his summer house. He kept the
gate locked, the Packard parked in front of it, Rex sitting with his feet
up on the dashboard, watching the road, but sometimes Rex dozed
off. One evening, someone walked up the road and slipped through
the gate. It was Haakon's wife, Karen, who had read Haakon's letter
announcing the divorce and had come to set things right. She walked
into the house, and in an upstairs bedroom she found Haakon asleep
with the black-haired woman. There were gunshots. As nearly as the
sheriff could figure out, Karen shot him in bed and then shot the
woman as she tried to climb out the window. Then Karen got into
bed, into the arms of her dead husband, and put the pistol to her temple and shot herself.

This happened in August 1932. Rex went for the sheriff, who came
out with the county coroner, and they put the three bodies into canvas bags, and Rex took them away.

The Tollefson twins were deeply affected by the deaths of their father and mother. The news reached them in Honduras, where they
were on tour with the carnival. "We are orphans now," they wrote to

their cousin Mildred in Lake Wobegon. "We are cut adrift, in a strange land, where we are loved only because we are freaks. Every time we look at each other, we think of Daddy—who despised us."

Donald started hitting the bottle hard. A quart of gin a day was his average, and through some physiological quirk unique to joined persons, it was David who woke up with the jagged headache and the sleazy stomach. This went on for years. One day in Mexico City in 1941, suffering from a terrible hangover, David came to the end of his tether.

In the show, the twins appeared with a baggy-pants clown, a *vagabundo*, who ran around shrieking as they swung baseball bats at him and he waved a pig bladder. It was low comedy all the way. He would belch, and a cloud of white dust came out of his mouth, and then he bent over and made a blatty sound as he squeezed a bulb in his pocket that made white dust blow out of his rear end. The Tollefsons hated him, and David had warned him against hitting them with the bladder, and this time he whacked them twice, and David pulled a derringer out of his shirt and fired two shots and killed the man on the spot, as the audience roared with laughter. Even when the police arrived, the audience thought it was great fun and stood and cheered the arrest.

The twins were charged with murder. The jury, unwilling to send an innocent man to prison in order to punish the guilty, acquitted both Tollefsons, and they returned to Buenos Aires, where they were separated by a surgeon—successfully, though each found it hard to walk and keep his balance without the other. And Donald's drinking got worse. His wife divorced him and took the house and children, and he found himself broke, unable to get carnival work as a single, too proud to live off his brother. He decided to return home to Minnesota and get his hands on Haakon's money.

He returned in the summer of 1952, by boat to Miami and bus to Chicago, where he bought a wreck of a car and headed north. Outside Menomonie, Wisconsin, he picked up a hitchhiker, a handsome young man in a broad-brimmed leather hat and a long green wool overcoat. When Donald said he was going all the way to Lake Wobegon, the man said, "That's where all those people were killed."

"How do you know about that?" said Donald.

"I knew someone from there. They say there's money in that house," the hitchhiker said. "He was a rich man and didn't trust banks. He kept boxes full of money around."

"What was the husband's name? I forget," said Donald, testing him.

"Haakon Tollefson. He was a publisher. His boat, the *Kristina*, won every race in its class at the Minnetonka regatta. He drove a black Packard and had a mistress. He befriended F. Scott Fitzgerald when he was down on his luck, gave him work writing Vanessa Van Swenson novels. One writer did the story, another did the descriptions, Fitzgerald wrote the dialogue."

"How do you know all this?" said Donald.

"My mother was a friend of the family maid," said the hitchhiker. "She said that Mr. Tollefson stashed two boxes full of money up over a false ceiling in an upstairs closet. The maid discovered it one day when she was looking for extra blankets. She bumped her head against the ceiling, and it dropped down, together with some bundles of hundred-dollar bills."

"She didn't take it?"

"No. She put it back."

"Why didn't she take the money?"

The hitchhiker was silent for a moment. "You want to know the truth?"

"Yes, of course."

He smiled a sickly smile and looked away. "The maid was sleeping with Mr. Tollefson, and she thought he intended to marry her. He told her he loved her. But he had a talent for being in love, and he could do it simultaneously with all sorts of people." The hitchhiker looked out the window at the darkening landscape. "If you wanted to go retrieve the money," he said, "it might be easier with two."

Donald's side still ached from the operation. He couldn't imagine reaching up for two heavy boxes squirreled away above a closet ceiling.

"I would do it for ten percent of the take," the hitchhiker said. "That's all you'd need to pay me." Donald said that sounded fine to him.

They reached Lake Wobegon at eight o'clock in the evening, when it was still light out, and Donald decided not to wait until morning. He drove through town and around the north side of the lake and found his father's old road, overgrown with sumac, and drove in until the car couldn't be seen from the highway and stopped. He and the hitchhiker plunged through the thick underbrush, the vines and bushes so dense they couldn't see six feet ahead. They traversed a cataract of grapevines and felt metal sprongs underfoot, the old gate, fallen to earth, half buried, and then they spotted the Packard, up to its axles in dirt, the upholstery rotted away, and then the hitchhiker tapped him on the shoulder and pointed, and there was the house, almost covered with vines, a birch tree poking up through the porch roof, the siding bone-gray from weathering, the front door falling off the hinges.

The hitchhiker stood and looked at the house for a long time. "His wife was a fine lady, you know, and a patron of the arts and the chairwoman of the Symphony Ball, but when she came here that night, she knew what she had to do and went straight in and did it. He was her husband, and he had betrayed her, and if she hadn't loved him, of course it wouldn't have mattered, but she did. So she shot him and the woman who seduced him, and then she lay down in his arms, where she belonged, and she killed herself. For balance. So that her murdering him would not be mere revenge. Few people today would understand such a thing."

Donald looked at the ruins where, one warm night twenty years before, his parents had met their end, one at the hand of the other. He had buried these horrible memories, and now they came leaping to mind again, the thought of his gentle mother, revolver in hand, climbing those stairs. He opened the front door, and it fell from the hinges and seemed to lunge at him. He ducked, and the hitchhiker put out a hand and caught it before it could fall on him. Inside was a parlor full of furniture covered with dust an inch thick, arms and legs broken, rotting wood and scraps of brocade and carpet, broken glass everywhere, and when Donald approached the staircase, he paused a moment to get up his courage. He said to himself, "This will take a few minutes, and it may be scary, but it's soon over, and at the end of it you'll have money again and you'll be able to fly back to Argentina. You can wear a good suit again. You can smoke a good cigar and have oysters and sirloin and an excellent 1901 Armagnac." And on the strength of the thought of a snifter of Armagnac, he headed up the stairs.

"Mind the broken treads," said the hitchhiker, but the stairway was solid oak; only the carpet had rotted away. At the top of the stairs, Donald stood in a wide hallway, the roof open to the sky, and he saw three doors, one open and two closed. Through the open door he saw an iron bed frame standing, a high iron spike at each corner, dirt and feathers on the floor. He opened the door to the second room, and a flock of pigeons rose up flapping and flew out the roof. That room was empty except for a split divan, weeds growing up from the stuffing, and bookcases, the books swollen. His heart pounded as he reached for the knob of the third door. He thought he might have a coronary thrombosis and fall down dead. And then he thought of the Armagnac, and he turned the knob, and the door was locked.

"Push it open," the hitchhiker said softly, and Donald heaved his shoulder against it, and the door fell from the rotted doorframe and landed on a mound of half-disintegrated wooden boxes. A rat scurried across the floor. Donald bent down and opened one of the boxes, and it was full of bundles of cash. He turned toward the hitchhiker and grinned, and the hitchhiker lifted his hat off and long blond hair fell out, and he took off his green overcoat and he was a woman in a black dress, with a red scarf, and her mouth was bleeding. It was his mother. Blood trickled from the corners of her mouth and down her chin. She did not wipe it away.

She said, "You're the same as him, aren't you. Not a bit of difference between you." And she untied her scarf, and she laughed, a soft, dry chuckle like leaves on a wood floor. "When I met your father, I expected there was honor among men, but there isn't, not a bit. The only difference is that some have more opportunity to cheat and some have less."

She reached into the overcoat and pulled out a Colt pistol. "This is the gun I used twenty years ago. I got him in his sleep and got her in the heat of terror. Mine was the hardest death of the three. I lay here listening to the chauffeur running up the stairs, and as he opened the door, that's when I fired. I had four bullets. One is left." Donald had been frozen with fear, but the sound of the gun clocking jolted him loose. He had seen his brother murder a man, and he knew how easily it could be done. He took three long strides and dove out the window and rolled down the porch roof and fell to the ground and landed on his side and got up running, though he had broken four ribs and his right arm, and he reached his car a quarter mile away and drove to Mildred's.

He knocked on the door and I opened it. I had not seen Donald for years, long before he was separated from his brother, and I couldn't place him exactly, though he had Uncle Haakon's long nose and deep-set eyes. He had a blanket wrapped around him, and he was shivering, though it was July. He said, "I'm Donald, Haakon's boy. May I come in?" and I said, "Of course." He told me the whole tale as I've told it to you, why he and David had gone to South America, and it touched me. Here he was, rejected by his own father, trying to recover his inheritance, haunted by the ghost of his mother. He opened his shirt and showed me the scar where the cartilage had been. I told him what I knew: that Haakon's will named John, Haakon's father, as sole beneficiary, with the bank as executor of the estate, and that John Tollefson had not touched one penny of this money, and when he died, he left everything to his son Einar, and Einar would have nothing to do with the money either, so there it sat, gathering 2 percent interest. Einar would most likely leave it to the church.

"I don't care about what's in the bank," he said. "All I want is what's out at the house." I said I would go out and get that money for him. "If you do," he said, "then you take what's in the bank. Bring it to Buenos Aires. My brother David will help you. We can disburse it from there as we see fit. But it doesn't belong in this town, I know that. This town was a torture to my father from the time he was old enough to walk. There was no love here for him. He thought the Lutheran Church was the coldest place on earth. He would be horrified—to be murdered and then see your fortune go to your old tormentors." He told me that Uncle Haakon would want me to take that money and have a good life with it. He was very persuasive.

I drove out to the summer house and went up to the room and got the boxes with the money. The place seemed quite peaceful to me. The sun shone down through a hole in the roof, into the upstairs bedrooms. The boxes were right there. The wooden box and a black steel box with a clasp. I brought them home and gave one to him and stowed the other under my bed. I managed to move Haakon's trust fund to another account, under Donald's name, and the money in the box I took to New York and made certain investments there. I must say, I did this with no trouble. The men of Lake Wobegon were the most benighted and ignorant people in the world, especially the ones at the bank, and this made me overconfident, and then the bank examiners sniffed me out and I had to leave town suddenly, a stroke of good luck. I escaped in more ways than one. We only took what was ours by right. Your mother told me to give it back, but it's my life and my cousins', and how can you give back your life? Your father said I should at least donate half to the Sons of Knute, but what would those old boogers do with money?

Mildred bought herself a white stone-and-stucco house behind a high brick wall, with a green-tiled swimming pool and a clay tennis court, an immaculate lawn with palm trees, where she lay on a chaise longue, her hair dyed with henna rinse, wearing a blue two-piece bathing suit and rhinestone-studded dark glasses, sipping a Daiquiri, talking with her boyfriend, Raymond, who had burned down his tavern in Des Moines for the insurance money. Around the elaborate stone fountain, in which naked cherubs peed into the air, was a wall made of pink shells and blue bricks. She enclosed a photograph of herself standing by the fountain, with Raymond's shadow extending into the picture.

Donald took his money and went to London, and a year later he was dead, run over by a taxi in the street, but it was a wonderful year for him. David lives here in Buenos Aires. What can I say? He is like any other Lutheran, except happier. Usually Lutherans take so long to die they have to start when they're young, but David is one of the Happy Lutherans. You know about them, don't you? I believe I am one of those too. We have continued Uncle Haakon's Solskin Press and publish erotic novels for sailors and truckdrivers, novels in which there are the expected vivid scenes, but we also slip in educational passages about botany, philosophy, architecture, first aid, and the removal of common stains.

Now, as to your request for financial assistance, here is the situation: some of this money is certainly yours by right, and you should have it, but due to the restrictions under which we foreigners live here, I cannot send you the money. You would have to come and spend it here in Argentina. I would say it amounts to about $60,000 at the current rate. Let me know what you wish to do. Love from your Aunt Mildred.

My lost inheritance had arrived, but I would have to fly down to Argentina to claim it. I could take a honeymoon, spend a week with Alida in a ritzy hotel, sky's-the-limit room service, a few bottles of wine so expensive I would have to close my eyes to sign the check. And we would buy diamond rings and wear them back to America.

TWENTY-TWO

Defeat

I dreaded going back to the radio station. I gave myself a pep talk, told myself to get dressed, that postponement only complicates matters, that it is shameful to give in to fear, and then I climbed back into bed and called Marian and left her a message to call me, and called Fawn and announced I was staying home.

"Are you really sick?" she said. "You don't sound sick. But if you'd rather stay home, I suppose that's your choice."

There was a tone of audacity in her voice. She said, "A lot has happened since you left. The staff has been meeting with Dean Baird to discuss the situation."

"Which situation is that, Fawn?"

"The one here," she said, "at WSJO. Which I believe you're aware of. We've discussed this in my group, and everyone agreed that you know what you're doing, and that's why I have to say it. You cannot power me down into a daughter role." Her voice broke, and she stopped. Obviously it was the tone of role-playing I heard in her voice. Someone had told her to be assertive, so now she was being assertive, even though it wasn't like her at all. She continued, in a shaky voice. "Professional work relationships have to exist on the basis of emotional and psychic equality. You have created an atmosphere of hostility and emotional domination. You make me feel inferior and incapable.

"This is not easy for me to say." She sounded on the verge of tears, and I thought that if she cried, I might like to join her, but she hung up. *She* was the one who had fingered me for the douche bag joke. She had taken her wounded Botticellian innocence to Dean Baird and had darkened my name, and now her adolescent misery would be used to wipe Mozart and Puccini off the airwaves, in place of which wounded people would drone about the slights and injustices and abuses they had suffered. Oh well. Mozart and Puccini knew how dangerous beautiful women could be.

I made a nest in bed, pillows and comforter, a quart of mineral water and a bag of blue-corn chips, and the phone rang. It was brother Bill. "How are you?" I said. "Fine," said Bill. It took him a long time to get to the point. He had to go down a long checklist of small talk, and then, of course, it turned out to be nothing at all. He was feeling down, he said, because he had figured up his retirement accounts and he would need to work for at least eight more years.

He and Elizabeth were considering a trip in June to upstate New York, and could they stay for a few days? Their therapist had recommended a trip.

"I may not be here in June," I said. "I am about to get fired."

"Oh, I'm sure it can't be all that bad," said Bill.

Marian called at noon. "The knives are out, honey," she said. "Poor baby. I don't think you're going to enjoy coming back."

"How bad is it?"

"The dean has set April first as the date to switch to a talk format. There was a long meeting about it. He and Susan Mack talked, and he's definitely got a bee up his butt about giving us niggers a voice."

"Have we heard from Miss LeWin at all?"

"Didn't you hear? She died. Almost a month ago. I guess she'd been ill, and she thought she didn't have long, so she treated herself to a steak dinner and took all her cats and went and sat in her Cadillac in the garage and turned on the engine while her CD player was doing the immolation scene from *Die Götterdämmerung*."

"The poor old thing." I thought of the old lady and her ailing Snowball. What a dark and grievous winter it must have been at The Poplars.

"Her will left a quarter of her estate to her nieces and nephews, and the rest to a guy in Syracuse who's starting an opera company. It was in the paper."

So Alan Dale had fought back. Good for him. He had survived my preemptive strike and had counterattacked and taken the field. He had given Miss LeWin a whiff of the sawdust and greasepaint and drawn lovely pictures in the air of great operatic spectacles and enchanted schoolchildren leaning forward in the dark.

Well, that settles your hash, I thought. I fired up the computer and wrote, and rewrote, a letter of resignation.

Dear President Postlethwaite:

It is clear to me that the direction St. James wishes to go with WSJO is one I cannot support, and so I am resigning as general manager. I feel that the station today is a priceless asset to our area. There are radio stations for the aging rock'n'rollers, the religious right, the audience with metal things stuck in their heads, the deer-hunting beer-drinking audience, and this one should be for folks who find spiritual sustenance in great music. Beethoven, Mozart, and Puccini are part of the broad humanistic tradition that we all draw water from, where we find centrist values such as tolerance, curiosity, a sense of justice, and humor. It is wrong to discard this tradition in favor of creating a Wailing Wall, a freak show like Speaker's Corner in Hyde Park, a radio zoo where people can hear lunatics foam and growl and rush at the bars.

Radio is capable of enlightening and amusing and touching the imagination in ways unique to itself. It should be allowed to rise to its own magnificent heights, not be consigned to social work.

Talk radio is part of the tide of dreariness slopping across America. Franchise architecture, generic shopping malls, popular music as ugly and empty as it's possible to be, and talk radio. The Cold War is over, the stock market booming, equity bursting at the seams, the twenty-first century winks and beckons, and yet the world's only superpower, America, the Nation of Nations, is in the dumps; gloom is playing on the sound track, the media wander, lost in narcissism and the fear of death and a slavish servility toward the rich and a knee-jerk contempt for leaders. If ever an era needed bucking up, it's this one—but academics have given up. You ask them for a vision, they give you dissenting opinions.

I thought, *Lighten up. You're thinking like an old fart.*

I called Alida. I had been saving her for last. When she picked up the phone, music was playing in the background and people were talking. It was an impromptu cocktail party. The chairman was there and a couple of graduate students and Ginger and Neil, who had separated for six months and were getting back together. Her friends Jens and Emily from Copenhagen were visiting her. The music and voices faded as Alida walked into her bedroom and closed the door.

"I can call back later," I said.

"Nonsense. You're the man I'm going to marry. I get to talk to you whenever I want. The guests can entertain themselves. They're smart enough."

Jens and Emily were perfect houseguests, she said, the kind who get up and fix their own breakfast and clean the kitchen and go away and amuse themselves all day and come home in the evening and tell you stories about things you never knew existed.

"I had no idea," she said, "that you could visit S. J. Perelman's apartment on Gramercy Park and see his collection of ascots and buskins and gaiters, his fedoras and dusters and dreadnoughts, tippets and dickeys, his smoking jackets, his dancing pumps, his old yellow MG parked in the garage. Or that the hotel on the Upper West Side where Holden Caulfield stayed—where the elevator man offered to get him a prostitute, remember?—was bought by J. D. Salinger ten years ago and turned into a shelter for streetwalkers, and every year they put on a floor show to raise money for the scholarship fund. It was last night. My friends happened to be walking past the front door and they went in, paid fifty dollars, and there was Salinger onstage in tux and black tie, the emcee, and according to them, he sang 'Love Walked In' and did a nice little soft-shoe routine in the middle of it. A charming man with silvery hair. I always thought he was a recluse, but that's New York for you. Full of surprises."

She asked if I had read the last chapter of her Balestrand book, which she gave me on the flight home from Minnesota. I had not. "I'm saving it for whenever I'm able to think straight," I said. "I'm resigning from my job tomorrow. They're holding meetings behind my back and switching the format to talk."

"Don't resign because of that. Resign because you want to move to New York and live with your wife."

"When do you want me to marry you?" I asked.

"In June," she said. And then the bedroom door opened and a man spoke to her. "There is a spoon stuck in the dishwasher," she said. "I'd better get it out."

I piled up pillows and pulled a quilt around me and read the chapter, a short one.

Balestrand left Washington after the war, an itinerant healer, traveling through New England and upstate New York by wagon, offering colonics and cold baths and poppy tea, and was especially popular among religious eccentrics and spinster ladies. He spent a week in Amherst and treated Emily Dickinson and her sister, Lavinia, and Emily wrote a poem for him:

A slender Fellow—is the Hose—
That comes—into—my Bed—
The Feeling—when the Water flows
The Ringing—in my Head.

The Roaring—of a Cataract
The Fog Bank—in the Room
As if an Arctic Glacier—Cracked—
And made—an Awful—Boom.

How like—a Thunderstorm—it was
And then Withdrew—from Me—
And Afterward—a Pleasant Buzz—
A lovely—Vacancy.

From Amherst, Balestrand traveled west. He was drinking too much opium tea, and his judgment was affected, and he moved in with a band of zealots on a farm near Great Barrington. They believed in an Absolute Being and Universal Omniscience that dwelt in all men but revealed its Sacred Oneness especially to those who ate whole grains and tubers and spoke softly and adhered to Higher Thought and maintained purity of purpose and wore dark colors. These people had no need of colonics; quite the contrary.

Balestrand showed up, a little pale and dizzy, and there was Susan B. Anthony. The great suffragist was visiting the tuberists to recharge her spiritual batteries and also to get away from Elizabeth Cady Stanton, whom she referred to as "the Bitch of Ithaca." They were having one of their frequent tiffs.

She and Balestrand fell for each other. She took his hand and he fainted dead away and she carried him to her hut, and that was that. He had practiced celibacy as part of his health regimen, believing that sexual congress weakened the system, and now that this seemed not to be true, he abandoned colonics and cold baths and took up love-making as a hobby.

The lovers felt giddy, surrounded by solemn moralists. In the evening, while the others gathered in the refectory to discuss nature and the soul, Susan and Bolle snuck off to the orchard, and Susan played her accordion and they drank mulberry wine and got silly, which put the tuberists in a terrific huff: they were willing to tolerate all sorts of ideas, but not silliness, and not accordions, and the lovers were asked to pack their things and leave. They traveled to Seneca Falls and lived with Elizabeth Cady Stanton for a time. But Susan and Elizabeth fought like cats, and always over trivial issues—a toothbrush left on the kitchen sink, a pair of scissors misplaced, a book borrowed and not returned, a coffee stain on a tablecloth. Bolle tried to be the peacemaker; he pointed out to the women that they shared a commitment to women's suffrage and the progressive cause. "Nonetheless," said Mrs. Stanton, "I hate her hair that way, bleached and curled into ringlets."

"What is liberation worth if a woman can't wear her hair as she likes?" Susan replied.

"It harms the cause of equal rights when you show up at speeches looking like a chippy," said Mrs. Stanton.

"If your followers judge everyone by her hair, they'll need more than a constitutional amendment to free them," Susan replied.

Balestrand decided that the constant company of women was not good for a man, that it sapped his innate optimism, and he left Susan a long note saying that he loved her but not under these circumstances and ran away and joined the army. He returned three years later, to find Susan wearing a black floor-length dress, her hair long and worn in a coil, her expression severe, her hands rough and dry. He embraced her, and she recoiled.

"Forgive my high spirits. When you have been left for dead, you become joyful and forget propriety," said Balestrand. "I want to marry you."

He explained that he had gone to St. Louis, enlisted in the Seventh Cavalry, and ridden at General Custer's side as an aide-de-camp on June 25, 1876, when they came over the rise and into the valley of the Little Big Horn and saw ten thousand Sioux and Cheyenne warriors gathered to meet them, and Custer turned to Corporal Balestrand and said, "Where was the staff work on this? Why am I the last person to find out about these things? Why can't we get better intelligence?" They dug in and prepared to defend themselves and Balestrand excused himself to go off in the bushes and move his bowels and moments later the Indians came whooping and screeching by and there was a rattle of gunfire and it was all over in five minutes. Meanwhile, the corporal lay in the bushes and pretended to be dead, and the Indians assumed from the smell of him that he was. He lay in the sun for six hours, and at sunset he snuck away and made it to Billings on foot and came east to New York, not telling a soul, out of fear that he might be court-martialed for desertion.

Mrs. Stanton was a shrewd promoter, and she guessed that the

Only Survivor of Custer's Last Stand might draw an audience of men to her suffrage rallies. And two nights later, she spoke on "The Moral Power of the Female" at the Ithaca Chautauqua to a mob of men who came to hear the Survivor and who smelled of ripe fruit. Bolle Balestrand took the stage after Mrs. Stanton, and a man yelled, "You've got bread crumbs for brains!" and the crowd rushed forward, hurling eggs and dead things, and hauled him off the stage and punched his lights out. They didn't want there to be a Survivor; they preferred a clean Massacre so they could imagine the heroic Custer, his golden hair flowing, standing amid the smoke and carnage, bright saber outstretched.

Bolle Balestrand curled up in a ball as they pounded on him. And then he blacked out. When he came to, he was riding over a bumpy road in the bottom of a junk wagon. He landed in Buffalo, took a job as a deckhand on a barge on the Erie Canal, and got to New York, where he shipped back to Norway and wrote his autobiography, *Jeg Var Ikke Saa Grei At Blive Kvit* (I Was Not So Easy to Get Rid Of), dedicated to Walt Whitman, which came out in 1918, and which nobody in Norway read. All the Norwegians who had any interest in America had already emigrated.

I sat in bed, drinking water and gazing out at the snowy backyard and thinking about the radio station and Dean Baird. In a few months, WSJO would change over, from classical music to talk: the *Gay-Lesbian Parenting Hour* at one P.M. and the *Men Dealing with Impotence Hour* at one-fifteen, the *Hearing Impaired Hour* at one-thirty, *Wounded Nephews of Distant Uncles* at one forty-five, *People in Grief for Former Lovers* at two, the *Herpes Hour* at two-fifteen, *People in Search of Closure* at two-thirty—each with its own smug host and tiny clientele, its own style of vacuity—and should I fight this? No, I did not think so.

Fighting is noble in theory, but when you look at the lives of battling visionaries—Joe Hill, Susan B. Anthony, Eugene Debs, Carry Nation, Father Coughlin, Dorothy Day, Martin Luther King, Ralph

Nader, Newt Gingrich—you see the price they paid, the loss of the private self, and how the inner fire that drove them to battle also made them not much fun to be with. Joe Hill's wife, Jill, married a florist after Joe's execution and happily gave up the labor movement for a life of Girl Scouting and literary teas in Muncie, Indiana, and hoped never to hear the word "solidarity" ever again. Eugene Debs, five-time Socialist candidate for President, was divorced by his wife, Debbie, who said that marriage to a great man was about as enjoyable as sleeping in a bed full of spruce boughs, and she found happiness raising Pomeranians and later playing Aunt Sis on *Friendly Neighbors*. Dorothy Day's husband, Ray, never accompanied her on her Catholic Worker tours or walked the picket line; his great passions were raising orchids and weaving baskets and maintaining his collection of Deanna Durbin memorabilia. Ralph Nader's wife, Nadine, tired of her husband's abstemiousness and fled to Santa Barbara and opened a gift shop. And poor Gingrich. The cost of leading the Republican Revolution was to become a man whom nobody but major donors cared to eat dinner with. Gingrich's first wife, Ginger, said that Newt was unable to focus on conversations not about himself, that he was afraid of small children and shrank back from them as if accosted by porcupines.

Warriors are great at creating myth and not so good at hanging around, and they are always trying to enlist you in their battles. A friend asks you to sign a harmless petition supporting medical research, and you do, and the next week there's a crowd on your front step, waving color photographs of disemboweled dogs, and one of them throws a rock through your window, and you run downstairs and trip on a loose rug and wind up with a lifetime of lower-back problems. And it wasn't even your battle.

I walked to the office in the morning, passing knots of students who seemed beaten down by school, or the cold, like prisoners in a work camp. They looked as if they had been up all night pecking out a particularly awful term paper, had suffered miserably for a C minus, and were now considering other options in life. Fawn looked up and grimaced when I came through the door. "The dean left you a letter," she said.

"What a coincidence. I just got done writing one to him," I said. "How are you doing?"

She snorted and looked down at her desk. "If you really wanted to know, I'd tell you, but you don't. So I'm fine."

"Good," I said. "So am I." Taped to the wall next to my office door was a notice advertising Holographic Repatterning—"a six-step process that enables you to access your negative unconscious patterns that keep you from your true potential."

My office seemed shrunken somehow. And it was cold. The thermostat was turned down to sixty-two. And someone had been working at my desk and had left some clippings about self-imaging. On *Morning Edition*, a man was lamenting the slaughter of songbirds by America's house cats and calling for a congressional investigation. The letter lay on my desk. It read: "Dear John, In consultation with the President of the College and the Faculty Advisory Committee on Broadcasting, I have come to the decision that a change of direction at WSJO would be in everyone's best interest. I am enclosing a letter of resignation for you to sign and deliver to my office at your earliest convenience. In return for your prompt signature, I am prepared to offer you six months of leave at full salary. This leave would begin immediately. This decision was made in full realization of your great contribution to WSJO, which will be recognized, upon receipt of your resignation, with the awarding of the College's Distinguished Achievement Medal at the spring commencement. Your presence at this event is not required, and the Medal can be mailed to you. With very best wishes, Edward Baird, Ph.D., Dean of Students, St. James College."

Well. I had wanted the pleasure of resigning on my own steam, with a statement of wounded virtue. But six months of paid leave— my, my, my: it was much too good a deal to turn down. I tore up my letter of resignation, signed the one the dean had written, and hiked over to the dean's office to hand it to him. The day was turning blustery. A gang of students swept by, including a pink-cheeked girl with close-cropped blond hair and pure blue eyes. I thought that what I would miss most at St. James was the pleasure of looking at young women.

When the dean's secretary saw me come through the door, she jumped up, all flustered, as if I were a terrorist, and blocked my way. She was tall, broad in the shoulders, and wore red-rimmed glasses.

"I came to turn in my resignation," I said.

She said, "He's not in. I'll take it."

Then I heard Dean Baird's voice thanking someone on the phone, someone hard of hearing. "My lawyer told me to make sure to hand it to him personally," I said, with a shrug. "You know lawyers." And I slipped into the dean's office. The dean sat in his leather swivel chair, his back to me, his legs crossed, his left hand holding the telephone and the other holding a yellow pencil and trying to pry something out of his right ear. I stood in the doorway. There were few books in the office; the shelves were full of seashells. Every year, Dean Baird took off for Florida, and he and Mrs. Baird roamed the beaches in search of specimens to add to their collection. I always thought of beaches as places to be stupefied by boredom.

"It was a beautiful ceremony, very simple and moving," said the dean, "and I'm sending you copies of the program, with your message on it, and again, all of us want to thank you for the gift—let me make sure I have your address," and he withdrew the pencil from his ear and swung around in the chair and saw me and froze. He repeated an address but didn't write it down: he was looking at me.

I advanced to the desk and set the letter down. The dean inquired as to the health of the caller's husband and other members of her family and then said goodbye and hung up. He looked at the letter. "Well," he said. "Good."

I stuck out my hand and the dean took it, none too happily, and we shook hands. "It was a wonderful job," I said, "and I'm glad to have had it. I enjoyed just about the whole time I've been here. And I certainly am going to miss the place. And thanks for the severance. It's very generous."

"It was the president's idea," said the dean. "It wasn't mine."

"Whatever," I said. "Who's your new manager? Anyone I know?"

"Susan Mack has agreed to take the job," he said. "By the way, she was not the one who complained about the douche bag joke, and your letter of apology was rather sophomoric, I must say."

"I suppose it was. I hope you don't get too much flak when you change the format," I said. "These classical music fans get pretty sour when you take away their station."

The dean smiled. "Whenever one does the right thing, one expects to be criticized for it. But face it: there is no point broadcasting classical music when everybody I know has CD players in their cars. And the unemployed, the people living in the trailer homes back in the woods, the fellows in the Embassy Bar—you don't reach out to those people with Mozart." He snorted at the thought.

"Well, I guess this is goodbye," I said. "Good luck." And I turned and walked out.

TWENTY-THREE

March

It felt good to be unemployed, free of the office nonsense. Felt digni-
fied. What freedom! It felt so good, I went straight from WSJO
around to Howard's house to shake hands, make peace, commiserate—
say, No hard feelings, better luck next time, see you around.

Howard's front walk was unshoveled, a path over packed snow, and
pages of newspaper littered the yard. I rapped on the door and
Anne opened it, a pencil in her hand. She wore bright-green shorts
and a Red Cliff jersey; she was on the phone, and it sounded as if
she was closing a sale involving magazine subscriptions. Shirts and
underwear lay in a heap at her feet. She pointed upstairs and mouthed
the words *He's up there*, and I climbed the stairs and knocked on the
bedroom door. I heard movie gunshots and squealing tires as I opened
the door. "What?" said Howard. He sat slumped in bed under a blue
knit coverlet, unshaven, in blue pajamas, his hair matted, drinking
from a can of Budweiser, watching television, a movie in which a man
and a woman were dashing down a long hallway of a building that

was disintegrating in flames behind them. He looked at me and muttered under his breath.

I told him that I'd come to patch things up. That it had been a rough couple of years. That I hoped we could put it behind us and start over and be friends again.

"What's the point?" said Howard. "You've kept me at arm's length for three years, you asshole. Why the sudden interest in friendship?"

I stood at the foot of the bed, next to the TV monitor on the rolling stand, the VCR slung below it, stacks of cassettes below that. One look at Howard, and it was clear why the restaurant had crashed. I switched off the TV.

"Howard, you need help," I said. "If you're not getting it, maybe you should be."

"Go away." Howard clicked the remote and the movie came back—the man and the woman running through dense underbrush, illuminated by flashes of exploding fuel tanks, heading toward a helicopter, its blades revving up for takeoff, as the man turned and fired a few bursts from an automatic rifle. I switched it off again.

Howard rose up in bed. "Look. I was in a partnership, John. You and me. We were, like, married, and you crawled into that protective shell of yours, and now it's over." His pajama top was open, revealing his belly, the whorl of dark hair around the deep pit of his navel. He jabbed his index finger at me. "You expected me to be the fixer, the doer of great deeds, but I'm only a lawyer, buddy! A lawyer is nothing but a high-class secretary. The restaurant was your idea, John. You could've made it work. And you walked away from it. You abdicated. Don't blame me. Now get out of my house."

I put a hand on the bedpost and looked Howard straight in his pinkish eyes and said, "Howard, you spent eight years as a mime. A mime, Howard. What training for a lawyer! You entertained tiny tots and you smoked industrial-strength reefer and you killed a lot of brain cells, Howard. I don't think you ever learned the fine points of contract law. You hired your old pal Steve, the Dr. Caligari of cabinetwork, and you handed him a contract that is like a bear trap with our heads inside it. It was an invitation to larceny! It gives the guy a contractor's fee of eight percent of whatever the project costs and no limit on what the cost should be! Does that make sense? I ask you."

Howard lay back against the pillows. "You signed that contract too!"

"You were my lawyer, Howard. You handed me the contract and told me it was okay. Howard, if I took that contract around to the state bar association and told them the story, you would be disbarred like *that*, for misfeasance to your fiduciary duty and violation of the canon of legal ethics and for sheer unbridled stupidity." I sensed a faint tremor in the bed at the mention of disbarment. "Disbarment, Howard. You stand in the public square at high noon, you and your weeping wife and children, and the president of the bar association rips the handle off your briefcase, and after that, Howard, you may have to wear a white smock and put price stickers on cans of vegetables for a living. You may have to wear a plaid sport coat and stand around in a tin-roofed shack at a used-car lot with plastic pennants whipping in the wind, like an owl waiting for mice. That's where disbarred attorneys go, Howard. They're forced farther down the food chain." I moved around to the side of the bed and sat down. "But I'm going to give you another chance, Howard. For your sister's sake. I want you to negotiate a surrender. Steve wins. But he ought to cut us in for a share of his profits. Simple as that. What do you say? Work it out and let's move on."

Howard looked at the dark screen, sulking. "I don't like it when people threaten me with disbarment," he said in a small voice.

"I was not threatening," I said. "I was only outlining alternative scenarios."

Howard shook his head. "I hope you're not going to marry my sister."

"I hope I am."

"You are making a big mistake. She'll eat you alive."

"She already has."

Howard plopped back against the pillows and looked up at the ceiling.

"I used to be a guy with a sense of trajectory," he said. "I had goals and I was terrified of failure, and lately I've been thinking that progress is essentially meaningless. There are no fixed points. Failure is actually a door to a different perception. What some people call success is the biggest failure of all, because they don't know it. Some people never figure that out. But I did. And that's what makes all of this worthwhile."

It was mime talk and it made no sense, but it seemed to relax Howard, and he went on chattering in that vein. I wished I could fast-forward, but the guy was hurting, he needed room. He talked about how he had felt trapped in other people's preconceptions and how dangerous it was to lose one's Inner Light, and when he came to a stopping place, I thanked him for the talk, told him to take care of himself, patted his shoulder, and left. Going down the stairs, I heard the helicopter take off, followed by bursts of ground fire.

Anne was off the phone. "I don't know what will become of us," she said. "He won't talk to me, and I don't know what to tell the kids, and we don't have any money—I'm borrowing from my parents just to pay the utility bills. I never imagined this could happen to people like us. Do you know if there's a pawnshop in Ithaca that takes jewelry?"

I told her to look in the Yellow Pages. She took my arm and looked pleadingly into my eyes and said, "You're one of the few people in this town I really trust, John." She seemed to want to tell me her troubles and hear something back that would clarify the situation.

"I've been fired, Anne, and I'm selling my house and moving to the city," I said. "I'm going to marry Alida. I'll be your brother-in-law. Let me know if there's anything I can do." I ducked out the door and drove home.

In celebration of losing my job, I fixed myself a hamburger, very rare, with a thick slice of raw onion and a dollop of mustard and horseradish. I made the patty to the Kyrie of a Haydn organ mass, and fried it to the Gloria in Excelsis Deo, a solo tenor singing a line in God's praise before the organ and orchestra and choir swept in—oh, glorious Haydn, who enlisted a ballet of angels in the worship of the Creator—and the hamburger wasn't bad either. I cranked up the volume for the Sanctus, the polyphonic voices like two sets of waves rocking an anchored boat from two directions, and then the levitation of the Agnus Dei. How lucky I am, praise God—how fortunate to have fixed points, like oarlocks, from which to fulcrum yourself forward through the water.

My House for Sale ad appeared in the next week's issue of the Red Cliff *Citizen*, along with an article announcing Susan Mack's elevation to general manager and a picture of her seated in my office, the big desk gone, replaced by a skinny table. Susan said that radio had a special obligation to the community of the disaffected and disconnected and those in pain and locked into lives of fear. Most Americans were burdened by secret shameful afflictions, and radio could allow them to break the silence of oppression.

What was Susan's shameful secret? I wondered. Did she stuff beans up her nose? Did she have a shopping obsession? Was her house crammed to the rafters with piles of junk?

There was also a photograph of Fawn Phillips, the new public affairs director, trying hard to look serious, her hair tied back tightly. She was hoping, she said, to create radio that did not make people feel inferior or uninformed but inspired them with a sense of their own creative potential. Dean Baird said that organizations needed continually to reinvent themselves. Mr. Tollefson, the story said, was leaving Red Cliff to take advantage of other opportunities.

Alida came up for the weekend, set her shopping bag on the floor, took off her dark glasses, put her arms around me, and said, "If the truth be told, I never cared for that bus trip, and I was never all that crazy about this house. And the town is a kitchen for clinical depression. I'm afraid you were the only attraction for me. How is my brother doing?"

"Having a breakdown, but he'll be okay."

"He takes after my mother. How soon can you move to the city? Do you need to wait for the house to sell?" she said.

"I'll be there before you know it," I said.

The last traces of snow melted during a three-day rain in late March, and the next week it was spring. One morning I awoke to the mulchy smell of dirt that the sun has been shining on, and after breakfast I spaded up the flower beds. The worms wriggled away from the light and plunged into crevices, safe from the eyes of robins. I put in tulip bulbs where the squirrels had dug up the old ones. I bought two yards of horse manure from the Red Cliff Nursery and had it delivered and raked it into a patch of dirt where I could set in tomato plants, though I knew I wouldn't be around to harvest them.

In the midst of fertilization, the phone rang, and it was Susan Mack, who wondered if I had a minute. Of course I did. I had many minutes, thousands of them.

"Do you mind if I ask you a question?" she said. "Is this uncomfortable—to talk?"

No, it wasn't, I said.

"Do you consider me neurotic?" she asked. "Is that why you were never comfortable around me?"

I said I had never had a problem being around her.

"Is that what you really think, or are you only being polite? Can we get beyond politeness? Can you be honest with me? Please?"

So I said that, yes, I did think she was the teeniest bit neurotic. "But hey, nobody's perfect."

"So you do think I'm neurotic," she said. "Why didn't you say so? In fact, you think I'm incredibly neurotic, don't you? And that was why you couldn't stand to be in the same room with me, wasn't it? I want to know."

"Oh, I suppose you bugged me a little bit."

"More than a little bit, didn't I? I know I did. But why? What was it? Was it that I asked too many questions? That I was never satisfied with the answers? That I was inquisitive? That I needed to know things? That I was not satisfied with pat answers? Was it the fact that I kept probing?"

I tried to think of a good answer. "Yes," I said.

"Then why didn't you tell me?" she said. "Why didn't you say something? Why did you keep it inside yourself?"

"I don't know," I said. "Fear, I guess. Fear of confrontation. It started when I got my teeth filled."

"Are you making fun of me now?" she said.

"Yes," I said. "I am."

I sold the house a few days later to a professor of French who lived two blocks away and had admired it for years, she said, especially after the fall it turned gold. I sold the Fiat. The used-book store bought half of my library and sent two teenagers to box it up, and the Salvation Army sent a truck for my clothes, and I held a sale in the house one Saturday, eight A.M., and sixty people came through, and by noon I had gotten rid of all the furniture, except the pendulum clock and the painting of Bergen. Jean came and bought the dining room table and the white china and the wineglasses. She said that she was living with a man she had known for a few years named Brad, who delivered her fuel oil. He was going through a nasty divorce, and his wife was putting Jean's name on thousands of mailing lists, and she was receiving bales of catalogues daily. "She calls me every day after work. She says the word 'whore' and hangs up. But I'm happy, so I don't mind. Are you happy, John?"

I thought for a moment. "Yes, in fact I am. Getting fired cleared up a lot of things for me."

In one week, I managed to whittle my earthly possessions down to what would fit in a rental minivan, an act of divestment that would have made Thoreau proud. I loaded the van on Sunday and cleaned the house, and in the evening I sat down on the kitchen floor with a half bottle of Chianti and a takeout submarine sandwich, and as I ate, the phone rang, and it was Mother, who, it turned out, had been divesting too. An antique dealer in Chicago had called about a mechanical organ of Dad's, and when she told him that everything in the house was for sale, he arrived the next day, did a quick appraisal, made an offer, and two days later, a semitrailer backed in, and six men packed everything in four hours, and it was gone. Dad's House o' Stuff was out of business. She was having the floors refinished, and Carl was coming in next week to paint the walls.

"Congratulations," I said.

"I'm sending you a check for your share," she said.

"Don't be silly."

"Byron was so sentimental," she said. "He loved those old things. It brought back memories for him, of Uncle Svend and bathing in a copper boiler in the kitchen on Saturday night, in front of a blazing woodstove, and down the hall was the parlor where the pastor was entertained and the women from church came to sit and roll bandages as somebody read to them from Thackeray. Oh, it was sweet how he loved those things. He kept those bobsled runners in the bedroom, and he'd go look at them and he'd remember the sleigh, and the horses named Scout and Prince jingling along, the sleigh packed with cousins, the fields all bright and still in the moonlight, and they'd wind up at Uncle Svend's, where uncles sat around the kitchen table, covered with a blue-checked oilcloth, and drank mugs of root beer and told lumberjack stories about the North Woods, and much later, after many hands of whist, an uncle took six of them on a hike out to the pasture, across the crusted snowdrifts, and pointed, and there was a silver wolf sitting under a tree a hundred yards away, perfectly still, looking at them. Your father remembered it so well as he got older. That world of order, in which Monday was different from Wednesday, and Saturday was its own day, and Sunday was completely set apart. Now everybody does as they please.

"I'm thinking of using my share to take a trip. What do you think of Greece?" She had gone to Travel Club on Monday, and Marilyn Hedlund did Greece and showed pictures of little villages of whitewashed houses rising up the dry rocky hills and served lamb shish kebob, and they danced to a recording of bouzouki music. "It'll give me something to study," she said. "The only problem is the dog. He's become very attached to me. When I put on my coat, he stands and trembles so badly his teeth chatter."

Ronnie and Serena had had a little boy and named him Ezekiel, she said. Ezekiel Tollefson. They were determined that he not be called Zeke, she said. She was going to Dallas to see him and then to Tucson to visit Diana and April, who were celebrating the third anniversary of their partnership on May 7.

"How do you celebrate a partnership?" I asked.

"They want to do something traditional," said Mother, "so they're going to say vows at a church—Unitarian, I guess—and then have a dinner at a restaurant. Diana wanted to wear my old wedding dress, but she's too big for it, I'm afraid. So I'm going to rip off the skirt and make a jacket out of it for her."

What with her travels, Mother guessed she wouldn't plant a garden this year, but that was all right. She said that at church that morning, there were weeds on the altar, burdock and horsetail and purslane and amaranth, showing that what man rejects, God finds beauty in. So she'd try weeds instead of vegetables. Besides, the freezer was still full from last year.

Speaking of church, David Ingqvist had flown to Texas to interview for a job as chaplain at the Dallas–Fort Worth airport. It paid well. Very well. And you'd be surprised, she said, at the problems people go through at airports. Marital problems, grief, separation—"missed connections," I added.

"Seriously," she said, "it sounds nice for him. There's a big chapel in the basement of the main terminal; he'd hold an interfaith service there twice a day and be available for counseling."

"An interfaith service is one where you sing hymns to nature and you talk about personal growth, right?"

She thought it would be good for him and Judy to have a change of scenery. "And you're moving too?" she said. A turbulent year for the Tollefsons. Uncle Henry and Aunt Allie were moving to Mexico. Had I heard? No? "I've been thinking of moving," Mother said. "I'm not ready to settle into being the old Tollefson widow. I had dinner with Herbert Anslinger the other night." She dropped that fact as one might drop a pebble into the pond to watch the rings.

"Are you asking my permission to date, Mother?"

She laughed. "Yes," she said. "May I?"

"With my blessings. And when the time comes, let me tell you about safe sex."

"His wife died three years ago, and he's starved for conversation," she said. "That's all it is. Two old people looking for someone to have a meal with."

Mother was something of a party girl in her teens, after her sister Dotty died. Herbert Anslinger was a rich boy who squired her around for a year. His father owned a department store in St. Cloud. Herbert took her driving in his LaSalle Phaeton, which could do 120 mph on pavement, and they went to roadhouses and drank sloe gin and danced to bands from Kansas City and Chicago. Her father's farm was lost, and she didn't have a dime, but a pretty girl can always make her way in the world, and Mother latched onto Herbert. Aunt Ray had shown me a picture of Mother posing at the wheel of the LaSalle, in a light cotton dress, her hair short and windblown, delicately holding a cigarette in her left hand, grinning, and Herbert standing, one foot up on the running board, a pleasant man in white pants and shirt and a sailor's cap, home for the summer from Yale. I think Aunt Ray was trying to build up Dad in my eyes by showing me the fellow he beat out. According to Aunt Ray, Herbert asked Mother to marry him, and his disapproving family threatened to send him away for a year, but she had already turned him down.

I can imagine Mother riding around the countryside, the top down, the wind in her hair, driving to clubs around Lake Minnetonka where black men in tuxedos and conked hair play the shimmy-sha-wobble, the Lindy, the fox walk, and she and Herbert waggle their butts and bump hips and writhe in each other's arms.

Years ago, on an August afternoon, after swimming with Leland and Swanson, I found her initials and Herbert's carved into a bench in the warming house at the skating rink, a long, dark-green shed where, in the summer, bathers changed into their suits, boys at the north end, girls at the south. Herbert and Mother swam together, I figured, and it made my scalp tingle to contemplate them, my own mother once desired by a young man who cut their initials deep enough in a pine plank to be legible for thirty years.

Herbert stood in that very room, I imagined, and took off his wet trunks and dried his privates and dressed, thinking about the slender naked girl on the other side of that wall, and then he reached into his trouser pocket for a knife. A hot day, and he had driven them over in the LaSalle for a swim before the Saturday night dance. They played around in the water and she did a headstand and he saw her slender legs rise in the air and he dove and kissed her underwater, a lingering kiss, bubbles streaming from their mouths, and later they did it again, under the diving dock, and he slipped his hand into her bodice and touched her bare breast, and she broke for the surface and treaded water, laughing, as he came up—" My, you are forward," she cried— and she pushed his head under, a mild reproof for such a bold over- ture, and this encouraged him to imagine more that might be possible later, on the way home. And now here he was, naked, with a knife in his hand, and he carved M.P. and H.A. and a heart around them with an arrow, taking his sweet time so that other boys would notice. I looked at the letters, stunned, contemplating what might have hap- pened other than what did. How odd to think of the fragile circum- stances that led to one's existence, the romance that might have flowered instead of the one with Dad that produced me.

Did Herbert park the LaSalle on a dirt road that night and did they sit in the 1938 twilight, her bare feet up on the dashboard, Herbert stroking her slender calves, and did they contemplate a life together as a wealthy young couple? Did he whisper to her a beautiful plan for the future, sailing on the *Normandie* for a summer on the Côte d'Azur and a tour of the Aegean, returning to St. Cloud and a hand- some residence overlooking the Mississippi? And did she for a mo- ment believe it? The glitter of moonlight on the lake, the gurgle of water lapping on the shore, the boughs rustling overhead, a train whistle blowing far away, the smell of new upholstery, the beating of her heart, his hand on her leg, his conversation, his clean boyish smell, his endearments in her left ear, and the sense of unending summer, that all of life would be like this night. I suppose it could have been delicious to believe in Herbert and his stories. But then she had to figure him out. Women had to be smarter then. You couldn't sleep with a man for a year or two and gradually decipher him; you had to size him up early and either drop him or sign on for life. And Mother sensed Herbert's weakness of character, smooth dancer though he was and good kisser and storyteller, and she dropped him. He went to work in the family store and married a clerk and never got out and saw the world. He turned into a plump man with soft hands and pomaded hair who was all sensitivity and no sense and ran the department store into the ground.

Mother dismissed Herbert in the fall, and after a decent interval, Dad came around and took her to the movies, and the following summer he proposed to her, on the lawn by the Sons of Knute temple on the Fourth of July, 1939, the municipal band tooting away, as Wobegonians wearing red, white, and blue caps formed the Living Flag on Main Street. He and Mother snuck off and kissed under a tree and he said (according to her), "I want to be next to you for the rest of my life." She was wearing a white dress with puff sleeves and flowers embroidered on the bodice and a broad-brimmed white straw hat, and he thought she looked like Joan Crawford.

I heard pieces of this story all my life. How it had been a hard day for Dad, because Mother was with her friends Virginia and Flora and Dorothy and Dorothy's brother Chappy, and Dad wasn't sure where he stood, if Mother was with him or with them.

DAD: I'd invited her. And here she was with this whole gay entourage of people I didn't know.

MOTHER: How can you invite someone to the Fourth of July? Everybody goes, invited or not. It's like inviting someone to drink from a water fountain.

DAD: I was hoping to be with you, that's all. Not a bunch of giggly girls.

MOTHER: You wanted me to tell them to go away?

DAD: Yes. Of course.

He hoped to kiss her if the opportunity presented itself, but her pals shared the blanket with them on the Lutheran church lawn for the picnic box lunch. Dad waited on her, fetched lemonade and extra napkins and cake, and then there was a moment of awkwardness when they all stood up and the sun was shining and she brushed the hair out of her eyes and asked, "Where are you going now?"—as if he would be going somewhere! as if she didn't want him to stay with her!—and he was deeply hurt and muttered, "Oh, I donno. Walk around." He could've said, "Walk around, and I'd like you to come with. Will you?" But Lutheran reserve prevented him from suggesting such a thing. So he said, "Where are you going?" and she replied,

"Oh, I donno. Go with my friends, I guess." And he said, "Well, maybe I'll see you later." "Sure," she said, and both turned away, feeling rejected, feeling a cold shadow come over the day. Maybe it was true, she thought, that Byron was conceited, as some people said. He thought, *She probably misses Herbert Anslinger. I'm not in his league. I should give it up now and not humiliate myself.*

He headed uptown for the carnival, which was set up in the parking lot of the ball field. There was a giant Ferris wheel and a carousel and pitch-penny games and a tent show with various freaks and a one-man band, and he had heard that you could buy a half pint of moonshine from the tent show barker. The barker wore a carpet vest and a top hat and he waved a white cane and talked up the sword swallower and the two-headed calf and the Wild Man of Borneo who ate live chickens, and you caught his eye and winked and waggled two fingers and he ducked down behind the flap and came back with a paper sack and you were in business. Dad was going to get a half pint and maybe catch a freight train for Worthington, work on a threshing crew there, work off his grief at having been thrown over by the only really wonderful girl he knew.

His life was saved by an old clown who sat on a bench suspended over a tank of water. The baseball toss. You paid a quarter to throw three baseballs at a bull's-eye and drop the bozo into the tank. The bozo kept up a stream of insults at passersby, goading them until they plunked down their quarters and tried to shut him up. He saw Dad strolling toward the tent show, and he drilled into him; he yelled, "Hey, ya little shrimp, ya got something hangin' out of yer nose, ya hayseed"—and Dad reached up to check his nostril, and the bozo cackled, "Oh, man, I have seen dumbos in my day, but you are the lamest-looking pea-brained rum-dum sad-sack Milquetoast mama's boy in this whole jerkwater town, Lake Wobble-gobble or whatever the hell. Lemme tell you, kid, compared to you, chickens are Ph.D.s. You are uglier than a mud fence"—and Dad stopped dead in his tracks and looked up at the bozo in wonderment, and the bozo screeched again and slapped his thigh and cried, "How come yer pants are droopin', boy? Huh, y' get excited, didja? Whew! Oh, I can smell it way up here! Oh, my! *That kid right there loaded his pants, folks! P.U.!* Looked at a pretty girl and got excited and next thing he knew, he had this warm, wonderful feeling in his shorts, right? Am I right? Am I right? Smell him!" And he cackled and whooped, and people edged away from Dad, not wanting to get in the line of fire, and the bozo yelled, "Hey, think y'kin see straight to throw a baseball? Whaddaya say, cream puff? Three tries for a quarter, rube." And Dad put down a quarter and got the baseballs and threw one, just wide, and threw again, a little wider, and the bozo was cackling and slapping his thigh and saying that Dad ought to go empty his pants, and the third pitch was a strike, and *whang* went the bull's-eye, and down went the bozo and came up dripping and sputtering and screamed, "*Lucky!* Had yer eyes shut! Let's see it again, fruit fly. Let's put some money on it, dumbo."

And Dad turned away. You could never beat people at that game. He could see that. The stream of insults that life directs at you cannot be vanquished by skill or cunning. You can't fight your way clear. You can't outsmart life. The only answer is to be loved so that nothing else matters so much. And he set out in search of Mother and found her with her four friends at the Sons of Knute Sing, in a crowd singing "With someone like you, a pal so good and true," and when Mother saw him, she held out her hand for him to join them. When he took her hand, he pulled, and she came with him out to the lawn, and he said, "I want to be next to you for the rest of my life," and kissed her under her big straw hat, and that was how they got together, that is where I come from, from that moment.

TWENTY-FOUR

New York City

I thought of the lovely girl in the white dress and straw hat and the farmhand in the white shirt with the rolled sleeves, his snap-brim cap, walking hand in hand on a July night in 1939 and sizing up their future together, after the dead ends and wrong turns that had brought them to that point. I thought of them as I took a last walk around Red Cliff. Nothing much had changed here since 1939. Pizza had come in, and massage, scented candles, foreign beer, sensitive greeting cards, holographic repatterning, but nothing of substance. I had not made much of an impact myself. The name Tollefson didn't ring many bells in Red Cliff. Oh well. It was a nice place to live while you tried to figure out something else. Long gentle springs, long golden falls. I drove to New York City, my possessions rattling in the back of the rented minivan. I took a slow route, over the Shawangunk Mountains, through little river villages not so different from my hometown. People in those towns were making the best of their situation, as people in Lake Wobegon do. Bad choices are inevitable, and given the opportunity, a man will dig a deep hole for himself, no doubt about it, but make the most of what you're stuck with and you'll do okay. That is the Lake Wobegon philosophy. I came into the Bronx and over the Triborough Bridge, for the view of the massed towers of Manhattan in the afternoon mist, and across Central Park on Ninety-seventh Street, to Riverside Drive, and parked around the corner from Alida's and went up, and she was lying on the couch, waiting for me to ring the bell. We celebrated in a French café on West Eighty-sixth, sitting by the window, a vase with two red roses on the table. I ordered a bottle of wine, a 1989 Rhône. Alida took my hand and kissed it on the knuckles, a kiss on each one, and said, "If you ever get angry at me, don't get so angry that you forget how it was today, at the beginning." She looked up, tears in her eyes. "I couldn't bear that," she said. "To see our loveliness ripped to tatters."

She wiped her eyes with my knuckles. "And promise me that we each get to be alone whenever we want simply by closing a door.

"And promise me that my mother won't be at the wedding," she said.

An old man and woman sat at a table in the corner. The woman's right arm hung down as if from a stroke, and he was cutting her breast of chicken into bite-sized pieces.

"So what do you want to talk about for the rest of our lives?"

"Whatever crosses our minds," she said. "Just don't go silent on me, okay?"

"Me? Silent?"

She studied her salad as the waitress ground pepper onto it. "It's a common trait among males of your ethnic persuasion," she said. "Studies have been done on this. They're sociable until the vows are said and the defloration occurs, and then the great Nordic twilight descends."

"We're a thoughtful people. We're not New Yorkers," I said.

"Don't knock New Yorkers. Especially now that you've become one."

The waitress poured the wine, and I tasted it and nodded. "New Yorkers talk as a nervous habit, the way other people drum their fingers on the table. They talk because silence makes them uneasy and because they need to keep the conversation on familiar ground. God forbid that anyone should bring up agriculture or mention

Minnesota—New Yorkers panic if anything about the Midwest comes into a conversation, because, one, they don't know anything about it and, two, they're not absolutely sure where it is."

She carefully composed a forkful of salad and ate it. "At least New Yorkers recognize that there is a social obligation," she said. "I have met people from your part of the country who seemed to think that you don't have to talk during a meal, that it's enough to enjoy your food and not spill."

"We are a people filled with beautiful inexpressible thoughts," I said.

"Tell me about it."

I held the glass of wine under my nose and breathed deeply and took a long sip. "What I feel for you and what I think about marrying you I cannot put in terms other than poetry, and poetry comes out of silence."

"Are you going to write me a poem for our wedding?" she said.

"I might do that."

In April and May, I got myself into a good routine, which an unemployed person should do, I think. You don't want to depend on improvisation; you might start improvising late-morning shots of sherry and marathon naps. I arose with Alida at six and fixed her breakfast— espresso, yogurt, wheat toast (unbuttered), and a glass of fresh juice from the juicer, custom-made according to the customer's specs (beet-carrot-apple-celery), and when she marched off to work, helmeted, backpacked, I made the bed and straightened the apartment, did my sit-ups and push-ups, showered, dressed, and got my breakfast at the bagel shop on Broadway, a poppy seed bagel with scallion cream cheese, a coffee (light), and brought it back to the little plaza in front of the firemen's fountain below Alida's apartment window, at the end of 100th Street.

The plaza was our porch, shared with eight or nine hundred other people in the course of a day, but thanks to the delicacy of New Yorkers, their skill at being private in public, it is a sweet and calming place to sit. The immense monument sequesters the plaza from the street, so it is quiet, and it is noble—dedicated "to the men of the Fire Department of the City of New York who died at the call of duty, soldiers in the war that never ends"—and on the plaza side, water pours from the granite into a pool. A tablet in the pavement, dated May 1927, honors "the horses that shared in valor and devotion and with mighty speed bore on the rescue," and three bronze steeds charge forward across a bronze tableau on the monument, on which goddesses representing Courage and Duty comfort a child and a dying man.

It is one of my favorite places in the city, right up there along with Lincoln Center and Times Square and the country road around the reservoir in Central Park, this peaceful plaza in honor of horrible death by smoke and fire and the collapse of bricks, with its tranquil air in the midst of traffic, the splash of cool water over the hum of cars and buses, the grandeur, the poetry about horses. I sat, eating my bagel and cream cheese, thinking about heroism, as New Yorkers came through the plaza and down the steps toward Riverside Park, men and women on dog-poop duty, joggers on their morning circuits, idlers like myself, and men in dark suits the color of their briefcases on their way to catch the same downtown subway that brought their cleaning ladies in from Harlem and Washington Heights, and once the actor William Hurt walked in and sat down and read the paper and drank a bottle of water. And once a woman in a black cocktail dress and high heels walked in, leading a large white poodle who lifted his leg and peed onto a corner of the monument, under Courage. I never saw anyone there who looked remotely like a fireman.

On Tuesdays and Thursdays, I went to St. Michael's Episcopal Church on Ninety-ninth to deliver hot food to people with AIDS. I spent two hours doing that, chatting with sick men, cutting their meat, sometimes walking their dogs or washing their dishes, did it as an exercise. Kindness isn't part of anyone's nature. You have to make yourself do it, like sit-ups. Then, having done some good, I hiked down Broadway from Ninety-ninth to Seventy-second, stopped in at Gray's Papaya for a hot dog, browsed in the magazine store across the street, and hiked back uptown, shopping for dinner.

New Yorkers are a ravenous people. Every hundred feet is a restaurant, coffee shop, or frozen yogurt stand, with bales of cardboard and mounds of garbage bags at the curb as proof of the appetites of the clientele. On almost every block is a fruit market, bins of oranges and apples, black grapes and nectarines, jutting out into the sidewalk to snag you, angled for your inspection. Heaps of Portobello mushrooms, heaps of greens and reds and yellows, thickets of cut flowers, watched over by tiny dark-skinned men, possibly Aztecs, men of royal lineage now trimming the stalks of tulips and daffodils. I carried a blue cotton shopping bag and dallied over the produce, contemplating dinner, choosing my salad carefully, finding the all-star potatoes, watching the passing parade.

Dozens of entrepreneurs work the street—hot-dog carts, gypsy cabs, Nigerians selling gold watches out of attaché cases, vendors of incense, curbside booksellers, and if it should start to rain, men will spring at you waving tiny collapsible umbrellas. Panhandlers come and go, including a legless man on a blanket with a cardboard sign that says VIETNAM VET and a thin black woman who will writhe and wail and keen and shake and make a scene so visceral and heart-rending that you'd gladly pay a dollar to avoid seeing it. There used to be a famously terrible Korean saxophonist, Dr. Wrong, who stood and honked in front of apartment buildings until offered financial incentive to move along. The man's playing was worse than car alarms. I liked the toothless lady in the stained gray sweater and black skirt who sometimes stood in front of Barnes & Noble, paper cup in hand, and opened the door for patrons, collecting tips, pretending to be deaf if the security guard spoke to her, until finally a store manager came out and dropped a twenty in her cup, and then she could knock off for the day.

All along Broadway are brand-new nondescript high-rise condominium buildings, and the people who come out their doors are young, and dressed in black, with sixty-dollar haircuts. The bars along Broadway are theme bars, with a prepackaged attitude, designed for young people trying out roles to see what might fit, the classic reason for coming to the city. You certainly don't care to experiment with a new persona in front of your old uncles—see how they like you as Southwestern Hombre, Bad Dude, Sullen Sophisticate, Preppy Heartthrob. So you move to the city and melt into the mass of the Young and Restless and seek out crowded joints like the Santa Monica Beach Club or the Cajun Café or Jamaica Joe's, where music pounds the floor late at night and passion rises like a bad perfume. New York is the great place for young adventurers. You can roam around, see incredibly weird things, be grossed out, learn the lingo, be glamorous in ways impossible back home, and have sex with anybody you like and be secret about it. New York offers the Young Punk's Dream—earn buckets of money, be attractive, have romantic dalliances with various inappropriate people, and then, in middle age, find a Good Person and beget offspring. The city breathes eroticism, from noon on. Even in the subway, you can sense men and women angling, sizing each other up. That is why New Yorkers maintain such a somber public demeanor, why everyone on the subway looks as if he or she is pondering a difficult math problem—it's to cover up a frank prurient interest in each other.

On June 1, Alida and I rode the subway downtown to the Municipal Building, near City Hall, and stood in line for an hour at the Marriage Bureau. The other couples in line seemed mostly to be immigrants—there was a whir of Spanish consonants in the air, the rumble of Russian, the twang of Korean. I wondered if only greenhorns come here for their license, if people in the know know a shortcut. I stood, one arm around Alida's waist, her head on my shoulder, and studied the couple at the head of the line. A couple in their twenties, plump and pale as raw turkeys, she in giant yellow shorts and a Mets sweatshirt, dull blond hair chopped short, and he in a loose red-flowered shirt, with long greasy black hair, dark glasses. You could imagine them emerging from their wedding a little unsteady from vodka sours, climbing into a car loaded with pickle dishes and serving trays, and driving home to Long Island and capsizing into bed and waking up with the dreadful knowledge that they had married in self-defense someone who shared their worst qualities.

Alida's book on Bolle Balestrand came out that same week of June and sank without a trace, unreviewed except in one scholarly journal, where a man from St. Olaf quoted two or three clumsy sentences from the book, pointed out a translation error and two factual discrepancies, pooh-poohed the Balestrand journals as a minor find that he and other scholars had been aware of for more than a decade, and said that a New York academic could hardly be expected to comprehend the subtle nuances, the overtones, the subtext, of the Norwegian experience in America.

I went into the Barnes & Noble at Eighty-second and Broadway and located two copies of *Bolle in America* by Alida Freeman on the bottom shelf of "New Nonfiction," between Al Franken and a biography of Annette Funicello, and reshelved Bolle at eye level, covers out, replacing *Dave Barry Turns Fifty*. Alida's publisher, Vandal-Pigeon, who had wanted to put a picture of her on the cover and call it *Lincoln's Cold Shower*, lost interest in the book when she balked at this, and the editor went off to vacation in Egypt. The book had a dark-blue cover, with pictures of Thoreau, Dickinson, Whitman, Lincoln, Anthony, and Custer, and looked like a fifth-grade history reader.

I strolled over to the magazine rack and stood for a few minutes, pretending to read the *Paris Review*, keeping an eye on Nonfiction, waiting for someone to take Alida's book off the shelf and open it and start reading. As I waited, I became gradually aware that a number of people around me were doing the same thing: hiding behind magazines, keeping an eye on the new-book shelves. There was a small, wolfish man with tiny black-rimmed glasses whom I recognized from a *Times* article about New Novelists; he had a book out called *Flotation Devices*, in which a boy falls down a mine shaft and is raised by moles and returns to the human world years later, blind, albino, but gifted with a preternatural sense of what people around him are thinking. Next to the wolfish man was a woman with a big white hat who (I was fairly sure) was Weaver Cleveland, author of a memoir about her dalliances with her father and her brother and her grandfather, *Kith*, and across the magazine rack from her was—yes, it was—the slight, boyish figure of Jonah Hadley, wearing wraparound dark glasses and a blue beret, holding a Zabar's bag, and peering from behind a copy of the *New York Review of Books* toward where his memoir, *Walking the River*, was stacked in a special section of books recommended by store employees. I followed his gaze and saw a handsome woman in a brown raincoat looking at *Walking the River*. She riffled through a few pages, set it back on the shelf, picked up a biography of Humphrey Bogart, and walked toward the cashiers. Jonah looked stricken, as if he'd been jilted, as if he might accost the woman and offer to discuss his book with her.

Walking the River was Jonah's account of the year he had to deal with turning forty at the same time as he began questioning his commitment to broadcasting and the terrible costs of being in the public eye. Every weekend or so for an entire year, he hiked along the Potomac River, recording the "evolving majesty of seasons, the movements of birds, the 'inner silence' of the natural world as it carries on the cycle of life even within a major metropolis, and finding in the common beauties of natural phenomena the strength to go on with his own working life," according to the jacket flap. I had glanced at the book, and it was slow going indeed, clots of purple prose combined with the shallowest sort of soul-searching.

I tapped Jonah on the shoulder, and the little man flinched and looked up at me. "Sir, do you mind if I check your bag?" I said in an authoritative voice. The little man froze in fear. I was about to say, "Just kidding, Jonah," when he dropped the Zabar's bag and brushed past me and slipped out the front door and ran up the sidewalk, head down, his little legs pumping. I looked in the bag. There was a sack of sugar doughnuts and a small white plastic bag with two videocassettes, *Locker Room Fantasies* and *Teasing the Teacher*. I put them back in the shopping bag and walked over to the small wolfish man and tapped him on the shoulder.

"Excuse me," I said. "I'm sorry to intrude on your privacy, but I'm a big, big fan, and I couldn't leave without telling you that your work has meant a lot to my wife and me, as she's been going through some medical problems, and I just want to say thanks for doing what you do and saying what you say. You're able to put things into words for a lot of us, and—I'd like to give you this. From both of us." And I handed the Zabar's bag to the novelist, who looked at me blankly as if he had never met a reader before in his life. As I turned to leave, I noticed a woman looking at Alida's book. A woman with wild black hair, in a white suit and black T-shirt, who read a couple pages, glanced at Alida's picture on the back flap, and put it under her arm. A reader! Someone who was actually going to sit and soak up those sentences so laboriously composed, eat that permanent banquet arranged at lavish expense.

A reader! I was overjoyed. I wanted to shake her hand. I wanted to invite her to the wedding.

We were married on a Saturday, after breakfast, in St. Michael's, Alida in a pale-green silk dress, I in a light-tan suit, carrying our gifts to each other in a paper bag. "Let's have it be just the two of us," she had said. "It has to either be the two of us or be four hundred of us. There's no middle ground."

We walked, hand in hand, to the church, Alida holding a bouquet of daisies, and as we turned up Ninety-ninth from Broadway, I saw a familiar figure in a tan raincoat waiting by the rectory gate. "She stayed at the St. Moritz last night. She wanted it to be a secret. I apologize for not telling you," said Alida.

As we approached, Mother smiled and took a camera out of her purse and snapped a picture of us. She kissed Alida and then me, and posed us at the gate, and took another picture. "Forgive me," she said. "I'm your mother. I know it's tacky, but I really had to be here—" And then she cried. "I'm sorry," she said. "I'm happy. I'll try to control myself."

"Don't say you're sorry," I said, my arm around her.

"I won't," she said. "I'm sorry."

We were going to get married in the cluttered office of the rector, an elegant young black man with a Caribbean accent, his secretary the witness, but when he saw Mother, he made a face and said, "This doesn't seem right to me." And turned away and motioned for us to follow. We traipsed through a narrow passageway that opened into a side chapel and the sanctuary, the long nave with a soaring roof, and he led us forward and up the steps toward the altar. High above was a stained-glass tableau of a gentle Pre-Raphaelite Christ and his apostles, all soft greens and browns and blues. We walked past the choir stalls to the steps at the altar rail, and he turned and smiled and said, "This is better."

His words seemed to continue on out and up into the twilight above, echoing as a sort of general benediction, and as he searched for the wedding service in the prayer book, we heard the beating of wings and looked up, to see a bird fluttering under the dome. It flew the length of the nave to the choir loft and then flew back and perched on a ledge above the altar.

"It's the Holy Spirit," said the rector. "We thought of everything."

He looked at Alida and at me, wondering (I thought) why such a beautiful woman was with such an ordinary man, and then he read the service. We made our vows to love each other, forsaking all others, and there was such poignance in the words. To have and to hold from this day forward, for better for worse, for richer for poorer, in sickness and in health, to love and to cherish, till death us do part—how many misbegotten journeys have started with these words, how many lonely people grasping at straws, hoping the words themselves have incantatory power to make a true love story out of a passing fancy, and having said them, the couple go lurching off into a marriage that is ritualized cruelty. And the alarm bells went off in my own head—Wrong! Wrong! Wrong!—and then I remembered what Jesus said: "If you have faith as a mustard seed, you would be able to move mountains," and there I stood, a faithless mountain, and then, having put the ring on Alida's finger, I kissed her, and kissed Mother, and the three of us walked down the aisle, toward a janitor who was waiting to sweep out the place.

"Don't be strangers," said the rector at the door. He kissed Alida. And we plunged out the door into the blazing noontime sun.

We walked down Broadway, through knots of strollers and shoppers, dog walkers, deliverymen with crates on handcarts, sales clerks on lunch hour, gangs of teenage boys out on a strut, bag ladies and lunatics of all persuasions, families walking four abreast, Orthodox Jews in dark suits, their sons trailing along, ancient men and women bundled in wheelchairs pushed by young black women, a mailman in shorts, and tourists—you can tell tourists by their slightly off-key dress, their purposeless gait, a general slackness about them. At the corner of Ninety-sixth and Broadway, an old man panhandling by the subway stairs noticed Alida's bouquet and took off his cap and bowed and said, "God bless you." I gave him a ten.

We walked down to Eighty-sixth Street, to the little French restaurant, and sat in the corner. Champagne was brought, three glasses of the best. "To the love of my life," I said. She smiled her broadest smile: "To my Norwegian." Mother said, "Long life to the both of you."

We exchanged gifts. She gave me a thesaurus and a watch, and I gave her a china bowl full of packets of seeds—Early Perfection Peas, Calypso Supersweet Jubilee Hybrid Sweet Corn, Early Prolific Straightneck Squash, Hale's Best Jumbo Cantaloupe, Brigadier Broccoli, Detroit Supreme Beets, American Purple-Top Rutabagas—and a white envelope containing a poem.

"I am sorry if this isn't a great poem. I was a history major, you know," I said.

"Hush," she said. She read it out loud.

I imagine you as you were those summer nights,
So fortunate and full of grace.
Above your head the heaven had hung its lights,
And I reached out my hand to touch your face.

I believe in impulse, fresh and green,
Believe in the foolish vision that comes out true,
Believe that all that is essential is unseen.
And for this lifetime, I believe in you,

All the sweet days and nights we made:
Nothing that is between us is a mistake.
All that we ever do for love's sake
Is not wasted and will never fade.

Love shines in every twinkling star
And is reflected in the silver moon:
If it's not here, it is not far;
It's coming and will be here soon.

She put it down and stood up and put her arms around me, and it was suddenly clear to me why men have written poems all these centuries—it is to impress a woman in hopes that she will sleep with you.

"I brought this gift for you," said Mother. I unwrapped it, a flat package, which contained a picture in a frame, and it was my great-grandfather John Tollefson, smiling at me.

"That is an unusual picture," she said. "They gave it to the sculptor after John died, to make the statue from. You know about that. It was Haakon's money." She looked at Alida. "Haakon was the one who made all the money. Anyway, this was in 1942, and the sculptor lost the picture, and instead he made a statue of a handsome youth pointing west and, on the base, the inscription 'Kan Du Glemme Gamle Norge?' which means 'Can You Forget Old Norway?' But of course they had forgotten Norway a long time before, and of course Norway isn't to the west unless you take the long way. And the youth didn't look like anybody they knew, so it came to be called the Unknown Norwegian. And years later, Byron found this portrait in an antique store in Wisconsin.

"It was taken when John was ninety-two. It was taken the morning of the day he died, as a matter of fact."

John Tollefson looked to be in good shape at ninety-two. He was using his own teeth, talking and making sense, the light was still on in his attic, and on his last day on earth, he walked into the Sidetrack Tap and enjoyed a hamburger and fried potatoes and two beers, won twenty-five cents at cribbage, which he put in the jukebox, and played three Glenn Miller tunes and danced to them with a waitress named DeeAnna, a comely woman. They danced close. And then he smiled to all in the room and waved goodbye and got in his car, drove home, sat down in his favorite chair, and died. Not that bad a deal, I thought.

He had a couple of beers and played cards and put some money in the jukebox and he danced with a pretty waitress. He was a Happy Lutheran, one of the few in Lake Wobegon. The others believed that humor is a disturbance of the natural order, that silence is the best policy, that every bright day contains a cloud if you look for it. But

John Tollefson, on his last day, enjoyed beer and victory at cards and held a young woman in his arms.

He was a cheerful stoic who left the lovely valley in Norway and booked passage to America and went to Lake Wobegon and settled on land that reminded him of Norway, forgetting that he had left Norway because the land was so poor. Stooped figures moved like clouds of doom through the town, and beautiful girls in summer dresses who looked Norwegian but spoke English, a harsh rumbly sound like a peanut grinder. But it could be worse. John looked at his champagne. He had a quarter in his pocket from cribbage. The sun was shining, and a lovely woman named Alida smiled across the table at him. It was 1942 and Hitler seemed to be riding high, but perhaps that would change in time. DeeAnna asked how everything was. "It's as good as it can be," I said. "It's better than I had any reason to expect. The music is calling, my dear. Would you care to dance?"